P9-EKY-215

The daughter of a town marshal, **Linda Lael Miller** is a #1 *New York Times* and *USA TODAY* bestselling author of more than one hundred historical and contemporary novels, most of which reflect her love of the West. Raised in Northport, Washington, she now lives in Spokane, Washington. Visit her at www.lindalaelmiller.com.

Brenda Jackson is a *New York Times* bestselling author of contemporary multicultural romance novels. Her books have earned awards from *RT Book Reviews* in 2010, 2011 and 2012, and she is a recipient of an RWA Lifetime Achievement Award. There are more than three million of her books currently in print. She is the first African American author to appear on the bestseller lists for the series romance genre and has won a number of awards for her work throughout her career. Her book *A Silken Thread* was a 2012 NAACP Image Award nominee. Visit her website at brendajackson.net.

#1 *New York Times* **Bestselling Author**

LINDA LAEL MILLER

SIERRA'S HOMECOMING

**HARLEQUIN
BESTSELLING
AUTHOR
COLLECTION**

**HARLEQUIN®
BESTSELLING
AUTHOR
COLLECTION**

Recycling programs
for this product may
not exist in your area.

ISBN-13: 978-1-335-00819-0

Sierra's Homecoming
First published in 2006. This edition published in 2023.
Copyright © 2006 by Linda Lael Miller

Star of His Heart
First published in 2010. This edition published in 2023.
Copyright © 2010 by Harlequin Enterprises ULC

For questions and comments about the quality of this book,
please contact us at CustomerService@Harlequin.com.

Harlequin Enterprises ULC
22 Adelaide St. West, 41st Floor
Toronto, Ontario M5H 4E3, Canada
www.Harlequin.com

Printed in U.S.A.

CONTENTS

Also by Linda Lael Miller

Canary Street Press

Painted Pony Creek

Country Strong
Country Proud
Country Born

The Carsons of Mustang Creek

A Snow Country Christmas
Forever a Hero
Always a Cowboy
Once a Rancher

The Brides of Bliss County

Christmas in Mustang Creek
The Marriage Season
The Marriage Charm
The Marriage Pact

McKettricks of Texas

McKettrick's Choice
A McKettrick Christmas
McKettricks of Texas: Tate
McKettricks of Texas: Garrett
McKettricks of Texas: Austin
A Lawman's Christmas
An Outlaw's Christmas

Visit her Author Profile page at Harlequin.com,
or lindalaelmiller.com, for more titles!

SIERRA'S HOMECOMING

Linda Lael Miller

To Little Angels Everywhere

Chapter 1

Present Day

"Stay in the car," Sierra McKettrick told her seven-year-old son, Liam.

He fixed her with an owlish gaze, peering through the lenses of his horn-rimmed glasses. "I want to see the graves, too," he told her, and put a mittened hand to the passenger-side door handle to make his point.

"Another time," she answered firmly. Part of her knew it was irrational to think a visit to the cemetery could provoke an asthma attack, but when it came to Liam's health, she was taking no chances.

A brief stare-down ensued, and Sierra prevailed, but barely.

"It's not fair," Liam said, yet he sounded resigned. He didn't normally give up so easily, but they'd just driven almost nonstop all the way from Florida to northern Arizona, and he was tired.

"Welcome to the real world," Sierra replied. She set the emergency brake, left the engine running with the heat on High, and got out of the ancient station wagon she'd bought on credit years before.

Standing ankle-deep in a patch of ragged snow, she took in her surroundings. Ordinary people were buried in churchyards and public cemeteries when they died, she reflected, feeling peevish. The McKettricks were a law unto themselves, living *or* dead. They weren't content with a mere plot, like other families. Oh, no. They had to have a place all their own, with a view.

And what a view it was.

Shoving her hands into the pockets of her cloth coat, which was nearly as decrepit as her car, Sierra turned to survey the Triple M Ranch, sprawling in every direction, well beyond the range of her vision. Red mesas and buttes, draped in a fine lacing of snow. Copses of majestic white oaks, growing at intervals along a wide and shining stream. Expanses of pastureland, and even the occasional cactus, a stranger to the high country, a misplaced wayfarer, there by mistake.

Like her.

A flash of resentment rose suddenly within Sierra, and a moment or two passed before she recognized the emotion for what it was: not her own opinion, but that of her late father, Hank Breslin.

When it came to the McKettricks, Sierra *had* no opinions that she could honestly claim, because she didn't know these people, except by reputation.

She'd taken their name for one reason and one reason only—because that was part of the deal. Liam needed health care, and she couldn't provide it. Eve McKettrick—Sierra's biological mother—had set up a medical trust fund for her grandson, but there were strings attached.

With the McKettricks, she heard her father say, as surely as if he were standing there beside her, *there are always strings attached.*

"Be quiet," Sierra said, out loud. She was grateful for Eve's help, and if she had to take the McKettrick name and live on the Triple M Ranch for a year to meet the conditions, so be it. It wasn't as if she had anyplace better to go.

Resolutely she approached the cemetery entrance, walked under the ornate metal archway forming the word "McKettrick" in graceful cursive.

A life-size bronze statue of a man on horseback, broad-shouldered and imposing, with a bandanna at his throat and a six-gun riding on his hip, took center stage.

Angus McKettrick, the patriarch. The founder of the Triple M, and the dynasty. Sierra knew little about him, but as she looked up into that hard, determined face, shaped by the rigors of life in the nineteenth century, she felt a kinship.

Ruthless old bastard, said the voice of Hank Breslin. *That's where McKettricks get their arrogance. From him.*

"Be quiet," Sierra repeated, thrusting her hands deeper into her coat pockets. She stood in silence for a long moment, listening to the rattle-throated hum of the station wagon's engine, the lonely cry of a nearby bird, the thrum of blood in her ears. A piney scent spiced the air.

Sierra turned, saw the marble angels marking the

graves of Angus McKettrick's wives—Georgia, mother
of Rafe, Kade and Jeb. Concepcion, mother of Kate.

Look for Holt and Lorelei, Eve had told her, the last
time they'd spoken over the telephone. *That's our part
of the family.*

Sierra caught sight of other bronze statues, smaller
than Angus's but no less impressive in their detail. They
were works of art, museum pieces, and if they hadn't
been solidly anchored in cement, they probably would
have been stolen. It said something about the McK-
ettrick legend, she supposed, that there had been no
vandalism in this lonely, wind-blown place.

Jeb McKettrick, the youngest of the brothers, was
represented by a cowboy with his six-gun drawn; his
wife, Chloe, by a slender woman in pioneer dress, shad-
ing her eyes with one hand and smiling. Their children,
grandchildren, great-and a few great-great-grandchil-
dren surrounded them, their costly headstones laid out
in neat rows, like the streets of a western town.

Next was Kade McKettrick, easy in his skin, wearing
a six-shooter, like his brother, but with an open book in
his hand. His wife, Mandy, wore trousers, a loose-fitting
shirt, boots and a hat, and held a shotgun. Like Chloe,
she was smiling. Judging by the number of other graves
around theirs, these two had also been prolific parents.

The statue of Rafe McKettrick revealed a big, powerfully built man with a stubborn set to his jaw. His bride,
Emmeline, stood close against his side; their arms were
linked and she rested her head against the outside of
his upper arm.

Sierra smiled. Again, their progeny was plentiful.

The last statue brought up an unexpected surge of
emotion in Sierra. Here, then, was Holt, half brother to

Rafe, Kade and Jeb, and to Kate. In his long trail coat, he looked both handsome and tough. A pair of very detailed ammunition belts criss-crossed his chest, and the badge pinned to his wide lapel read Texas Ranger.

Sierra stared into those bronze eyes and, once again, felt something stir deep inside her. *I came from this man,* she thought. *We've got the same DNA.*

Liam gave a jarring blast of the car horn, impatient to get to the ranch house that would be their home for the next twelve months.

Sierra waved in acknowledgment but moved on to the statue of Lorelei. She was mounted on a mule, long, lace-trimmed skirts spilling on either side of her impossibly small waist, face shadowed, not by a sunbonnet but by a man's hat. Her spirited gaze rested lovingly on her husband, Holt.

Liam laid on the horn.

Fearing he might decide to take the wheel and drive to the ranch house on his own, Sierra turned reluctantly from the markers and followed a path littered with pine needles and the dead leaves of the six towering white oaks that shared the space, heading back to the car.

Back to her son.

"Are all the McKettricks *dead?*" Liam asked, when Sierra settled into the driver's seat and fastened the belt.

"No," Sierra answered, waiting for some stray part of herself to finish meandering among those graves, making the acquaintance of ancestors, and catch up. "*We're* McKettricks, and we're not dead. Neither is your grandmother, or Meg." She knew there were cousins, too, descended from Rafe, Kade and Jeb, but it was too big a subject to explain to a seven-year-old boy.

Besides, she was still trying to square them all away in her own mind.

"I thought my name was Liam *Breslin*," the little boy said practically.

It should have been Liam Douglas, Sierra thought, remembering her first and only lover. As always, when Liam's father, Adam, came to mind, she felt a pang, a complicated mixture of passion, sorrow and helpless fury. She and Adam had never been married, so she'd given Liam her maiden name.

"We're McKettricks now," Sierra said with a sigh. "You'll understand when you're older."

She backed the car out carefully, keenly aware of the steep descent on all sides, and made the wide turn that would take them back on to the network of dirt roads bisecting the Triple M.

"I can understand *now*," Liam asserted, having duly pondered the matter in his solemn way. "After all, I'm *gifted*."

"You may be gifted," Sierra replied, concentrating on her driving, "but you're still seven."

"Do I get to be a cowboy and ride bucking broncs and stuff like that?"

Sierra suppressed a shudder. "No," she said.

"That bites," Liam answered, folding his arms and settling deeper into the heavy nylon coat she'd bought him on the road, when they'd reached the first of the cold-weather states. "What's the good of living on a ranch if you can't be a cowboy?"

Chapter 2

The elderly station wagon banged into the yard, bald tires crunching half-thawed gravel, and came to an obstreperous stop. Travis Reid paused behind the horse trailer hitched to Jesse McKettrick's mud-splattered black truck, pushed his hat to the back of his head with one leather-gloved finger and grinned, waiting for something to fall off the rig. Nothing did, which just went to prove that the age of miracles was not past.

Jesse appeared at the back of the trailer, leading old Baldy by his halter rope. "Who's that?" he asked, squinting in the wintry late afternoon sunshine.

Travis spared him no more than a glance. "A long-lost relative of yours, unless I miss my guess," he said easily.

The station wagon belched some smoke and died. Travis figured it for a permanent condition. He looked on with interest as a good-looking woman climbed out from behind the wheel, looked the old car over, and gave the driver's-side door a good kick with her right foot.

She was a McKettrick, all right. Of the female persuasion, too.

Jesse left Baldy standing to jump down from the bed of the trailer and lower the ramp to the ground. "Meg's half sister?" he asked. "The one who grew up in Mexico with her crazy, drunken father?"

"Reckon so," Travis said. He and Meg communicated regularly, most often by email, and she'd filled him in on Sierra as far as she could. Nobody in the family knew her very well, including her mother, Eve, so the information was sparse. She had a seven-year-old son—now getting out of the car—and she'd been serving cocktails in Florida for the last few years, and that was about all Travis knew about her. As Meg's caretaker and resident horse trainer, not to mention her friend, Travis had stocked the cupboards and refrigerator, made sure the temperamental furnace was working and none of the plumbing had frozen, and started up Meg's SUV every day, just to make sure it was running.

From the looks of that station wagon, it was a good thing he'd followed the boss-lady's orders.

"You gonna help me with this horse," Jesse asked testily, "or just stand there gawking?"

Travis chuckled. "Right now," he said, "I'm all for gawking."

Sierra McKettrick was tall and slender, with short, gleaming brown hair the color of a good chestnut horse. Her eyes were huge and probably blue, though she was still a stride or two too far away for him to tell.

Jesse swore and stomped back up the ramp, making plenty of noise as he did so. Like most of the McKettricks, Jesse was used to getting his way, and while he was a known womanizer, he'd evidently dismissed Sierra out of hand. After all, she was a blood relative—no sense driving his herd into *that* canyon.

Travis took a step toward the woman and the boy, who was staring at him with his mouth open.

"Is this Meg's house?" Sierra asked.

"Yes," Travis said, putting out his hand, pulling it back to remove his work gloves, and offering it again. "Travis Reid," he told her.

"Sierra Bres—McKettrick," she replied. Her grip was firm. And her eyes were definitely blue. The kind of blue that pierces something in a man's middle. She smiled, but tentatively. Somewhere along the line, she'd learned to be sparing with her smiles. "This is my son, Liam."

"Howdy," Liam said, squaring his small shoulders.

Travis grinned. "Howdy," he replied. Meg had said the boy had health problems, but he looked pretty sound to Travis.

"That sure is an ugly horse," Liam announced, pointing towards the trailer.

Travis turned. Baldy stood spraddle-footed, midway down the ramp, a miserable gray specimen of a critter with pink eyes and liver-colored splotches all over his mangy hide.

"Sure is," Travis agreed, and glowered at Jesse for palming the animal off on him. It was like him to pull off a dramatic last-minute rescue, then leave the functional aspects of the problem to somebody else.

Jesse flashed a grin, and for a moment, Travis felt territorial, wanted to set himself between Sierra and her boy, the pair of them, and one of his oldest friends. He felt off balance, somehow, as though he'd been ambushed. What the hell was *that* all about?

"Is that a buckin' bronc?" Liam asked, venturing a step toward Baldy.

Sierra reached out quickly, caught hold of the fur-trimmed hood on the kid's coat and yanked him back. Cold sunlight glinted off the kid's glasses, making his eyes invisible.

Jesse laughed. "Back in the day," he said, "Baldy was a rodeo horse. Cowboys quivered in their boots when they drew him to ride. Now, as you can see, he's a little past his prime."

"And you would be—?" Sierra asked, with a touch of coolness to her tone. Maybe she was the one woman out of a thousand who could see Jesse McKettrick for what he was—a good-natured case of very bad news.

"Your cousin Jesse."

Sierra sized him up, took in his battered jeans, work shirt, sheepskin coat and very expensive boots. "Descended from…?"

The McKettricks talked like that. Every one of them could trace their lineage back to old Angus, by a variety of paths, and while there would be hell to pay if anybody riled them as a bunch, they mostly kept to their own branch of the family tree.

"Jeb," Jesse said.

Sierra nodded.

Liam's attention remained fixed on the horse. "Can I ride him?"

"Sure," Jesse replied.

"No way," said Sierra, at exactly the same moment.

Travis felt sorry for the kid, and it must have shown in his face, because Sierra's gaze narrowed on him.

"We've had a long trip," she said. "I guess we'll just go inside."

"Make yourselves at home," Travis said, gesturing toward the house. "Don't worry about your bags. Jesse and I'll carry them in for you."

She considered, probably wondering if she'd be obligated in any way if she agreed, then nodded. Catching Liam by the hood of his coat again, she got him turned from the horse and hustled him toward the front door.

"Too bad we're kin," Jesse said, following Sierra with his eyes.

"Too bad," Travis agreed mildly, though privately he didn't believe it was such a bad thing at all.

The house was a long, sprawling structure, with two stories and a wraparound porch. Sierra's most immediate impression was of substance and practicality, rather than elegance, and she felt a subtle interior shift, as if she'd been a long time lost in a strange, winding street, thick with fog, and suddenly found herself standing at her own front door.

"Those guys are *real cowboys,*" Liam said, once they were inside.

Sierra nodded distractedly, taking in the pegged wood floors, gleaming with the patina of venerable age, the double doors and steep staircase on the right, the high ceilings, the antique grandfather clock ticking ponderously beside the door. She peeked into a spacious living room, probably called a parlor when the house was new, and admired the enormous natural-rock fireplace, with its raised hearth and wood-nook. Worn but

colorful rugs gave some relief to the otherwise uncom-
promisingly masculine decor of leather couches and
chairs and tables of rough-hewn pine, as did the piano
set in an alcove of floor-to-ceiling windows.

An odd nostalgia overtook Sierra; she'd never set
foot on the Triple M before that day, let alone entered
the home of Holt and Lorelei McKettrick, but she might
have, if her dad hadn't snatched her the day Eve filed
for divorce, and carried her off to San Miguel de Al-
lende to share his expatriate lifestyle. She might have
spent summers here, as Meg had, picking blackberries,
wading in mountain streams, riding horses. Instead,
she'd run barefoot through the streets of San Miguel,
with no more memory of her mother than a faint scent
of expensive perfume, sometimes encountered among
the waves of tourists who frequented the markets, shops
and restaurants of her home town.

Liam tugged at the sleeve of her coat. "Mom?"

She snapped out of her reverie, looked down at him,
and smiled. "You hungry, bud?"

Liam nodded solemnly, but brightened when the
door bumped open and Travis came in, lugging two
suitcases.

Travis cleared his throat, as though embarrassed.
"Plenty of grub in the kitchen," he said. "Shall I put
this stuff upstairs?"

"Yes," Sierra said. "Thanks." At least that way she'd
know which rooms were hers and Liam's without having to ask. She might have been concerned, sharing
the place with Travis, but Meg had told her he lived in
a trailer out by the barn. What Meg hadn't mentioned
was that her resident caretaker was in his early thirties,
not his sixties, as Sierra had imagined, and too attrac-

tive for comfort, with his lean frame, blue-green eyes
and dark-blond hair in need of a trim.

She blushed as these thoughts filled her mind, and
shuffled Liam quickly toward the kitchen.

It was a large room, with the same plank floors she'd
seen in the front of the house and modern appliances,
strangely juxtaposed with the black, chrome-trimmed
wood cookstove occupying the far-left-hand corner. The
table was long and rustic, with benches on either side
and a chair at each end.

"Tables like that are a tradition with the McK-
ettricks," a male voice said from just behind her.

Sierra jumped, startled, and turned to see Jesse in
the doorway.

"Sorry," he said. He was handsome, Sierra thought.
His coloring was similar to Travis's, and so was his
build, and yet the two men didn't resemble each other
at all.

"No problem," Sierra said.

Liam wrenched open the refrigerator. "Bologna!" he
yelled triumphantly.

"Whoopee," Sierra replied, with a dryness that was
lost on her son. "If there's bologna, there must be white
bread, too."

"Jesse!" Travis's voice, from the direction of the front
door. "Get out here and give me a hand!"

Jesse grinned, nodded affably to Sierra and vanished.

Sierra took off her coat, hung it from a peg next to
the back door, and gestured for Liam to remove his,
too. He complied, then went straight back to the bologna. He found a loaf of bread in a colorful polka-dot
bag and started to build a sandwich.

Watching him, Sierra felt a faint brush of sorrow

against the back of her heart. Liam was good at doing things on his own; he'd had a lot of practice, with her working the night shift at the club and sleeping days. Old Mrs. Davis from the apartment across the hall had been a conscientious babysitter, but hardly a mother figure.

She put coffee on to brew, once Liam was settled on a bench at the table. He'd chosen the side against the wall, so he could watch her moving about the kitchen.

"Cool place," he observed, between bites, "but it's haunted."

Sierra took a can of soup from a shelf, opened it and dumped the contents into a saucepan, placing it on the modern gas stove before answering. Liam was an imaginative child, often saying surprising things. Rather than responding instantly, Sierra usually tried to let a couple of beats pass before she answered.

"What makes you say that?"

"Don't know," Liam said, chewing. They'd had a drive-through breakfast, but that had been hours ago, and he was obviously starving.

Another jab of guilt struck Sierra, keener than the one before. "Come on," she prodded. "You must have had a reason." Of course he'd had a reason, she thought. They'd just been to a graveyard, so it was natural that death would be on his mind. She should have waited, made the pilgrimage on her own, instead of dragging Liam along.

Liam looked thoughtful. "The air sort of...buzzes," he said. "Can I make another sandwich?"

"Only if you promise to have some of this soup first."

"Deal," Liam said.

An old china cabinet stood against a far wall, near

the cookstove, and Sierra approached it, even though she didn't intend to use any of the dishes inside. Price-less antiques, every one.

Her family had eaten off those dishes. Generations of them.

Her gaze caught on a teapot, sturdy looking and, at the same time, exquisite. Spellbound, she opened the glass doors of the cabinet and reached inside to touch the piece, ever so lightly, with just the tips of her fingers.

"Soup's boiling over," Liam said mildly.

Sierra gasped, turned on her heel and rushed back to the modern stove to push the saucepan off the flame.

"Mom," Liam interjected.

"What?"

"Chill out. It's only soup."

The inside door swung open, and Travis stuck his head in. "Stuff's upstairs," he said. "Anything else you need?"

Sierra stared at him for a long moment, as though he'd spoken in an alien language. "Uh, no," she said finally. "Thanks." Pause. "Would you like some lunch?"

"No, thanks," he said. "Gotta see to that damn horse." With that, he ducked out again.

"How come I can't ride the horse?" Liam asked.

Sierra sighed, setting a bowl of soup in front of him. "Because you don't know how."

Liam's sigh echoed her own, and if they'd been talking about anything but the endangerment of life and limb, it would have been funny.

"How am I supposed to *learn* how if you won't let me try? You're being overprotective. You could scar my psyche. I might develop psychological problems."

"There are times," Sierra confessed, sitting down

across from him with her own bowl of soup, "when I wish you weren't quite so smart."

Liam waggled his eyebrows at her. "I got it from you."

"Yeah right," Sierra said. Liam had her eyes, her thick, fine hair, and her dogged persistence, but his remarkable IQ came from his father.

Don't think about Adam, she told herself.

Travis Reid sidled into her mind.

Even worse.

Liam consumed his soup, along with a second sandwich, and went off to explore the rest of the house while Sierra lingered thoughtfully over her coffee.

The telephone rang.

Sierra got up to fetch the cordless receiver and pressed Talk with her thumb. "Hello?"

"You're there!" Meg trilled.

Sierra noticed that she'd left the china cabinet doors open and went in that direction, intending to close them. "Yes," she said. Meg had been kind to her, in a long-distance sort of way, but Sierra had only been two when she'd last seen her half sister, and that made them strangers.

"How do you like it? The ranch house, I mean?"

"I haven't seen much of it," Sierra answered. "Liam and I just got here, and then we had lunch…." Her hand went, of its own accord, to the teapot, and she imagined she felt just the faintest charge when she touched it. "Lots of antiques around here," she said, thinking aloud.

"Don't be afraid to use them," Meg replied. "Family tradition."

Sierra withdrew her hand from the teapot, shut the doors. "Family tradition?"

"McKettrick rules," Meg said, with a smile in her voice. "Things are meant to be used, no matter how old they are."

Sierra frowned, uneasy. "But if they get broken—"

"They get broken," Meg finished for her. "Have you met Travis yet?"

"Yes," Sierra said. "And he's not at all what I expected."

Meg laughed. "What did you expect?"

"Some gimpy old guy, I guess," Sierra admitted, warming to the friendliness in her sister's voice. "You said he took care of the place and lived in a trailer by the barn, so I thought—" She broke off, feeling foolish.

"He's cute and he's single," Meg said.

"Even the teapot?" Sierra mused.

"Huh?"

Sierra put a hand to her forehead. Sighed. "Sorry. I guess I missed a segue there. There's a teapot in the china cabinet in the kitchen—I was just wondering if I could—"

"I know the one," Meg answered, with a soft fondness in her voice. "It was Lorelei's. She got it for a wedding present."

Lorelei. The matriarch of the family. Sierra took a step backward.

"*Use* it," Meg said, as if she'd seen Sierra's reflexive retreat.

Sierra shook her head. "I couldn't. I had no idea it was that old. If I dropped it—"

"Sierra," Meg said, "it's not china. It's cast iron, with an enamel overlay."

"Oh."

"Kind of like the McKettrick women, Mom always

says." Meg went on. "Smooth on the outside, tough as iron on the inside."

Mom. Sierra closed her eyes against all the conflicting emotions the word brought up in her, but it didn't help.

"We'll give you time to settle in," Meg said gently, when Sierra was too choked up to speak. "Then Mom and I will probably pop in for a visit. If that's okay with you, of course."

Both Meg and Eve lived in San Antonio, Texas, where they helped run McKettrickCo, a multinational corporation with interests in everything from software to communication satellites, so they wouldn't be "popping in" without a little notice.

Sierra swallowed hard. "It's your house," she said.

"And yours," Meg pointed out, very quietly.

After that, Meg made Sierra promise to call if she needed anything. They said goodbye, and the call ended.

Sierra went back to the china cabinet for the teapot.

Liam clattered down the back stairs. "I *told* you this place was haunted!" he crowed, his small face shining with delight.

The teapot was heavy—definitely cast iron—but Sierra was careful as she set it on the counter, just the same. "What on earth are you talking about?"

"I just saw a kid," Liam announced. "Upstairs, in my room!"

"You're imagining things."

Liam shook his head. "I *saw* him!"

Sierra approached her son, laid her hand to his forehead. "No fever," she mused, worried.

"Mom," Liam protested, pulling back. "I'm not sick—and I'm not delusional, either."

Delusional. How many seven-year-olds used that word? Sierra sighed and cupped Liam's eager face in both hands. "Listen. It's fine to have imaginary friends, but—"

"He's *not* imaginary."

"Okay," Sierra responded, with another sigh. It was possible, she supposed, that a neighbor child had wandered in before they arrived, but that seemed unlikely, given that the only other houses on the ranch were miles away. "Let's investigate."

Together they climbed the back stairs, and Sierra got her first look at the upper story. The corridor was wide, with the same serviceable board floors. The light fixtures, though old-fashioned, were electric, but most of the light came from the large arched window at the far end of the hallway. Six doors stood open, an indication that Liam had visited each room in turn after leaving the kitchen the first time.

He led her into the middle one, on the left side.

No one was there.

Sierra let out her breath, admiring the room. It was spacious, perfect quarters for a boy. Two bay windows overlooked the barn area, where Baldy, the singularly unattractive horse, stood stalwartly in the middle of the corral, looking as though he intended to break loose at any second and do some serious bucking. Travis was beside Baldy, stroking the animal's neck as he eased the halter off over its head.

A quivery sensation tickled the pit of Sierra's stomach.

"Mom," Liam said. "He was here. He had on short pants and funny shoes and suspenders."

Sierra turned to look at her son, feeling fretful again.

Liam stood near the other window, examining an antique telescope, balanced atop a shining brass tripod. "I believe you," she said.

"You don't," Liam argued, jutting out his chin. "You're *humoring* me."

Sierra sat down on the side of the bed positioned between the windows. Like the dressers, it was scarred with age, but made of sturdy wood. The headboard was simply but intricately carved, and a faded quilt provided color. "Maybe I am, a little," she admitted, because there was no fooling Liam. He had an uncanny knack for seeing through anything but the stark truth. "I don't know what to think, that's all."

"Don't you believe in ghosts?"

I don't believe in much of anything, Sierra thought sadly. "I believe in you," she said, patting the mattress beside her. "Come and sit down."

Reluctantly, he sat. Stiffened when she slipped an arm around his shoulders. "If you think I'm going to take a nap," he said, "you're dead wrong."

The word *dead* tiptoed up Sierra's spine to dance lightly at her nape. "Everything's going to be all right, you know," she said gently.

"I like this room," Liam confided, and the hopeful uncertainty in his manner made Sierra's heart ache. They'd always lived in apartments or cheap motel rooms. Had Liam been secretly yearning to call a house like this one home? To settle down somewhere and live like a normal kid?

"Me, too," Sierra said. "It has friendly vibes."

"Is that supposed to be like a closet?" Liam asked, indicating the huge pine armoire taking up most of one wall.

Sierra nodded. "It's called a wardrobe."

"Maybe it's like the one in that story. Maybe the back of it opens into another world. There could be a lion and a witch in there." From the smile on Liam's face, the concept intrigued rather than troubled him.

She ruffled his hair. "Maybe," she agreed.

His attention shifted back to the telescope. "I wish I could look through that and see Andromeda," he said. "Did you know that the whole galaxy is on a collision course with the Milky Way? All hell's going to break loose when it gets here, too."

Sierra shuddered at the thought. Most parents worried that their kids played too many video games. With Liam, the concern was the Discovery and Science Channels, not to mention programs like *Nova*. He thought about things like Earth losing its magnetic field and had nightmares about creatures swimming in dark oceans under the ice covering one of Jupiter's moons. Or was it Saturn?

"Don't get excited, Mom," he said, with an understanding smile. "It's going to be something like five billion years before it happens."

"Before what happens?" Sierra asked, blinking.

"The *collision*," he said tolerantly.

"Right," Sierra said.

Liam yawned. "Maybe I *will* take a nap." He studied her. "Just don't get the idea it's going to be a regular thing."

She mussed his hair again, kissed the top of his head. "I'm clear on that," she said, standing and reaching for the crocheted afghan lying neatly folded at the foot of the bed.

Liam kicked off his shoes and stretched out on top

of the blue chenille bedspread, yawning again. He set his glasses on the night stand with care.

She covered him, resisted the temptation to kiss his forehead, and headed for the door. When she looked back from the threshold, Liam was already asleep.

1919

Hannah McKettrick heard her son's laughter before she rode around the side of the house, toward the barn, a week's worth of mail bulging in the saddlebags draped across the mule's neck. The snow was deep, with a hard crust, and the January wind was brisk.

Her jaw tightened when she saw her boy out in the cold, wearing a thin jacket and no hat. He and Doss, her brother-in-law, were building what appeared to be a snow fort, their breath making white plumes in the frigid air.

Something in Hannah gave a painful wrench at the sight of Doss; his resemblance to Gabe, his brother and her late husband, invariably startled her, even though they lived under the same roof and she should have been used to him by then.

She nudged the mule with the heels of her boots, but Seesaw-Two didn't pick up his pace. He just plodded along.

"What are you doing out here?" Hannah called.

Both Tobias and Doss fell silent, turning to gaze guiltily in her direction.

The breath plumes dissipated.

Tobias set his feet and pushed back his narrow shoulders. He was only eight, but since Gabe's coffin had arrived by train one warm day last summer, draped in an

American flag and with Doss for an escort, her boy had taken on the mien of a man.

"We're just making a fort, Ma," he said.

Hannah blinked back sudden, stinging tears. A soldier, Gabe had died of influenza in an army infirmary, without ever seeing the battleground. Tobias thought in military terms, and Doss encouraged him, a fact Hannah did not appreciate.

"It's cold out here," she said. "You'll catch your death."

Doss shifted, pushed his battered hat to the back of his head. His face hardened, like the ice on the pond back of the orchard where the fruit trees stood, bare-limbed and stoic, waiting for spring.

"Go inside," Hannah told her son.

Tobias hesitated, then obeyed.

Doss remained, watching her.

The kitchen door slammed eloquently.

"You've got no business putting thoughts like that in his head," Doss said, in a quiet voice. He took old Seesaw's reins and held him while she dismounted, careful to keep her woolen skirts from riding up.

"That's a fine bit of hypocrisy, coming from you," Hannah replied. "Tobias had pneumonia last fall. We nearly lost him. He's fragile, and you know it, and as soon as I turn my back, you have him outside, building a snow fort!"

Doss reached for the saddlebags, and so did Hannah. There was a brief tug-of-war before she let go. "He's a kid," Doss said. "If you had your way, he'd never do anything but look through that telescope and play checkers!"

Hannah felt as warm as if she were standing close to a hot stove, instead of Doss McKettrick. Their breaths melded between them. "I fully intend to have my way,"

she said. "Tobias is my son, and I will not have you telling me how to raise him!"

Doss slapped the saddlebags over one shoulder
and stepped back, his hazel eyes narrowed. "He's my
nephew—my brother's boy—and I'll be damned if I'll let
you turn him into a sickly little whelp hitched to your
apron strings!"

Hannah stiffened. "You've said quite enough," she told
him tersely.

He leaned in, so his nose was almost touching hers. "I
haven't said the half of it, Mrs. McKettrick."

Hannah sidestepped him, marching for the house, but
the snow came almost to her knees and made it hard to
storm off in high dudgeon. Her breath trailed over her
right shoulder, along with her words. "Supper's in an
hour," she said, without turning around. "But maybe you'd
rather eat in the bunkhouse."

Doss's chuckle riled her, just as it was no doubt meant
to do. "Old Charlie's a sight easier to get along with than
you are, but he can't hold a candle to you when it comes
to home cooking. Anyhow, he's been gone for a month,
in case you haven't noticed."

She felt a flush rise up her neck, even though she was
shivering inside Gabe's old woolen work coat. His scent
was fading from the fabric, and she wished she knew a
way to hold on to it.

"Suit yourself," she retorted.

Tobias shoved a chunk of wood into the cookstove as
she entered the house, sending sparks snapping up the
gleaming black chimney before he shut the door with
a clang.

"We were only building a fort," he grumbled.

Hannah was stilled by the sight of him, just as if somebody had thrown a lasso around her middle and pulled it tight. "I could make biscuits and sausage gravy," she offered quietly.

Tobias ignored the olive branch. "You rode down to the road to meet the mail wagon," he said, without meeting her eyes. "Did I get any letters?" With his hands shoved into the pockets of his trousers and his brownish-blond hair shining in the wintry sunlight flowing in through the windows, he looked the way Gabe must have, at his age.

"One from your grandpa," Hannah said. Methodically, she hung her hat on the usual peg, pulled off her knitted mittens and stuffed them into the pockets of Gabe's coat. She took that off last, always hating to part with it.

"Which grandpa?" Tobias lingered by the stove, warming his hands, still refusing to glance her way.

Hannah's family lived in Missoula, Montana, in a big house on a tree-lined residential street. She missed them sorely, and it hurt a little, knowing Tobias was hoping it was Holt who'd written to him, not her father.

"The McKettrick one," she said.

"Good," Tobias answered.

The back door opened, and Doss came in, still carrying the saddlebags. Usually he stopped outside to kick the snow off his boots so the floors wouldn't get muddy, but today he was in an obstinate mood.

Hannah went to the stove and ladled hot water out of the reservoir into a basin, so she could wash up before starting supper.

"Catch," Doss said cheerfully.

She looked back, saw the saddlebags, burdened with mail, fly through the air. Tobias caught them ably with a grin.

When was the last time he'd smiled at her that way?

The boy plundered anxiously through the bags, brought out the fat envelope postmarked San Antonio, Texas. Her in-laws, Holt and Lorelei McKettrick, owned a ranch outside that distant city, and though the Triple M was still home to them, they'd been spending a lot of time away since the beginning of the war. Hannah barely knew them, and neither did Tobias, for that matter, but they'd kept up a lively correspondence, the three of them, ever since he'd learned to read, and the letters had been arriving on a weekly basis since Gabe died.

Gabe's folks had come back for the funeral, of course, and in the intervening months Hannah had been secretly afraid. Holt and Lorelei saw their lost son in Tobias, the same as she did, and they'd offered to take him back to Texas with them when they left. She hadn't had to re-fuse—Tobias had done that for her, but he'd clearly been torn. A part of him had wanted to leave.

Hannah's heart had wedged itself up into her throat and stayed there until Gabe's mother and father were gone. Whenever a letter arrived, she felt anxious again.

She glanced at Doss, now shrugging out of his coat. He'd gone away to the army with Gabe, fallen sick with influenza himself, recovered and stayed on at the ranch after he brought his brother's body home for burial. Though no one had come right out and said so, Hannah knew Doss had remained on the Triple M, instead of join-ing the folks in Texas, mainly to look after Tobias.

Maybe the McKettricks thought she'd hightail it home to Montana, once she got over the shock of losing Gabe, and they'd lose track of the boy.

Now Tobias stood poring over the letter, devouring

every word with his eyes, getting to the last page and starting all over again at the beginning.

Deliberately Hannah diverted her attention, and that was when she saw the teapot, sitting on the counter. She looked toward the china cabinet, across the room. She hadn't touched the piece, knowing it was special to Lorelei, and she couldn't credit that Doss or Tobias would have taken it from its place, either. They'd been playing in the snow while she was gone to fetch the mail, not throwing a tea party.

"Did one of you get this out?" she asked casually, getting a good grip on the pot before carrying it back to the cabinet. It was made of metal, but the pretty enamel coating could have been chipped, and Hannah wasn't about to take the risk.

Tobias barely glanced her way before shaking his head. He was still intent on the letter from Texas.

Doss looked more closely, his gaze rising curiously from the teapot to Hannah's face. "Nope," he said at last, and busied himself emptying the contents of the coffeepot down the sink before pumping in water for a fresh batch.

Hannah closed the doors of the china cabinet, frowning.

"Odd," she said, very softly.

Chapter 3

Present Day

Sierra descended the rear staircase into the kitchen, being extra quiet so she wouldn't wake Liam up. He hadn't had an asthma attack in almost a month, but he needed his rest.

Intending to brew herself some tea and spend a few quiet minutes restoring her equilibrium, she chose a mug from one of the cupboards, located a box of orange pckoe, and reached for the heirloom teapot.

It was gone.

She glanced toward the china cabinet and saw Lorelei's teapot sitting behind the glass.

Jesse or Travis must have come inside while she was upstairs, she reasoned, and put it away.

But that seemed unlikely. Men, especially cowboys,

didn't usually fuss with teapots, did they? Not that she knew that much about men in general or cowboys in particular.

She'd seen Travis earlier, from Liam's bedroom window, working with the horse, and she was sure he hadn't been back in the house after carrying in the bags.

"Jesse?" she called softly, half-afraid he might jump out at her from somewhere.

No answer.

She moved to the front of the house, peered between the lace curtains in the parlor. Jesse's truck was gone, leaving deep tracks in the patchy mud and snow, rapidly filling with gossamer white flakes.

Bemused, Sierra returned to the kitchen, grabbed her coat and went out the back door, shoving her hands into her pockets and ducking her head against the thickening snowfall and the icy wind that accompanied it. Nothing in her life had prepared her for high-country weather; she'd been raised in Mexico, moved to San Diego after her father died and spent the last several years living in Florida. She supposed it would be a while before she adjusted to the change in climate, but if there was one thing she'd learned to do, on the long journey from then to now, it was adapt.

The doors of the big, weathered-board barn stood open, and Sierra stepped inside, shivering. It was warmer there, but she could still see her breath.

"Mr. Reid?"

"Travis" came the taciturn answer from a nearby stall. "I don't answer to much of anything else."

Sierra crossed the sawdust floor and saw Travis on the other side of the door, grooming poor old Baldy with long, gentle strokes of a brush. He gave her a sidelong glance and grinned slightly.

"Settling in okay?" he asked.

"I guess," she said, leaning on the stall door to watch him work. There was something soothing about the way he attended to that horse, almost as though he were touching her own skin….

Perish the thought.

He straightened. A quiver went through Baldy's body. "Something wrong?" Travis asked.

"No," Sierra said quickly, attempting a smile. "I was just wondering…"

"What?" Travis went back to brushing again, though he was still watching Sierra, and the horse gave a contented little snort of pleasure.

Suddenly the whole subject of the teapot seemed silly. How could she ask if he or Jesse had moved it? And, so what if they had? Jesse was a McKettrick, born and raised, and the things in that house were as much a part of his heritage as hers. Travis was clearly a trusted family friend—if not more.

Sierra found that possibility unaccountably disturbing. Meg had said he was single and free, but she obviously trusted Travis implicitly, which might mean there was a deeper level to their relationship.

"I was just wondering…if you ever drink tea," Sierra hedged lamely.

Travis chuckled. "Not often, unless it's the electric variety," he replied, and though he was smiling, the expression in his eyes was one of puzzlement. He was probably asking himself what kind of nut case Meg and Eve had saddled him with. "Are you inviting me?"

Sierra blushed, even more self-conscious than before. "Well...yes. Yes, I guess so."

"I'd rather have coffee," Travis said, "if that's all right with you."

"I'll put a pot on," Sierra answered, foolishly relieved. She should have walked away, but she seemed fixed to the spot, as though someone had smeared the soles of her shoes with superglue.

Travis finished brushing down the horse, ran a gloved hand along the animal's neck and waited politely for Sierra to move, so he could open the stall door and step out.

"What's really going on here, Ms. McKettrick?" he asked, when they were facing each other in the wide aisle, Baldy's stall door securely latched. Along the aisle, other horses nickered, probably wanting Travis's attention for themselves.

"Sierra," she said. She tried to sound friendly, but it was forced.

"Sierra, then. Somehow I don't think you came out here to ask me to a tea party or a coffee klatch."

She huffed out a breath and pushed her hands deeper into her coat pockets. "Okay," she admitted. "I wanted to know if you or Jesse had been inside the house since you brought the baggage in."

"No," Travis answered readily.

"It would certainly be all right if you had, of course—"

Travis took a light grip on Sierra's elbow and steered her toward the barn doors. He closed and fastened them once they were outside.

"Jesse got in his truck and left, first thing," he said. "I've been with Baldy for the last half an hour. Why?"

Sierra wished she'd never begun this conversation. Never left the warmth of the kitchen for the cold and the questions in Travis's eyes. She'd done both those things, though, and now she would have to explain. "I took a teapot out of the china cabinet," she said, "and set it on the counter. I went up to Liam's room, to help him settle in for a nap, and when I came downstairs—"

A startling grin broke over Travis's features like a flash of summer sunlight over a crystal-clear pond. "What?" he prompted. He moved to Sierra's other side, shielding her from the bitter wind, increasing his pace, and therefore hers, as they approached the house.

"It was in the cabinet again. I would swear I put it on the counter."

"Weird," Travis said, kicking the snow off his boots at the base of the back steps.

Sierra stepped inside, shivering, took off her coat and hung it up.

Travis followed, closed the door, pulled off his gloves and stuffed them into the pockets of his coat before hanging it beside Sierra's, along with his hat. "Must have been Liam," he said.

"He's asleep," Sierra replied. The coffee she'd made earlier was still hot, so she filled two mugs, casting an uneasy glance toward the china cabinet as she did so. Liam couldn't have gotten downstairs without her seeing him, and even if he had, he wouldn't have been able to reach the high shelf in the china closet without dragging a chair over. She would have heard the scraping sound and, anyway, Liam being Liam, he wouldn't have put the chair back where he found it. There would have been evidence.

Travis accepted the cup Sierra offered with a nod of

thanks, took a sip. "You must have put it away your-self, then," he said reasonably. "And then forgotten."

Sierra sat down in the chair closest to the wood-burning cookstove, suddenly yearning for a fire, while Travis made himself comfortable nearby, on the bench facing the wall.

"I know I didn't," she said, biting her lower lip.

Travis concentrated on his coffee for some moments before turning his gaze back to her face. "It's a strange house," he said.

Sierra blinked.

Cool place, Liam had said, right after they arrived, *but it's haunted.*

"What do you mean, 'It's a strange house'?" she asked. She made no attempt to keep the skepticism out of her voice.

"Meg's going to kill me for this," Travis said.

"I beg your pardon?"

"She doesn't want you scared off."

Sierra frowned, waiting.

"It's a good place," Travis said, taking the homey kitchen in with a fond glance. Clearly, he'd spent a lot of time there. "Odd things happen sometimes, though."

Sierra heard Liam's voice again. *I saw a kid, up-stairs in my room.*

She shook off the memory. "Impossible," she mut-tered.

"If you say so," Travis replied affably.

"What *kind* of 'odd things' happen in this house?"

Travis smiled, and Sierra had the sense that she was being handled, skillfully managed, in the same way as the horse. "Once in a while, you'll hear the piano play-ing by itself. Or you walk into a room, and you get the feeling you passed somebody on the threshold, even though you're alone."

Sierra shivered again, but this time it had nothing to do with the icy January weather. The kitchen was snug and warm, even without the cookstove lit. "I would appreciate it," she said, "if you wouldn't talk that kind of nonsense in front of Liam. He's…impressionable."

Travis raised an eyebrow.

Suddenly, strangely, Sierra wanted to tell him what Liam had said about seeing another little boy in his room, but she couldn't quite bring herself to do it. She wouldn't have Travis Reid—or anybody else, for that matter—thinking Liam was…different. He got enough of that from other kids, being so smart, and his asthma set him apart, too.

"I must have moved the teapot myself," Sierra said, at last, "and forgotten. Just as you said."

Travis looked unconvinced. "Right," he agreed.

1919

Tobias carried the letter to the table, where Doss sat comfortably in the chair everyone thought of as Holt's. "They bought three hundred head of cattle," the boy told his uncle excitedly, handing over the sheaf of pages. "Drove them all the way from Mexico to San Antonio, too."

Doss smiled. "Is that right?" he mused. His hazel eyes warmed in the light of a kerosene lantern as he read. The place had electricity now, but Hannah tried to save on it where she could. The last bill had come to over a dollar, for a mere two months of service, and she'd been horrified at the expense.

Standing at the stove, she turned back to her work,

stood a little straighter, punched down the biscuit dough with sharp jabs of the wooden spoon. Apparently, it hadn't occurred to Tobias that she might like to see that infernal letter. She was a McKettrick, too, after all, if only by marriage.

"I guess Ma and Pa liked that buffalo you carved for them," Doss observed, when he'd finished and set the pages aside. Hannah just happened to see, since she'd had to pass right by that end of the table to fetch a pound of ground sausage from the icebox. "Says here it was the best Christmas present they ever got."

Tobias nodded, beaming with pride. He'd worked all fall on that buffalo, even in his sick bed, whittling it from a chunk of firewood Doss had cut for him special. "I reckon I'll make them a bear for next year," he said. Not a word about carving something for her parents, Hannah noted, even though they'd sent him a bicycle and a toy fire engine back in December. The McKettricks, of course, had arranged for a spotted pony to be brought up from the main ranch house on Christmas morning, all decked out in a brand-new saddle and bridle, and though Tobias had dutifully written his Montana grandparents to thank them for their gifts, he'd never played with the engine. Just set it on a shelf in his room and forgotten all about it. The bicycle wouldn't be much use before spring, that was true, but he'd shown no more interest in it once the pony had arrived.

"Wash your hands for supper, Tobias McKettrick," Hannah said.

"Supper isn't ready," he protested.

"Do as your mother says," Doss told him quietly.

He obeyed immediately, which should have pleased Hannah, but it didn't.

Doss, meanwhile, opened the saddle bags, took out the usual assortment of letters, periodicals and small parcels, which Hannah had already looked through before the mail wagon rounded the bend in the road. She'd been both disappointed and relieved when there was nothing with her name on it. Once, in the last part of October, when the fiery leaves of the oak trees were falling in puddles around their trunks like the folds of a discarded garment, she'd gotten a letter from Gabe. He'd been dead almost four months by then, and her heart had fairly stopped at the sight of his handwriting on that envelope.

For a brief, dizzying moment, she'd thought there'd been a mistake. That Gabe hadn't died of the influenza at all, but some stranger instead. Mix-ups like that happened during and after a war, and she hadn't seen the body, since the coffin was nailed shut.

She'd stood there beside the road, with that letter in her hand, weeping and trembling so hard that a good quarter of an hour must have passed before she broke the seal and took out the thick fold of vellum pages inside. She'd come to her practical senses by then, but seeing the date at the top of the first page still made her bellow aloud to the empty countryside: March 17, 1918.

Gabe had still been well when he wrote that letter. He'd been looking forward to coming home. It was about time they added to their family, he'd said, and got cattle running on their part of the Triple M again.

She'd dropped to her knees, right there on the hard-packed dirt, too stricken to stand. The mule had wandered home, and presently Doss had come looking for her. Found her still clutching that letter to her chest, her throat so raw with sorrow that she couldn't speak.

He'd lifted her into his arms, Doss had, without saying a word. Set her on his horse, swung up behind her and taken her home.

"Hannah?"

She blinked, came back to the kitchen and the biscuit batter, the package of sausage in her hands.

Doss was standing beside her, smelling of snow and pine trees and man. He touched her arm.

"Are you all right?" he asked.

She swallowed, nodded.

It was a lie, of course. Hannah hadn't been all right since the day Gabe went away to war. Like as not, she would never be all right again.

"You sit down," Doss said. "I'll attend to supper."

She sat, because the strength had gone out of her knees, and looked around blankly. "Where's Tobias?"

Doss washed his hands, opened the sausage packet, and dumped the contents into the big cast iron skillet waiting on the stove. "Upstairs," he answered.

Tobias had left the room without her knowing?

"Oh," she said, unnerved. Was she losing her mind? Had her sorrow pushed her not only to absent-minded distraction, but beyond the boundaries of ordinary sanity as well?

She considered the mysterious movement of her mother-in-law's teapot.

Adeptly, Doss rolled out the biscuit dough, cut it into circles with the rim of a glass. Lorelei McKettrick had taught her boys to cook, sew on their own buttons and make up their beds in the morning. You could say that for her, and a lot of other things, too.

Doss poured Hannah a mug of coffee, brought it to her. Started to rest a hand on her shoulder, then thought better of it and pulled back. "I know it's hard," he said.

Hannah couldn't look at him. Her eyes burned with tears she didn't want him to see, though she reckoned he knew they were there anyhow. "There are days," she said, in a whisper, "when I don't think I can go another step. But I have to, because of Tobias."

Doss crouched next to Hannah's chair, took both her hands in his own and looked up into her face. "There's been a hundred times," he said, "when I wished it was me in that grave up there on the hill, instead of Gabe. I'd give anything to take his place, so he could be here with you and the boy."

A sense of loss cut into Hannah's spirit like the blade of a new ax, swung hard. "You mustn't think things like that," she said, when she caught her breath. She pulled her hands free, laid them on either side of his earnest, handsome face, then quickly withdrew them. "You mustn't, Doss. It isn't right."

Just then Tobias clattered down the back stairs.

Doss flushed and got to his feet.

Hannah turned away, pretended to have an interest in the mail, most of which was for Holt and Lorelei, and would have to be forwarded to San Antonio.

"What's the matter, Ma?" Tobias spoke worriedly into the awkward silence. "Don't you feel good?"

She'd hoped the boy hadn't seen Doss sitting on his haunches beside her chair, but obviously he had.

"I'm fine," she said briskly. "I just had a splinter in my finger, that's all. I got it putting wood in the fire, and Doss took it out for me."

Tobias looked from her to his uncle and back again.

"Is that why you're making supper?" he asked Doss.

Doss hesitated. Like Gabe, he'd been raised to abhor any kind of lie, even an innocent one, designed to soothe a boy who'd lost his father and feared, in the depths of his dreams, losing his mother, too.

"I'm making supper," he said evenly, "because I can."

Hannah closed her eyes, opened them again.

"Set the table, please," Doss told Tobias.

Tobias hurried to the cabinet for plates and silverware.

Hannah met Doss's gaze across the dimly lit room.

A charge seemed to pass between them, like before, when Hannah had come back from getting the mail and found Tobias outside, in the teeth of a high-country winter, building a snow fort.

"It's too damn dark in this house," Doss said. He walked to the middle of the room, reached up, and pulled the beaded metal cord on the overhead light. The bare bulb glowed so brightly it made Hannah blink, but she didn't object.

Something in Doss's face prevented her from it.

Present Day

Travis had long since finished his coffee and left the house by the time Liam got up from his nap and came downstairs, tousle-haired and puffy-eyed from sleep.

"That boy was in my room again," he said. "He was sitting at the desk, writing a letter. Can I watch TV? There's a nice setup in that room next to the front door. A computer, too, with a big, flat-screen monitor."

Sierra knew about the fancy electronics, since she'd explored the house after Travis left. "You can watch TV for an hour," she said. "Hands off the computer, though. It doesn't belong to us."

Liam's shoulders slumped slightly. "I *know* how

to use a computer, Mom," he said. "We had them at school."

Between rent, food and medical bills, Sierra had never been able to scrape together the money for a PC of their own. She'd used the one in the office of the bar she worked in, back in Florida. That was how Meg had first contacted her. "We'll get one," she said, "as soon as I find another job."

"My mailbox is probably full," Liam replied, unappeased. "All the kids in the Geek Program were going to write to me."

Sierra, in the midst of putting a package of frozen chicken breasts into the microwave to thaw, felt as though she'd been poked with a sharp stick. "Don't call it the Geek Program, please," she said.

Liam shrugged one shoulder. "Everybody else does."

"Go watch TV."

He went.

A rap sounded at the back door, and Sierra peered through the glass, since it was dark out, to see Travis standing on the back porch.

"Come in," she called, and headed for the sink to wash her hands.

Travis entered, carrying a fragrant bag of take-out food in one hand. The collar of his coat was raised against the cold, his hat brim pulled low over his eyes.

"Fried chicken," he said, lifting the bag as evidence.

Sierra paused, shut off the faucet, dried her hands. The timer on the microwave dinged. "I was about to cook," she said.

Travis grinned. "Good thing I got to you in time," he answered. "If you're anything like your sister, you shouldn't be allowed to get near a stove."

If you're anything like your sister.

The words saddened Sierra, settled bleak and heavy over her heart. She didn't know whether she was like her sister or not; until Meg had emailed her a smiling picture a few weeks ago, she wouldn't have recognized her on the street.

"Did I say something wrong?" Travis asked.

"No," Sierra said quickly. "It was—thoughtful of you to bring the chicken."

Liam must have heard Travis's voice, because he came pounding into the room, all smiles.

"Hey, Travis," he said.

"Hey, cowpoke," Travis replied.

"The computer's making a dinging noise," Liam reported.

Travis smiled, set the bag of chicken on the counter but made no move to take off his hat and coat. "Meg's got it set to do that, so she'll remember to check her email when she's here," he said.

"Mom won't let me log on," Liam told him.

Travis glanced at Sierra, turned to Liam again. "Rules are rules, cowpoke," he said.

"Rules bite," Liam said.

"Ninety-five percent of the time," Travis agreed.

Liam recovered quickly. "Are you going to stay and eat with us?"

Travis shook his head. "I'd like that a lot, but I'm expected somewhere else for supper," he answered.

Liam looked sorely disappointed.

Sierra wondered where that "somewhere else" was, and with whom Travis would be sharing a meal, and was irritated with herself. It was none of her business, and besides, she didn't care what he did or who he did it with anyway. Not the least little bit.

"Maybe another time," Travis said.

Liam sighed and retreated to the study and his allotted hour of television.

"You shouldn't have," Sierra said, indicating their supper with a nod.

"It's your first night here," Travis answered, opening the door to leave. "Seemed like the neighborly thing to do."

"Thank you," Sierra said, but he'd already closed the door between them.

Travis started up his truck, just in case Sierra was listening for the engine, drove it around behind the barn and parked. After stopping to check on Baldy and the three other horses in his care, he shrugged down into the collar of his coat and slogged to his trailer.

The quarters were close, smaller than the closet off his master bedroom at home in Flagstaff, but he didn't need much space. He had a bed, kitchen facilities, a bathroom and a place for his laptop. It was enough.

More than Brody was ever going to have.

He took off his hat and coat and tossed them on to the built-in, padded bench that passed for a couch. He tried not to think about Brody, and in the daytime, he stayed busy enough to succeed. At night, it was another matter. There just wasn't enough to do after dark, especially out here in the boonies, once he'd nuked a frozen dinner and watched the news.

He thought about Sierra and the boy, in there in the big house, eating the chicken and fixings he'd picked up in the deli at the one and only supermarket in Indian

Rock. He'd never intended to join them, since they'd just arrived and were settling in, but he could picture himself sitting down at that long table in the kitchen, just the same.

He rooted through his refrigerator, something he had to crouch to do, and chose between Salisbury steak, Salisbury steak and Salisbury steak.

While the sectioned plastic plate was whirling round and round in the lilliputian microwave that came with the trailer, he made coffee and remembered his last visit from Rance McKettrick. Widowed, Rance lived alone in the house *his* legendary ancestor, Rafe, had built for his wife, Emmeline, and their children, back in the 1880s. He had two daughters, whom he largely ignored.

"This place is just a fancy coffin," Rance had observed, in his blunt way, when he'd stepped into the trailer. "Brody's the one that's dead, Trav, not you."

Travis rubbed his eyes with a thumb and forefinger. Brody was dead, all right. No getting around that. Seventeen, with everything to live for, and he'd blown himself up in the back room of a slum house in Phoenix, making meth.

He looked into the window over the sink, saw his own reflection.

Turned away.

His cell phone rang, and he considered letting voice mail pick up, but couldn't make himself do it. If he'd answered the night Brody called...

He fished the thing out, snapped it open and said, "Reid."

"Whatever happened to 'hello'?" Meg asked.

The bell on the microwave rang, and Travis reached in to retrieve his supper, burned his hand and cursed.

She laughed. "Better and better."

"I'm not in the mood for banter, Meg," he replied, turning on the water with his free hand and then switching to shove his scorched fingers into the flow.

"You never are," she said.

"The horses are fine."

"I know. You would have called me if they weren't."

"Then what do you want?"

"My, my, we *are* testy tonight. I called, you big grouch, to ask about my sister and my nephew. Are they okay? How do they look? Sierra is so private, she's almost standoffish."

"You can say that again."

"Thank you, but in the interest of brevity, I won't."

"Since when do you give a damn about brevity?" Travis inquired, but he was grinning by then.

Once again Meg laughed. Once again Travis wished he'd been able to fall in love with her. They'd tried, the two of them, to get something going, on more than one occasion. Meg wanted a baby, and he wanted not to be alone, so it made sense. The trouble was, it hadn't worked.

There was no chemistry.

There was no passion.

They were never going to be anything more than what they were—the best of friends. He was mostly resigned to that, but in lonely moments, he ached for things to be different.

"Tell me about my sister," Meg insisted.

"She's pretty," Travis said. *Real* pretty, added a voice in his mind. "She's proud, and overprotective as hell of the kid."

"Liam has asthma," Meg said quietly. "According to Sierra, he nearly died of it a couple of times."

Travis forgot his burned fingers, his Salisbury steak and his private sorrow. *"What?"*

Meg let out a long breath. "That's the only reason Sierra's willing to have anything to do with Mom and me. Mom put her on the company health plan and arranged for Liam to see a specialist in Flagstaff on a regular basis. In return, Sierra had to agree to spend a year on the ranch."

Travis stood still, absorbing it all. "Why here?" he asked. "Why not with you and Eve in San Antonio?"

"Mom and I would love that," Meg said, "but Sierra needs…distance. Time to get used to us."

"Time to get used to two McKettrick women. So we're talking, say, the year 2050, give or take a decade?"

"Very funny. Sierra *is* a McKettrick woman, remember? She's up to the challenge."

"She is definitely a McKettrick," Travis agreed ruefully. And very definitely a woman. "How did you find her?"

"Mom tracked her and Hank down when Sierra was little," Meg answered.

Travis dropped on to the edge of his bed, which was unmade. The sheets were getting musty, and every night, the pizza crumbs rubbed his hide raw. One of these days he was going to haul off and change them.

"'Tracked her down'?"

"Yes," Meg said, with a sigh. "I guess I didn't tell you about that part."

"I guess you didn't." Travis had known about the kidnapping, how Sierra's father had taken off with her the day the divorce papers were served, and that the two of them had ended up in Mexico. "Eve knew, and she still didn't lift a finger to get her own daughter back?"

"Mom had her reasons," Meg answered, withdrawing a little.

"Oh, well, then," Travis retorted, "that clears everything up. What *reason* could she possibly have?"

"It's not my place to say, Trav," Meg told him sadly. "Mom and Sierra have to work it all through first, and it might be a while before Sierra's ready to listen."

Travis sighed, shoved a hand through his hair. "You're right," he conceded.

Meg brightened again, but there was a brittleness about her that revealed more than she probably wanted Travis to know, close as they were. "So," she said, "what would you say Mom's chances are? Of reconnecting with Sierra, I mean?"

"The truth?"

"The truth," Meg said, without enthusiasm.

"Zero to zip. Sierra's been pleasant enough to me, but she's as stubborn as any McKettrick that ever drew breath, and that's saying something."

"Gee, thanks."

"You said you wanted the truth."

"How can you be so sure Mom won't be able to get through to her?"

"It's just a hunch," Travis said.

Meg was quiet. Travis was famous for his hunches. Too bad he hadn't paid attention to the one that said his little brother was in big trouble, and that Travis ought to drop everything and look for Brody until he found him.

"Look, maybe I'm wrong," he added.

"What's your real impression of Sierra, Travis?"

He took his time answering. "She's independent to

a fault. She's built a wall around herself and the kid, and she's not about to let anybody get too close. She's jumpy, too. If it wasn't for Liam, and the fact that she probably doesn't have two nickels to rub together, she definitely wouldn't be on the Triple M."

"Damn," Meg said. "We knew she was poor, but—"

"Her car gave out in the driveway as soon as she pulled in. I took a peek under the hood, and believe me, the best mechanic on the planet couldn't resurrect that heap."

"She can drive my SUV."

"That might take some convincing on your part. This is not a woman who wants to be obliged. It's probably all she can do not to grab the kid and hop on the next bus to nowhere."

"This is depressing," Meg said.

Travis got up off the bed, peeled back the plastic covering his dinner, and poked warily at the faux meat with the tip of one finger. Talk about depressing.

"Hey," he said. "Look on the bright side. She's here, isn't she? She's on the Triple M. It's a start."

"Take care of her, Travis."

"As if she'd go along with that."

"Do it for me."

"Oh, please."

Meg paused, took aim and scored a bull's-eye. "Then do it for Liam."

Chapter 4

1919

Doss left the house after supper, ostensibly to look in on the livestock one last time before heading upstairs to bed, leaving the dishwashing to Tobias and Hannah. He stood still in the dooryard, raising the collar of his coat against the wicked cold. Stars speckled the dark, wintry sky.

In those moments he missed Gabe with a piercing intensity that might have bent him double, if he wasn't McKettrick proud. That was what his mother called the quality, anyhow. In the privacy of his own mind, Doss named it stubbornness.

Thinking of his ma made his pa come to mind, too. He missed them almost as sorely as he did Gabe. His uncles, Rafe and Kade and Jeb, along with their wives, were all down south, around Phoenix, where the weather was more hospitable to their aging bones. Their sons, to a man, were still in the army, even though the war was over, waiting to be mustered out. Their daughters had all married, every one of them keeping the McKettrick name, and lived in places as far-flung as Boston, New York and San Francisco.

There was hardly a McKettrick left on the place, save himself and Hannah and Tobias. It deepened Doss's loneliness, knowing that. He wished everybody would just come back home, where they belonged, but it would have been easier to herd wild barn cats than that bunch.

Doss looked back toward the house. Saw the lantern glowing at the kitchen window. Smiled.

The moment he'd gone outside, Hannah must have switched off the bulb. She worried about running short of things, he'd noticed, even though she'd come from a prosperous family, and certainly married into one.

His throat tightened. He knew she'd been different before he brought Gabe home in a pine box, but then, they all had. Gabe's going left a hole in the fabric of what it meant to be a McKettrick, and not a tidy one, stitched at the edges. Rather, it was a jagged tear, and judging by the raw newness of his own grief, Doss had little hope of it ever mending.

Time heals, his mother had told him after they'd laid Gabe in the ground up there on the hill, with his Grandpa Angus and those that had passed after him, but she'd had tears in her eyes as she said it. As for his pa, well, he'd stood a long time by the grave. Stood there until Rafe and Kade and Jeb brought him away.

Doss thrust out a sigh, remembering. "Gabe," he said, under his breath, "Hannah says it's wrong of me, but I still wish it had been me instead of you."

He'd have given anything for an answer, but wherever Gabe was, he was busy doing other things. Maybe they had fishing holes up there in the sky, or cattle to round up and drive to market.

"Take care of Hannah and my boy," Gabe had told him, in that army infirmary, when they both knew there would be no turning the illness around. "Promise me, Doss."

Doss had swallowed hard and made that promise, but it was a hard one to keep. Hannah didn't seem to want taking care of, and every morning when Doss woke up, he was afraid this would be the day she'd decide to go back to her own people, up in Montana, and stay gone for good.

The back door opened, startling Doss out of his musings. He hesitated for a moment, then tramped in the direction of the barn, trying to look like a man bent on a purpose.

Hannah caught up, bundled into a shawl and carrying a lighted lantern in one hand.

"I think I'm going mad," she blurted out.

Doss stopped, looked down at her in puzzled concern. "It's the grief, Hannah," he told her gruffly. "It will pass."

"You don't believe that any more than I do," Hannah challenged, catching up with herself. The snow was deep and getting deeper, and the wind bit straight through to the marrow.

Doss moved to the windward side, to be a buffer for her. "I've got to believe it," he said. "Feeling this bad forever doesn't bear thinking about."

"I put the teapot away," Hannah said, her breath coming in puffs of white. "I know I put it away. But I must have gotten it out again, without knowing or remembering, and that scares me, Doss. That really scares me."

They reached the barn. Doss took the lantern from her and hauled open one of the big doors one-handed. It wasn't easy, since the snow had drifted, even in the short time since he'd left off feeding and watering the horses and the milk cow and that cussed mule Seesaw. The critter was a son of Doss's mother's mule, who'd borne the same name, and he was a son of something else, too.

"Maybe you're a mite forgetful these days," Doss said, once he'd gotten her inside, out of the cold. The familiar smells and sounds of the darkened barn were a solace to him—he came there often, even when he didn't have work to do, which was seldom. On a ranch, there was always work to do—wood to chop, harnesses to mend, animals to look after. "That doesn't mean you're not sane, Hannah."

Don't say it, he pleaded silently. Don't say you might as well take Tobias and head for Montana.

It was a selfish thought, Doss knew. In Montana, Hannah could live a city life again. No riding a mule five miles to fetch the mail. No breaking the ice on the water troughs on winter mornings, so the cattle and horses could drink. No feeding chickens and dressing like a man.

If Hannah left the Triple M, Doss didn't know what he'd do. First and foremost, he'd have to break his promise to Gabe, by default if not directly, but there was more to it than that. A lot more.

"There's something else, too," Hannah confided.

To keep himself busy, Doss went from stall to stall, looking in on sleepy horses, each one confounded and blinking in the light of his lantern. He was giving Hannah space, enough distance to get out whatever it was she wanted to say.

"What?" he asked, when she didn't speak again right away.

"Tobias. He just told me—he told me—"

Doss looked back, saw Hannah standing in the moonlit doorway, rimmed in silver, with one hand pressed to her mouth.

He went back to her. Set the lantern aside and took her by the shoulders. "What did he tell you, Hannah?"

"Doss, he's seeing things."

He tensed on the inside. Would have shoved a hand through his hair in agitation if he hadn't been wearing a hat and his ears weren't bound to freeze if he took it off. "What kind of things?"

"A boy." She took hold of his arm, and her grip was strong for such a small woman. It did curious things to him, feeling her fingers on him, even through the combined thickness of his coat and shirt. "Doss, Tobias says he saw a boy in his room."

Doss looked around. There was nothing but bleak, frozen land for miles around. "That's impossible," he said.

"You've got to talk to him."

"Oh, I'll talk to him, all right." Doss started for the house, so fixed on getting to Tobias that he forgot all about keeping Hannah sheltered from the wind. She had to lift her skirts to keep pace with him.

Present Day

"Tell me about the boy you saw in your room," Sierra said, when they'd eaten their fill of fried chicken, macaroni salad, mashed potatoes with gravy, and corn on the cob.

Liam's gaze was clear as he regarded her from his side of the long table. "He's a ghost," he replied, and waited, visibly expecting the statement to be refuted.

"Maybe an imaginary playmate?" Sierra ventured. Liam was a lonely little boy; their lifestyle had seen to that. After her father had died, drunk himself to death in a back-street cantina in San Miguel, the two of them had wandered like gypsies. San Diego. North Carolina, Georgia, and finally Florida.

"There's nothing imaginary about him," Liam said staunchly. "He wears funny clothes, like those kids on those old-time shows on TV. He's a *ghost,* Mom. Face it."

"Liam—"

"You never believe anything I tell you!"

"I believe *everything* you tell me," Sierra insisted evenly. "But you've got to admit, this is a stretch." Again she thought of the teapot. Again she pushed the recollection aside.

"I never lie, Mom."

She moved to pat his hand, but he pulled back. The set of his jaw was stubborn, and his gaze drilled into her, full of challenge. She tried again. "I know you don't lie, Liam. But you're in a strange new place and you miss your friends and—"

"And you won't even let me see if they sent me emails!" he cried.

Sierra sighed, rested her elbows on the tabletop and rubbed her temples with the fingertips of both hands. "Okay," she relented. "You can log on to the internet. Just be careful, because that computer is expensive, and we can't afford to replace it."

Suddenly Liam's face was alight. "I won't break it," he promised, with exuberance.

Sierra wondered if he'd just scammed her, if the whole boy-in-the-bedroom thing was a trick to get what he wanted.

In the next instant she was ashamed. Liam was direct to a fault. He *believed* he'd seen another child in his empty bedroom. She'd call his new doctor in Flagstaff in the morning, talk to the woman, see what a qualified professional made of the whole thing. She offered a silent prayer that her car would start, too, because the doctor was going to want to see Liam, pronto.

Meanwhile, Liam got to his feet and scrambled out of the room.

Sierra cleared away the supper mess, then followed him, as casually as she could, to the room at the front of the house.

He was already online.

"Just what I thought!" he crowed. "My mailbox is *bulging.*"

The TV was still on, a narrator dolefully describing the effects of a second ice age, due any minute. Run for the hills. Sierra shut it off.

"Hey," Liam objected. "I was listening to that."

Sierra approached the computer. "You're only seven," she said. "You shouldn't be worrying about the fate of the planet."

"Somebody's got to," Liam replied, without looking at her. "*Your* generation is doing a lousy job." He was staring, as if mesmerized, into the computer screen. Its bluish-gray light flickered on the lenses of his glasses, making his eyes disappear. "Look! The whole Geek Group wrote to me!"

"I asked you not to—"

"Okay," Liam sighed, without looking at her. "The brilliant children in the gifted program are engaging in communication."

"That's better," Sierra said, sparing a smile.

"You've got a few emails waiting yourself," Liam announced. He was already replying to the cybermissives, his small fingers ranging deftly over the keyboard. He'd skipped the hunt-and-peck method entirely, as had all the other kids in his class. Using a computer came naturally to Liam, almost as if he'd been born knowing how, and she knew this was a common phenomenon, which gave her some comfort.

"I'll read them later," Sierra answered. She didn't have that many friends, so most of her messages were probably sales pitches of the penis-enlargement variety. How had she gotten on that kind of list? It wasn't as if she visited porn sites or ordered battery-operated boyfriends online.

"They get to watch a real rocket launch!" Liam cried, without a trace of envy. *"Wow!"*

"Wow indeed," Sierra said, looking around the room. According to Meg, it had originally been a study. Old books lined the walls on sturdy shelves, and there was a natural rock fireplace, too, with a fire already laid.

Sierra found a match on the mantelpiece, struck it and lit the blaze.

A chime sounded from the computer.

"Aunt Meg just IM'd you," Liam said.

Where had he gotten this "Aunt Meg" thing? He'd never even met the woman in person, let alone established a relationship with her. "'IM'd'?" she asked.

"Instant Messaged," Liam translated. "Guess you'd better check it out. Just make it quick, because I've still got a *pile* of mail to answer."

Smiling again, Sierra took the chair Liam so reluctantly surrendered and read the message from Meg.

Travis tells me your car died. Use my SUV. The keys are in the sugar bowl beside the teapot.

Sierra's pride kicked in. Thanks, she replied, at a fraction of Liam's typing speed, but I probably won't need it. My car is just... She paused. Her car was just what? Old? tired, she finished, inspired.

The SUV won't run when I come back if somebody doesn't charge up the battery. It's been sitting too long, Meg responded quickly. She must have been as fast with a keyboard as Liam.

Is Travis going to report on everything I do? Sierra wrote. She made so many mistakes, she had to retype the message before hitting Send, and that galled her.

Yes, Meg wrote. Because I plan to nag every last detail out of him.

Sierra sighed. It won't be that interesting, she answered, taking her time so she wouldn't have to revise. She was out of practice, and if she hoped to land anything better than a waitressing job in Indian Rock, she'd better polish her computer skills.

Meg sent a smiley face, followed by, Good night, Sis. (I've always wanted to say that.)

Sierra bit her lower lip. Good night, she tapped out, and rose from the chair with a glance at the clock on the mantel above the now-snapping fire.

Why had she lit it? She was exhausted, and now she would either have to throw water on the flames or wait until they died down. The first method, of course, would make a terrible mess, so that was out.

"Hurry up and finish what you're doing," she told Liam, who had plopped in the chair again the moment Sierra got out of it. "Half an hour till bedtime."

"I had a *nap,*" Liam reminded her, typing simultaneously.

"Finish," Sierra repeated. With that, she left the study,

climbed the stairs and went into Liam's room to get his favorite pajamas from one of the suitcases. She meant to put them in the clothes dryer for a few minutes, warm them up.

Something drew her to the window, though. She looked down, saw that the lights were on in Travis's trailer and his truck was parked nearby. Evidently, he hadn't stayed long in town, or wherever he'd gone.

Why did it please her so much, knowing that?

1919

Hannah stood in the doorway of Tobias's room, watching her boy sleep. He looked so peaceful, lying there, but she knew he had bad dreams sometimes. Just the night before, in the wee small hours, he'd crawled into bed beside her, snuggled as close as his little-boy pride would allow, and whispered earnestly that she oughtn't die anytime soon.

She'd been so choked up, she could barely speak.

Now she wanted to wake him, hold him tight in her arms, protect him from whatever it was in his mind that made him see little boys that weren't there.

He was lonely, that was all. He needed to be around other children. Way out here, he went to a one-room school, when it wasn't closed on account of snow, with only seven other pupils, all of whom were older than he was.

Maybe she should take him home to Montana. He had cousins there. They'd live in town, too, where there were shops and a library and even a moving-picture theater. He could ride his bicycle, come spring, and play baseball with other boys.

Hannah's throat ached. Gabe had wanted his son

raised here, on the Triple M. Wanted him to grow up the way he had, rough-and-tumble, riding horses, rounding up stray cattle, part of the land. Of course, Gabe hadn't expected to die young—he'd meant to come home, so he and Hannah could fill that big house with children. Tobias would have had plenty of company then.

A tear slipped down Hannah's cheek, and she swatted it away. Straightened her spine.

Gabe was gone, and there weren't going to be any more children.

She heard Doss climbing the stairs, and wanted to move out of the doorway. He thought she was too fussy, always hovering over Tobias. Always trying to protect him.

How could a man understand what it meant to bear and nurture a child?

Hannah closed her eyes and stayed where she was.

Doss stopped behind her, uncertain. She could feel that, along with the heat and sturdy substance of his body.

"Leave the child to sleep, Hannah," he said quietly.

She nodded, closed Tobias's door gently and turned to face Doss there in the darkened hallway. He carried a book under one arm and an unlit lantern in his other hand.

"It's because he's lonesome," she said.

Doss clearly knew she was referring to Tobias's hallucination. "Kids make up playmates," he told her. "And being lonesome is a part of life. It's a valley a person has to go through, not something to run away from."

No McKettrick ever ran from anything. Doss didn't have to say it, and neither did she. But she wasn't a McKettrick, not by blood. Oh, she still wrote the word, whenever she had to sign something, but she'd stopped owning the name the day they put Gabe in the ground.

She wasn't sure why. He'd been so proud of it, like all the rest of them were.

"Do you ever wish you could live someplace else?" Hannah heard herself say.

"No," Doss said, so quickly and with such gravity that Hannah almost believed he'd been reading her mind. "I belong right here."

"But the others—your uncles and cousins—they didn't stay...."

"Ask any one of them where home is," Doss answered, "and they'll tell you it's the Triple M."

Hannah started to speak, then held her tongue. Nodded. "Good night, Doss," she said.

He inclined his head and went on to his own room, shut himself away.

Hannah stood alone in the dark for a long time.

She'd been so happy on the Triple M when Gabe was alive, and even after he'd gone into the army, because she'd never once doubted that he'd return. Come walking up the path with a duffel bag over one shoulder, whistling. She'd rehearsed that day a thousand times in her mind—pictured herself running to meet him, throwing herself into his arms.

It was never going to happen.

Without him, she might as well have been alone on the barren landscape of the moon.

Her eyes filled.

She walked slowly to the end of the hall, into the room where Gabe had brought her on their wedding night. He'd been conceived and born in the big bed there, just as Tobias had. As so many other babes would have been, if only Gabe had lived.

Hannah didn't undress after she closed the door behind her. She didn't let her hair down and brush it, like usual, or wash her face at the basin on the bureau.

Instead, she sat down in Lorelei's rocking chair and waited. Just waited.

For what, she did not know.

Present Day

After Liam had gone to bed, Sierra went back downstairs to the computer and scanned her email. When she spotted Allie Douglas-Fletcher's return address, she wished she'd waited until morning. She was always stronger in the mornings.

Allie was Adam's twin sister. Liam's aunt. After Adam was murdered, while on assignment in South America, Allie had been inconsolable, and she'd developed an unhealthy fixation for her brother's child.

After taking a deep breath and releasing it slowly, Sierra opened the message. Typically, there was no preamble. Allie got right to the point.

The guest house is ready for you and Liam. You know Adam would want his son to grow up right here in San Diego, Sierra. Tim and I can give Liam everything—a real home, a family, an education, the very best medical care. We're willing to make a place for you, too, obviously. If you won't come home, at least tell us you arrived safely in Arizona.

Sierra sat, wooden, staring at the stark plea on the screen. Although Allie and Adam had been raised in relative poverty, both of them had done well in life. Adam had been a photojournalist for a major magazine; he and Sierra had met when he did a piece on San Miguel.

Allie ran her own fund-raising firm, and her husband was a neurosurgeon. They had everything—except what they wanted most. Children.

You can't have Liam, Sierra cried, in the silence of her heart. *He's mine.*

She flexed her fingers, sighed, and hit Reply. Allie was a good person, just as Adam had been, for all that he'd told Sierra a lie that shook the foundations of the universe. Adam's sister sincerely believed she and the doctor could do a better job of raising Liam than Sierra could, and maybe they were right. They had money. They had social status.

Tears burned in Sierra's eyes.

Liam is well. We're safe on the Triple M, and for the time being, we're staying put.

It was all she could bring herself to say.

She hit Send and logged off the computer.

The fire was still flourishing on the hearth. She got up, crossed the room, pushed the screen aside to jab at the burning wood with a poker. It only made the flames burn more vigorously.

She kicked off her shoes, curled up in the big leather chair and pulled a knitted afghan around her to wait for the fire to die down.

The old clock on the mantel tick-tocked, the sound loud and steady and almost hypnotic.

Sierra yawned. Closed her eyes. Opened them again.

She thought about turning the TV back on, just for the sound of human voices, but dismissed the idea. She was so tired, she was going to need all her energy just to go upstairs and tumble into bed. There was none to spare for fiddling with the television set.

Again, she closed her eyes.

Again, she opened them.

She wondered if the lights were still on in Travis's trailer.

Closed her eyes.

Was dragged down into a heavy, fitful sleep.

She knew right away that she was dreaming, and yet it was so real.

She heard the clock ticking.

She felt the warmth of the fire.

But she was standing in the ranch house kitchen, and it was different, in subtle ways, from the room she knew.

She was different.

Her eyes were shut, and yet she could see clearly.

A bare light bulb dangled overhead, giving off a dim but determined glow.

She looked down at herself, the dream-Sierra, and felt a wrench of surprise.

She was wearing a long woolen skirt. Her hands were smaller—chapped and work worn—someone else's hands.

"I'm dreaming," she insisted to herself, but it didn't help.

She stared around the kitchen. The teapot sat on the counter.

"Now what's that doing there?" asked this other Sierra. "I know I put it away. I know for sure I did."

Sierra struggled to wake up. It was too intense, this dream. She was in some other woman's body, not her own. It was sinewy and strong, this body. She felt the heartbeat, the breath going in and out. Felt the weight of long hair, pinned to the back of her head in a loose chignon.

"Wake up," she said.

But she couldn't.

She stood very still, staring at the teapot.

Emotions stormed within her, a loneliness so wretched and sharp that she thought she'd burst from the inside and shatter. Longing for a man who'd gone away and was never coming home, an unspeakable sorrow. Love for a child, so profound that it might have been mourning.

And something else. A forbidden wanting that had nothing to do with the man who'd left her.

Sierra woke herself then, by force of will, only to find her face wet with another woman's tears.

She must have been asleep for a while, she realized. The flames on the hearth had become embers. The room was chilly.

She shivered, tugged the afghan tighter around her, and got out of the chair. She went to the window, looked out. Travis's trailer was dark.

"It was just a dream," she told herself out loud.

So why was her heart breaking?

She made her way into the kitchen, navigating the dark hallway as best she could, since she didn't know where the light switches were. When she reached her destination, she walked to the middle of the room, where she'd stood in the dream, and suppressed an urge to reach up for the metal-beaded cord she knew wasn't there.

What she needed, she decided, was a good cup of tea.

She found a switch beside the back door and flipped it.

Reality returned in a comforting spill of light.

She found an electric kettle, filled it at the sink and plugged it in to boil. Earlier she'd been too weary to get out of that chair in the study and turn on the TV. Now she knew it would be pointless to try to sleep.

Might as well do this up right, she thought.

She went to the china cabinet, got the teapot out, set it on the table. Added tea leaves and located a little strainer in one of the drawers. The kettle boiled.

She was sitting quietly, sipping tea and watching fat snowflakes drift past the porch light outside the back door, when Liam came down the back stairway in his pajamas. Blinking, he rubbed his eyes.

"Is it morning?" he asked.

"No," Sierra said gently. "Go back to bed."

"Can I have some tea?"

"No, again," Sierra answered, but she didn't protest when Liam took a seat on the bench, close to her chair. "But if there's cocoa, I'll make you some."

"There is," Liam said. He looked incredibly young, and so very vulnerable, without his glasses. "I saw it in the pantry. It's the instant kind."

With a smile, Sierra got out of the chair, walked into the pantry and brought out the cocoa, along with a bag of semihard marshmallows. Thanks to Travis's preparations for their arrival, there was milk in the refrigerator and, using the microwave, she had Liam's hot chocolate ready in no time.

"I like it here," he told her. "It's better than any place we've ever lived."

Sierra's heart squeezed. "You really think so? Why?"

Liam took a sip of hot chocolate and acquired a liquid mustache. One small shoulder rose and fell in a characteristic shrug. "It feels like a real home," he said. "Lots of people have lived here. And they were all McKettricks, like us."

Sierra was stung, but she hid it behind another smile. "Wherever we live," she said carefully, "is a real home, because we're together."

Liam's expression was benignly skeptical, even tolerant. "We never had so much room before. We never had a barn with horses in it. And we never had *ghosts*." He whispered the last word, and gave a little shiver of pure joy.

Sierra was looking for a way to approach the ghost subject again when the faint, delicate sound of piano music reached her ears.

Chapter 5

"Do you hear that?" she asked Liam.

His brow furrowed as he shifted on the bench and took another sip of his cocoa. "Hear what?"

The tune continued, flowing softly, forlornly, from the front room.

"Nothing," Sierra lied.

Liam peered at her, perplexed and suspicious.

"Finish your chocolate," she prompted. "It's late."

The music stopped, and she felt relief and a paradoxical sorrow, reminiscent of the all-too-vivid dream she'd had earlier while dozing in the big chair in the study.

"What was it, Mom?" Liam pressed.

"I thought I heard a piano," she admitted, because she knew her son wouldn't let the subject drop until she told him the truth.

Liam smiled, pleased. "This house is so cool," he

said. "I told the Geek—the kids—that it's haunted. Aunt Allie, too."

Sierra, in the process of lifting her cup to her mouth, set it down again, shakily. "When did you talk to Allie?" she asked.

"She sent me an email," he replied, "and I answered."

"Great," Sierra said.

"Would my dad really want me to grow up in San Diego?" Liam asked seriously. The idea had, of course, come from Allie. While Sierra wasn't without sympathy for the woman, she felt violated. Allie had no business trying to entice Liam behind her back.

"Your dad would want you to grow up with me," Sierra said firmly, and she knew that was true, for all that Adam had betrayed her.

"Aunt Allie says my cousins would like me," Liam confided.

Liam's "cousins" were actually half sisters, but Sierra wasn't ready to spring that on him, and she hoped Allie wouldn't do it, either. Although Adam had told Sierra he was divorced when they met, and she'd fallen immediately and helplessly in love with him, she'd learned six months later, when she was carrying his child, that he was still living with his wife when he wasn't on the road. It had been Allie, earnest, meddling Allie, who traveled to San Miguel, found Sierra and told her the truth.

Sierra would never forget the family photos Allie showed her that day—snapshots of Adam with his arm around his smiling wife, Dee. The two little girls in matching dresses posed with them, their eyes wide with innocence and trust.

"Forget him, kiddo," Hank had said airily, when Sierra went to him, in tears, with the whole shameful story. "It ain't gonna fly."

She'd written Adam immediately, but her letter came back, tattered from forwarding, and no one answered at any of the telephone numbers he'd given her.

She'd given birth to Liam eight weeks later, at home, attended by Hank's long-time mistress, Magdalena. Three days after that, Hank brought her an American newspaper, tossed it into her lap without a word.

She'd paged through it slowly, possessed of a quiet, escalating dread, and come across the account of Adam Douglas's death on page four. He'd been shot to death, according to the article, on the outskirts of Caracas, after infiltrating a drug cartel to take pictures for an exposé he'd been writing.

"Mom?" Liam snapped his fingers under Sierra's nose. "Are you hearing the music again?"

Sierra blinked. Shook her head.

"Do you think my cousins would like me?"

She reached out, her hand trembling only slightly, and ruffled his hair. "I think *anybody* would like you," she said. When he was older, she would tell him about Adam's other family, but it was still too soon. She took his empty cup, carried it to the sink. "Now, go upstairs, brush your teeth again and hit the sack."

"Aren't you going to bed?" Liam asked practically.

Sierra sighed. "Yes," she said, resigned. She didn't think she'd sleep, but she knew Liam would wonder if she stayed up all night, prowling around the house. "You go ahead. I'm just going to make sure the front door is locked."

Liam nodded and obeyed without protest.

Sierra considered marking the occasion on the calendar.

She went straight to the front room, and the piano, the moment Liam had gone upstairs. The keyboard cover was down, the bench neatly in place. She switched on a lamp and inspected the smooth, highly polished wood for fingerprints. Nothing.

She touched the cover, and her fingers left distinct smudges.

No one had touched the piano that night, unless they'd been wearing gloves.

Frowning, Sierra checked the lock on the front door. Fastened.

She inspected the windows—all locked—and even the floor. It was snowing hard, and anybody who'd come in out of that storm would have left some trace, no matter how careful they were—a puddle somewhere, a bit of mud.

Again, there was nothing.

Finally she went upstairs, found a nightgown, bathed and got ready for bed. Since Travis had left her bags in the room adjoining Liam's, she opened the connecting door a crack and crawled between sheets worn smooth by time.

She was asleep in an instant.

1919

Hannah closed the cover over the piano keys, stacked the sheet music neatly and got to her feet. She'd played as softly as she could, pouring her sadness and her yearning into the music, and when she returned to the upstairs corridor, she saw light under Doss's door.

She paused, wondering what he'd do if she went in, took off her clothes and crawled into bed beside him.

Not that she would, of course, because she'd loved her husband and it wouldn't be fitting, but there were times when her very soul ached within her, she wanted so badly to be touched and held, and this was one of them.

She swallowed, mortified by her own wanton thoughts.

Doss would send her away angrily.

He'd remind her that she was his brother's widow—if he ever spoke to her again at all.

For all that, she took a single, silent step toward the door.

"Ma?"

Tobias spoke from behind her. She hadn't heard him get out of bed, come to the threshold of his room.

Thanking heaven she was still fully dressed, she turned to face him.

"What is it?" she asked gently. "Did you have another bad dream?"

Tobias shook his head. His gaze slipped past Hannah to Doss's door, then back to her face, solemn and worried. "I wish I had a pa," he said.

Hannah's heart seized. She approached, pulled the boy close, and he allowed it. During the day, he would have balked. "So do I," she replied, bending to kiss the top of his head. "I wish your pa was here. Wish it so much it hurts."

Tobias pulled back, looked up at her. "But Pa's dead," he said. "Maybe you and Doss could get hitched. Then he wouldn't be my uncle anymore, would he? He'd be my pa."

"Tobias," Hannah said very softly, praying Doss hadn't overheard somehow. "That wouldn't be right."

"Why not?" Tobias asked.

She crouched, looked up into her son's face. One day, he'd be handsome and square-jawed, like the rest of the McKettrick men. For now he was still a little boy, his features childishly innocent. "I was your pa's wife. I'll love him for the rest of my days."

"That might be a long time," Tobias said, with a measure of dubiousness, as well as hope. He dropped his voice to a whisper. "I don't want Doss to marry somebody else, Ma," he said. "All the women in Indian Rock are sweet on him, and one of these days he might take a notion to get himself a wife."

"Tobias," Hannah reasoned, "you must put this foolishness out of your head. If Doss chooses to take a bride, that's certainly his right. But it won't be me he marries. It's too hard to explain right now, but Doss was your pa's brother. I couldn't—"

"You'd marry some man in Montana, though, wouldn't you?" Tobias demanded, suddenly angry, and this time, he made no effort to keep his voice down. "Some stranger who wears a suit to work!"

"Tobias!"

"I won't go to Montana, do you hear me? I won't leave the Triple M unless Doss goes, too!"

Hannah reddened with embarrassment and anger—Doss had surely heard—and rose to her full height. "Tobias McKettrick," she said sternly, "you go to bed this instant, and don't you ever talk to me like that again!"

Tobias's chin jutted out, in the McKettrick way, and his eyes flashed. "You go anyplace you want to," he told her, turning on one bare heel to flee into his room, "but I'm not going with you!" With that, he slammed the door in her face.

Hannah took a step toward it, even reached for the knob. But in the end she couldn't face her son.

"Hannah."

Doss.

She stiffened but didn't turn. Doss would see too much if she did. Guess too much.

He caught hold of her arm, brought her gently around.

She whispered his name, despondent.

He took her hand, led her to the opposite end of the hall, opened the last door on the right, the one where she kept her sewing machine.

"What are you—?"

Doss stepped over the threshold first, turned, and drew her in behind him. Reached around her to shut the door.

She leaned against the panel. It was hard at her back.

"Doss," she said.

He cupped her face in his hands, bent his head, and kissed her, full on the mouth.

A sweet shock went through her. She knew she ought to break away, knew he wouldn't force himself on her if she uttered the slightest protest, but she couldn't say a word. Her body came alive as he pressed himself against her. His weight was hard and warm and blessedly real.

Doss reached behind her head, pulled the pins from her hair, let it fall around her shoulders, to her waist. He groaned, buried his face in it, burrowed through to take her earlobe between his lips and nibble on it.

Hannah gasped with guilty pleasure. Her knees went weak, and Doss held her upright with the lower part of his body.

She moaned softly.

"We can't," she whispered.

"We'd damn well better," Doss answered, "before we both go crazy."

"What if Tobias…?"

Doss leaned back, opened the buttons on her bodice, put his hands inside, under her camisole, to take the weight of her breasts. Chafed the nipples lightly with the sides of his thumbs.

"He won't hear," he said.

He bent to find a nipple, take it into his mouth. Suckled in the same nibbling, teasing way he'd tasted her earlobe.

Hannah plunged her fingers into his hair, groaned and tilted her head back, already surrendering. Already lost.

She tried to bring Gabe's face to her mind, hoping the image would give her the strength to stop—stop—before it was too late, but it wouldn't come.

Doss made free with her breasts, tonguing them until she was in a frenzy.

She sank against the door, barely able to breathe.

And then he knelt.

Hannah trembled. Even though the room was cold, perspiration broke out all over her body. She made a slight whimpering sound when Doss lifted her skirts, went under them and pulled down her drawers.

She felt him part her private place with his fingers, felt his tongue touch her, like fire. Sobbed his name, under her breath.

He took her full in his mouth, hungrily.

Her hips moved frantically, seeking him, and her knees buckled.

He braced her securely against the door, put her legs over his shoulders, first one, and then the other, and through all that, he drew on her.

She writhed against him, one hand pressed to her

mouth so that the guttural cries pounding at the back of her throat wouldn't get out.

He suckled.

She felt a surge of heat, radiating from her center into every part of her, then stiffened in a spasm of release so violent that she was afraid she would splinter into pieces.

"Doss," she pleaded, because she knew it was going to happen again, and again.

And it did.

When it was over, he ducked out from under the hem of her skirt and held her as she sagged, spent, to her knees. They were facing each other, her breasts bared to him, her body still quivering with an ebbing tide of passion.

"We can stop here," he said quietly.

She shook her head. They'd gone past the place of turning back.

Doss opened his trousers, reached under her skirt and petticoat to take hold of her hips. Lifted her onto him.

She slid along his length, letting him fill her, exalting in the size and heat and slick hardness of him. She gave a loud moan, and he covered her mouth with his, kissed her senseless, even as he raised and lowered her, raised and lowered her. The friction was slow and exquisite. Hannah dug her fingers into his shoulders and rode him shamelessly until satisfaction overtook her again, convulsed her, like some giant fist, and didn't let go until she was limp with exhaustion.

Only when she wept with relief did Doss finish. She felt him erupt inside her, swallowed his groans as he gave himself up to her.

He brushed away her tears with his thumbs, still inside

her, and looked deep into her eyes. "It's all right, Hannah," he said gruffly. "Please, don't cry."

He didn't understand.

She wasn't weeping for shame, though that would surely come, but for the most poignant of joys.

"No," she said softly. She plunged her fingers into his hair, kissed him boldly, fervently. "It's not that. I feel..."

He was growing hard within her again.

"Oh," she groaned.

He played with her nipples. And got harder still.

"Doss," she gasped. "Doss—"

Present Day

Sierra awakened with a start, sounding from the depths of a dream so erotic that she'd been on the verge of climax. The light dazzled her, and the muffled silence seemed to fill not only her bedroom, but the world beyond it.

She lay still for a long time, recovering. Listening to her own quick, shallow breathing. Waiting for her heartbeat to slow down.

Liam peeked through the doorway linking her room to his.

"Mom?"

"Come in," Sierra said.

He bounded across the threshold. "It snowed!" he whooped, heading straight for the window. "I mean, it *really* snowed!"

Sierra smiled, sat up in bed and put her feet on the floor.

A jolt of cold went through her.

"It's *freezing* in here!"

Liam turned from the window to grin at her. "Travis says the furnace is out."

"Travis?"

"He's downstairs," Liam said. "He'll get it going."

A dusty-smelling whoosh rose from the nearest heat vent, as if to illustrate the point.

"What's he doing here?" Sierra asked, scrambling through her suitcases for a bathrobe. All she had was a thin nylon thing, and when she saw it, she knew it would be worse than nothing, so she pulled the quilt off the bed and wrapped herself in that instead.

"Don't be a grump," Liam replied. "Travis is doing us a *favor,* Mom. We'd probably be icicles by now if it wasn't for him. Did you know that old stove downstairs *works?* Travis built a fire in it, and he put the coffee on, too. He said to tell you it will be ready in a couple of minutes and we're snowed in."

"Snowed in?"

"Keep up, Mom," Liam chirped. "There was a *blizzard* last night. That's why Travis came to make sure we were all right. I heard him knock, and I let him in."

Sierra joined Liam at the window and drew in her breath.

The whiteness of all that snow practically blinded her, but it was beautiful, too, in an apocalyptic way. She'd never seen anything like it before and, for a long moment, she was spellbound. Then her sensible side kicked in.

"Thank God the power didn't go out," she said, easing a little closer to the vent, which was spewing deliciously warm air.

"It *did,*" Liam informed her happily. "Travis got the

generator started right away. We don't have lights or anything, but he said the furnace is all that matters."

She frowned. "How could he have made coffee?"

"On the *cookstove,* Mom," Liam said, with a roll of his eyes.

For the first time Sierra noticed that Liam was fully dressed.

He headed for the door. "I'd better go help Travis bring in the wood," he said. "Get some *clothes* on, will you?"

Five minutes later Sierra joined Travis and Liam in the kitchen, which was blessedly warm. Her jeans would do well enough, but she'd had to raid Meg's room for socks and a thick sweatshirt, because her tank tops weren't going to cut it.

"Are we *stranded* here?" she demanded, watching as Travis poured coffee from a blue enamel pot that looked like it came from a stash of camping gear.

He grinned. "Depends on how you look at it," he said. "Liam and I, we see it as an adventure."

"Some adventure," Sierra grumbled, but she took the coffee he offered and gave a grateful nod of thanks.

Travis chuckled. "Don't worry," he said. "You'll adjust."

Sierra hastened over to stand closer to the cookstove. "Does this happen often?"

"Only in winter," Travis quipped.

"Hilarious," she drawled.

Liam laughed uproariously.

"You are *enjoying* this," she accused, tousling her son's hair.

"It's *great!*" Liam cried. "Snow! Wait till the Geeks hear about this!"

"Liam," Sierra said.

He gave Travis a long-suffering look. "She hates it when I say 'geek,'" he explained.

Travis picked up his own mug of coffee, took a sip, his eyes full of laughter. Then he headed toward the door, put the cup on the counter and reclaimed his coat down from the peg.

"You're *leaving?*" Liam asked, horrified.

"Gotta see to the horses," Travis said, putting on his hat.

"Can I go with you?" Liam pleaded, and he sounded so desperately hopeful that Sierra swallowed the "no" that instantly sprang from her vocal cords.

"Your coat isn't warm enough," she said.

"Meg's got an old one around here someplace," Travis said carefully. "Hall closet, I think."

Liam dashed off to get it.

"I'll take care of him, Sierra," Travis told her quietly, when the boy was gone.

"You'd better," Sierra answered.

1919

Hannah knew by the profound silence, even before she opened her eyes, that it had been snowing all night. Lying alone in the big bed she'd shared with Gabe, she burrowed deeper into the covers and groaned.

She was sore.

She was satisfied.

She was a trollop.

A tramp.

She'd practically thrown herself at Doss the night be-

fore. She'd let him do things to her that no one else besides Gabe had ever done.

And now it was morning and she'd come to her senses
and she would have to face him.

For all that, she felt strangely light, too.

Almost giddy.

Hannah pulled the covers up over her head and giggled.

Giggled.

She tried to be stern with herself.

This was serious.

Downstairs the stove lids rattled.

Doss was building a fire in the cookstove, the way he
did every morning. He would put the coffee on to boil,
then go out to the barn to attend to the livestock. When
he got back, she'd be making breakfast, and they'd talk
about how cold it was, and whether he ought to bring in
extra wood from the shed, in case there was more snow
on the way.

It would be an ordinary ranch morning.

Except that she'd behaved like a tart the night before.

Hannah tossed back the covers and got up. She wasn't
one to avoid facing things, no matter how awkward they
were. She and Doss had lost their heads and made love.
That was that.

It wouldn't happen again.

They'd just go on, as if nothing had happened.

The water in the pitcher on the bureau was too cold
to wash in.

Hannah decided she would heat some for a bath, after
the breakfast dishes were done. She'd send Tobias to the
study to work at his school lessons, and Doss to the barn.

She dressed hastily, brushed her hair and wound it

into the customary chignon at the back of her head. Just before she opened the bedroom door to step out into the new day, the pit of her stomach quivered. She drew a deep breath, squared her shoulders and turned the knob resolutely.

Doss had not left for the barn, as she'd expected. He was still in the kitchen, and when she came down the back stairs and froze on the bottom step, he looked at her, reddened and looked away.

Tobias was by the back door, pulling on his heaviest coat. "Doss and me are fixing to ride down to the bend and look in on the widow Jessup," he told Hannah matter-of-factly, and he sounded like a grown man, fit to make such decisions on his own. "Could be her pump's frozen, and we're not sure she has enough firewood."

Out of the corner of her eye, Hannah saw Doss watching her.

"Go out and see to the cow," Doss told Tobias. "Make sure there's no ice on her trough."

It was an excuse to speak to her alone, Hannah knew, and she was unnerved. She resisted an urge to touch her hair with both hands or smooth her skirts.

Tobias banged out the back door, whistling.

"He's not strong enough to ride to the Jessups' place in this weather," Hannah said. "It's four miles if it's a stone's throw, and you'll have to cross the creek."

"Hannah," Doss said firmly, grimly. "The boy will be fine."

She felt her own color rise then, remembering all they'd done together, on the spare room floor, herself and this man. She swallowed and lifted her chin a notch, so he wouldn't think she was ashamed.

"About last night—" Doss began. He looked distraught.

Hannah waited, blushing furiously now. Wishing the floor would open, so she could fall right through to China and never be seen or heard from again.

Doss shoved a hand through his hair. "I'm sorry," he said.

Hannah hadn't expected anything except shame, but she was stung by it, just the same. "We'll just pretend—" She had to stop, clear her throat, blink a couple of times. "We'll just pretend it didn't happen."

His jaw tightened. "Hannah, it did happen, and pretending won't change that."

She intertwined her fingers, clasped them so tightly that the knuckles ached. Looked down at the floor. "What else can we do, Doss?" she asked, almost in a whisper.

"Suppose there's a child?"

Hannah hadn't once thought of that possibility, though it seemed painfully obvious in the bright, rational light of day. She drew in a sharp breath and put a hand to her throat.

How would they explain such a thing to Tobias? To the McKettricks and the people of Indian Rock?

"I'd have to go to Montana," she said, after a long time. "To my folks."

"Not with my baby growing inside you, you wouldn't," Doss replied, so sharply that Hannah's gaze shot back to his face.

"Doss, the scandal—"

"To hell with the scandal!"

Hannah reached out, pulled back Holt's chair at the table and sank into it. "Maybe I'm not. Surely just once—"

"Maybe you are," Doss insisted.

Hannah's eyes smarted. She'd wanted more children, but not like this. Not out of wedlock, and by her late husband's brother. Folks would call her a hussy, with considerable justification, and they'd make Tobias's life a plain misery, too. They'd point and whisper, and the other kids would tease.

"What are we going to do, then?" she asked.

He crossed the room, sat astraddle the long bench next to the table, so close she could feel the warmth of his body, glowing like the fresh fire blazing inside the cookstove.

His very proximity made her remember things better forgotten.

"There's only one thing we can do, Hannah. We'll get married."

She gaped at him. "Married?"

"It's the only decent thing to do."

The word decent stabbed at Hannah. She was a proud person, and she'd always lived a respectable life. Until the night before. "We don't love each other," she said, her voice small. "And anyway, I might not be—expecting."

"I'm not taking the chance," Doss told her. "As soon as the trail clears a little, we're going into Indian Rock and get married."

"I have some say in this," Hannah pointed out.

Outside, on the back porch, Tobias thumped his boots against the step, to shake off the snow.

"Do you?" Doss asked.

Chapter 6

Present Day

While Travis and Liam were in the barn, Sierra inspected the wood-burning stove. She found a skillet, set it on top, took bacon and eggs from the refrigerator, which was ominously dark and silent, and laid strips of the bacon in the pan. When the meat began to sizzle, she felt a little thrill of accomplishment.

She was actually *cooking* on a stove that dated from the nineteenth century. Briefly, she felt connected with all the McKettrick women who had gone before her.

When the electricity came on, with a startling revving sound, she was almost sorry. Keeping an eye on breakfast, she switched on the small countertop TV to catch the morning news.

The entire northern part of Arizona had been inundated in the blizzard, and thousands were without power. She watched as images of people skiing to work flashed across the screen.

The telephone rang, and she held the portable receiver between her shoulder and ear to answer. "Hello?"

"It's Eve," a gracious voice replied. "Is that you, Sierra?"

Sierra went utterly still. Travis and Liam tramped in from outside, laughing about something. They both fell silent at the sight of her, and neither one moved after Travis pushed the door shut.

"Hello?" Eve prompted. "Sierra, are you there?"

"I'm… I'm here," Sierra said.

Travis took off his coat and hat, crossed the room and elbowed her away from the stove. "Go," he told her, cocking a thumb toward the center of the house. "Liam and I will see to the grub."

She nodded, grateful, and hurried out of the warm kitchen. The dining room was frigid.

"Is this a bad time to talk?" Eve asked. She sounded uncertain, even a little shy.

"No—" Sierra answered hastily, finally gaining the study. She closed the door and sat in the big leather chair she'd occupied the night before, waiting for the fire to go out. Now she could see her breath, and she wished the blaze was still burning. "No, it's fine."

Eve let out a long breath. "I see on the Weather Channel that you've been hit with quite a storm up there," she said.

Sierra nodded, remembered that her mother—this woman she didn't know—couldn't see her. "Yes," she replied. "We have power again, thanks to Travis. He got the generator running right away, so the furnace would work and—"

She swallowed the rush of too-cheerful words. She'd been blathering.

"Poor Travis," Eve said.

"Poor Travis?" Sierra echoed. "Why?"

"Didn't he tell you? Didn't Meg?"

"No," Sierra said. "Nobody told me anything."

There was a long pause, then Eve sighed. "I'm probably speaking out of turn," she said, "but we've all been a little worried about Travis. He's like a member of the family, you know. His younger brother, Brody, died in an explosion a few months ago. It really threw Travis. He walked away from the company and just about everyone he knew. Meg had to talk fast to get him to come and stay on the ranch."

Sierra was very glad she'd brought the phone out of the kitchen. "I didn't know," she said.

"I've already said more than I should have," Eve told her ruefully. "And anyway, I called to see how you and Liam are doing. I know you're not used to cold weather, and when I saw the storm report, I had to call."

"We're okay," Sierra said. Had she known the woman better, she might have confided her worries about Liam—how he claimed he'd seen a ghost in his room. She still planned to call his new doctor, but driving to Flagstaff for an appointment would be out of the question, considering the state of the roads.

"I hear some hesitation in your voice," Eve said. She was treading lightly, Sierra could tell, and she would be a hard person to fool. Eve ran McKettrickCo, and hundreds of people answered to her.

Sierra gave a nervous laugh, more hysteria than

amusement. "Liam claims the house is haunted," she admitted.

"Oh, that," Eve answered, and she actually sounded relieved.

"'Oh, that'?" Sierra challenged, sitting up straighter.

"They're harmless," Eve said. "The ghosts, I mean. If that's what they are."

"You know about the ghosts?"

Eve laughed. "Of course I do. I grew up in that house. But I'm not sure *ghosts* is the right word. To me, it always felt more like sharing the place than its being haunted. I got the sense that they—the other people— were as alive as I was. That they'd have been just as surprised, had we ever come face-to-face."

Sierra's mind spun. She squeezed the bridge of her nose between a thumb and forefinger. The piano notes she'd heard the night before tinkled sadly in her memory. "You're not saying you actually *believe*—"

"I'm saying I've had experiences," Eve told her. "I've never seen anyone. Just had a strong sense of someone else being present. And, of course, there was the famous disappearing teapot."

Sierra sank against the back of the chair, both relieved and confounded. Had she told Meg about the teapot? She couldn't recall. Perhaps Travis had mentioned it—called Eve to report that her daughter was a little loony?

"Sierra?" Eve asked.

"I'm still here."

"I would get the teapot out," Eve recounted, "and leave the room to do something else. When I came back, it was in the china cabinet again. The same thing used to happen to my mother, and my grandmother, too. They thought it was Lorelei."

"How could that be?"

"Who knows?" Eve asked, patently unconcerned. "Life is mysterious."

It certainly is, Sierra thought. Little girls get separated from their mothers, and no one even comes looking for them.

"I'd like to come and see you," Eve went on, "as soon as the weather clears. Would that be all right, Sierra? If I spent a few days at the ranch? So we could talk in person?"

Sierra's heart rose into her throat and swelled there. "It's your house," she said, but she wanted to throw down the phone, snatch Liam, jump into the car and speed away before she had to face this woman.

"I won't come if you're not ready," Eve said gently.

I may never be ready, Sierra thought. "I guess I am," she murmured.

"Good," Eve replied. "Then I'll be there as soon as the jet can land. Barring another snowstorm, that should be tomorrow or the next day."

The jet? "Should we pick you up somewhere?"

"I'll have a car meet me," Eve said. "Do you need anything, Sierra?"

I could have used a mother when I was growing up. And when I had Liam and Dad acted as though nothing had changed—well, you would have come in handy then, too, Mom. "I'm fine," she answered.

"I'll call again before I leave here," Eve promised. Then, after another tentative pause and a brief goodbye, she rang off.

Sierra sat a long time in that chair, still holding the

phone, and might not have moved at all if Liam hadn't come to tell her breakfast was on the table.

1919

It was a cold, seemingly endless ride to the Jessup place, and hard going all the way. More than once Doss glanced anxiously at his nephew, bundled to his eyeballs and jostling patiently alongside Doss's mount on the mule, and wished he'd listened to Hannah and left the boy at home.

More than once, he attempted to broach the subject that was uppermost in his mind—he'd been up half the night wrestling with it—but he couldn't seem to get a proper handle on the matter at all.

I mean to marry your ma.

That was the straightforward truth, a simple thing to say.

But Tobias was bound to ask why. Maybe he'd even raise an objection. He'd loved his pa, and he might just put his old uncle Doss right square in his place.

"You ever think about livin' in town?" Tobias asked, catching him by surprise.

Doss took a moment to change directions in his mind. "Sometimes," he answered, when he was sure it was what he really meant. "Especially in the wintertime."

"It's no warmer there than it is here," Tobias reasoned. Whatever he was getting at, it wasn't coming through in his tone or his manner.

"No," Doss agreed. "But there are other folks around. A man could get his mail at the post office every day, instead of waiting a week for it to come by wagon, and take a meal in a restaurant now and again. And I'll admit that library is an enticement, small as it is." He thought fondly of the books lining the study walls back at the ranch house. He'd read all of them, at one time or another, and most several times. He'd borrowed from his uncle Kade's collection, and his ma sent him a regular supply from Texas. Just the same, he couldn't get enough of the damn things.

"Ma's been talking about heading back to Montana," Tobias blurted, but he didn't look at Doss when he spoke. Just kept his eyes on the close-clipped mane of that old mule. "If she tries to make me go, I'll run away."

Doss swallowed. He knew Hannah thought about moving in with the homefolks, of course, but hearing it said out loud made him feel as if he'd not only been thrown from his horse, but stomped on, too. "Where would you go?" he asked, when he thought he could get the words out easy. He wasn't entirely successful. "If you ran off, I mean?"

Tobias turned in the saddle to look him full in the face. "I'd hide up in the hills somewhere," he said, with the conviction of innocence. "Maybe that canyon where Kade and Mandy faced down those outlaws."

Doss suppressed a smile. He'd grown up on that story himself, and to this day, he wondered how much of it was fact and how much was legend. Mandy was a sharpshooter, and she'd given Annie Oakley a run for her money, in her time. Kade had been the town marshal, with an office in Indian Rock back then, so maybe it had happened just the way his pa and uncles related it.

"Mighty cold up there," he told the boy mildly. "Just a cave for shelter, and where would you get food?"

Tobias's shoulders slumped a little, under all that wool Hannah had swaddled him in. If the kid took a spill from the mule, he'd probably bounce. "I could hunt," he said. "Pa taught me how to shoot."

"McKettricks," Doss replied, "don't run away."

Tobias scowled at him. "They don't live in Missoula, either."

Doss chuckled, in spite of the heavy feeling that had settled over his heart after he and Hannah had made love and stayed there ever since. Gabe was dead, but it still felt as if he'd betrayed him. "They live in all sorts of places," Doss said. "You know that."

"I won't go, anyhow," Tobias said.

Doss cleared his throat. "Maybe you won't have to."

That got the boy's full attention. His eyes were full of questions.

"I wonder what you'd say if I married your ma."

Tobias looked as though he'd swallowed a lantern with the wick burning. "I'd like that," he said. "I'd like that a lot!"

Too bad Hannah wasn't as keen on the prospect as her son. "I thought you might not care for the idea," Doss confessed. "My being your pa's brother and all."

"Pa would be glad," Tobias said. "I know he would."

Secretly, Doss knew it, too. Gabe had been a practical man, and he'd have wanted all of them to get on with their lives.

Doss's eyes smarted something fierce, all of a sudden, and he had to pull his hat brim down. Look away for a few moments.

Take care of Hannah and my boy, Gabe had said. *Promise me, Doss.*

"Did Ma say she'd hitch up with you?" Tobias asked, frowning so that his face crinkled comically. "Last night I said she ought to, and she said it wouldn't be right."

Doss stood in the stirrups to stretch his legs. "Things can change," he said cautiously. "Even in a night."

"Do you love my ma?"

It was a hard question to answer, at least aloud. He'd loved Hannah from the day Gabe had brought her home as his bride. Loved her fiercely, hopelessly and honorably, from a proper distance. Gabe had guessed it right away, though. Waited until the two of them were alone in the barn, slapped Doss on the shoulder and said, Don't you be ashamed, little brother. It's easy to love my Hannah.

"Of course I do," Doss said. "She's family."

Tobias made a face. "I don't mean like that."

Doss's belly tightened. The boy was only eight, and he couldn't possibly know what had gone on last night in the spare room.

Could he?

"How do you mean, then?"

"Pa used to kiss Ma all the time. He used to swat her on the bustle, too, when he thought nobody was looking. It always made her laugh, and stand real close to him, with her arms around his neck."

Doss might have gripped the saddle horn with both hands, because of the pain, if he'd been riding alone. It wasn't the reminder of how much Hannah and Gabe had loved each other that seared him, though. It was the loss of his brother, the way of things then, and it all being over for good.

"I'll treat your mother right, Tobias," he said, after more hat-brim pulling and more looking away.

"You sound pretty sure she'll say yes," the boy commented.

"She already has," Doss replied.

Present Day

More snow began to fall at mid-morning and, worried that the power would go off again, and stay off
this time, Sierra gathered her and Liam's dirty laundry and threw a load into the washing machine. She'd
telephoned Liam's doctor in Flagstaff, from the study,
while he and Travis were filling the dishwasher, but she
hadn't mentioned the hallucinations. She'd heard the
piano music herself, after all, and then Eve had made
such experiences seem almost normal.

Sierra didn't know precisely what was happening,
and she was still unsettled by Liam's claims of seeing
a boy in old-time clothes, but she wasn't ready to bring
up the subject with an outsider, whether that outsider
had a medical degree or not.

Dr. O'Meara had reviewed Liam's records, since
they'd been expressed to her from the clinic in Florida, and she wanted to make sure he had an inhaler on
hand. She'd promised to call in a prescription to the
pharmacy in Indian Rock, and they'd made an appointment for the following Monday afternoon.

Now Liam was in the study, watching TV, and Travis
was outside splitting wood for the stove and the fire-
places. If the power went off again, she'd need firewood
for cooking. The generator kept the furnace running,
along with a few of the lights, but it burned a lot of gas
and there was always the possibility that it would break
down or freeze up.

Travis came in with an armload just as she was starting to prepare lunch.

Watching him, Sierra thought about what Eve had
said on the phone earlier. Travis's younger brother had

died horribly, and very recently. He'd left his job, Travis had, and come to the ranch to live in a trailer and look after horses.

He didn't look like a man carrying a burden, but appearances were deceiving. Nobody knew that better than Sierra did.

"What kind of work did you do, before you came here?" she asked, and then wished she hadn't brought the subject up at all. Travis's face closed instantly, and his eyes went blank.

"Nothing special," he said.

She nodded. "I was a cocktail waitress," she told him, because she felt she ought to offer him something after asking what was evidently an intrusive question.

Standing there, beside the antique cookstove and the wood box, in his leather coat and cowboy hat, Travis looked as though he'd stepped through a time warp, out of an earlier century.

"I know," he said. "Meg told me."

"Of course she did." Sierra poured canned soup into a saucepan, stirred it industriously and blushed.

Travis didn't say anything more for a long time. Then, "I was a lawyer for McKettrickCo," he told her.

Sierra stole a sidelong glance at him. He looked tense, standing there holding his hat in one hand. "Impressive," she said.

"Not so much," he countered. "It's a tradition in my family, being a lawyer, I mean. At least, with everyone but my brother, Brody. He became a meth addict instead, and blew himself to kingdom-come brewing up a batch. Go figure."

Sierra turned to face Travis. Noticed that his jaw

was hard and his eyes even harder. He was angry, in pain, or both.

"I'm so sorry," she said.

"Yeah," Travis replied tersely. "Me, too."

He started for the door.

"Stay for lunch?" Sierra asked.

"Another time," he answered, and then he was gone.

1919

It was near sunset when Doss and Tobias rode in from the Jessup place, and by then Hannah was fit to be tied. She'd paced for most of the afternoon, after it started to snow again, fretting over all the things that could go wrong along the way.

The horse or the mule could have gone lame or fallen through the ice crossing the creek.

There could have been an avalanche. Just last year, a whole mountainside of snow had come crashing down on to the roof of a cabin and crushed it to the ground, with a family inside.

Wolves prowled the countryside, too, bold with the desperation of their hunger. They killed cattle and sometimes people.

Doss hadn't even taken his rifle.

When Hannah heard the horses, she ran to the window, wiped the fog from the glass with her apron hem. She watched as they dismounted and led their mounts into the barn.

She'd baked pies that day to keep from going crazy, and the kitchen was redolent with the aroma. She smoothed her skirts, patted her hair and turned away so she wouldn't be caught looking if Doss or Tobias happened to glance toward the house.

Almost an hour passed before they came inside—they'd done the barn chores—and Hannah had the table set, the lamps lighted and the coffee made. She wanted to fuss over Tobias, check his ears and fingers for frostbite and his forehead for fever, but she wouldn't let herself do it.

Doss wasn't deceived by her smiling restraint, she could see that, but Tobias looked downright relieved, as though he'd expected her to pounce the minute he came through the door.

"How did you find Widow Jessup?" she asked.

"She was right where we left her last time," Doss said with a slight grin.

Hannah gave him a look.

"She was fresh out of firewood," Tobias expounded importantly, unwrapping himself, layer by layer, until he stood in just his trousers and shirt, with melted snow pooling around his feet. "It's a good thing we went down there. She'd have froze for sure."

Doss looked tired, but his eyes twinkled. "For sure," he confirmed. "She got Tobias here by the ears and kissed him all over his face, she was so grateful that he'd saved her."

Tobias let out a yelp of mortification and took a swing at Doss, who sidestepped him easily.

"Stop your roughhousing and wash up for supper," Hannah said, but it did her heart good to see it. Gabe used to come in from the barn, toss Tobias over one shoulder and carry him around the kitchen like a sack of grain. The boy had howled with laughter and pummeled Gabe's chest with his small fists in mock resistance. She'd missed the ordinary things like that more than anything except being held in Gabe's arms.

She served chicken and dumplings, in her best Blue Willow dishes, with apple pie for dessert.

Tobias ate with a fresh-air, long-ride appetite and nearly fell asleep in his chair once his stomach was filled.

Doss got up, hoisted him into his arms and carried him, head bobbing, toward the stairs.

Hannah's throat went raw, watching them go.

She poured a second cup of coffee for Doss, had it waiting when he came back a few minutes later.

"Did you put Tobias in his nightshirt and cover him with the spare quilt?" she asked, when Doss appeared at the bottom of the steps. "He mustn't take a chill—"

"I took off his shoes and threw him in like he was," Doss interrupted. That twinkle was still in his eyes, but there was a certain wariness there, too. "I made sure he was warm, so stop fretting."

Hannah had put the dishes in a basin of hot water to soak, and she lingered at the table, sipping tea brewed in Lorelei's pot.

Doss sat down in his father's chair, cupped his hands around his own mug of steaming coffee. "I spoke to Tobias about our getting married," he said bluntly. "And he's in favor of it."

Heat pounded in Hannah's cheeks, spawned by indignation and something else that she didn't dare think about. "Doss McKettrick," she whispered in reproach, "you shouldn't have done that. I'm his mother and it was my place to—"

"It's done, Hannah," Doss said. "Let it go at that."

Hannah huffed out a breath. "Don't you tell me what's

done and ought to be let go," she protested. "I won't take orders from you now or after we're married."

He grinned. "Maybe you won't," he said. "But that doesn't mean I won't give them."

She laughed, surprising herself so much that she slapped a hand over her mouth to stifle the sound. That gesture, in turn, brought back recollections of the night before, when Doss had made love to her, and she'd wanted to cry out with the pleasure of it.

She blushed so hard her face burned, and this time it was Doss who laughed.

"I figure we're in for another blizzard," he said. "Might be spring before we can get to town and stand up in front of a preacher. I hope you're not looking like a watermelon smuggler before then."

Hannah opened her mouth, closed it again.

Doss's eyes danced as he took another sip of his coffee.

"That was an insufferably forward thing to say!" Hannah accused.

"You're a fine one to talk about being forward," Doss observed, and repeated back something she'd said at that very height of her passion.

"That's enough, Mr. McKettrick."

Doss set his cup down, pushed back his chair and stood. "I'm going out to the barn to look in on the stock again. Maybe you ought to come along. Make the job go faster, if you lent a hand."

Hannah squirmed on the bench.

Doss crossed the room, took his coat and hat down from the pegs by the door. "Way out there, a person could holler if they wanted to. Be nobody to hear."

Hannah did some more squirming.

"Fresh hay to lie in, too," Doss went on. "Nice and

soft, and if a man were to spread a couple of horse blankets over it—"

Heat surged through Hannah, brought her to an aching
simmer. She sputtered something and waved him away.

Doss chuckled, opened the door and went out, whistling merrily under his breath.

Hannah waited. If Doss McKettrick thought he was
going to have his way with her—in the barn, of all
places—well, he was just…

She got up, went to the stove and banked the fire
with a poker.

He was just right, that was what he was.

She chose her biggest shawl, wrapped herself in it,
and hurried after him.

Present Day

As soon as Sierra put supper on the table that night,
the power went off again. While she scrambled for candles, Liam rushed to the nearest window.

"Travis's trailer's dark," he said. "He'll get *hypo-
thermia* out there."

Sierra sighed. "I'll bet he comes back to see to the
furnace, just like he did this morning. We'll ask him to
have supper with us."

"I see him!" Liam cried gleefully. "He's coming out
of the barn, with a lantern!" He raced for the door,
and before Sierra could stop him, he was outside, with
no coat on, galloping through the deepening snow and
shouting Travis's name.

Sierra pulled on her own coat, grabbed Liam's and
hurried after him.

Travis was already herding him toward the house.

"Mom made meat loaf, and she says you can have some," Liam was saying, as he tramped breathlessly along.

Sierra wrapped his coat around him, and would have scolded him, if her gaze hadn't collided unexpectedly with Travis's.

Travis shook his head.

She swallowed all that she'd been about to say and hustled her son into the house.

"I'll start the generator," Travis said.

Sierra nodded hastily and shut the door.

"Liam McKettrick," she burst out, "what were you thinking, going out in that cold without a coat?"

In the candlelight, she saw Liam's lower lip wobble. "Travis said it isn't the cowboy way. He was about to put his coat on me when you came."

"*What* isn't the 'cowboy way'?" she asked, chafing his icy hands between hers and praying he wouldn't have an asthma attack or come down with pneumonia.

"Not wearing a coat," Liam replied, downcast. "A cowboy is always prepared for any kind of weather, and he never rushes off half-cocked, without his gear."

Sierra relaxed a little, stifled a smile. "Travis is right," she said.

Liam brightened. "Do cowboys eat meat loaf?"

"I'm pretty sure they do," Sierra answered.

The furnace came on, and she silently blessed Travis Reid for being there.

He let himself into the kitchen a few minutes later. By then Sierra had set another place at the table and lit several more candles. They all sat down at the same time, and there was something so natural about their gathering that way that Sierra's throat caught.

"I hope you're hungry," she said, feeling awkward.

"I'm starved," Travis replied.

"Cowboys eat meat loaf, right?" Liam inquired.

Travis grinned. "This one does," he said.

"This one does, too," Liam announced.

Sierra laughed, but tears came to her eyes at the same time. She was glad of the relative darkness, hoping no one would notice.

"Once," Liam said, scooping a helping of meat loaf onto his plate, his gaze adoring as he focused on Travis, "I saw this show on the Science Channel. They found a cave man, in a block of ice. He was, like *fourteen thousand* years old! I betcha they could take some of his DNA and clone him if they wanted to." He stopped for a quick breath. "And he was all blue, too. That's what you'll look like, if you sleep in that trailer tonight."

"You're not a kid," Travis teased. "You're a forty-year-old wearing a pygmy suit."

"I'm *really* smart," Liam went on. "So you ought to listen to me."

Travis looked at Sierra, and their eyes caught, with an almost audible click and held.

"The generator's low on gas," Travis said. "So we have two choices. We can get in my truck and hope there are some empty motel rooms at the Lamplight Inn, or we can build up the fire in that cookstove and camp out in the kitchen."

Liam had no trouble at all making the choice. "Camp out!" he whooped, waving his fork in the air. "Camp out!"

"You can't be serious," Sierra said to Travis.

"Oh, I'm serious, all right," he answered.

"Lamplight Inn," Sierra voted.

"Roads are bad," Travis replied. "*Real* bad."

"Once on TV, I saw a thing about these people who froze to death right in their car," Liam put in.

"Be quiet," Sierra told him.

"Happens all the time," Travis said.

Which was how the three of them ended up bundled in sleeping bags, with couch and chair cushions for a makeshift mattress, lying side by side within the warm radius of the wood-burning stove.

Chapter 7

1919

Hannah and Doss returned separately from the barn, by tacit agreement. Hannah, weak-kneed with residual pleasure and reeling with guilt, pumped water into a bucket to pour into the near-empty reservoir on the cookstove, then filled the two biggest kettles she had and set them on the stove to heat. She was adding wood to the fire when she heard Doss come in.

She blushed furiously, unable to meet his gaze, though she could feel it burning into her flesh, right through the clothes he'd sweet-talked her out of just an hour before, laying her down in the soft, surprisingly warm hay in an empty stall, kissing and caressing and nibbling at her until she'd begged him to take her.

Begged him.

She'd carried on something awful while he was at it, too.

"Look at me, Hannah," he said.

She glared at Doss, marched past him into the pantry and dragged out the big wash tub stored there under a high shelf. She set it in front of the stove with an eloquent clang.

"Hannah," Doss repeated.

"Go upstairs," she told him, flustered. "Leave me to my bath."

"You can't wash away what we did," he said.

She whirled on him that time, hands on her hips, fiery with temper. "Get out," she ordered, keeping her voice down in case Tobias was still awake or even listening at the top of the stairs. "I need my privacy."

Doss raised both hands to shoulder height, palms out, but his words were juxtaposed to the gesture. "If we're going to talk about what you need, Hannah, it's not a bath. It's a lot more of what we just did in the barn."

"Tobias might hear you!" Hannah whispered, outraged. If the broom hadn't been on the back porch, she'd have grabbed it up and whacked him silly with it.

"He wouldn't know what we were talking about even if he did," Doss argued mildly, lowering his hands. He approached, plucked a piece of straw from Hannah's hair and tickled her under the chin with it.

She felt as though she'd been electrified, and slapped his hand away.

He laughed, a low, masculine sound, leaned in and nibbled at her lower lip. "Good night, Hannah," he said.

A hot shiver of renewed need went through her. How could that be? He'd satisfied her that night, and the one before. Both times he'd taken her to heights she hadn't even reached with Gabe.

The difference was, she'd been Gabe's wife, in the eyes of God and man, and she'd loved him. She not only wasn't married to Doss, she didn't love him. She just wanted him, that was all, and the realization galled her.

"You've turned me into a hussy," she said.

Doss chuckled, shook his head. "If you say so, Hannah," he answered, "it must be true."

With that, he kissed her forehead, turned and left the kitchen.

She listened to the sound of his boot heels on the stairs, heard his progress along the second-floor hallway, even knew when he opened Tobias's door to look in on the boy before retiring to his own room. Only when she'd heard his door close did Hannah let out her breath.

When the water in the kettles was scalding hot, Hannah poured it into the tub, sneaked upstairs for a towel, a bar of soap and a nightgown. By the time she'd put out all the lanterns in the kitchen and stripped off her clothes, her bathwater had cooled to a temperature that made her sigh when she stepped into it.

She soaked for a few minutes, and then scrubbed with a vengeance.

It turned out that Doss had been right.

She tried but she couldn't wash away the things he'd made her feel.

A tear slipped down her cheek as she dried herself off, then donned her nightgown. She dragged the tub to the back door and on to the step, drained it over one side and dashed back in, covered with gooseflesh from the chill.

"I'm sorry, Gabe," she said, very quietly, huddling by the stove. "I'm sorry."

Present Day

Travis was building up the fire when Sierra opened her eyes the next morning. "Stay in your sleeping bag," he told her. "It's colder than a meat locker in here."

Liam, lying between them throughout the night, was still asleep, but his breathing was a shallow rattle. Sierra sat bolt-upright, watchful, holding her own breath. Not feeling the external chill at all, except as a vague biting sensation.

Liam opened his eyes, blinked. "Mom," he said. "I can't—"

Breathe, Sierra finished the sentence for him, replayed it in her mind.

Mom, I can't breathe.

She bounded out of the sleeping bag, scrambled for her purse, which was lying on the counter and rummaged for Liam's inhaler.

He began to wheeze, and when Sierra turned to rush back to him, she saw a look of panic in his eyes.

"Take it easy, Liam," she said, as she handed him the inhaler.

He grasped it in both hands, all too familiar with the routine, and pressed the tube to his mouth and nose.

Travis watched grimly.

Sierra dropped on to her knees next to her boy, put an arm loosely around his shoulders. *Let it work,* she prayed silently. *Please let it work!*

Liam lowered the inhaler and stared apologetically up into Sierra's eyes. He could barely get enough wind to speak. He was, in essence, choking. "It's—I think it's broken, Mom—"

"I'll warm up the truck," Travis said, and banged out of the house.

Desperate, Sierra took the inhaler, shook it and shoved it back into Liam's hands. It *wasn't* empty—she wouldn't have taken a chance like that—but it must have been clogged or somehow defective. "Try again," she urged, barely avoiding panic herself.

Outside, Travis's truck roared audibly to life. He gunned the motor a couple of times.

Liam struggled to take in the medication, but the inhaler simply wasn't working.

Travis returned, picked Liam up in his arms, sleeping bag and all, and headed for the door again. Sierra, frightened as she was, had to hurry to catch up, snatching her coat from the peg and her purse from the counter on the way out.

The snow had stopped, but there must have been two feet of it on the ground. Travis shifted the truck into four-wheel drive and the tires grabbed for purchase, finally caught.

"Take it easy, buddy," he told Liam, who was on Sierra's lap, the seat belt fastened around both of them. "Take it real easy."

Liam nodded solemnly. He was drawing in shallow gasps of air now, but not enough. *Not enough.* His lips were turning blue.

Sierra held him tight, but not too tight. Rested her chin on top of his head and prayed.

The roads hadn't been plowed—in fact, except for sloping drifts on either side, Sierra wouldn't have known where they were. Still, the truck rolled over them as easily as if they were bare.

What if we'd been alone, Liam and me? Sierra

thought frantically. Her old station wagon, a snow-covered hulk in the driveway in front of the house, probably wouldn't have started, and even if it had by some miracle, the chances were good that they'd have ended up in the ditch somewhere along the way to safety.

"It's going to be okay," she heard Travis say, and she'd thought he was talking to Liam. When she glanced at him, though, she knew he'd meant the words for her.

She kept her voice even. "Is there a hospital in Indian Rock?" She and Liam had passed through the town the day they arrived, but she didn't remember seeing anything but houses, a diner or two, a drugstore, several bars and a gas station. She'd been too busy trying to follow the hand-drawn map Meg had scanned and sent to her by email—the McKettricks' private cemetery was marked with an X, and the ranch house an uneven square with lines for a roof.

"A clinic," Travis said. He looked down at Liam again, then turned his gaze back to the road. The set of his jaw was hard, and he pulled his cell phone from the pocket of his coat and handed it to Sierra.

She dialed 911 and asked to be connected.

When a voice answered, Sierra explained the situation as calmly as she could, keeping it low-key for Liam's sake. They'd been through at least a dozen similar episodes during his short life, and it never got easier. Each time, Sierra was hysterical, though she didn't dare let that show. Liam was taking his cues from her. If she lost it, he would, too, and the results could be disastrous.

The clinic receptionist seemed blessedly unruffled. "We'll be ready when you get here," she said.

Sierra thanked the woman and ended the call, set the phone on the seat.

By the time they arrived at the town's only medical facility, Liam was struggling to remain conscious. Travis pulled up in front, gave the horn a hard blast and was around to Sierra's side with the door open before she managed to get the seat belt unbuckled.

Two medical assistants, accompanied by a gray-haired doctor, met them with a gurney. Liam was whisked away. Sierra tried to follow, but Travis and one of the nurses stopped her.

Her first instinct was to fight.

"My son needs me!" She'd meant it for a scream, but it came out as more of a whimper.

"We'll need your name and that of the patient," a clerk informed her, advancing with a clipboard. "And of course there's the matter of insurance—"

Travis glared the woman into retreat. "Her *name*," he said, "is McKettrick."

"Oh," the clerk said, and ducked behind her desk.

Sierra needed something, anything, to do, or she was going to rip apart every room in that place until she found Liam, gathered him into her arms. "My purse," she said. "I must have left it in the truck—"

"I'll get it," Travis said, but first he steered her toward a chair in the waiting area and sat her down.

Tears of frustration and stark terror filled her eyes. What was happening to Liam? Was he breathing? Were they forcing the hated tube down into his bronchial passage even at that moment?

Travis cupped her face between his hands, for just a moment, and his palms felt cold and rough from ranch work.

The sensation triggered something in Sierra, but she was too distraught to know what it was.

"I'll be right back," he promised.

And he was.

Sierra snatched her bag from his hands, scrabbled through it to find her wallet. Found the insurance card Eve had sent by express the same day Sierra agreed to take the McKettrick name and spend a year on the Triple M, with Liam. She might have kissed that card, if Travis hadn't been watching.

The clerk nodded a little nervously when Sierra walked up to the desk and asked for the papers she needed to fill out.

Patient's Name. Well, that was easy enough. She scrawled Liam Bres—crossed out the last part, and wrote McKettrick instead.

Address? She had to consult Travis on that one. Everybody in Indian Rock knew where the Triple M was, she was sure, but the people in the insurance company's claims office might not.

Occupation? Child.

Damn it, Liam was a little boy, hardly more than a baby. Things like this shouldn't happen to him.

Sierra printed her own name, as guarantor. She bit her lip when asked about her job. Unemployed? She couldn't write that.

Travis, watching, took the clipboard and pen from her and inserted, Damn good mother.

The tears came again.

Travis got up, with the forms and the clipboard and the insurance card, inscribed with the magical name and carried them over to the waiting clerk.

He was halfway back to Sierra when the doctor reappeared.

"Hello, Travis," he said, but his gaze was on Sierra's face, and she couldn't read it, for all the practice she'd had.

"I'm Sierra McKettrick," she said. The name still felt like a garment that didn't quite fit, but if it would help Liam in any way, she would use it every chance she got. "My son—"

"He'll be fine," the doctor said kindly. His eyes were a faded blue, his features craggy and weathered. "Just the same, I think we ought to send him up to Flagstaff to the hospital, at least overnight. For observation, you understand. And because they've got a reliable power source up there."

"Is he awake?" Sierra asked anxiously.

"Partially sedated," replied the doctor, exchanging glances with Travis. "We had to perform an intubation."

Sierra knew how Liam hated tubes, and how frightened he probably was, sedated or not. "I have to see him," she said, prepared for an argument.

"Of course" was the immediate and very gentle answer.

Sierra felt Travis's hand close around hers. She clung, instead of pulling away, as she would have done with any other virtual stranger.

A few minutes later they were standing on either side of Liam's bed in one of the treatment rooms. His eyes widened with recognition when he saw Sierra, and he pointed, with one small finger, to the mouthpiece of his oxygen tube.

She nodded, blinking hard and trying to smile. Took his hand.

"You have to spend the night in the hospital in Flagstaff," she told him, "but don't be scared, okay? Because I'm going with you."

Liam relaxed visibly. Turned his eyes to Travis. Sierra's heart twisted at the hope she saw in her little boy's face.

"Me, too," Travis said hoarsely.

Liam nodded and drifted off to sleep.

The doctor had ordered an ambulance, and Sierra rode with Liam, while Travis followed in the truck.

There was more paperwork to do in Flagstaff, but Sierra was calmer now. She sat in a chair next to Liam's bed and filled in the lines.

Travis entered with two cups of vending-machine coffee, just as she was finishing.

"Thank you," Sierra said, and she wasn't just talking about the coffee.

"Wranglers like Liam and me," he replied, watching the boy with a kind of fretful affection, "we stick together when the going gets tough."

She accepted the paper cup Travis offered and set the ubiquitous clipboard aside to take a sip. Travis drew up a second chair.

"Does this happen a lot?" he asked, after a long and remarkably easy silence.

Sierra shook her head. "No, thank God. I don't know what we would have done without you, Travis."

"You would have coped," he said. "Like you've been doing for a long time, if my guess is any good. Where's Liam's dad, Sierra?"

She swallowed hard, glanced at the boy to make sure he was sleeping. "He died a few days before Liam was born," she answered.

"You've been alone all this time?"

"No," Sierra said, stiffening a little on the inside,

where it didn't show. Or, at least, she *hoped* it didn't. "I had Liam."

"You know that isn't what I meant," Travis said.

Sierra looked away, made herself look back. "I didn't want to—complicate things. By getting involved with someone, I mean. Liam and I have been just fine on our own."

Travis merely nodded, and drank more of his coffee.

"Don't you have to go back to the ranch and feed the horses or something?" Sierra asked.

"Eventually," Travis answered with a sigh. He glanced around the room again and gave the slightest shudder.

Sierra remembered his younger brother. The wounds must be raw. "I guess you probably hate hospitals," she said. "Because of—" the name came back to her in Eve's telephone voice "—Brody."

Travis shook his head. His eyes were bleak. "If he'd gotten this far—to a hospital, I mean—it would have meant there was hope."

Sierra moved to touch Travis's hand, but just before she made contact, his cell phone rang. He pulled it from the pocket of his western shirt. "Travis Reid."

He listened. Raised his eyebrows. "Hello, Eve. I wouldn't have thought even *your* pilot could land in this kind of weather."

Sierra tensed.

Eve said something, and Travis responded. "I'll let Sierra explain," he said, and held out the phone to her.

Sierra swallowed, took it. "Hello, Eve," she said.

"Where are you?" her mother asked. "I'm at the ranch. It looks as if you've been sleeping in the kitchen—"

"We're in Flagstaff, in a hospital," Sierra told her. Only then did she realize that she and Travis were both wearing the clothes they'd slept in. That she hadn't combed her hair or even brushed her teeth.

All of a sudden she felt incredibly grubby.

Eve drew in an audible breath. "Oh, my *God*—Liam?"

"He had a pretty bad asthma attack," Sierra confirmed. "He's on a breathing machine, and he has to stay until tomorrow, but he's okay, Eve."

"I'll be up there as soon as I can. Which hospital?"

"Hold on," Sierra said. "There's really no need for you to come all this way, especially when the roads are so bad. I'm pretty sure we'll be home tomorrow—"

"Pretty sure?" Eve challenged.

"Well, he'll need his medication adjusted, and the inflammation in his bronchial tubes will have to go down."

"This sounds serious, Sierra. I think I should come. I could be there—"

"Please," Sierra interrupted. "Don't."

A thoughtful silence followed. "All right, then," Eve said finally, with a good grace Sierra truly appreciated. "I'll just settle in here and wait. The furnace is running and the lights are on. Tell Travis not to rush back—I can certainly feed the horses."

Sierra could only nod, so Travis took the phone back.

Evidently, a barrage of orders followed from Eve's end.

Travis grinned throughout. "Yes, ma'am," he said. "I will."

He ended the call.

"You will what?" Sierra inquired.

"Take care of you and Liam," Travis answered.

1919

That morning the world looked as though it had been carved from a huge block of pure white ice. Hannah marveled at the beauty of it, staring through the kitchen window, even as she longed with bittersweet poignancy for spring. For things to stir under the snowbound earth, to put out roots and break through the surface, green and growing.

"Ma?"

She turned, troubled by something she heard in Tobias's voice. He stood at the base of the stairs, still wearing his nightshirt and barefoot.

"I don't feel good," he said.

Hannah set aside her coffee with exaggerated care, even took time to wipe her hands on her apron before she approached him. Touched his forehead with the back of her hand.

"You're burning up," she whispered, stricken.

Doss, who had been rereading last week's newspaper at the table, his barn work done, slowly scraped back his chair.

"Shall I fetch the doc?" he asked.

Hannah turned, looked at him over one shoulder, and nodded. If you hadn't insisted on taking him with you to the widow Jessup's place, she thought—

But she would go no further.

This was not the time to place blame.

"You get back into bed," she told Tobias, briskly efficient and purely terrified. The bout of pneumonia that had nearly killed him during the fall had started like this. "I'll make you a mustard plaster to draw out the congestion, and your uncle Doss will go to town for Dr. Willaby. You'll be right as rain in no time at all."

Tobias looked doubtful. His face was flushed, and his nightshirt was soaked with perspiration, even though the kitchen was a little on the chilly side. The boy seemed dazed, almost as though he were walking in his sleep, and Hannah wondered if he'd taken in a word she'd said.

"I'll be back as soon as I can," Doss promised, already pulling on his coat and reaching for his hat. "There's whisky left from Christmas. It's in the pantry, behind that cracker tin," he added, pausing before opening the door. "Make him a hot drink with some honey. Pa used to brew up that concoction for us when we took sick, and it always helped."

Doss and Gabe, along with their adopted older brother, John Henry, had never suffered a serious illness in their lives, if you didn't count John Henry's deafness. What did they know about tending the sick?

Hannah nodded again, her mouth tight. She'd lost three sisters in childhood, two to diphtheria and one to scarlet fever; only she and her younger brother, David, had survived.

She was used to nursing the afflicted.

Doss hesitated a few moments on the threshold, as though there was something he wanted to say but couldn't put into words, then went out.

"You change into a dry nightshirt," Hannah told Tobias. His sheets were probably sweat-soaked, too, so she added, "And get into our bed."

Our bed.

Meaning Gabe's and hers.

And soon, after they were married, Doss would be sleeping in that bed, in Gabe's place.

She could not, would not, consider the implications of that.

Not now. Maybe not ever.

She was like the ranch woman she'd once read about in a Montana newspaper, making her way from the house to the barn and back in a blinding blizzard, with only a frozen rope to hold on to. If she let go, she'd be lost.

She had to attend to Tobias. That was her rope, and she'd follow it, hand over hand, thought over thought.

Hannah retrieved an old flannel shirt from the rag bag and cut two matching pieces, approximately twelve inches square. These would serve to protect Tobias's skin from the heat of the poultice, but like as not, he would still have blisters. She kept a mixture on hand for just such occasions, in a big jar with a wire seal. She dumped a big dollop of the stuff on to one of the bits of flannel, spread it like butter, and put the second cloth on top, her nose twitching at the pungent odors of mustard seed, pounded to a pulp, and camphor.

When she got upstairs, she found Tobias huddled in the middle of her bed, and his eyes grew big with recollection when he saw what she was carrying in her hands.

"No," he protested, but weakly. "No mustard plaster." He'd begun to shiver, and his teeth were chattering.

"Don't fuss, Tobias," Hannah said. "Your grandfather swears by them."

Tobias groaned. "My Montana grandfather," he replied. "My grandpa Holt wouldn't let anybody put one of those things on him!"

"Is that a fact?" Hannah asked mildly. "Well, next time you write to the almighty Holt McKettrick, you ask. I'll bet he'll say he wouldn't be without one when he's under the weather."

Tobias made a rude sound, blowing through his lips, but he rolled on to his back and allowed Hannah to open the top buttons of his nightshirt and put the poultice in place.

"Grandpa Holt," he said, bearing the affliction stalwartly, "would probably make me a whisky drink, just like he did for Pa and Uncle Doss."

Hannah sighed. Privately she thought there was a good deal of the roughneck in the McKettrick men, and while she wouldn't call any of them a drunk, they used liquor as a remedy for just about every ill, from snakebite to the grippe. They'd swabbed it on old Seesaw's gashes, when he tangled with a sow bear, and rubbed it into the gums of teething babies.

"What you're going to have, Tobias McKettrick, is oatmeal."

He made a face. "This burns," he complained, pointing to the mustard plaster.

Hannah bent and kissed his forehead. He didn't pull away, like he'd taken to doing of late, and she found that both reassuring and worrisome.

She glanced at the window, saw a scallop of icicles dangling from the eave. It might be many hours—even tomorrow—before Doss got back from Indian Rock with Dr. Willaby. The wait would be agony, but there was nothing to do but endure.

When Tobias closed his eyes and slept, Hannah left the room, descended the stairs and went into the pantry again. She moved the cracker tin aside, looked up at the bottle of whisky hidden behind it, gave a disdainful sniff, and took a canned chicken off the shelf instead. It was a treasure, that chicken—she'd been saving it for some celebration, so she wouldn't have to kill one of her laying hens—but it would make a fine, nourishing soup.

After gathering onions, rice and some of her spices—which she cherished as much as preserved meat, given how costly they were—Hannah commenced to make soup.

She was surprised when, only an hour after he'd ridden out, Doss returned with another man she recognized as one of the ranch hands down at Rafe's place. She frowned, watching from the window as Doss dismounted and left the newcomer to lead both horses inside.

That was odd. Doss hadn't been to Indian Rock yet; he couldn't have covered the distance in such a short time. Why would he ask someone to put up his horse?

Puzzled, impatient and a little angry, Hannah was waiting at the door when Doss came in.

"Bundle the boy up warm," he said, without any preamble at all. "Willie's going to stay here and look after the horses and the place. Once I've hitched the draft horses to the sleigh, we'll go overland to Indian Rock."

Hannah stared at him, confounded. "You're suggesting that we take Tobias all the way to Indian Rock?"

"I'm not 'suggesting' anything, Hannah," Doss interposed. "I met Seth Baker down by the main house, when I was about to cross the stream, and he hailed me, wanted to know where I was headed. I told him I was off to fetch Doc Willaby, because Tobias was feeling poorly. Seth said Willaby was down with the gout, but his nephew happened to be there, and he's a doctor, too. He's looking after the doc's practice, in town, so he wouldn't be inclined to come all the way out here."

Hannah's throat clenched, and she put a hand to it. "A ride like that could be the end of Tobias," she said.

Doss shook his head. "We can't just sit here," he countered, grim-jawed. "Get the boy ready or I'll do it myself."

"May I remind you that Tobias is my son?"

"He's a McKettrick," Doss replied flatly, as though that were the end of it—and for him, it probably was.

Chapter 8

Travis waited until Sierra had drifted off into a fitful sleep in her chair next to Liam's hospital bed. Then he got a blanket from a nurse, covered Sierra with it and left.

A few minutes later, he was behind the wheel of his truck.

The roads were sheer ice, and the sky looked gray, burdened with fresh snow. After consulting the GPS panel on his dashboard, he found the nearest Wal-Mart, parked as close to the store as he could and went inside.

Shopping was something Travis endured, and this was no exception. He took a cart and wheeled it around, choosing the things Sierra and Liam would need if this hitch in Flagstaff turned out to be longer than expected.

He'd spent the night at his own place, a few miles from the hospital, showered and changed there.

When he got back from his expedition—a January Santa Claus burdened down with bulging blue plastic bags—he made his way to Liam's room.

Sierra was awake, blinking and befuddled, and so was Liam. A huge teddy bear, holding a helium balloon in one paw, sat on the bedside table. The writing on the balloon said Get Well Soon in big red letters.

"Eve?" Travis asked, indicating the bear with a nod of his head.

Sierra took in the bags he was carrying. "Eve," she confirmed. "What have you got there?"

Travis grinned, though he felt tired all of a sudden, as though ten cups of coffee wouldn't keep him awake. Maybe it was the warmth of the hospital, after being out in the cold.

"A little something for everybody," he said.

Liam was sitting up, and the breathing tube had been removed. His words came out as a sore-throated croak, but he smiled just the same, and Travis felt a pinch deep inside. The kid was so small and so brave. "Even me?"

"Especially you," Travis said. He handed the boy one of the bags, watched as he pulled out a portable DVD player, still in its box, and the episodes of *Nova* he'd picked up to go with it.

"Wow," Liam said, his voice so raw that it made Travis's throat ache in sympathy. "I've always wanted one of these."

Sierra looked worried. "It's way too expensive," she said. "We can't accept it."

Liam hugged the box close against his little chest,

obstinately possessive. Everything about him said, I'm not giving this up.

Travis ignored Sierra's statement and tossed her another of the bags, this one fat and light. "Take a shower," he told her. "You look like somebody who just went through a harrowing medical emergency."

She opened her mouth, closed it again. Peeked inside the bag. He'd bought her yoga pants and a hoodie, guessing at the sizes, along with toothpaste, a brush, soap and a comb.

She swallowed visibly. "Thanks."

He nodded.

While Sierra was in Liam's bathroom, showering, Travis helped the boy get the DVD player out of the box, plugged in and running.

"Mom might not let me keep it," Liam said sadly.

"I'm betting she will," Travis assured him.

Liam was engrossed in an episode about killer bees when Sierra came out of the bathroom, looking scrubbed and cautiously hopeful in her dark-blue sweats. Her hair was still wet from washing, and the comb had left distinct ridges, which Travis found peculiarly poignant.

Complex emotions fell into line after that one, striking him with the impact of a runaway boxcar, but he didn't dare explore any of them right away. He'd need to be alone to do that, in his truck or with a horse. For now, he was too close to Sierra to think straight.

She glanced at Liam, softened noticeably as she saw how much he was enjoying Travis's gift. His small hands clasped the machine on either side, as though he feared someone would wrench it away.

Something similar to Travis's thoughts must have

gone through her mind, because he saw a change in her face. It was a sort of resignation, and it made him want to take her in his arms—though he wasn't about to do that.

"I could use something to eat," he said.

"Me, too," Sierra admitted. She tapped Liam on the shoulder, and he barely looked away from the screen, where bees were swarming. Music from the speakers portended certain disaster. "You'll be all right here alone for a while, if Travis and I go down to the cafeteria?"

The boy nodded distractedly, refocused his eyes on the bees.

Sierra smiled with a tiny, forlorn twitch of her lips.

They were well away from Liam's room, and waiting for an elevator, when she finally spoke.

"I'm grateful for what you did for Liam and me," she said, "but you shouldn't have given him something that cost so much."

"I won't miss the money, Sierra," Travis responded. "He's been through a lot, and he needed something else to think about besides breathing tubes, medical tests and shots."

She gave a brief, almost clipped nod.

That McKettrick pride, Travis thought. It was something to behold.

The elevator came, and the doors opened with a cheerful chiming sound. They stepped inside, and Travis pushed the button for the lower level. Hospital cafeterias always seemed to be in the bowels of the building, like the morgues.

Downstairs, they went through the grub line with trays, and chose the least offensive-looking items from the stock array of greasy green beans, mock meat loaf, brown gravy and the like.

Sierra chose a corner table, and they sat down, facing each other. She looked like a freshly showered angel from some celestial soccer team in the athletic clothes he'd provided, and Travis wondered if she had any idea how beautiful she was.

"I'm surprised Eve hasn't shown up," he said, to get the conversation started.

Sierra's cheeks pinkened a little, and she avoided his gaze. Poked at the faux meat loaf with a water-spotted fork.

"I don't know what I'm going to say to her," she said. "Beyond 'thank you,' I mean."

"How about, 'hello'?" Travis joked.

Sierra didn't look amused. Just nervous, like a rat cornered by a barn cat.

He reached across the table, closed his hand briefly over hers. "Look, Sierra, this doesn't have to be hard. Eve will probably do most of the talking, at least in the beginning, and she'll feed you your lines."

She smiled again. Another tentative flicker, there and gone.

They ate in silence for a while.

"It's not as if I hate her," Sierra said, out of the blue. "Eve, I mean."

Travis waited, knowing they were on uneven ground. Sierra was as skittish as a spring fawn, and he didn't want to speak at the wrong time and send her bolting for the emotional underbrush.

"I don't know her," Sierra went on. "My own mother. I saw her picture on the McKettrickCo website, but she told me it didn't look a thing like her."

Still, Travis waited.

"What's she like?" Sierra asked, almost plaintively. "Really?"

"Eve is a beautiful woman," Travis said. *Like you,* he added silently. "She's smart, and when it comes to negotiating a business deal, she's as tough as they come. She's remarkable, Sierra. Give her a chance."

Sierra's lower lip wobbled, ever so slightly. Her blue, blue eyes were limpid with feelings Travis could only guess at. He wanted to dive into them, like a swimmer, and explore the vast inner landscape he sensed within her.

"You know what happened, don't you?" she asked, very softly. "Back when my mother and father were divorced."

"Some of it," Travis said, cautious, like a man touching a tender bruise.

"Dad took me to Mexico when I was two," she said, "right after someone from Eve's lawyer's office served the papers."

Travis nodded. "Meg told me that much."

"As little as I was, I remembered what she smelled like, what it felt like when she held me, the sound of her voice." A spasm of pain flinched in Sierra's eyes. "No matter how I tried, I could never recall her face. Dad made sure there weren't any pictures, and—"

He ached for her. The soupy mashed potatoes went pulpy in his mouth, and they went down like so much barbed wire when he swallowed. "What kind of man would—"

He caught himself.

None of your business, Trav.

To his surprise she smiled again, and warmth rose

in her eyes. "Dad was never a model father, more like a buddy. But he took good care of me. I grew up with the kind of freedom most kids never know—running the streets of San Miguel in my bare feet. I knew all the vendors in the marketplace, and writers and artists gathered at our *casita* almost every night. Dad's mistress, Magdalena, home-schooled me. I attracted stray dogs wherever I went, and Dad always let me keep them."

"Not a traumatic childhood," Travis observed, still careful.

She shook her head. "Not at all. But I missed my mother desperately, just the same. For a while, I thought she'd come for me. That one day a car would pull up in front of the *casita*, and there she'd be, smiling, with her arms open. Then when there was no sign of her, and no letters came—well, I decided she must be dead. It was only after I got old enough to surf the internet that I found her."

"You didn't call or write?"

"It was a shock, realizing she was alive—that if I could find her, she could have found me. And she didn't. With the resources she must have had—"

Travis felt a sting of anger on Sierra's behalf. Pushed away his tray. "I used to work for Eve," he said. "And I've known her for most of my life. I can't imagine why she wouldn't have gone in with an army, once she knew where you were."

Sierra bit her lower lip again, so hard Travis almost expected it to bleed. Her eyes glistened with tears she was probably too proud to shed, at least for herself. She'd wept plenty for Liam, he suspected, alone and in secret. It paralyzed him when a woman cried, and yet in that moment he'd have rewritten history if he could have. He'd have been there, in the thick of Sierra's sorrows, whatever they were, to put his arms around her, promise that everything would be all right and move heaven and earth to make it so.

But the plain truth was, he hadn't been.

"I'd better get back to Liam," she said.

He nodded.

They carried their trays to the dropping-off place, went upstairs again, entered Liam's room.

He was asleep, with the DVD player still running on his lap.

Travis went to speak to one of the nurses, a woman he knew from college, and when he came back, he found Sierra stretched out beside her son, dead to the world.

He sighed, watching the pair of them.

He'd kept himself apart, even before Brody died, busy with his career. Dated lots of women and steered clear of anything heavy.

Now, without warning, the whole equation had shifted, and there was a good chance he was in big trouble.

1919

The air was so cold it bit through the bearskin throws and Hannah's many layers of wool to her flesh. She could see her breath billowing out in front of her, blue white, like Doss's. Like Tobias's.

Her boy looked feverishly gleeful, nestled between her and Doss, as the sleigh moved over an icy trail, drawn by the big draft horses, Cain and Abel. The animals usually languished in the barn all winter; in the spring, they pulled plows in the hayfields, in the fall, harvest wagons.

Summers, they grazed. They seemed spry and vigorous to Hannah, gladly surprised to be working.

Where other horses or even mules might have floundered in the deep, crusted snow, the sons of Adam, as Gabe liked to call them, pranced along as easily as they would over dry ground.

Doss held the reins in his gloved hands, hunkered down into the collar of his sheepskin-lined coat, his ear-lobes red under the brim of his hat. Once in a while he glanced Hannah's way, but mostly when he spared a look, it was for Tobias.

"You warm enough?" he'd asked.

And each time Tobias would nod. If his blood had been frozen in his veins, he'd have nodded, Hannah knew that, even if Doss didn't. He idolized his uncle, always had.

Would he forget Gabe entirely, once she and Doss were married?

Everything within Hannah rankled at the thought.

Why hadn't she left for Montana before it was too late?

Now she was about to tie herself, for good, to a man she lusted after but would never love.

Of course she could still go home to her folks—she knew they'd welcome her and Tobias—but suppose she was carrying Doss's child? Once her pregnancy became apparent, they'd know she'd behaved shamefully. The whole world would know.

How could she bear that?

No. She would go ahead and marry Doss, and let sharing her bed with him be her private consolation. She'd find a way to endure the rest, like his trying to give her orders all the time and maybe yearning after other women because he'd taken a wife out of honor, not choice.

She'd be his cross to bear, and he would be hers.

There was a perverse kind of justice in that.

They reached the outskirts of Indian Rock in the late afternoon, with the sun about to go down. Doss drove straight to Dr. Willaby's big house on Third Street, secured the horses and reached into the sleigh for Tobias before Hannah got herself unwrapped enough to get out of the sleigh.

Doc Willaby's daughter, Constance, met them at the door. She was a beautiful young woman, and she'd pursued Gabe right up to the day he'd put a gold band on Hannah's finger. Now, from the way she looked at Doss, she was ready to settle for his younger brother.

The thought stirred Hannah to fury, though she'd have buttered, baked and eaten both her shoes before admitting it.

"We have need of a doctor," Doss said to Constance, holding Tobias's bundled form in both arms.

"Come in," Constance said. She had bright-auburn hair and very green eyes, and her shape, though slender, was voluptuous. What, Hannah wondered, did Doss think when he looked at her? "Papa's ill," the other woman went on, "but my cousin is here, and he'll see to the boy."

Hannah put aside whatever it was she'd felt, seeing Constance, for relief. Tobias would be looked after by a real doctor. He'd be all right now, and nothing else mattered but that.

She would darn Doss McKettrick's socks for the rest of her life. She would cook his meals and trim his hair and wash his back. She would take him water and sandwiches in summer, when he was herding cattle or working in the hayfields. She'd bite her tongue, when he galled her, which would surely be often, and let him win at cards on winter nights.

The one thing she would never do was love him—her heart would always belong to Gabe—but no one on earth, save the two of them, was ever going to know the plain, regrettable truth.

"It's a bad cold," the younger doctor said, after carefully examining Tobias in a room set aside for the purpose. He was a very slender man, almost delicate, with dark hair and sideburns. He wore a good suit and carried a gold watch, which he consulted often. He was a city dweller, Hannah reflected, used to schedules. "I'd recommend taking a room at the hotel for a few days, though, because he shouldn't be exposed to this weather."

Doss took out his wallet, like it was his place to pay the doctor bills, and Hannah stepped in front of him. She was Tobias's mother, and she was still responsible for costs such as these.

"That'll be one dollar," the doctor said, glancing from Hannah's face, which felt pink with conviction and cold, to Doss's.

Hannah shoved the money into his hand.

"Give the boy whisky," the physician added, folding the dollar bill and tucking it into the pocket of his fine tailored coat. "Mixed with honey and lemon juice, if the hotel dining room's got any such thing on hand."

Doss, to his credit, did not give Hannah a triumphant look at this official prescription for a remedy he'd already suggested and she'd disdained, but she elbowed him in the ribs anyway, just as if he had.

They checked into the Arizona Hotel, which, like many of the businesses in Indian Rock, was McKettrick owned. Rafe's mother-in-law, Becky Lewis, had run the place for years, with the help of her daughter, Emmeline. Now it was in the hands of a manager, a Mr. Thomas Crenshaw, hired out of Phoenix.

Doss was greeted like a visiting potentate when he walked in, once again carrying Tobias. A clerk was dispatched to take the sleigh and horses to the livery stable, and they were shown, the three of them, to the best rooms in the place.

The quarters were joined by a door in between, and Hannah would have preferred to be across the hall from Doss instead, but she made no comment. While Mr. Crenshaw hadn't gone quite so far as to put them all in the same room, it was clearly his assumption, and probably that of the rest of Indian Rock, too, that she and Doss were intimate. She could imagine how the reasoning went: Doss and his brother's widow shared a house, after all, way out in the country, and heaven only knew what they were up to, with only the boy around. He'd be easy to fool, being only eight years old.

Hannah went bright red as these thoughts moved through her mind.

Doss dismissed the manager and put Tobias on the nearest bed.

"I'll go downstairs and fetch that whisky concoction," he said, when it was just the three of them.

Tobias had never stayed in a hotel and, sick as he was, he was caught up in the experience. He nestled down in the bearskins, cupped his hands behind his head and gazed smiling up at the ceiling.

"Do as you please," Hannah told Doss, removing her heavy cloak and bonnet and laying them aside.

He sighed. "While we're in town, we'd best get married," he said.

"Yes," Hannah agreed acerbically. "And let's not forget to place an order at the feed-and-grain, buy groceries, pay the light bill and renew our subscription to the newspaper."

Doss gave a ragged chuckle and shook his head. "Guess I'd better dose you up with whisky, too," he replied. "Maybe that way you'll be able to stand the honeymoon."

Hannah's temper flared, but before she could respond, Doss was out the door, closing it smartly behind him.

"I like this place," Tobias said.

"Good," Hannah answered irritably, pulling off her gloves.

"What's a honeymoon," Tobias asked, "and how come you need whisky to stand it?"

Hannah pretended she hadn't heard the question.

She'd packed hastily before leaving the house, things for Tobias and for herself, but nothing for a wedding and certainly nothing for a wedding night. If the valises had been brought upstairs, she'd have something to do, shaking out garments, hanging them in the wardrobes, but as it was, her choices were limited. She could either pace or fuss over Tobias.

She paced, because Tobias would not endure fussing.

Doss returned with their bags, followed by a woman from the kitchen carrying two steaming mugs on a tray. She set the works down on a table, accepted a gratuity from Doss, stole a boldly speculative look at Hannah and bustled out.

"Drink up," Doss said cheerfully, handing one mug to Hannah and carrying the other to Tobias, who sat up eagerly to accept it.

Hannah sniffed the whisky mixture, took a tentative sip and was surprised at how good the stuff tasted. "Where's yours?" she asked, turning to Doss.

"I'm not the one dreading tonight," he answered.

Hannah's hands trembled. She set the mug down, beckoned for Doss to follow, and swept into the adjoining room. "What do you mean, tonight?" she whispered, though of course she knew.

Doss closed the door, examined the bed from a distance and proceeded to walk over to it and press hard on the mattress several times, evidently testing the springs.

Hannah's temper surged again, but she was speechless this time.

"Good to know the bed won't creak," Doss observed.

She found her voice, but it came out as a sputter. "Doss McKettrick—"

He ran his eyes over her, which left a trail of sensation, just as surely as if he'd stripped her naked and caressed her with his hands. "The preacher will be here in an hour," he said. "He'll marry us downstairs, in the office behind the reception desk. If Tobias is well enough to attend, he can. If not, we'll tell him about it later."

Hannah was appalled. "You made arrangements like that without consulting me first?"

"I thought we'd said all there was to say."

"Maybe I wanted time to get used to the idea. Did you ever think of that?"

"Maybe you'll never get used to the idea," Doss reasoned, sitting now, on the edge of the bed he clearly intended to share with her that very night. He stood, stretched in a way that could only have been called risqué. "I'm going out for a while," he announced.

"Out where?" Hannah asked, and then hated herself for caring.

He stepped in close—too close.

She tried to retreat and found she couldn't move.

Doss hooked a finger under her chin and made her look at him. "To buy a wedding band, among other things," he said. She felt his breath on her lips, and it made them tingle. "I'll send a wire to my folks and one to yours, too, if you want."

Hannah swallowed. Shook her head. "I'll write to Mama and Papa myself, when it's over," she said.

Sad amusement moved in Doss's eyes. "Suit yourself," he said.

And then he left her standing there.

She heard him speak quietly to Tobias, then the opening and closing of a door. After a few moments she returned to the next room.

Tobias had finished his medicinal whisky, and his eyelids were drooping. Hannah tucked the covers in around him and kissed his forehead. Whatever else was happening, he seemed to be out of danger. She clung to that blessing and tried not to dwell on her own fate.

He yawned. "Will Uncle Doss be my pa, once you and him are married?" he asked drowsily.

"No," Hannah said, her voice firm. "He'll still be your uncle." Tobias looked so disheartened that she added, "And your stepfather, of course."

"So he'll be sort of my father?"

"Sort of," Hannah agreed, relenting.

"I guess we won't be going to Montana now," Tobias mumbled, settling into his pillow.

"Maybe in the spring," Hannah said.

"You go," Tobias replied, barely awake now. "I'll stay here with Uncle Pa."

It wounded Hannah that Tobias preferred Doss's company to hers and that of her family, but the boy was ill and she wasn't going to argue with him. "Go to sleep, Tobias," she told him.

As if he'd needed her permission, the little boy lapsed into slumber.

Hannah sat watching him sleep for a long time. Then, seeing snow drift past the windows in the glow of a gas streetlamp, she stood and went to stand with her hands resting on the wide sill, looking out.

It was dark by then, and the general store, the only place in Indian Rock where a wedding band could be found, had probably been closed for an hour. All Doss would have to do was rap on the door, though, and they'd open the place to him. Same as the telegraph office, or any other establishment in town.

After all, he was a McKettrick.

A tear slipped down her cheek.

She was a bride, and she should be happier.

Instead she felt as if she was betraying Gabe's memory. Letting down her folks, too, because they'd hoped she'd come home and eventually marry a local man, though they hadn't actually come out and said that last part. Now, because she'd been foolish enough, needy enough, to lie with Doss, not once but twice, she'd have to stay on the Triple M until she died of old age.

A tear slipped down her cheek, and she wiped it away quickly with the back of one hand.

"You made your bed, Hannah McKettrick," she told her reflection in the cold, night-darkened glass of the window, "and now you'll just have to lie in it."

By the time Doss returned, she'd washed her face, taken her hair down for a vigorous brushing and pinned it back up again. She'd put on a fresh dress, a prim but practical gray wool, and pinched some color into her cheeks.

He had on a brand-new suit of clothes, as fancy as the ones the doctor's nephew wore, and he'd gotten a haircut and a shave, too.

She was strangely touched by these things.

"I'd have bought you a dress for the wedding," he told her, staring at her as though he'd never seen her before, "but I didn't know what would fit, and whether you'd think it proper to wear white."

She smiled, feeling a tender sort of sorrow. "This dress will do just fine," she said.

"You look beautiful," Doss told her.

Hannah blushed. It was nonsense, of course—she probably looked more like a schoolmarm than anything else in her stern gray frock with the black buttons coming up to her throat—but she liked hearing the words. Had almost forgotten how they sounded, with Gabe gone.

Doss took her hand, and there was an uncharacteristic shyness in the gesture that made her wonder if he was as frightened and reluctant as she was.

"You don't have to go through with this, Doss," she said.

He ran his lips lightly over her knuckles before letting her hand go. "It's the right thing to do," he answered.

She swallowed, nodded.

"I guess the preacher must be here."

Doss nodded. "Downstairs, waiting. Shall we wake Tobias?"

Hannah shook her head. "Better to let him sleep."

"I'll fetch a maid to watch over him while we're gone," Doss said.

Now it was Hannah who nodded.

He left her again, and this time she felt it as a tearing-away, sharp and prickly. He came back with a plump, older woman clad in a black uniform and an apron, and then he took Hannah's hand once more and led her out of the room, down the stairs and into the office where she would become Mrs. McKettrick, for the second time.

At least, she thought philosophically, she wouldn't have to get used to a new name.

Chapter 9

Present Day

The weather hadn't improved, Sierra noted, standing at the window of Liam's hospital room the next morning. Orderlies had wheeled in a second bed the night before, and she'd slept in a paper gown. Now she was back in the sweats Travis had bought for her, rested and restored.

Dr. O'Meara had already been in to introduce herself, check on Liam's progress and do a work-up of her own, and she'd signed the release papers, too. Sierra liked and trusted the woman, though she was younger than expected, no more than thirty-five years old, with delicate features, very long brown hair held back by a barrette and a trim figure.

Armed with a prescription, Sierra was ready to take her son and leave.

Ready to face Eve, and all the emotional spade work involved.

Or not.

Just as she turned from the window, Travis entered the room, wearing slacks and a blue pullover sweater that accentuated the color of his eyes. He'd said he owned a house in Flagstaff, and Sierra knew he'd gone there to spend the night.

There was so much she *didn't* know about his life, and this was unsettling, although she didn't have the time or energy to pursue it at the moment.

"Travis!" Liam crowed, as though he hadn't expected to see his friend ever again. "I get to go home today!"

The word *home* caught in Sierra's heart like a fish hook. The ranch house on the Triple M was Eve's home, and it was Meg's, but it didn't belong to her and Liam. They were temporary guests, and it had troubled Sierra all along to think Liam might become attached to the place and be hurt when they left.

Travis approached the bed, grinned and ruffled Liam's hair. "That's great," he said. "According to reports, the power is back on, the pantry is bulging, and your grandmother is waiting to meet you."

Sierra felt a wrench at the reminder. So much for thinking she was prepared to deal with Eve McKettrick.

Liam inspected Travis speculatively. "You don't look like a cowboy today," he declared.

Travis laughed. "Neither do you," he countered.

"Yeah, but I *never* do," Liam said, discouraged.

"We'll have to do something about that one of these days soon."

Sierra bristled. She and Liam were committed to staying on the ranch for a year, that was the bargain. Twelve months. The time would surely pass quickly, and she didn't want her son putting down roots only to be torn from that hallowed McKettrick ground.

"Liam looks fine the way he is," she said.

Travis gave her a long, thoughtful look. "True enough," he said mildly. "My buddy Liam is one handsome cowpoke. In fact, he looks a lot like Jesse did, at his age."

Another connection to the storied McKettrick clan. Uncomfortable, Sierra averted her eyes. She'd already gathered Liam's things, but now she rearranged them busily, just for something to do.

Half an hour later, the three of them were in Travis's truck, headed back to the ranch. Liam, buckled in between Travis and Sierra, promptly fell asleep, but his hands were locked around his DVD player. Mentally Sierra clutched the new inhaler, prescribed by Dr. O'Meara, purchased at the hospital pharmacy and tucked away in her bag, just as anxiously.

She had been silent for most of the ride, gazing out at the winter landscape as it whipped past the passenger window.

Travis said little or nothing, concentrating on navigating the icy roads, but Sierra was fully aware of his presence just the same, and in a way that disturbed her. He'd been a rock since Liam's asthma attack, and she was grateful but she couldn't afford to become dependent on him, emotionally or in any other way, and she didn't want her son to, either.

Trouble was, it might be too late for Liam. He adored Travis Reid, and there was no telling what fantasies he'd cooked up in that high-powered little brain of his. He and Travis riding the range, probably. Wearing baseball mitts and playing catch. Going fishing in some pristine mountain lake.

All the things a boy did with a dad.

"Sierra?"

She didn't dare look at Travis, for fear he might see the vulnerability she was feeling. All her nerves seemed to be on the outside of her skin, and they were doing the jingle-bell rock. "What?"

"I was just wondering what you were thinking."

She couldn't tell him, of course. He'd think she was attracted to him, and she wasn't.

Much.

So she lied. "All about Eve," she said.

He chuckled at the flimsy joke, but Sierra gave him points for recognizing an obscure reference to an old movie. Maybe they had a thing or two in common after all.

"I imagine the lady's on pins and needles herself, right about now. She wants to see you and Liam more than anything, I'd guess, but it won't be easy for her."

"I don't *want* it to be easy for her," Sierra answered.

Travis hesitated only a beat or two. "Maybe she has good reasons for what she did."

Sierra's silence was eloquent.

"Give her a chance, Sierra."

She glanced at him. "I'm doing that," she said. "I drove all the way here from Florida. I agreed to stay on the Triple M for a full year."

"Would you have done it if it weren't for the insurance?"

Damn it. He *was* a lawyer. "Probably not," she admitted.

"You'd do just about anything for Liam."

"Not 'just about,'" Sierra said. "*Anything* covers it."

"What about yourself? What would you do for Sierra?"

"Are we going to talk about me in the third person?"

"Stop hedging. I understand your devotion to Liam. I'd just like to know what you'd be doing right now if you didn't have a child, especially one with medical problems."

Sierra glanced at Liam, making sure he was asleep. "Don't talk about him as though he were somehow… deficient."

"I'm not. He's a great kid, and he'll grow up to be an exceptional man. And I'm still waiting to hear what your dreams are for yourself."

She gave a desultory little chuckle. "Nothing spectacular. I'd like to survive."

"Not much of a life. Not for you and not for Liam."

Sierra squirmed. "Maybe I've forgotten how to dream," she said.

"And that doesn't concern you?"

"Up until now, it hasn't been a factor."

"That's unfortunate. Liam will pattern his attitudes after yours. Is that what you want for him? Just survival?"

"Are you channeling some disincarnate life coach?" Sierra demanded.

Travis laughed, low and quiet. "Not me," he said.

"You're just playing the cowboy version of Dr. Phil, then?"

"Okay, Sierra," Travis conceded. "I'll back off. For now."

"What are *your* dreams, hotshot?" Sierra retorted, too nettled to let the subject alone. "You have a law degree, but you train horses and shovel out stalls for a living."

This time there was no laughter. Travis's glance was utterly serious, and the pain Sierra saw in it made her ashamed of the way she'd spoken to him.

"I guess I had that coming," he said quietly. "And here's my answer. I'd like to be able to dream again. *That's* my dream."

"I'm sorry," Sierra told him, after a few moments had passed. The man had lost his brother in a very tragic way. He was probably doing the best he could, like almost everybody else. "I didn't mean to be unkind. I was just feeling—"

"Cornered?"

"That's a good word for it."

"You must have been burned pretty badly," Travis observed. "And not just by Eve." He looked down at Liam. "Maybe by this little guy's dad?"

"Maybe," Sierra said.

After that, conversation fell by the wayside again, but Sierra did plenty of thinking.

When they arrived at the ranch, all the lights in the house seemed to be on, even though it was barely noon. A glowing tangle of color loomed in the parlor window, and Sierra squinted, sure she must be seeing things.

Travis followed her gaze and chuckled. "Uh-oh," he said. "Looks as if Christmas sneaked back in while we weren't around."

Liam's eyes popped open at the magic word. "Christmas?"

Sierra smiled, in spite of the knot of worry lying heavily in the pit of her stomach. What was Eve up to?

Travis pulled up close to the back door, and Sierra braced herself as it sprang open. There was Eve McKettrick, standing on the top step, a tall, slender woman, breathtakingly attractive in expensive slacks and a blue silk blouse.

"Is *that* my grandma?" Liam asked. "She looks like a movie star!"

She *did* look like a movie star, a young Maureen O'Hara. And Sierra was suddenly, stunningly aware that she'd seen this woman before, in San Miguel, not once, but several times. She'd been a periodic guest at one of the better B&Bs when Sierra was small, and they'd had ice cream together at a sidewalk café near the *casita*, several times.

For a moment Sierra forgot how to breathe.

The Lady. She'd always called Eve "the Lady," and she'd secretly believed she was an angel. But it had been years since she'd given the memory conscious house room.

Now it all came flooding back, in a breathtaking rush.

Travis shut off the truck and opened the door to get out. "Sierra?" he prompted, when she didn't move.

"Hello!" Liam yelled, delighted, from his place next to Sierra. "My name is Liam and I'm seven!"

Eve smiled, and her vivid green eyes glistened with emotion. "My name is Eve," she said quietly, "and I'm fifty-three. Come here and give me a hug."

Sierra finally came unstuck, opened the passenger-side door and climbed down, planting her feet in the crusty snow. Liam scrambled past her so quickly that he generated a slight breeze.

Eve leaned down to gather her grandson in her arms. She kissed the top of his head and met Sierra's gaze again as she straightened.

"I'll see to the horses," Travis said.

"Don't go," Sierra blurted, before she could stop herself.

Eve steered Liam into the kitchen, watching with interest as Travis rounded the front end of the truck and stood close to Sierra.

"You'll be all right," he told her.

She bit her lower lip, feeling like a fool. It was still all she could do not to grab one of his hands with both of hers and cling like some crazy codependent girlfriend about to be hustled out of town on the last bus of the day.

So long. It's been real.

For a few long moments she and Travis just stared into each other's eyes. He was determined; she was scared. And something *else* was happening, too, something a lot harder to define.

Finally Travis broke the impasse by turning and striding off toward the barn.

Sierra drew a deep breath and marched toward the open door of the kitchen and the woman who waited on the threshold.

"There's a surprise in the living room," Eve said to Liam, once they were all inside and she'd shut the door against the unrelenting cold.

He raced to investigate.

"You're the Lady," Sierra said, stricken.

"The Lady?" Eve echoed, but Sierra could see by

the expression in her mother's eyes that it was mere rhetoric.

"The one I used to see in San Miguel."

"Yes," Eve said. "Sit down, Sierra. I'll make tea, and we'll chat."

"Wow!" Liam yelled, from the living room. "Mom, there *is* a Christmas tree in here, with *major* presents under it!"

"Oh, Lord," Sierra said, and sank on to one of the benches at the table.

"They're *all* for me!" Liam whooped.

Sierra watched her mother take Lorelei's teapot from the cabinet, spoon tea leaves into it, fill and plug in the electric kettle. "Christmas presents?" she asked.

Eve smiled a little guiltily. "I had seven years of grandmothering to make up for," she said. "Cut me a break, will you?"

Sierra would have tallied the numbers differently, but there was no point in saying so. "I thought you were an angel," she confessed. "In San Miguel, I mean."

Eve busied herself with the tea-brewing process, stealing the occasional hungry glance at Sierra. "You've certainly grown up to be a beautiful woman," she said. Finally she stopped her puttering, clasped her hands together and practically gobbled Sierra up with her eyes. "It's…it's so wonderful to see you."

Sierra didn't answer.

Liam pounded in from the living room. "Can I open my presents?"

"If it's all right with your mother," Eve said.

Sierra sighed. "Go ahead. And calm down, please. You just got out of the hospital, remember? Overexcitement and asthma do not mix."

Liam gave a shout of delight and thundered off again, ignoring her admonition completely.

The electric kettle whistled, and Eve poured the contents into the antique teapot, and brought it to the table. She selected two cups and saucers from the priceless collection and carried those over, too. Then, at last, looking as nervous as Sierra felt, Eve sat down in the chair at the end of the table.

"How's Liam?" she asked.

"He's fine," Sierra answered. "But he's just getting over a crisis, as you know, so he's going to bed as soon as he finishes opening his presents." The bear and the balloon were in the back of Travis's truck, under the heavy plastic cover, and she imagined her mother ordering them for a grandson she'd never seen.

"So many things to say," Eve fretted, "and I haven't the first idea where to start."

Suddenly Sierra was tired. And *not* so suddenly she was overwhelmed. "Why didn't you tell me who you were—when we met in San Miguel?"

Eve poured tea, warmed beautifully manicured and bejeweled hands around a translucent china cup. "Nothing like cutting to the chase," she said, with rueful appreciation.

"Nothing like it," Sierra agreed implacably.

"If I'd told you who I was, you would have told Hank, and he might have taken you and disappeared again. It took me almost five years to find you the first time, so I wasn't about to let that happen."

Sierra absorbed her mother's words quietly. She *had* mentioned "the Lady" to her father, at least after the first encounter, but if he'd suspected anything, he'd probably dismissed the accounts as flights of a child's imagination. Besides, elegant tourists were common in San Miguel, and they were generous to local children.

"If I'd been in that situation—if it were Liam who'd been snatched away and I'd found him—I'd have taken him home with me."

Eve's eyes filled with tears, but she blinked them back. "Would you?" she challenged softly. "Even if he seemed happy and healthy, and you knew he didn't remember you? Would you simply kidnap him—tear him away from everyone and everything he knew? Without thought for any of the psychological repercussions?"

Sierra blinked. She *would* have been terrified if Eve had stolen her back from Hank, whisked her out of the country in some clandestine way. And she would have had to do exactly that, because even though Sierra's father seemed benignly disinterested most of the time, word would have gotten back to him quickly, had Eve tried to spirit her away. He would have called out the *federales,* as well as the municipal authorities, many of whom were his friends, and Eve would probably *still* be languishing in a Mexican jail.

And she'd had another daughter to consider, as well as a home and a business.

"I've been grown up for quite some time," Sierra pointed out, after long reflection. "What stopped you from contacting me after Dad died and Liam and I came to the States?"

Eve looked down into her cup.

Liam burst into the room, making both women start.

"Look, Mom!" he cried, clutching an expensive telescope in both arms, already attached to its tripod. "I'll be able to see all the way back to the Big Bang with this thing!"

"You're getting too excited," Sierra reiterated, sparing a glance for Eve before rising from her chair. "You'd better go and lie down for a while."

Liam balked, of course. He was seven, faced with unexpected largesse. "But I haven't even opened half my presents!"

"Later," Sierra said. She got up, put a hand on her son's shoulder and steered him toward the back stairs.

He protested all the way, clutching Eve's telescope in the same way he had Travis's DVD player. The stuff *she'd* given him for Christmas, all bought on sale with her tips from the bar, paled by comparison to this bounty, and even though she was glad for him, she also felt a deep slash of resentment.

"Look at it this way," she said a few minutes later, tucking him into bed in a fresh pair of pajamas, the telescope positioned in front of the window, beside the antique one that had been there when they arrived. "You've still got a lot of loot downstairs. Rest awhile, and you can tear into it again."

"Do you promise?" Liam asked suspiciously. "You won't make my grandma take it all back to the store or something?"

"When have I ever lied to you?"

"When you said there was a Santa Claus."

Sierra sighed. "Okay. Name one other time."

"You said we didn't have any family. We've got Grandma and Aunt Meg."

"I give up," Sierra said, spreading her hands. "I'm a shameless prevaricator."

Liam grinned. "If that boy comes back, I'm going to show him *my* telescope!"

A tiny chill moved down Sierra's spine. "Liam," she insisted, "there *is* no boy."

"That's what *you* think," Liam replied, and he looked damnably smug as he settled back into his pillows. "This is his room. This is his bed, and that's his old telescope."

Sierra took off the boy's shoes, tucked him under the faded quilt and sat with him until he drifted off to sleep.

And even then she didn't move, because she didn't want to go downstairs again and hear more well-rehearsed reasons why her mother had abandoned her when she was smaller than Liam.

1919

Hannah couldn't help comparing her second wedding to her first, at least in the privacy of her mind. She and Gabe had been married in the summer, in the side yard at the main ranch house. Gabe's grandfather, Angus, had been alive then and, as head of the McKettrick clan, he'd issued a decree to that effect. There had been a big cake and a band and long improvised tables burdened with food. There had been guests and gifts and dancing.

After the celebration, Gabe had driven her to town in a surrey, and they'd stayed right here at the Arizona Hotel, caught the next day's train out of Indian Rock. Traveled all the way to San Francisco for a honeymoon. Tobias had been conceived during that magical time, and the box of photographs commemorating the trip was one of Hannah's most treasured possessions.

Now she found herself standing in the cramped and cluttered office behind the reception desk, a widow about to become a bride. Only, this time there was no cake, no honeymoon trip to look forward to, and certainly no music and dancing.

Those things wouldn't have mattered, Hannah was certain, if she'd loved Doss and known he loved her. It wasn't the modesty of the ceremony that troubled her, but the coldly practical reasons behind it.

While the preacher droned the sacred words, with Mr. Crenshaw and one of the maids for witnesses, Hannah stole the occasional sidelong glance at her groom.

Doss looked stalwart, determined and impossibly handsome.

What will become of us? Hannah wondered, in silent and stoic despair. She'd pasted a wobbly smile on her face, because she wouldn't have the preacher gossiping afterward, saying she'd looked like a deer with one foot stuck in a railroad track, and the train about to come clackety-clacking round the bend at full throttle.

Oh, no. If she did what she really wanted to do, which was either run or break down and cry, that self-righteous old coot would spread the news from one end of the state to the other, and what a time folks would have with that.

A weeping bride.

A grimly resigned groom.

The talk wouldn't die down for years.

So Hannah endured.

She repeated her vows, when she was prompted, and kept her chin high, her backbone straight and her eyes bone dry. The ordeal was almost over when suddenly the office door banged open and Doss's uncle Jeb strolled in. He was still handsome, though well into middle age, and he grinned as he took in the not-so-happy couple.

"Thought I'd missed it," he said.

Doss laughed, evidently pleased to set eyes on another blood-McKettrick.

The minister cleared his throat, not entirely approving of the interruption, it would seem.

"I now pronounce you man and wife," he said quickly.

"Kiss your bride," Jeb prompted, watching his nephew closely.

Hannah blushed.

Doss kissed her, and she wondered if he'd have remembered to do it at all, if his uncle hadn't provided a verbal nudge.

"No flowers?" Jeb asked, after Doss had paid the preacher and the man had gone. He looked around the office. "No guests?"

"It was a hasty decision," Doss explained.

Hannah blushed again.

"Oh," Jeb said. He shook Doss's hand, whacked him once on the shoulder and then turned to Hannah, gently kissing her cheek. "Be happy, Hannah," he whispered, close to her ear. "Gabe would want that."

Tears brimmed in Hannah's eyes, and this after she'd held up so well, made such an effort to play the happy bride. Did her true feelings show? Or was Jeb McKettrick just perceptive?

She nodded, unable to speak.

"I thought you were down in Phoenix," Doss said to his uncle. If he'd noticed Hannah's tears, he was keeping the observation to himself.

"I came up here to take care of some business at the Cattleman's Bank," Jeb explained. "Arrived on the afternoon train. It's a long ride out to the ranch, and the meeting ran long, so I decided to spend the night here at the hotel and head back to Phoenix tomorrow. I was sitting in the dining room, taking my supper, when somebody mentioned that the two of you were shut up in here with a preacher." He glanced at Hannah again, and she saw concern flash briefly in his eyes. "I decided to invite myself to the festivities. Of course when I tell Chloe about it, she'll say I ought to learn a few manners. After all this time, my wife still hasn't given up on grinding off my rough edges."

Doss slipped an arm around Hannah's waist. "We're glad you came," he told Jeb. "Aren't we, Hannah?"

She didn't answer right away, and he had the gall to pinch her lightly under her ribs, through the fabric of her sadly practical gray dress.

"Yes," she said.

"Where's Tobias?" Jeb asked. "Chloe'll skin me if I don't bring back a detailed report. That woman likes to know everything about everybody. How much the boy's grown, how he's doing with his lessons, and all that."

"He's down with a cold," Doss said. "That's why we brought him to town. So he could see the doctor."

"And you just decided to get married while you were here?"

Doss colored up.

Hannah was stricken to silence again.

Jeb smiled. "The boy's here in the hotel, then?"

Hannah nodded, still mute.

Jeb's gaze shifted to Doss. "Why don't you go up there and see if he's agreeable to a visit from his old Uncle Jeb?" he said.

Doss hesitated, then nodded and left the room.

"I'm going to ask Doss the same thing I'm about to ask you," Jeb said, the moment they were alone with the door closed. "What's going on here?"

Hannah swallowed painfully. "Well, it just seemed sensible for us to get married."

"Sensible?"

"Both of us living out there on the ranch, I mean. You know how folks…speculate about things like that."

"I know, all right," Jeb answered. "Chloe and I stirred up plenty of talk in our day. I guess I just figured if there'd been a wedding in the offing, the family would have heard something about it before now."

"Doss wired his folks, and I was going to write to mine—"

"You're both adults and it's your business what you do," Jeb said. "Do you love Doss, Hannah?"

She fell back on something she'd said to Tobias, out at the ranch, when he'd asked a similar question. "He's family," she replied.

"He's also a man. A young one, with his whole life ahead of him. He deserves a wife who's glad to be his wife."

Hannah lifted her chin. "A few minutes ago you told me Gabe would want this. Doss and me married, I mean. And you're probably right. So I did it as much for him as anybody."

"There's only one person you ought to please in a situation like this, Hannah, and that's yourself."

"Tobias needs Doss."

"I don't doubt that's true. Losing Gabe was hard on everybody in this family, but it was worse for you and Tobias. The question on my mind right now is, do you need Doss, Hannah?"

Hannah needed her new husband, all right, but not in a way she was going to discuss with his uncle—or anyone else on the face of the earth, for that matter. "I'll see that he's happy, if that's what you're worried about," she said, and felt her cheeks burn again, fearing she'd revealed exactly what she'd been so determined to keep secret.

"He'll be happy," Jeb said, with such remarkable certainty that Hannah wondered if he knew something she didn't. "Will you?"

"I'll learn to be," she answered.

Jeb placed his hands on her shoulders, squeezed lightly and kissed her forehead. Then, without another word, he went out, leaving Hannah standing there alone, full of confusion and sorrow.

She was waiting in the lobby when Doss came downstairs, some minutes later, looking shy as a schoolboy. Evidently, Jeb had already spoken to him and was with Tobias now.

Doss tried to smile but fell a little short. Now that they were actually married, he apparently didn't know what to say, and neither did Hannah. They were making the best of things, both of them, and it shouldn't have been that way.

"I guess we ought to have some supper," Doss said. "Tobias has already eaten. The maid went down to the kitchen and brought him up a meal while we were—"

Hannah looked down at her feet. "You deserve somebody who loves you," she said softly, miserable with shame.

Doss put a finger under her chin and raised her head, so he could look into her eyes. "I don't know if your mind and heart love me, Hannah McKettrick," he said solemnly, with no trace of arrogance, "but your body does. And maybe it will teach the rest of you to feel the same way."

She took a gentle hold on the lapels of his new suit,

bought just for the wedding. "Gabe would want this," she said. "Our being married, I mean."

Doss swallowed. "I loved my brother," he told her gravely, "but I don't want to talk about him. Not tonight."

Hannah wept inside, even though her eyes were dry. "All right," she agreed.

He led her into the dining room, and they both ordered fried chicken dinners. It was an occasion, to eat a restaurant meal, almost as unusual, in Hannah's life, as getting married. She was starved, after a long and hectic day, and yet the food tasted like sawdust from the first bite.

Jeb appeared, just as they were trying to choke down dessert. Chocolate cake, normally Hannah's favorite, with powdered sugar icing.

"Tobias," Jeb announced, "is spending the night in the room next to mine. I've already made arrangements for the maid to stay with him."

Hannah laid down her fork, relieved not to have to pretend to eat any longer. It was almost as hard as pretending to be happy, and she didn't think she could manage both.

"I guess that's all right," she allowed.

Doss looked down at his plate. He hadn't eaten much more than Hannah had, though, like her, he'd made a good show of it. Making illicit love on the ranch was one thing, she realized, and being married was quite another. Was he as nervous about the night to come as she was?

Jeb congratulated them both and left.

Their plates were cleared away.

Doss paid the bill.

And then there was nothing to do but go upstairs and get on with their wedding night.

Chapter 10

Tobias's bed was empty, and his things had been removed. Hannah glanced nervously at Doss, now her husband, and put a hand to her throat.

He sighed and loosened his string tie, then unbuttoned his collar. If there had been whisky in that hotel room, Hannah was sure he would have poured himself a double and downed it in a gulp. She felt moved to touch his arm, soothe him somehow, but the urge died aborning. Instead she stood rigid upon the soles of her practical high-button shoes, and wished she'd put her foot down while there was still time, called the whole idea of getting married for the damn fool notion that it was, stopped the wedding and let the gossips say what they would.

She was miserable.

Doss was miserable.

What in the world had possessed them?

"We could get an annulment," she said shakily.

Doss's gaze sliced to her, sharp enough to leave the thick air quivering in its wake. "Oh, I'd say we were past that," he retorted coldly. "Wouldn't you?"

Hannah's cheeks burned as smartly as if they'd been chapped by the bitter wind even then rattling at the windows and seeping in as a draft. "I only meant that we haven't…well…consummated the marriage, and—"

He narrowed his eyes. "I remember it a little differently," he said.

Damn him, Hannah thought fiercely. He'd been so all-fired set on going through with the ceremony—it had been his idea to exchange vows, not hers—and now he was acting as though he'd been wooed, enticed, trapped.

"I will thank you to remember this, Doss McKettrick—I didn't seduce you. You seduced me!"

He hooked a finger in his tie and jerked at it. Took an angry step toward her and glared down into her face. "You could have said no at any time, Hannah," he reminded her, making a deliberate effort to keep his voice down. "My recollection is that you didn't. In fact, you—"

"Stop," Hannah blurted. "If you're any kind of gentleman, you won't throw that in my face! I was—we were both—lonely, Doss. We lost our heads, that's all. We could find the preacher, tell him it was a mistake, ask him to tear up the license—"

"You might as well stand in the middle of Main Street, ring a cowbell to draw a crowd, and tell the whole damn town what we did as do that!" Doss seethed. "And what's going to happen in six months or so, when your belly is out to here with my baby?"

Hannah's back teeth clamped together so hard that she had to will them apart. "What makes you so sure there is a baby?" she demanded. "Gabe and I wanted more children after Tobias, but nothing happened."

Doss opened his mouth, closed it again forcefully. Whatever he'd been about to say, he'd clearly thought better of it. All of a sudden Hannah wanted to reach down his throat and haul the words out of him like a bucket from a deep well, even though she knew she'd be just as furious to hear them spoken as she was right then, left to wonder.

For what seemed to Hannah like a very long time, the two of them just stood there, practically nose to nose, glowering at each other.

Hannah broke first, shattered against that McKettrick stubbornness the way a storm-tossed ship might shatter on a rocky shore. With a cry of sheer frustration, she turned on one heel, strode into the next room and slammed the door hard behind her.

There was no key to turn the lock, and nothing to brace under the knob to keep Doss from coming after her. So Hannah paced, arms folded, until some of her fury was spent.

Her gaze fell on her nightgown, spread by some thoughtful soul—probably the maid who had looked after Tobias while she and Doss were downstairs ruining their lives—across the foot of the bed.

Resignation settled over Hannah, heavy and cold as a wagonload of wet burlap sacks.

I might as well get this over with, she thought, trying to ignore the unbecoming shiver of excitement she felt at the prospect of being alone with Doss, bared to him, surrendering and, at the same time, conquering.

Resolutely she took off her clothes, donned the nightgown and unpinned her hair.

And waited.

Where was Doss?

She sat down on the edge of the mattress, twiddling her thumbs.

He didn't arrive.

She got up and paced.

Still no Doss.

She was damned if she'd open the door and invite him in after the way he'd acted, but the waiting was almost unbearable.

Finally Hannah sneaked across the room, bent and peered through the keyhole. Her view was limited, and while she couldn't actually see Doss, that didn't mean he wasn't there. If he'd left, she would have heard him—wouldn't she?

She paced again, briskly this time, muttering under her breath.

The room was growing cold, and not just because there was no fire to light. She marched over to the radiator, under the window, and cranked on the handle until she heard a comforting hiss. Something caught her eye, through the night-darkened glass, as she straightened, and she wiped a peephole in the steam with the sleeve of her nightgown. Squinted.

Was that Doss, standing in the spill of light flowing over the swinging doors of the Blue Garter Saloon down at the corner? His shape and stance were certainly familiar, but the clothes were wrong—or were they? Doss had worn a suit to the wedding, and this man was dressed for the open range.

Hannah stared harder, and barely noticed when the tip of her nose touched the icy glass. Then the man struck a match against the saloon wall, and lit a cheroot, and she saw his face clearly in the flare of orange light.

It was Doss, and he was looking in her direction, too. He'd seen her, watching him from the hotel room window like some woebegone heroine in a melodrama.

No. It couldn't be him.

They had a lot to settle, it was true, but this was their wedding night.

Hannah clenched her fists and turned from the window for a few moments, struggling to regain her composure as well as her dignity. By now everyone in Indian Rock knew about the hurry-up wedding, knew they ought to be honeymooning, she and Doss, even if they hadn't gotten any further than the Arizona Hotel. If Doss passed the evening in the Blue Garter Saloon, tonight of all nights—

She whirled, fumbling to pull up the sash, meaning to call out to him, though God only knew what she'd say. But before she could open the window, he turned his back on her and went right through those saloon doors. Hannah watched helplessly as they swung on their hinges and closed behind him.

Present Day

Sierra stood with her hands on her hips, studying the January Christmas tree. The lights shimmered and the colors blurred as she took in the mountain of gifts still to be unwrapped, the wads of bright paper, the expensive loot Liam had already opened.

Sweaters. A leather coat, reminiscent of Travis's. Cowboy boots and a hat. A set of toy pistols. Why, there was more stuff there than she'd been able to give Liam in all seven years of his life, let alone for one Christmas.

Eve had done it all, of course. The decorating, anyway. She might have brought the presents with her from Texas, after sending some office minion out to ransack the high-end stores.

Did it mean she genuinely cared, Sierra wondered, or was she merely trying to buy some form of absolution?

Sierra sensed Eve's presence almost immediately, but it was a few moments before she could look her in the eye.

"The pistols might have been an error in judgment," Eve conceded quietly, poised in the doorway as though unsure whether to bolt or stay and face the music. "I should have asked."

"The whole thing is an error in judgment," Sierra responded, her insides stretched so taut that they seemed to hum. "It's too much." She turned, at last, and faced her mother. "You had no right."

"Liam is my grandson," Eve pointed out, and the very rationality of her words snapped hard around Sierra's heart, like some giant rubber band, yanked to its limits and then let go.

"You had no right!" Sierra repeated, in a furious undertone.

To her credit, Eve didn't flinch. "What are you so afraid of, Sierra? That he'll like me?"

Sierra swayed a little, suddenly light-headed. "Don't you understand? I can't give Liam things like this. I don't want him getting used to this way of life—it will be too hard on him later, when we have to leave it all behind."

"What way of life?" Eve persisted. Her attitude

wasn't confrontational, but it was obvious that she intended to stand her ground. It was all so easy for her, with her money and her power. She could make grand gestures, but Sierra would be the one picking up the pieces when she and Liam made a hard—and inevitable—landing in the real world.

"The *McKettrick* way of life!" Sierra burst out. "This big house, the land, the money—"

"Sierra, you *are* a McKettrick, and so is Liam."

Sierra closed her eyes for a moment, struggling to regain her composure. "I agreed to come here for one reason and one reason only," she finally said, with hard-won moderation, "because my son needs medical attention, and I can't afford to provide it. But the agreement was for one year—*one year,* Eve—and we won't be here a single day after that condition is met!"

"And after that one year is up, you think I'm just going to forget that I have a second daughter and a grandson? Whether you're still too blasted stubborn to accept my help or not?"

"I don't *need* your help, Eve!"

"Don't you?"

Sierra shook her head, more in an effort to clear her mind than to deny Eve's meaning, found a chair and sank slowly into it. "I appreciate what you're doing," she said, after a few slow, deep breaths. "I really do. But if you expect anything beyond what we agreed to, there's a problem."

Eve moved to the fireplace, took a long match from the mantel and lit the newspaper and kindling already stacked in the grate. She waited until the flames caught, crackling merrily, then added more wood from the basket next to the hearth. "What did Hank tell you about me, Sierra?" she asked quietly, turning back to study Sierra's face. "Did he tell you I was dead? Or did he say I didn't want you?"

"He didn't have to say you didn't want me. That was perfectly obvious."

"Was it?" Eve dusted off a place on the raised hearth and sat down, folding her hands loosely in her lap. "I want to know what he told you, Sierra. After all these years, after all he took from me, I think I have the right to ask."

"He never said you didn't want me. He said you didn't want *him*."

"Well, that was certainly true enough."

Sierra swallowed. "I guess I was five or six before I noticed that other little girls had mothers, not just fathers. I started asking a lot of questions, and I guess he got tired of it. He said there'd been an accident, that you'd been badly hurt and you'd probably have to go to heaven."

Eve lowered her head then, wiped furtively at her cheek with the back of one hand. "Who would have thought Hank Breslin would say *two* true things out of three in the same lifetime?"

Sierra slid to the edge of her chair, eager and tense at the same time.

Don't get sucked in, she heard Hank say, as clearly as if he'd been standing in the room, taking part in the conversation.

"There *was* an accident?" Sierra asked on a breath, mentally shushing her father. Just asking the question meant a part of her hadn't believed Hank, but this, like so many other things, would have to be considered later, when she was alone. And calm.

Eve nodded.

"What kind of accident?"

Eve visibly collected herself, sitting up a little straighter. Her eyes seemed focused on a past Sierra hadn't been a part of. "I was having lunch at an outdoor café in San Antonio—with my lawyer, as it happens. We'd found you after two years of searching, or at least the investigators we'd hired had, and I'd seen you with my own eyes, in San Miguel. Spoken to you. I wanted to contact Hank, work out some kind of arrangement—"

A peculiar, buzzing sensation dimmed Sierra's hearing.

"Your father had to be handled very carefully. I knew that. It would have been like Hank to take you deeper into Mexico—even into South America—if he'd gotten spooked, and he'd have been a lot more careful to disappear for good the second time."

Sierra waited, willing her head to clear, listening with everything in her. "The accident?" she prompted, very softly.

"A car jumped the curb, crashed through the stucco wall between the tables and the street. We were sitting just on the other side. My lawyer—his name was Jim Furman and he had a wife and five children—was killed instantly. I was in traction for weeks, and it took me another year and a half just to walk again."

The incident sounded like something from a soap opera, and yet Sierra knew it was true. Her stomach churned as horrific images, complete with a soundtrack of crashes and screams, flashed through her mind.

"By the time I recovered," Eve went on, after a few long moments of silence, "I knew it was too late, that I'd have to wait until you were older, when you could make choices for yourself. You were happy and healthy and very bright. You were still so young. I couldn't just waltz into your life and say, 'Hello, I'm your mother.' I was still afraid of what Hank might do, and I was struggling to rebuild my life after the accident. Meg was spending most of her time with nannies as it was, and I had to turn the company over to the board of directors because I couldn't seem to focus my mind on anything. With all that going on, how could I take you away from the only home you knew, only to turn around and leave you in the care of strangers?"

Sierra sat quietly, drawing careful, measured breaths, taking it all in. "Okay," she said, finally. "I can buy all that. But there's still a pretty big gap between then and six weeks ago, when you finally contacted me."

Eve was silent.

So I was right, Sierra thought bitterly. There's more.

"I was ashamed," Eve said.

"Ashamed?"

Silence.

"Eve?"

"After the accident," Eve went on, her voice pitched so low that Sierra had to lean forward to hear, "I took a lot of pain pills. They became less and less effective, while the pain seemed to get worse, so I started washing them down with alcohol."

Sierra's mouth dropped open. "Meg never mentioned—"

"Of course she wouldn't," Eve said. "It was my place to tell you and, besides, you don't just email something like that to somebody. What was she supposed to say? 'Oh, by the way, Mother is a pill-freak and a drunk'?"

"My God," Sierra whispered.

"I was intermittently clean and sober," Eve went on. "But I always fell off the wagon eventually. If Rance hadn't stepped in after I took control of the company again, God bless him, I probably would have run McKettrickCo into the ground."

"Rance?"

"Your cousin."

Sierra struggled to hit a lighter note, because they both needed that. "Which branch of the family tree was *he* hatched in?"

Eve smiled weakly, but with a kind of gratitude that pinched Sierra's heart in one of the tenderest places. "Rance is descended from Rafe and Emmeline," she answered. "Rafe was old Angus's son."

"It took you all this time to get your life back together?" Sierra asked tentatively, after yet another lengthy silence had run its course.

"No," Eve said. Color stained her cheeks. "No, I've been on the straight-and-narrow for ten years or so. I said it before, Sierra—I was ashamed. So much time had gone by, and I didn't know what to say. Where to start. It became a vicious cycle. The longer I put it off, the harder it was to take the risk."

"But you finally tracked me down again. What changed?"

"I didn't have to track you down. I always knew where you were." Eve sighed, and her shoulders stooped a little. "I found out about Liam's asthma, and I couldn't wait any longer." She paused, straightened her back again. "Fair is fair, Sierra. I've answered the hard questions, though I realize there will be more. Now, it's your turn. Why did you spend your life moving from place to place, serving cocktails, instead of putting down roots somewhere and making something of your life?"

Sierra considered her past and felt something sink within her. She'd taken a few night courses, here and there. She'd used her fluent Spanish with customers and volunteered, when she could, at some of Liam's schools. But she'd never had roots or any direction except "away."

"There's nothing wrong with serving cocktails," she said, trying not to sound defensive and not quite succeeding.

"Of course there isn't," Eve readily agreed. "But why didn't you go to college?"

Sierra smiled ruefully. "There are only twenty-four hours in a day, Eve. I had a child to support."

Eve nodded reflectively. And waited.

Sierra waited, too.

"That doesn't explain all the moving from place to place," Eve said at last.

"I wish I had a ready answer," Sierra said, after considerable searching. "I guess I just always had this low-grade anxiety, like I was trying to outrun something."

Eve took that in silently.

"Why did you divorce my father?" Sierra asked. She hadn't seen the question coming, but she knew it had been fermenting in the back of her mind for a long time. Whenever it arose, she pushed it down, told herself it didn't matter, but this was a time for truth, however painful it might be.

"Hank," Eve replied carefully, "was one of those men who believe they're entitled to call the shots, by virtue of possessing a penis. He quit his job a month after we were married—he sold condominiums—planning to become a golf pro at the country club. He never actually got around to applying, of course, and it would have been quite a trick to get hired anyway, since there wasn't an opening and he didn't know a nine-iron from a putter."

Sierra moistened her lips, uncomfortable.

"He was an emotional lightweight," Eve went on, quietly relentless. "But you knew that, didn't you, Sierra?"

She *had* known, but admitting it aloud was beyond her. She did manage a stiff nod, though.

"How did he earn a living?" Eve asked. "Even in Mexico, there's rent to pay, and food costs money."

Sierra blushed. Hank had tended bar at the corner cantina on occasion, and played a lot of backroom poker. The house they'd lived in belonged to Magdalena. "He just seemed to...coast," she said.

"But you had clothes, shoes. Medical care. Birthday cakes. Toys at Christmas?"

Sierra nodded. Her childhood had been marked by two things—a vague, pervasive loneliness, and a bohemian kind of freedom. At last, realization struck. "*You* were sending him money somehow."

"I was sending *you* money, through Hank's sister, from the day he took you away. Nell, your aunt, was pretty clever. She always cashed the check, then wired it to Hank, through various places—sometimes a bank, sometimes the courtesy desk in a supermarket, sometimes a convenience store. Eventually my investigators picked up the trail, but it wasn't so easy in those days."

Sierra flashed on a series of memories—her dad walking away from one of the many *cambio* outlets in San Miguel, where tourists cashed traveler's checks and exchanged their own currency for *pesos*. She'd been very small, but she'd seen him folding a wad of bills and tucking it into his pocket, and she'd wondered. Now she felt a stab of shame on his behalf, recalling his small, secret smile.

Eve was right. Hank Breslin had felt *entitled* to that money, and while he'd always made sure Sierra had the necessities, he'd never been overly generous. In fact, it had been Magdalena not Hank, who had provided extras. Sweet, plump, spice-scented Magdalena of the patient smile and manner.

Sierra's emotions must have been clearly visible in her face. Eve rose, came over to her and laid a hand on her shoulder. Then, without another word, she turned and left the room.

Sierra had loved her father, for all his shortcomings, and seeing him in this light destroyed a lot of fantasies. Even worse, she knew that Adam, Liam's father, had been a younger version of Hank. Oh, he'd had a career. But she'd been an amusement to him and nothing more. He'd been willing to sell her out, sell out his own wife and daughters, for a good time. Like Hank, he'd felt entitled to whatever pleasures happened to be available, and to hell with all the people who got hurt in the process.

For a moment she hated Adam, hated Hank, hated all men.

She'd been attracted to Travis Reid.

Now she took an internal step back, and an enormous *no!* boiled up from her depths, spewing like a geyser and then freezing solid at its height.

Chapter 11

1919

Doss returned to the room well after midnight, smelling of cigar smoke and whisky. Hannah lay absolutely still, playing possum, watching through her lashes as he shed his hat and coat and kicked off his boots. Maybe he knew she was awake, and maybe he was fooled. She wasn't about to give herself away by speaking to him and, besides, she didn't trust herself not to tear into him like a shrew. Once the first word tumbled out of her mouth, others would follow, like a raging horde with swords and cudgels.

On the other hand, if he had the pure audacity to think, for one blessed moment, that he was going to enjoy his husbandly privileges, she'd come up out of that bed like a tigress, claws bared and slashing.

She breathed slowly, deeply and regularly, making her body soft.

Doss moved to the bureau, filled the china wash basin from the pitcher provided, and washed. She waited, in delicious dread, for him to undress, since he obviously intended to sleep in that room, in that bed, with her.

To her surprise, relief and complete annoyance, he remained fully clothed, sat down on the edge of the bed, and stretched out on top of the covers.

"I know you're not asleep," he said.

Hannah bit down hard on her lower lip. Though her eyes were shut tight, tears squeezed beneath her lids. Gabe would never have done such a thing to her, never have gone out on their wedding night to smoke and drink whisky and carouse with bad companions. Never have subjected her to such a public humiliation.

A sob shook her body. "I hate you, Doss McKettrick," she said.

He sighed, sounding resigned. If he'd apologized, if he'd put his arm around her and held her close, she would have felt better, in spite of it all, but he didn't. He kept to his own side of the bed, a weight atop the blankets, within touching distance and yet as remote from Hannah as Indian Rock was from the Eastern Seaboard.

"We'll have to make the best of things," he told her.

She rolled on to her side, with her back to him. "No, we won't," she whispered snappishly, "because as soon as Tobias is well enough, he and I are getting on the train and leaving for good."

"If it's a comfort to you," Doss replied, "then you just go ahead and think that. The truth of the matter is, you're my wife now, and as long as there's a chance you're carrying my baby, you're not going anywhere."

"I hate you," Hannah repeated.

"So you said," Doss answered, with a long-suffering sigh.

"I'll leave if I want to."

"I'll bring you back. And believe me, Hannah, I can keep up the game as long as you can."

"Then you mean to keep me prisoner." Hannah spoke into the darkness, and it seemed like a shadow, cast by her very soul, that gloom, rather than mere night, with the moon following its ancient course and the stars in their right places. It was, in that moment, as if the sun would never rise again.

"I won't lock you in the cellar, if that's what you mean," Doss told her. "I won't mistreat you or force my attentions on you, and I'll be civil as long as you are. But until I know whether you're pregnant or not, you're staying right here."

Hannah huddled deeper into the covers, feeling small, and wiped away a tear with the edge of the sheet. "I hope I'm not," she whispered. "I hope I'm not carrying your baby."

Even as she said the words, though, she knew they were the frayed and tattered weavings of a lie. She longed for another child, a girl this time, yearned to feel a life growing and stirring under her heart. She just didn't want Doss McKettrick to be the father, that was all.

She cried quietly, lying there next to Doss. Cried till her pillow was wet. She'd have bet money she wouldn't sleep a wink, but at some point she succumbed.

The next thing she knew, it was morning.

Doss's side of the bed was empty, and fat, lazy flakes of snow drifted past the window. The room was cold, but she could hear voices in the next room and the clattering of silverware against dishes. The aroma of bacon teased her nose; her stomach clenched with hunger, and then she was nauseous.

"No," she said, in a whisper, sitting bolt-upright.

Yes, her body replied. She'd had the same reaction within ten days of Tobias's conception.

Tobias appeared in the doorway, with Doss standing just behind him.

"You want some breakfast, Ma?" the boy asked. He looked slightly feverish, but stronger, too, and he was wearing a new suit of clothes—black woolen trousers, a blue-and-white-plaid flannel shirt, even suspenders.

The whole picture turned hazy, and the mention of food, let alone the smell, sent bile scalding into the back of Hannah's throat. Avoiding Doss's gaze, she gulped and shook her head.

Doss laid a hand on Tobias's shoulder and gently steered him back into the other room. He pulled the door closed, too, and the instant he did, Hannah rolled out of bed, pulled the chamber-pot out from underneath, distractedly grateful that it was clean, and threw up until she collapsed onto the hooked rug, utterly spent.

She heard the door open again, heard Doss say her name, but she couldn't respond. She just lay there, on her side, wretched and empty, as though she'd lost her soul as well as the remains of her wedding supper.

Doss knelt, gathered her in his arms, and put her back into bed, covering her gently. He fetched a basin of tepid water from the other room, along with a washcloth, and cleaned her up. When that was done, he handed her a glass, and she rinsed her mouth, then spat into the basin.

"I'll get the doctor," he said.

She shook her head. "Don't," she answered, and the word came out raspy and raw. "I just need to rest."

Doss drew up a chair, sat beside the bed, keeping a silent vigil. Hannah wished he'd go away, and at the same time she dreaded his leave-taking with the whole echoing hollowness of her being.

A maid came in, replacing the fouled chamber pot, washing out the basin, taking the pitcher away and bringing it back full. Although she cast the occasional worried glance in Hannah's direction, the woman never said a word, and when she was gone, Doss remained.

He plumped the pillows behind Hannah's back and adjusted the radiator to warm the room.

"I thought I'd bundle Tobias up," Doss ventured, at some length, "and take him down to the general store. Get him some things to play with, maybe a book to read."

Hannah was in a strange, dazed state, weak all over. "You see that he doesn't take a chill," she muttered. Common sense said Tobias ought to stay in, out of the weather, and if she'd been herself, she would have insisted on that. As things stood, she didn't have the strength, and anyway she knew the boy was desperate to get out, if only for a little while.

Doss stood, tucked the covers in around her. To look at them, Hannah thought, anybody would have thought they were a normal husband and wife, people who loved each other. "Can I bring you something back?"

"No," she said, and closed her eyes, drifting.

When she opened them again, Doss was back, with the chilly scent of fresh air surrounding him. She could hear Tobias in the next room, chatting with somebody.

"Feeling better?" Doss asked. He was holding a parcel in his hands, wrapped in brown paper and tied with string.

"Thirsty," Hannah murmured.

Doss nodded, set the package aside and brought her another glass of water, this time from the pitcher on the bureau.

She drank it down, waited, and was pathetically pleased when it didn't come right back up.

"You'd best have something to eat, if you can," Doss said.

Hannah nodded. Suddenly she was ravenous.

He left again, was gone so long that she wondered if he meant to hunt down the food, skin it, and cook it over a slow fire. Tobias wandered in, cheeks pink from the cold, eyes bright. "Uncle Jeb wants to buy me a sandwich," he told her. "Downstairs, in the restaurant. Is it all right if I go?"

Hannah smiled. "Sure it is," she said.

Tobias drew a step nearer, moving tentatively, as though approaching something fragile enough to fall over and break at the slightest touch. "Doss says you're not dying," he said.

"He's right," Hannah answered.

"Then what's the matter? You never stay in bed in the daytime."

Hannah extended her hand, and after hesitating Tobias took it. "I'm being lazy," she said, giving his fingers a squeeze.

He clung for a moment, then let go. His eyes were wide and worried. "I heard you being sick," he told her.

A door opened in the distance, and Hannah heard Doss and Jeb exchange quiet words, though she couldn't make them out. "I'll be fine by tomorrow," she promised. "You go and have that sandwich. It isn't every day you get to eat in a real restaurant."

Tobias relaxed visibly. He smiled, planted a kiss on her

forehead and fled, nearly colliding with Doss in the doorway. Doss tightened his grip on the tray of food he was
carrying. A teapot, with steam wisping from the spout.
A bowl of something savory and fragrant.

Hannah's nose twitched, and her formerly rebellious
stomach growled an audible welcome.

"Chicken and dumplings," Doss said, with a grin.

He set the tray carefully on Hannah's lap. Poured her
a cup of tea and probably would have spoon-fed her, too,
if she hadn't taken charge of the situation.

"Thank you," she said, trying to square this attentive
man with the one who had left her alone on their wedding night to visit the Blue Garter Saloon.

"You're welcome," he replied. He sat down to watch
her eat, and his gaze strayed once or twice to the package
on the nightstand, still wrapped and mysterious.

Hannah did not assume it was for her, since she'd
clearly refused Doss's earlier offer to bring her something from the mercantile, but she was curious, just the
same. The shape was booklike, and before she'd married
Gabe, she'd read so much her mother and father used to
fret that her eyes might go bad. After she became a wife,
she was too busy, and when Gabe went away to war, she
found she couldn't concentrate on the printed word. Letters were all she'd been able to manage then.

She ate what she could and sipped her tea, hot and
sweet and pale with milk, and Doss took the tray away,
set it on the bureau. Jeb and Tobias had long since gone
downstairs for their midday meal, and except for the
sounds of wagons passing in the street below and the
faint hiss of the radiator, the room was silent.

Doss cleared his throat and shifted uncomfortably in
his chair. "Hannah, about last night—"

"Stop," Hannah said quickly, and with as much force as she could manage, given her curiously fragile state. The teacup rattled in its saucer, and Doss leaned forward to take it from her, set it next to the parcel. He looked resigned, and a little impatient.

Hannah leaned back on her pillows, fighting another spate of tears. She would have sworn she'd cried them all out the night before, after Doss came back from the Blue Garter and told her he wouldn't let her go home to Montana, but here they were, burning behind her eyes, threatening to spill over.

"I figure you know what this means, your being sick like this," Doss said presently, and in a tone that said he wouldn't be silenced before he'd finished his piece. "That's the only reason I didn't bring the doctor over here, first thing."

Hannah closed her eyes. Nodded.

"I know you'd rather it was Gabe sitting here," he went on. "That he'd be the one who fathered that child, the one taking you home to the ranch, the one bringing Tobias up to be a man. But the plain fact of the matter is, it'll be me doing those things, Hannah, and you might as well make peace with that."

She didn't speak, because she couldn't. She tried to summon up Gabe's image in her mind, but it wouldn't come to her. All she saw was Doss, coming in after a night at the Blue Garter, taking off his coat and hat and boots, lying down beside her on the bed, keeping a careful distance.

He retrieved the parcel from the nightstand and laid it in her lap. She listened, despondent, as he left the room, closed the door quietly behind him.

She ought to refuse the package, throw it against the

wall or into Doss's face when he came back. But some part of her wanted a gift, something frivolous and impractical, chosen purely to bring a smile to her face.

She barely remembered what it was like to smile, without thinking about it first, without deciding she ought to, because it was called for or expected.

Her hands trembled as she undid the string, wound it into a little ball to keep, turned back the brown paper, which she would carefully fold and save against some future need, to find that Doss had indeed given her a book. Her breath caught at the beauty of the green leather cover. The title, embossed in shining gold, seemed to sing beneath the tips of her fingers.

The Flowers of Western America, Native and Imported: An Illustrated Guide.

Hannah held the thick volume reverently, savoring the anticipation for a few moments before opening it to look at the title page, memorize the author's name, as well as that of the artist who'd done the original woodcuttings and metal etchings for the pictures.

When she couldn't bear to wait another moment, Hannah turned that page, expecting to read the table of contents. Instead, there was a note, written in Doss's strong, clear handwriting.

On the occasion of our marriage, and
because I know you long for spring, and your garden.
Doss McKettrick
January 17, 1919

An emotion Hannah could not recognize swelled in her throat, fairly cutting off her breath. She traced his name with her eyes and then with the tip of her index finger. Doss McKettrick. As if men by that name were common as thorns in a blackberry thicket, and any one of them might be her husband. As if he had to be sure she knew which one would give her a book and which had noticed how fiercely, how desperately she craved that first green stirring in the cold earth and in the bare-limbed branches of trees.

Did he know how she listened for the breaking of the ice on the pond far back in the woods behind the house? How she watched the frigid sky for the first brave birds, carrying back the merry little songs she pined for, in the secret regions of her heart, when the snow was just beginning to seep into the ground?

Hannah closed the book, held it against her chest.

Then she opened it again and carefully turned to the first illustration, a lovely colored woodcut of purple crocuses, blooming above a thin snowfall. She drank them in, surfeited herself on lilacs and climbing roses, sweet williams and peonies.

Doss had given her flowers, in the dead of winter. Just looking at the pictures, she could imagine their distinctive scents, the shape of their petals, the depth upon depth of their various colors—everything from the palest of whites to the fathomless purples and crimsons.

She gobbled them all greedily with her eyes, page after page of them, tumbled flower-drunk into sleep and dreamed of them. Dreamed of spring, of trout quickening in the creeks, of green grass and of fresh, warm breezes teasing her hair and tingling on her skin.

When she wakened, drowsy and confused, the room was lavender with twilight, and a rim of golden light edged the lower part of the door. She heard Doss and Tobias talking in the next room, knew by a series of decisive clicks that they were playing checkers. Tobias gave a shout of triumphant laughter, and the sound seemed so poignant to Hannah that tears thickened in her throat.

She got up, used the chamber pot, washed her hands at the basin. She rummaged for her flannel wrapper, pulled it on and crossed the cold wooden floor to the door.

Opened it.

Tobias and Doss both turned to look at her.

Tobias smiled, delighted.

Doss looked shy, as though they'd just met. He got up suddenly, came to her, took her arm. Escorted her to a chair.

"Don't fuss," she scolded, but it was after the fussing was through.

"I beat Uncle Doss four times!" Tobias crowed.

"Did you?" Hannah asked, deliberately widening her eyes.

Doss went over to the other bed, pulled the quilt off, made Hannah stand, wrapped her up like renderings in a sausage skin and sat her down again.

What am I to make of you, Doss McKettrick? she asked silently.

"I'll go down and order us some supper," Doss said.

"Has your uncle Jeb gone?" Hannah asked Tobias, when they were alone.

Tobias nodded, kneeling on the floor, stacking checker pieces into red and black towers that teetered on the wooden board. "He took the afternoon train back to Phoenix. Said to tell you he hoped you'd be feeling better soon."

"I wish I could have said goodbye," Hannah said, but it wasn't the complete truth. She'd not been eager to face Doss's uncle; he was half again too wise and, besides, he

must have known that her new husband had spent much
of their wedding night in a saloon, just to avoid her. He'd
never have mentioned it, of course, but she'd have seen
the knowledge in his eyes.

Would he tell his wife, Chloe, when he got home? Would
she, in turn, tell Emmeline and Mandy and the other McK-
ettrick women? Get them all feeling sorry for poor Hannah?

She'd know soon enough. Concerned letters would
begin arriving, probably in the next batch of mail, full
of wary congratulations and carefully worded questions.
The Aunts, as both Gabe and Doss had always referred to
them, were not gossips, so she needn't fear scandal from
that quarter, but they would have plenty of private discus-
sions among themselves, and they'd give Doss what for
when they returned to the Triple M in the spring, settling
into their houses on all parts of the ranch, throwing open
windows and doors, planting gardens and entertaining a
steady stream of children and grandchildren.

Hannah thought she would have welcomed even their
curiosity, if it meant the long winter was over.

"Ma?"

Hannah realized she'd let her mind wander and turned
her attention to Tobias, who was studying her closely
and clearly had something of moment to say. "Yes, sweetheart?"

"Is Uncle Doss my pa, now that you and him are married?"

Hannah blinked. Took in a slow breath and took her
time letting it out. "I told you before, Tobias. Doss is still
your uncle. Your father will always be—your father."

Tobias's forehead creased as he frowned. "But Pa's
dead," he said.

Hannah sighed. "Yes."

"Uncle Doss is alive."

"He certainly is."

"I want a pa. Somebody to take me fishin' and teach me how to shoot."

"Uncles can do those things." Hannah didn't want Tobias within a mile of a gun, but she didn't have the strength to fight that battle just then, so she let it go.

"It isn't the same," Tobias reasoned.

"Tobias, there are some things in this life a person has to accept. Your father is gone. Doss is your uncle, not your pa. You'll just have to make the best of that."

"The best would be if he was my pa instead of my uncle."

"Tobias."

"You said once that Uncle Doss would be my stepfather if you got married. Now, you're his wife. So if you leave off the 'step' part, that makes him my pa."

Hannah rubbed her temples with her fingertips.

Tobias beamed. Eight years old, and he could argue like a senior senator at a campaign picnic.

The door to the corridor opened, and Doss came in, followed by two maids carrying trays laden with food.

"Pa's back," Tobias said.

Hannah's gaze locked with Doss's. Something passed between them, silent and charged.

Hannah looked away first.

Chapter 12

Present Day

"You need time to absorb all this," Eve told Sierra the next morning at the breakfast table. Eve had made waffles for them all, and everyone had eaten with a hearty appetite. Now Liam was upstairs, dressing for his first visit to Indian Rock Elementary School—Sierra planned to register him but wasn't sure he was ready for a full day of class—and Travis had given the ranch house a wide berth ever since their return from Flagstaff the previous afternoon. "So I'm going to leave," Eve finished, gently decisive.

Sierra, who had spent a largely sleepless night, had mixed feelings about Eve's going away. On the one hand, there were so many things she wanted to know about her mother—things that had nothing to do with their long separation. What kind of books did she read? What places had she visited? Had she loved anyone before or after Hank Breslin? What made her laugh? Did she cry at sad movies, or was she a stone-realist, prone to saying, "It's only a story"?

On the other, Sierra craved solitude, to think and reflect and sort what she had learned into some kind of sensible order. She wanted to huddle up somewhere, with her arms around her knees and decide what she believed and what she didn't.

"Okay," she said.

"There is one thing I want to show you before I go," Eve said, rising from the kitchen table and crossing to the china cabinet to lean down and open one of the drawers. She brought out a large, square object, wrapped in soft blue flannel, and set it before Sierra, who had shoved her plate and coffee cup aside in the meantime and wiped her part of the tabletop clean with a checkered cloth napkin.

Sierra's heart raced a little and, at a nod from Eve, she folded back the flannel covering to reveal an old photo album.

"These are your people, Sierra," Eve said quietly. "Your ancestors. There are journals and other photographs in the attic, and they need cataloging. It would be a great favor to me if you would gather them and make sure they're properly preserved."

"I can do that," Sierra said. Her hand, resting on the album cover, trembled a little, with both anticipation and a certain reluctance to get involved. Biologically she had a connection with the faces and names between the battered leather covers of the book, but in terms of real life, she was just passing through. She couldn't afford to forget that.

Eve laid a hand on her shoulder. "Sorry about the Christmas tree," she said with a slight smile. "I was the one who put it up, and I should be the one to take it down, but the plane will be arriving in an hour, so there isn't time. The corresponding boxes are in the basement, at the bottom of the steps."

Sierra nodded a second time. Liam had finished opening his presents the night before, and the mess had been cleaned up. Putting away the tree, like sorting photos and journals, would be a bittersweet enterprise. She hadn't looked closely at the ornaments, but she supposed they were heirlooms, like so many other things in that house, each one with a meaning she could never fully understand.

So many McKettrick Christmases, and she hadn't been a part of any of them. With Hank the holiday had gone almost unnoticed, although there were always a few gifts. Sierra hadn't felt deprived at the time, because she hadn't known that other people made more of a fuss.

The McKettricks, most likely, made a lot of fuss, not just over Christmas, but other holidays, too. They'd probably kept happy secrets at Yuletide, sung carols around that haunted piano, toasted each other with eggnog poured into cut-glass cups that were older than any of them....

Enough, Sierra told herself sternly. *That time is gone. You missed it. Get over wishing you hadn't.*

Eve bent to kiss Sierra on top of the head, then went upstairs to the big master bedroom, to pack up her things.

Sierra cleared the table and loaded the dishwasher,

but her gaze kept straying to the album. It was as though the people in the photographs, all long dead, were calling to her.

Get to know us.

We are part of you. We are part of Liam.

Sierra shook off the feeling as a nostalgic whim. She was as much a Breslin as a McKettrick, after all. She knew how to be Hank's daughter, but being Eve's was a whole new ball game. It was as though she had an entirely separate and unfamiliar identity, and that person was a stranger to her.

Liam bounded down the back stairs as she was rinsing out the coffee carafe, beaming at the prospect of starting school. He'd been thrilled to learn, through the research he and Sierra had done on Meg's computer, after last night's present-unwrapping frenzy, that there was no "Geek Program" at Indian Rock Elementary.

He wanted to be an "ordinary" kid.

Not sick.

Not gifted.

"Just regular" as he'd put it.

Sierra's heart ached with love and empathy. As a child, home taught by Magdalena, she'd yearned to go to a real school, but Hank had forbidden it.

Now she realized Hank had been hiding her, probably fearful that some visitor, expatriate parent or teacher might catch on to the fact that he'd snatched her, and look into the matter.

For a moment she indulged in a primitive anger so deep that it was visceral, causing her stomach to clench and her jaws to tighten.

"Grandma says we'd better take Meg's car into town today, because ours is a heap, not to mention a veritable eyesore," Liam reported cheerfully. "When are we going to get a new car?"

"When I win the lottery or get a job," Sierra said, deliberately relaxing her shoulders, which had immediately tensed, and taking Liam's new "cowboy" coat, as he'd dubbed it, down from the peg. While she would have objected if she'd known Eve was out buying all those gifts, let alone wrapping them and putting them under a fully decorated Christmas tree, she was glad of this one. It was made of leather and lined with sheepskin, well beyond her budget, and it would definitely keep her little boy warm.

Just then Eve came back, bundled up for winter weather herself, and carrying a small, expensive suitcase in one hand. Her coat was full length and black, elegantly cut and probably cashmere.

"We're in the process of opening a branch office of McKettrickCo in Indian Rock," she announced, evidently unabashed that she'd been eavesdropping. "Keegan is heading it up, but I'm sure there will be a place for you in the organization if you want one. You do speak Spanish, don't you?"

"Keegan," Sierra mused mildly, letting the indirect job offer slide, along with the reference to her language skills, at least for the moment. "Another McKettrick cousin?"

"Descended from Kade and Mandy," Eve confirmed, smiling slightly and nodding toward the album. "It's all in the book."

"How are you getting back to the airstrip—or wherever your jet is landing?" Sierra asked, shrugging into her coat, which looked like something from the bottom of a grungy bin at a thrift store, compared to the ones Eve and Liam were decked out in.

"Travis is taking me in his truck," Eve said, setting her suitcase down by the door, heading to the china cabinet to pluck a set of keys from a sugar bowl, taking Sierra's hand, opening it and placing them on her palm. "Use the SUV. That wreck of yours won't make it out of the driveway, if it starts at all."

Sierra hesitated a moment before closing her fingers around the keys. "Not to mention that it's a veritable eyesore," she said pointedly, but with a little smile.

"You said it," Eve replied brightly. "I didn't."

"Yes, you did," Liam countered. "Upstairs, you told me—"

Outside Travis honked the truck horn.

Eve touched her grandson's neatly groomed hair. "Give your old granny a hug," she said. "I'll be back in a few weeks, and if the weather is good, maybe you'd like to take a ride in the company jet."

Liam let out a whoop.

Sierra didn't get a chance to protest, because Travis rapped lightly, opened the back door and took up Eve's suitcase. He gave Sierra a nod for a greeting and grinned down at Liam.

"Hey, cowpoke," he said. "Lookin' good in that new gear."

Liam preened, showing off the coat. "I wanted to wear the hat, too," he replied, "but Mom said I might lose it at school."

"The world," Travis replied, with a longer glance at Sierra, "is full of hats."

"What's that supposed to mean?" Sierra asked, feeling defensive again.

Travis sighed. A look passed between him and Eve.

Then he simply turned, without answering and headed for the truck.

Eve hugged Liam, then Sierra.

Moments later she and Travis were in the truck and barreling away.

Sierra found the door leading into the garage—cleverly hidden in back of the pantry, like the architectural afterthought it surely was—and assessed her sister's shining red SUV. Liam strained to reach the button on the wall, and the garage door grumbled up on its rollers, letting in a shivery chill.

Her station wagon was parked outside, behind the SUV, and Sierra muttered as she started Meg's vehicle, after she and Liam were both buckled in, and maneuvered around the eyesore.

1919

Despite the bitter cold, Hannah sat well away from Doss as they drove home in the sleigh two days after the wedding, Tobias cosseted between them.

She was married.

Each time her thoughts drifted in that direction, she started inwardly, surprised all over again.

She was a wife—but she certainly didn't feel like one.

Doss remained silent for the greater part of the journey, his gloved hands gripping the reins with the ease of long practice. Hannah felt his gaze on her a couple of times, but when she looked in his direction, he was always watching the snow-packed trail ahead.

By the time they reached the ranch, Hannah sorely wished she could simply crawl into bed, pull the covers up over her head and remain there until something changed.

It was an indulgence ranch women were not afforded.

Doss drew the team and sleigh up close to the house, lifted a half-sleeping Tobias from the seat and carried him in. Hannah got down on her own, bringing her valise, the flower book tucked safely inside among her dirty clothes, and followed stalwartly.

The kitchen was frigidly cold.

Doss pulled the string on the lightbulb in the middle of the room as he passed, heading for the stairs with Tobias.

Hannah rose above an inclination to turn it right back off again. She set her valise down and made for the stove. By the time Doss returned, she had a fire going and lamps lighted. She'd fetch some eggs from the spring house, she decided, provided that Willie had gathered them during their absence, and make an omelet for their supper. Perhaps she'd fry up some of the sausage she'd preserved last fall, and make biscuits and gravy, too.

"I'll see to the team," Doss said.

"Where do you suppose Willie's got to?" Hannah asked. She'd seen no sign of the hired man when they were driving in, and she feared for her chickens, along with the livestock in the barn. Like many laborers, Willie was a drifter, and might have taken it into his head to kick off the traces and take to the road anywhere along the line.

"I saw him when we came in," Doss answered, opening the door to go out again. "Out by the bunkhouse, stacking firewood."

Hannah gave a sigh of relief. In the next moment, she wanted to tell Doss to stay inside where it was warm, that she'd have the coffee ready in a few minutes, but it would have been a waste of breath. He was a rancher, born and bred, and that meant he looked after the cattle and horses first and saw to his own comforts later, when the work was done.

"Supper will be on the table in half an hour," she said, as though she were a landlady in a boarding house and he a paying guest, planning the briefest of stays. "Willie's welcome to join us, if he wants."

Doss nodded, raised his coat collar around his ears and went out.

Sometime later, he returned alone. Hannah had already fetched the eggs from the spring house, and they were scrambled, cooked and waiting on a platter in the warming oven above the stove. The kitchen was snug, and the softer light of lanterns glowed, replacing the glare of the overhead bulb.

"Willie's gone on back to the main ranch house," he said. "But he thanks you kindly for the invite to supper."

Hannah wiped her hands on her apron and took plates from the china cabinet to set the table. That was when she noticed the album lying there, as though someone had been perusing it and intended to come back and look some more later.

She stopped in her tracks.

Doss, in the act of shedding his coat and hat, followed her gaze.

"What's the matter, Hannah?" he asked, with a quiet alertness in his voice.

"The album," she said.

"What about it?" Doss asked, passing her to approach the stove. He poured himself a cup of coffee and came to stand beside her.

"Willie wouldn't have gone through our things, would he?"

Doss shook his head. "Not likely it would even have occurred to him to do that," he said. "Judging by how cold it was in here when we got home, he probably didn't set foot in the house once he'd finished off that chicken soup you made before we left."

Hannah wrung her hands, took a step toward the table and then paused. "Do you...do you ever get the feeling we're not alone in this house?" she asked, almost whispering the words.

"No," Doss said, with conviction.

"It was bad enough when the teapot kept moving. Now, the album—"

"Hannah." He touched her arm. "You sound like Tobias, going on about seeing a boy in his room."

"Maybe," Hannah ventured to speculate, almost breathless with the effort of speaking the words aloud, "he's not imagining things. Maybe it wasn't the fever."

Doss cupped Hannah's elbow in one hand and steered her to the table, letting go only to pull back a chair. It was pure fancy, of course, but as Hannah sat down, it seemed to her that the album, fairly new and reverently cared for, was very old. The sensation lasted only a moment or so, but it was so powerful that it left her feeling weak.

"We've all been under a strain, Hannah," Doss reasoned. "One of us must have gotten the album out and forgotten about it."

She looked up into his face. "Did you?" she challenged softly.

He paused, shook his head.

"I know I didn't," she insisted.

"Tobias, then," Doss said.

"No," Hannah replied. "He was too sick."

Doss set his coffee on the table, sat astride the bench, facing her. "There's a simple explanation for this, Hannah. Somebody might have come up from one of the other places, let themselves in."

As close as the McKettricks were, they didn't go into each other's houses when no one was at home. If one of them had wanted to see the album, they'd have said so. Anyway, the aunts and uncles were all in Phoenix, their children grown and gone. The people who looked after their places wouldn't have considered snooping like this, even if they'd been interested, which seemed unlikely.

"The biscuits will burn if you don't take them out of the oven," Hannah said, staring at the album, almost expecting it to move on its own, float through the air like a spirit medium's trumpet at a séance.

Doss got up, crossed the room and rescued the biscuits. The sausage gravy was done, warming at the back of the stove, so he retrieved one of the plates Hannah had gotten out, filled it for her and brought it to the table.

"Tobias will be hungry," she said, thinking aloud.

"I'll see to him," Doss answered. "Eat."

Hannah moved the album out of the way and pulled the plate toward her, resigned to taking her supper, even though she didn't want it. Doss brought her silverware, then filled another plate for Tobias and took it downstairs.

When he returned, he dished up his own meal and joined Hannah at the table. She was still staring at her scrambled eggs, sausage gravy and biscuits.

"Eat," he repeated.

She took up a fork. "There's someone here," she said. "Someone we can't see. Someone who moves the teapot and now the album, too."

"Let's assume, for a moment, that that's true," Doss ruminated, tucking into his food with an energy Hannah envied. "What do you plan to do about it?"

Hannah swallowed a bite of tasteless food. "I don't know," she answered, but it wasn't the complete truth. An idea was already brewing in her mind.

They finished their supper.

Hannah cleared the table, put the album back in its drawer in the china cabinet, and went upstairs to look in on Tobias while Doss washed the dishes.

Her son was sitting up in bed when she entered his room, his supper half-eaten and set aside on the bedside table. "The boy's not here," he said. "I wonder if he's gone away."

Hannah frowned. "What boy?" she asked, even though she knew.

"The one I see sometimes. With the funny clothes."

Hannah stroked her boy's hair. Sat down on the edge of his bed. "Does this boy ever speak to you? Does he have a name?"

Tobias shook his head. His eyes were large in his pale face. The trip back from Indian Rock had been hard on him, and Hannah was both worried about her son and determined not to let on.

"We mostly just look at each other. I reckon he's as surprised to see me as I am to see him."

"Next time he shows up, will you tell me?"

Tobias bit his lower lip, then nodded. "You believe me?"

"Of course I do, Tobias."

"Pa said he was imaginary. When we talked about it, I mean."

Hannah sighed. "Tobias, Doss is your uncle, not your pa."

Suddenly, Tobias's eyes glistened with unshed tears.

"Why won't you let him be my pa?" he asked. "He's your husband, isn't he? If you can have a husband, why can't I have a pa?"

Had Tobias been older, Hannah thought, she might have explained that Doss wasn't a real husband, that theirs was a marriage of convenience, but he was still far too young to understand.

In point of fact, she didn't entirely understand the situation herself.

"A woman can have more than one husband," she said cautiously. "A boy has only one father. And your father was Gabriel Angus McKettrick. I don't want you to forget that."

"I won't forget," Tobias said. "You can wash my mouth out with soap, if you want to, but I'm still going to call Uncle Doss my pa. I've got enough uncles—Jeb and Kade and Rafe, and John Henry, too. What I need is a pa."

Hannah was too exhausted to argue, and she knew she wouldn't win anyhow. "So long as you promise me you will never forget who your real father is," she said. "And I would appreciate it if you would include your uncle David—my brother—in that list of relations you just mentioned."

Tobias brightened and put out one small hand for a shake. "It's a deal," he agreed. "I like Uncle David. He can spit a long way."

"Go to sleep," Hannah told him with a smile, reaching to turn down the wick in the lantern next to his bed.

"I didn't wash my face or brush my teeth," he confessed, settling back on to his pillows.

"Just this once we'll pretend you did," she said.

The lamp went out.

She kissed his forehead, found it blessedly cool and

tucked the covers in close around him. "Good night, To-bias," she said.

"Good night, Ma," Tobias replied with a yawn.

He was probably asleep before she reached the door.

She'd hoped Doss would have turned in by the time she went downstairs, so she wouldn't have to be alone with him in the intimacy of evening, but he was right there in the kitchen, with the bathtub set out in the middle of the floor and buckets and kettles of water heating on the stove.

"I just came down to say good night," she lied. Actually, she'd been planning to sit up awhile, pondering her plan. It wasn't much, but she was bound and determined to find out something about the strange goings-on in that house.

"You can have this bath if you want," Doss told her. "I can always take one later."

"You have it," Hannah said, even though she would have loved to soak the chill out of her bones in a tub of hot water. She wondered if he was planning to share her bed, but she'd have broken the ice on top of the horse trough and stripped bare for a dunking before asking him outright.

He simply nodded.

"Don't forget to bank the fire," she said.

He grinned. "I never do, Hannah," he reminded her.

She turned, blushing a little, and went back upstairs. Entering her room, the one she'd shared with Gabe, she exchanged her clothes for a nightgown. She took her hair down, brushed it, plaited it into a long braid, trying all the while not to imagine Doss right downstairs, naked as the day he was born, lounging in that tub in front of the stove.

Would he join her later?

He was her legal husband, and he had every right to

sleep beside her. She, on the other hand, had every right to turn him away, wedding band or none.

Would she?

She honestly didn't know, and in the end, it didn't matter.

She put out her lamp, threw back the covers on her bed and stretched out, waiting and listening.

Presently she heard Doss climb the stairs, walk along the hallway and pass her room.

His door closed moments later.

Hannah told herself she was relieved, and then cried herself into a fitful sleep.

Present Day

The roads had been plowed, and Sierra was secretly proud of the way she handled the SUV. She'd grown up in Mexico, after all, and spent the last few years in Florida, which precluded driving in snow. This was an accomplishment.

At the elementary school, she got Liam registered and watched as he rushed off to join his class before she could even suggest that he start slowly. His eagerness left her feeling a little bereft.

She shook that off. He had his inhaler. The school nurse had been apprised of his asthma. She had to let go.

She would be living on the Triple M for a year, per her agreement with Eve. Might as well drive around a bit, see what the town was like.

Thirty minutes later she'd seen it all.

The supermarket. The library. The Cattleman's Bank. Two cafés, three bars, a gas station. A dry cleaners, and the ubiquitous McDonald's. The Indian Rock Historical Society. A real estate firm. A few hundred houses, many of them old and, at the edge of town, a spanking-new office complex with the word McKettrickCo inlaid in colored stone over a gleaming set of automatic doors.

I'm sure there will be a place for you in the organization, if you want one, she heard Eve's voice say.

Slowing the car, she studied the place, imagined herself going inside, in her jeans, sweatshirt and ratty coat, her hair combed in a slap-dash method, no mirror required. Face bare of makeup. "Hi, there," she would say to her cousin Keegan, who would no doubt be less than thrilled to see her but manage a polite greeting, anyway. "My name is Sierra and, what do you know? Turns out, I'm a McKettrick, just like you. Go figure. Oh, and by the way, my mother says you're to give me a job. Top-dollar salary and all the fringe benefits, if you don't mind."

She smiled ruefully at the thought. "Of course, all I know how to do is serve cocktails and speak Spanish," she might add. "No problem, I'm sure."

She pulled up in front of the Cattleman's Bank, patted her purse, which contained a few hundred dollars in traveler's checks, all the money she had in the world, and went in to open a checking account.

"You already have one, Ms. McKettrick," a perky young teller told her, after a few taps on her computer keyboard. The girl's eyes widened as she peered at the screen. "It's pretty substantial, too."

Sierra frowned, momentarily puzzled. "There must be some mistake. I've only been in town a few days, and I haven't—"

And then it struck her. Eve had been up to her tricks again.

The teller turned her pivoting monitor around so Sierra could read the facts for herself. The bottom line made her catch hold of the counter with both hands, lest she faint dead away.

Two million dollars?

"Of course you'll need to sign a signature card," the clerk said, still chipper. "Do you have two forms of personal identification?"

"I need to use your telephone," Sierra managed to say. The floor was still at an odd tilt, and her knuckles hurt where she gripped the edge of the counter.

The teller blinked. "You don't carry a cell phone?" she marveled, in a tone usually reserved for people who think they've been abducted by aliens and subjected to a lot of very painful and explicit medical procedures.

"No," Sierra said, trying not to hyperventilate, "I do not carry a cell phone."

"Over there," the teller said, pointing to a friendly looking nook marked off in brass letters as the Customer Comfort area.

Sierra made her way to the telephone, rummaged through her purse for Eve's cell number and dialed. The operator came on and informed her the call was long distance, and there would be charges.

"Make it collect," Sierra snapped.

One ring. Two. Eve was probably still in flight, aboard the company jet, with her phone shut off. Sierra was about to give up when, after the third ring, her mother chimed, "Eve McKettrick."

"I have a bank account with two million dollars in

it!" Sierra whispered into the receiver, bent around it like someone calling a 900 number during a church service.

"Yes, dear," Eve said sweetly. "I know."

"I will not accept—"

"Your trust fund?"

Sierra sucked in her breath. Almost choked on it. "My *trust fund?*"

"Yes," Eve answered. "You also have a share in McKettrickCo, of course."

Sierra swallowed, carefully this time. "I will not take your charity."

"Tell it to your grandfather," Eve responded, unruffled. "Of course, you'll need a clairvoyant to help, because he's been dead for fifteen years."

Sierra held the receiver away from her, stared at it, jammed it to her ear again. "My grandfather left me *two million* dollars?"

"Yes," Eve said. "We kept it safely tucked away in Switzerland, so your father wouldn't get his paws on it."

Sierra closed her eyes.

"Sweetheart?" her mother asked, sounding concerned now. "Are you still there?"

"Yes," Sierra breathed. She could have walked away from all that money. She really could have—if not for Liam. "Why didn't you tell me about this, when you were at the house?"

"Because I knew you weren't ready to hear it, and I didn't want to waste precious time arguing."

Sierra swallowed. "How come you can talk on a cell phone in flight?"

Eve laughed. "Because I patch the number into

the phone onboard the plane before takeoff," she answered. "I'm quite the technological whiz. Any more questions?"

"Yes. What am I supposed to do with two million dollars?"

Chapter 13

1919

By the time Hannah came downstairs, Doss had built up the fire, brewed the coffee and left for the barn, like he did every morning. She put on Gabe's old coat—there was nothing of his scent left in it now—and made a trip to the privy, then the chicken house. She was washing her hands in a basin of hot water when Doss came in from doing the chores.

"I guess I'll drive the sleigh down and look in on the widow Jessup again," he said. "This cold snap might outlast her firewood."

"You'll have a good, hot breakfast first," Hannah told him. "While I'm fixing it, why don't you get some preserves from the pantry and pack them up? Mrs. Jessup especially loves those cinnamon pears and pickled crab apples I put up for Christmas."

Doss nodded, a grin crooking one corner of his mouth in a way that made Hannah feel sweetly flustered. "How's Tobias today?"

"He's sleeping in," she said, cracking eggs into a bowl, keeping her gaze averted with some difficulty. "And don't think for a moment you're going to take him with you. It's too cold and he's worn-out from yesterday."

She'd thought Doss was in the pantry, but all of a sudden his hands closed over her shoulders, startling her so that she stiffened.

He turned her around to face him. Looked straight into her eyes.

Her heart beat a little faster.

Was he about to kiss her?

Say something important?

She held her breath, hoping he would. Hoping he wouldn't.

"Before he went back to Phoenix, Uncle Jeb said we ought to help ourselves to some hams from the smoke-house down at Rafe and Emmeline's place," he said. "A side of bacon, too. That means I'll be gone a little longer than usual."

Hannah merely nodded.

They stood, the two of them facing each other for a long moment.

Then Doss let go of Hannah's shoulders, and she turned to whip the eggs and slice bread for toasting. He found a crate and filled it with provisions for the widow Jessup.

After he'd gone, Hannah carried a plate up to Tobias,

who seemed content to stay in bed with one of his many picture books.

"I'm getting worried about that boy," Tobias told Hannah solemnly. "He ought to be back by now."

"I'm sure you'll see him again soon," Hannah said moderately. "Remember, you promised to let me know right away when you do."

He nodded, looking glum.

She kissed his forehead and went out, leaving the door open so she'd hear if he called for her. What he needed most right now was rest, and good food to build his strength. When Doss got back with the bacon and hams, she'd make up a special meal.

Downstairs Hannah tidied the kitchen, washed the dishes, dried them and put them away. When that was done, she built up the fire and went to the china cabinet to open the top drawer. The album was there, where it belonged, but a little shiver went up her spine at the sight of it, just the same.

She reached past it, found the small leather-bound remembrance book Lorelei and Holt had sent her for a Christmas present. The cover was a rich shade of blue, the pages edged in shiny gold.

She hadn't written a word in the journal, hadn't even opened it. She hadn't wanted to record her grief, hadn't wanted to make it real by writing it down in dark, formal letters.

Now she had something very different in mind. She carried the remembrance book to the table, and then went to the study for a bottle of ink and a pen. The room was chilly. She rarely went there, because it always brought back memories of Gabe, sitting at the desk, reading or pondering over a ledger.

It was especially empty that day; though, strangely, it was Doss's absence Hannah felt most keenly, not Gabe's. She collected the items she needed and hurried out again.

Back in the kitchen she found a rag to wipe the pen clean. When she was finished she opened the ink and turned to the first page.

She bit her lower lip, dipped the pen, summoned up all her resolve and began to write.

My name is Hannah McKettrick. Today's date is January 19, 1919...

Present Day

The first thing Sierra noticed when she got back to the house later that morning—with a load of groceries and a head spinning with possibilities now that she was rich—was that Travis wasn't around. The second thing was that the album Eve had brought out to show her was gone.

She'd left it on the kitchen table, and it had vanished.

She paused, holding her breath. Listening. Was there someone in the house?

No, it was empty. She didn't need to search the rooms, open closet doors, peer under beds, to know that.

Her practical side took over. She brought in the rest of the supermarket bags and put everything away. Put on a pot of coffee. Made a tuna salad sandwich and ate it.

Only when she'd rinsed the plate and put it in the dishwasher did she walk over to the china cabinet and open the top drawer, as Eve had done earlier that morning.

The album was back in its place.

Sierra frowned.

Invisible fingers played a riff on her spine, touching every vertebra.

She closed the drawer again.

She would look at the photographs later. Combine that with the job of cataloging the ones stored in the attic.

She brought the Christmas boxes up from the basement, carried them into the living room. Carefully and methodically removed and wrapped each ornament. Some were obviously expensive, others were the handiwork of generations of children.

By the time she'd put them all away and dismantled the silk tree, it was time to drive into town and pick Liam up at school. Backing the SUV out of the garage, she almost ran over Travis, who had the hood up on the station wagon and was standing to one side, fiddling with one of its parts.

He leaped out of her path, grinning.

She slammed on the brakes, buzzed down the window on the passenger side. "You scared me," she said.

Travis laughed, leaning in. "*I* scared *you?*"

"I wasn't expecting you to be standing there."

"I wasn't expecting *you* to come shooting out of the garage at sixty-five miles an hour, either."

Sierra smiled. "Do you always argue about everything?"

"Sure," he said, with an affable shrug of his impressive shoulders. "Gotta stay sharp in case I ever want to practice law again. Where are you headed in such a hurry, anyway?"

"Liam's about to get out of school for the day."

"Right," Travis said, stepping back.

"Do you want to come along?"

Now what made her say *that?* She liked Travis Reid well enough, and certainly appreciated all he'd done to help, but he also made her poignantly uncomfortable.

He must have seen her thoughts playing out in her face. "Maybe another time," he said easily. "Eve told me you were going to take down the Christmas tree. It's a big sucker, so I'll lug it back to the basement if you want."

"That would be good. The coffee's on—help yourself."

Travis grinned. Nodded. Stepped back from the side of the SUV with exaggerated haste.

As she drove away, Sierra wasn't thinking about her two-million-dollar trust fund, the vanishing teapot, the piano that played itself, teleporting photo album or even Liam.

She was thinking about the hired help.

Peering through his new telescope at the night sky, Liam felt that familiar shiver in the air. He knew, even before he turned around to look, that the boy would be there.

And he was. Lying in the bed, staring at Liam.

"What's your name?" the boy asked.

For a moment, Liam couldn't believe his ears. He wasn't scared, but his throat got tight, just the same. He'd planned on telling the boy all about his first day at the new school, and a lot of other things, too, as soon as he showed up, but now the words got stuck and wouldn't come out.

"Mine's Tobias."

"I'm Liam."

"That's an odd name."

Liam straightened his back. "Well, 'Tobias' is pretty weird, too," he countered.

Tobias tossed back the covers and got out of bed. He was wearing a funny flannel nightgown, more suited to a girl than a boy. It reached clear past his knees. "What's that?" he asked, pointing to Liam's telescope.

Liam patiently explained the obvious. "Wanna look? You can see all the way to Saturn with this thing."

Tobias peered through the viewer. "It's bouncing around. And it's *blue!*"

"Yep," Liam agreed. "How come you're wearing a nightie?"

Tobias looked up. His eyes flashed, and his cheeks got red. "This," he said, "is a night*shirt.*"

"Whatever," Liam said.

Tobias gave him the eyeball. "Those are mighty peculiar duds," he announced.

"Thanks a lot," Liam said, but he wasn't mad. He figured "duds" must mean clothes. "Are you a ghost?"

"No," Tobias said. "I'm a boy. What are you?"

"A boy," Liam answered.

"What are you doing in my room?"

"This is *my* room. What are *you* doing here?"

Tobias grinned, poked a finger into Liam's chest, as though testing to see if it would go right through. "My ma told me to let her know first thing if I saw you again," he said.

Liam put out his own finger and found Tobias to be as solid as he was.

"Are you going to?" he asked.

"I don't know," Tobias said. He put his eye to the

viewer again. "Is that *really* Saturn, or is this one of those moving-picture contraptions?"

1919

Hannah blew on the ink until it dried. Then she wiped the pen clean, sealed the ink bottle and closed the remembrance book.

Now that she'd written in it, she felt a little foolish, but what was done was done. She took the book back to the china cabinet and placed it carefully beneath the top cover of the family album.

She was just mounting the steps to go and check on Tobias when she realized he was talking to someone. She couldn't make out the words, just the conversational tone of his voice. He spoke with an eager lilt she hadn't heard in a long time.

She stood absolutely still, straining to listen.

"Ma!" he yelled suddenly.

She bolted up the stairs, along the hallway, into his room.

She found him lying comfortably in bed, wide awake, his eyes shining with an almost feverish excitement. "I saw the boy," he said. "His name is Liam and he showed me Saturn."

"Liam," Hannah repeated stupidly, because anything else was quite beyond her.

"I said it was a strange name, Liam, I mean, and he said Tobias was a weird thing to be called, too."

Hannah opened her mouth, closed it again. Twisted the hem of her apron in both hands. Her knees felt as though they'd turned to liquid, and even though she'd asked Tobias to let her know straight away if he saw the boy again, she realized she hadn't been prepared to hear it. She wished Doss were there, even though he'd probably be a hindrance, rather than a help.

"Ma?" Tobias sounded worried, and his eyes were great in his face.

She hurried to his bed, sat down on the edge of the mattress, touched a hand to his forehead.

He squirmed away. "I'm not sick," he protested. "I saw Saturn. It's blue, and it really does have rings."

Hannah withdrew her hand, and it came to rest, fluttering, at the base of her throat.

"You don't believe me!" Tobias accused.

"I don't know what to believe," Hannah admitted softly. "But I know you're not lying, Tobias."

"I'm not seeing things, either!"

"I— It's just so strange."

Tobias subsided a little, falling back on to his pillows with a sigh. "He told me lots of stuff, Ma," he said, his voice small and uncertain.

Hannah took his hand, squeezed it. Tried to appear calm. "What 'stuff,' Tobias?" she managed, after a few slow, deep breaths.

"That Saturn has moons, just like the earth does. Only, it's got four, instead of just one. One of them is covered in ice, and it might even have an ocean underneath, full of critters with no eyes."

Hannah swallowed a slight, guttural cry of pure dismay. "What else?"

"People have boxes in their houses, and they can watch all kinds of stories on them. Folks act them out, like players on a stage."

Tears of pure panic burned in Hannah's eyes, but she blinked them back. "You must have been dreaming, Tobias," she said, fairly croaking the words, like a frog in a fable. "You fell asleep, and it only seemed real—"

"No," Tobias said flatly. "I saw Liam. I talked to him. He said it was the twenty-first century, where he lives. I told him he was full of sheep dip—that it was 1919, and I'd get the calendar to prove it. Then he said if I was eight years old in 1919, I was probably dead or in a nursing home someplace in his time." He paused. "What's a nursing home, Ma? And how could I be two places at once? A kid here, and an old man somewhere else?"

Dizzy, Hannah gathered her boy in both arms and held him so tightly that he struggled.

"Let me go, Ma," he said. "You're fair smothering me!"

With a conscious effort, Hannah broke the embrace. Let her arms fall to her sides.

"What's happening to us?" she whispered.

"I need to use the chamber pot," Tobias announced.

Hannah stood slowly, like a sleepwalker. She moved out of that room, closed the door behind her and got as far as the top of the back stairs before her legs gave out and she had to sit down.

She was still there when Doss came in, back from his travels to the smokehouse and the widow Jessup's place. As though he'd sensed her presence, he came to the foot of the steps, still in his coat and hat.

"Hannah? What's the matter? Is Tobias all right?"

"He's...yes."

Doss tossed his hat away, came up the steps, sat down next to Hannah and put an arm around her shoulders. She sagged against his side, even as she despised herself for the weakness. Turned her face into his cold-weather-and-leather-scented shoulder and wept with confusion and relief and a whole tangle of other emotions.

He held her until the worst of it had passed.

She sniffled and sat up straight. Even tried to smile. "How was the widow Jessup?" she asked.

Present Day

That night Sierra invited Travis to supper. Just marched right out to his trailer, knocked on the door and, the moment he opened it, blurted, "We're having spaghetti tonight. It's Liam's favorite. It would mean a lot to him if you came and ate with us."

Travis grinned. Evidently, he'd been changing clothes, because his shirt was half-unbuttoned. "If you're trying to make up for almost running over me backing out of the garage this afternoon, it's okay," he teased. "I'm still pretty fast on my feet."

Sierra was doing her level best not to admire what she could see of his chest, which was muscular. She wondered what it would be like to slide her hands inside that shirt, feel his skin against her palms and her splayed fingers.

Then she looked up into his eyes again, saw the knowing smile there and blushed. "It's more about thanking you for taking the Christmas tree downstairs," she fibbed.

"At your service," he said with a slight drawl.

Was that a double entendre?

Don't be silly, she told herself. Of course it wasn't.

"There's wine, too," she blurted out, and then blushed again. At this rate, Travis would think she'd already had a few nips.

"Everything but music," he quipped.

Afraid to say another word, she turned and hurried

back toward the house, and she distinctly heard him chuckle before he closed the trailer door.

Liam was strangely quiet at supper. He usually gobbled spaghetti, but tonight he merely nibbled. He had a perfect opportunity to talk "cowboy" with Travis, or chatter on about his first day of school; instead, he asked to be excused so he could take a bath and get to bed early. At Sierra's nod, he murmured something and fled.

"He must be sick," Sierra fretted, about to go after him.

"Let him go," Travis counseled. "He's all right."

"But—"

"He's *all right,* Sierra." He refilled her wineglass, then his own.

They finished their meal, cleared the table together, loaded the dishwasher. When Sierra would have walked away, Travis caught hold of her arm and gently stopped her. Switched on the countertop radio with his free hand.

Soft, smoky music poured into the room.

The next thing she knew, Sierra was in Travis's arms, close against that chest she'd admired earlier at the door of his trailer, and they were slow dancing.

Why didn't she pull away?

Maybe it was the wine.

"Relax," he said. His breath was warm in her hair.

She giggled, more nervous than amused. What was the matter with her? She was attracted to Travis, had been from the first, and he was clearly attracted to her. They were both adults. Why not enjoy a little slow dancing in a ranch-house kitchen?

Because slow dancing led to other things, especially when it was wine powered. She took a step back and felt the counter flush against her lower back. Travis naturally came with her, since they were holding hands and he had one arm around her waist.

Simple physics.

Then he kissed her.

Physics again—this time, not so simple.

"Yikes," she said, when their mouths parted.

He grinned. "Nobody's ever said that after I kissed them."

She felt the heat and substance of his body pressed against hers, right where it counted. If Liam hadn't been just upstairs, and likely to come back down at any moment, she might have wrapped her legs around Travis's waist and kissed him nuclear-style.

"It's going to happen, isn't it?" she heard herself whisper.

"Yep," Travis answered.

"But not tonight," Sierra said on a sigh.

"Probably not," Travis agreed, grinding his hips a little. His erection burned into her abdomen like a firebrand.

"When, then?"

He chuckled, gave her a slow, nibbling kiss. "Tomorrow morning," he said. "After you drop Liam off at school."

"Isn't that...a little...soon?"

"Not soon enough," Travis answered. He cupped a hand around her breast, and even through the fabric of her shirt and bra, her nipple hardened against the chafing motion of his thumb. "Not nearly soon enough."

After Travis had gone, Sierra felt like an idiot.

She looked in on Liam, who was sound asleep, and then took a cool shower. It didn't help.

She would come to her senses by morning, she told herself, as she stood at her bedroom window, gazing down at the lights burning in Travis's trailer.

She'd get a good night's sleep. That was all she needed.

She slept, as it happened, like the proverbial log, but she woke up thinking about Travis. About the way she'd felt when he kissed her, when he backed her up against the counter...

She made breakfast.

Took Liam to school.

Zoomed straight back to the ranch, even though she'd intended to drive around town for a while, giving herself a chance to cool down.

Instead, she was on autopilot.

But it wasn't as if she gave up easily. She raised every argument she could think of. It was *way* too soon. She didn't know Travis well enough to sleep with him.

She would regret this in the morning.

No, long *before* then.

The truth was, she'd denied herself so much, for so long, that she couldn't stand it anymore.

She didn't even bother to park the SUV in the garage. She shut it down between the house and Travis's trailer, up to the wheel wells in snow, jumped out, and double-timed it to his door.

Knocked.

Maybe he's not home, she thought desperately.

Let him be here.

Let him be in China.

His truck was parked in its usual place, next to the barn.

The trailer door creaked open.

He grinned down at her. "Hot damn," he said.

Sierra shoved her hands into her coat pockets. Wished she could dig her toes right into the ground somehow and hold out against the elemental forces that were driving her.

Travis stepped back. "Come in," he said.

So much for the toehold. She was inside in a single bound.

He leaned around her to pull the door shut.

"This is crazy," she said.

He began unbuttoning her coat. Slipped it back off her shoulders. Bent his head to taste her earlobe and brush the length of her neck with his lips.

She groaned.

"Talk some sense into me," she pleaded. "Say this is stupid and we shouldn't do it."

He laughed. "You're kidding, right?"

"It's wrong."

"Think of it as therapy."

She trembled as he tossed her coat aside. "For whom? You or me?"

He opened her blouse, undid the catch at the front of her bra, caught her breasts in his hands when they sprang free.

"Oh, I think we'll both benefit," he said.

Sierra groaned again. He sat her down on the side of his bed, crouched to pull off her snow boots, peel off her socks. Then he stood her up again, and undressed her, garment by garment. Blouse...bra...jeans...and, finally, her lacy underpants.

He suckled at her breasts, somehow managing to shed his own clothes in the process; Sierra was too dazed, and too aroused, to consider the mechanics of it.

He laid her down on the bed, gently. Eased two pillows under her bottom. Knelt between her legs.

"Oh, God," she whimpered. "You're not going to—?"

Travis kissed his way from her mouth to her neck.

"I sure am," he mumbled, before pausing to enjoy one of her breasts, then the other.

He kept moving downward, stroking the tender flesh on the insides of her thighs. He plumped up the pillows, raising her higher.

Sierra moaned.

He parted the nest of moist curls at the junction of her thighs. Breathed on her. Touched her lightly with the tip of his tongue.

She arched her back and gave a low, throaty cry of need.

"I thought so," Travis said, almost idly.

"You—thought—what?" Sierra demanded.

"That you needed this as much as I do." He took her full into his mouth.

She welcomed him with a sob and an upward thrust of her hips.

He slid his hands under her buttocks and lifted her higher still.

She was about to explode, and she fought it. It wasn't as though she had orgasms every day. She wanted this experience to *last*.

He drove her straight over the edge.

She convulsed with the power of her release— once—twice—three times.

It was over.

But it wasn't.

Before she had time to lament, he was taking her to a new level.

She came again, voluptuously, piercingly, her legs over his shoulders now. And before she could begin the breathless descent, he grasped the undersides of her knees and parted them, tongued her until she climaxed yet again. Only, this time she couldn't make a sound. She could only buckle in helpless waves of pleasure.

And still it wasn't over.

He waited until she'd opened her eyes. Until her breathing had evened out. After all of the frenzy, he waited until she nodded.

He entered her in a long, slow, deep stroke, supporting himself with his hands pressing into the narrow mattress on either side of her shoulders, gazing intently down into her face. Taking in every response.

She began the climb again. Rasped his name. Clutched at his shoulders.

He didn't increase his pace.

She pumped, growing more and more frantic as the delicious friction increased, degree by degree, toward certain meltdown.

The wave crashed over her like a tsunami, and when she stopped flailing and shouting in surrender—and only then—she saw him close his eyes. His neck corded, like a stallion's, as he threw back his head and let himself go.

His powerful body flexed, and flexed again, every muscle taut, and Sierra almost wept as she watched his control give way.

Afterward he lowered himself to lie beside her, wrapping her close in his arms. Kissed her temple, where the hair was moist with perspiration. Stroked her breasts and her belly.

She listened as his breathing slowed.

"You're not going to fall asleep, are you?" she asked.

He laughed. "No," he said. He rolled on to his back, pulling her with him, so that she lay sprawled on top of him. Caressed her back, her shoulders, her buttocks.

She nestled in. Buried her face in his neck. Popped her head up again, suddenly alarmed. "Did you use…?"

"Yes," he said.

She snuggled up again. "That was…great," she confessed, and giggled.

He shifted beneath her. She felt some fumbling.

"We can't possibly do that again," she said.

"Wanna bet?" He eased her upright, set her knees on either side of his hips.

Felt him move inside her, sleek and hard.

A violent tremor went through her, left her shuddering.

He cupped her breasts in his hands, drew her forward far enough to suck her breasts. All the while, he was raising and lowering her along his length. She took him deeper.

And then deeper still.

And then the universe dissolved into shimmering particles and rained down on them both like atoms of fire.

Chapter 14

Sierra slept, snuggled against Travis's side, one arm draped across his chest, one shapely leg flung over his thighs.

Travis pulled the quilt up over them both, so she wouldn't get cold, and considered his situation.

He'd been to bed with a lot of women in his time.

He knew how to give and receive pleasure.

He said goodbye as easily as hello.

But this was different.

Different feeling. Different woman.

He'd been a dead man up until now, and this trailer had been his coffin.

Rance had sure been right about that.

Sierra McKettrick, who had probably expected no more from this encounter than he had—a roll in the hay, some much-needed satisfaction, a break in the monotony—had resurrected him. Probably inadvertently, but the effect was the same.

"Shit," he whispered. He'd *needed* that all-pervasive numbness and the insulation it provided. Needed *not* to feel.

Sierra had awakened everything inside him, and it hurt, to the center of his soul, like frost-bitten flesh thawing too fast.

She stirred against him, uttered a soft, hmmm sound, but didn't awaken.

He held her a little closer and thought about Brody. His little brother. Brody would never make love to a woman like Sierra. He'd never watch the moon rise over a mountain creek, the water purple in the twilight, or choke up at the sight of a ragged band of wild horses racing across a clearing for no other reason than that they had legs to run on. He'd never throw a stick for a faithful old dog to fetch, watch Fourth-of-July fireworks with a kid perched on his shoulders or eat pancakes swimming in syrup in a roadside café while hokey music played on the jukebox.

There were so many things Brody would never do.

Travis's throat went raw, and his eyes stung.

The loss yawned inside him, a black hole, an abyss.

He'd thought losing his brother would be the hardest thing he'd ever had to do, but now he knew it wasn't. Dying inside was easy—it was having the guts to *live* that was hard.

He shifted.

Sierra sighed, raised her head, looked straight into his face.

It was too much to hope, he figured, that she wouldn't

notice the tear that had just trickled out of the corner of his eye to streak toward his ear.

If she saw, she had the good grace not to comment, and the depth of his gratitude for that simple blessing was downright pathetic, by his reckoning.

"What time is it?" she asked, looking anxious and womanly.

Real womanly.

He stretched, groped for his watch on the little shelf above the bed. "Twelve-thirty," he answered gruffly. He wanted to say a whole lot more, but he wasn't sure what it was. He'd have to say it all to himself first, and make sense of it, before he could tell it to anyone else.

Especially Sierra.

Not that he loved her or anything. It was too early for that.

But he sure as hell felt *something,* and he wished he didn't.

"You okay?" she asked, raising herself on to one elbow and studying his face a lot more intently than he would have liked.

"Fine," he lied.

"This doesn't have to change anything," Sierra reasoned, hurrying her words a little—pushing them along, like rambunctious cattle toward a narrow chute. Was she trying to convince him, or herself?

"Right," he said.

She pulled away, sat on the backs of her thighs, the quilt pulled up to her chin. "I'd better—get back to the house."

He nodded.

She nodded.

Neither of them moved.

"What just happened here?" Sierra asked, after a long time had passed, with the two of them just staring at each other.

Whatever had happened, it had been a lot more than the obvious. He was sure of that, if nothing else.

"I'll be damned if I know," Travis said.

"Me, neither," Sierra said. Then she bent and kissed his forehead, before scrambling out of bed.

He sat up, watched as she gathered her scattered clothes and shimmied into them. He wished he smoked, because lighting a cigarette would have given him something to do. Something to distract him from the rawness of what he felt and his frustration at not being able to wrestle it down and give it a name.

"I guess you must think I do things like this all the time," she said. Maybe he wasn't alone in being confused. The idea stirred a forlorn hope within him. "And I don't. I *don't* sleep with men I barely know, and I don't—"

He smiled. "I believe you, Sierra," he said. He did, too. Anybody who came with the kind of sensual abandon she had, on a regular basis, would be superhuman, dead of exhaustion or both.

Actually, he admired her stamina, and her uncommon passion.

And she was up, moving around, dressing. He wasn't entirely sure he could stand.

She sat on the side of the bed, keeping a careful if subtle distance, to pull on her socks and boots. "Travis?" she said without looking at him. He saw a pink glow along the edge of her cheek, and thought of a summer dawn, rimming a mountain peak.

"What?"

"It was good. What we did was good. Okay?"

He swallowed. Reached out and squeezed her hand briefly before letting it go. "Yeah," he agreed. "It was good."

She left then, and Travis felt her absence like a vacuum.

He cupped his hands behind his head, lay back and began making a list in his mind.

All the things he had to do before he left the Triple M for good.

She'd made a damn fool of herself.

Sierra let herself into the house, closed the door behind her and leaned back against it.

What had she been thinking, throwing herself at Travis that way? She'd been like a woman possessed—and a *stupid* woman, at that.

Sierra McKettrick, the sexual sophisticate.

Right.

Sierra McKettrick, who had been intimate with exactly two men in her life—one of whom had fathered her child, lied to her and left her behind, apparently without a second thought.

What if Travis hadn't been telling the truth when he said he used protection?

What if she was pregnant again?

"Get a grip," she told herself out loud. Travis had clearly had a lot of experience in these matters, unlike her. Furthermore he was a lawyer. He might not have given a damn whether *she* was protected or not, but he surely would have covered his *own* backside, if only to avoid a potential paternity suit.

She stood still, breathing like a woman in the early

stages of labor, until she'd regained some semblance of composure. She had to pull herself together. In a couple of hours she'd be picking Liam up at school.

He'd want to tell her all about his class. The other kids. The teachers.

There would be supper to fix and homework to oversee.

She was a *mother*, for God's sake, not some bimbo in a soap opera, sneaking off to have prenoon monkey sex in a trailer with a virtual stranger.

She straightened.

Her own voice echoed in her mind.

It was good. What we did was good. Okay?

And it *had* been good, just not in the noble sense of the word.

Sierra went slowly upstairs, took a long, hot shower, dressed in fresh jeans and a white cotton blouse. Borrowed one of Meg's cardigans, to complete the "Mom" look.

By the time she was finished, she still had more than an hour until she had to leave for town.

Her gaze strayed to the china cabinet.

She would look at the pictures in the album. Get a frame of reference for all those McKettricks that had gone before. Try to imagine herself as one of them, a link in the biological chain.

She heard Travis's truck start up, resisted an urge to go to the window and watch him drive away. There was too much danger that she would morph into a desperate housewife, smile sweetly and wave.

Not gonna happen.

Keeping her thoughts and actions briskly business-like, she retrieved the album, carried it to the table, sat down and lifted the cover.

A small blue book was tucked inside, its corners curled with age.

A tremor of something went through Sierra like a wash of ice water, some premonition, some subconscious awareness straining to reach the surface.

She opened the smaller volume.

Focused on the beautifully scripted lines, penned in ink that had long since faded to an antique brown.

My name is Hannah McKettrick.
I know you're here. I can sense it. You've moved the teapot, and the album in which I've placed this remembrance book.
   Please don't harm my boy. His name is Tobias. He's eight years old.
   He is everything to me.

Sierra caught her breath. There was more, but her shock was such that, for the next few moments, the remaining words might as well have been gibberish.

Was this woman, probably long dead, addressing her from another century?

Impossible.

But then, it was impossible for teapots and photograph albums to move by themselves, too. It was impossible for an ordinary piano to play itself, with no one touching the keys.

It was impossible for Liam to see a boy in his room.

Sierra swallowed, lowered her eyes to the journal again. The words had been written so very long ago, and yet they had the immediacy of an email.

How could this be happening?

She sucked in another breath. Read on.

I must be losing my mind. Doss says it's grief, over
Gabe's dying. I don't even know why I'm writing
this, except in the hope that you'll write something
back. It's the only way I can think of to speak to you.

Sierra glanced at the clock. Only a few minutes had
passed since she sat down at the table, but it seemed
like so much longer.

She got out of her chair, found a pen in the junk
drawer next to the sink. This was *crazy.* She was about
to deface what might be an important family record.
And yet there was something so plaintive in Hannah's
plea that she couldn't ignore it.

My name is Sierra McKettrick. I have a son, too,
and his name is Liam. He's seven, and he has
asthma. He's the center of my life.
    You have nothing to fear from me. I'm not a
ghost, just an ordinary flesh-and-blood woman.
A mother, like you.

The telephone rang, jolting Sierra out of the spell.

Conditioned to unexpected emergencies, because
of Liam's illness, she hurried to answer, squinting at
the caller ID.

"Indian Rock Elementary School."

The room swayed.

"This is Sierra McKettrick," she said. "Is my son
all right?"

The voice on the other end of the line was blessedly

calm. "Liam is just a little sick at his stomach, that's all," the woman said. "The school nurse thinks he ought to come home. He'll probably be fine in the morning."

"I'll be right there," Sierra answered, and hung up without saying goodbye.

Liam is safe, she told herself, but she felt panicky, just the same.

She deliberately closed Hannah McKettrick's journal, put it back inside the album. Placed the album inside the drawer.

Then she raced around the kitchen, frantically searching for the car keys, before remembering that she'd left them in the ignition earlier, when she'd come back from town. She'd been so focused on having an illicit tryst with Travis Reid....

She grabbed her coat, dashed out the door, jumped into the SUV.

The roads were icy, and by the time Sierra sped into Indian Rock, huge flakes of snow were tumbling from a grim gray sky. She forced herself to slow down, but when she reached the school parking lot, she almost forgot to shut off the motor in her haste to get inside, find her son.

Liam lay on a cot in the nurse's office, alarmingly pale. Someone had laid a cloth over his forehead, presumably cool, but he was all by himself.

How could these people have left him alone?

"Mom," he said. "My stomach hurts. I think I'm gonna hurl again."

She went to him. He rolled on to his side and vomited onto her shoes.

"I'm sorry!" he wailed.

She stroked his sweat-dampened hair. "It's all right, Liam. Everything is going to be all right."

He threw up again.

Sierra snatched a handful of paper towels from the wall dispenser, wet them down at the sink and washed his face.

"My coat!" he lamented. "I don't want to leave my cowboy coat—"

"Don't worry about your coat," Sierra said, wondering distractedly how she could possibly be the same woman who'd spent half the morning naked in Travis's bed.

The nurse, a tall blond woman with kindly blue eyes, stepped into the room, carrying Liam's coat and backpack. Silently she laid the things aside in a chair and came to assist in the cleanup effort.

Sierra went to get the coat.

"No!" Liam cried out, as she approached him with it. "What if I puke on it?"

"Sweetheart, it's cold outside, and we can always have it cleaned—"

The nurse caught her eye. Shook her head. "Let's just bundle Liam up in a couple of blankets. I'll help you get him to the car. This coat is important to him— *so* important that, sick as he was, he insisted I go and get it for him."

Sierra bit her lip. She and the nurse wrapped Liam in the blankets, and Sierra lifted him into her arms. He was getting so big. One day soon, she probably wouldn't be able to carry him anymore.

The main doors whooshed open when Sierra reached them.

"Oh, great," Liam moaned. "Everybody's looking. Everybody knows I *ralphed*."

Sierra hadn't noticed the children filling the corridor. The dismissal bell must have rung, but she hadn't heard it.

"It's okay, Liam," she said.

He shook his head. "No, it *isn't!* My *mom* is carrying me out of the school in a bunch of *blankets,* like a *baby!* I'll never live this down!"

Sierra and the nurse exchanged glances.

The nurse smiled and shifted Liam's coat and backpack so she could pat his shoulder. "When you get back to school," she said, "you come to my office and I'll tell you *plenty* of stories about things that have happened in this school over the years. You're not the first person to throw up here, Liam McKettrick, and you won't be the last, either."

Liam lifted his head, apparently heartened. "Really?"

The nurse rolled her eyes expressively. "If you only *knew,*" she said, in a conspiratorial tone, opening the door of the SUV on the passenger side, so Sierra could set Liam on the seat and buckle him in. "I wouldn't name names, of course, but I've seen kids do a lot worse than vomit."

Sierra shut the door, turned to face the nurse.

"Thanks," she said. Liam peered through the window, his face a greenish, bespectacled moon, his hair sticking out in spikes. "You have a unique way of comforting an embarrassed kid, but it seems to be effective."

The nurse smiled, put out her hand. "My name is Susan Yarnia," she said. "If you need anything, you call me, either here at the school or at home. My husband's name is Joe, and we're in the book."

Sierra nodded. Took the coat and backpack and put them into the rig, after ferreting for Liam's inhaler, just in case he needed it on the way home. "Do you think I should take him to the clinic?" she asked in a whisper, after she'd closed the door again.

"That's up to you, of course," Susan said. "There's been a flu bug going around, and my guess is Liam caught it. If I were you, I'd just take him home, put him to bed and make a bit of a fuss over him. See that he drinks a lot of liquids, and if you can get him to swallow a few spoonfuls of chicken soup, so much the better."

Sierra nodded, thanked the woman again and rounded the SUV to get behind the wheel.

"What if I spew in Aunt Meg's car?" Liam asked.

"I'll clean it up," Sierra answered.

"This whole thing is *mortifying.* When I tell Tobias—"

Tobias.

If Sierra hadn't been pulling out on to a slick road, she probably would have slammed on the brakes.

Please don't harm my boy, Hannah McKettrick had written, eighty-eight years ago, in her journal. *His name is Tobias. He's eight years old.*

"Who is Tobias?" Sierra asked moderately, but her palms were so wet on the steering wheel that she feared her grip wouldn't hold if she had to make a sudden turn.

"The. Boy. In. My. Room," Liam said very carefully, as though English were not even Sierra's *second* language, let alone her first. "I told you I saw him."

"Yeah," Sierra replied, her stomach clenching so hard that she wasn't sure *she* wouldn't be the next one to throw up, "but you didn't mention having a conversation with him."

Liam turned away from her, rested his forehead against the passenger-side window, probably because it was cool. "I thought you'd freak," he said. "Or send me off to some bug farm."

Sierra drove past the clinic where she and Travis had taken Liam the day of his asthma attack. It was all she could do not to pull in and demand that he be put on life support, or air-lifted to Stanford.

It's stomach flu, she insisted to herself, and kept driving by sheer force of will.

"When have I ever threatened to send you *anywhere,* let alone to a 'bug farm'?"

"There's always a first time," Liam reasoned.

"You were sick last night," Sierra realized aloud. "That's why you were so quiet at supper."

"I was quiet at supper because I figured Tobias would be there when I went upstairs."

"Were you scared?"

Liam flung her a scornful look. "No," he said. And then his cheeks puffed out, and he made a strangling sound.

Sierra pulled to the side of the road, got out of the SUV and barely got around to open the door before he decorated her shoes again.

This is your real life, she thought pragmatically.

Not the two million dollars.

Not great sex in a cowboy's bed.

It's a seven-year-old boy, barfing on your shoes.

The reflections were strangely comforting, given the circumstances.

When Liam was through, she wiped off her boots with handfuls of snow, got back into the car and drove to the nearest gas station, where she bought him a bottle of Gatorade so he could rinse out his mouth, spit gloriously onto the pavement, and hopefully retain enough electrolytes to keep from dehydrating.

Twilight was already gathering by the time she pulled into the garage at the ranch house, having noticed, in spite of herself, that Travis was back from wherever he'd gone, and the lights were glowing golden in the windows of his trailer.

Not that it mattered.

In fact, she wasn't the least bit relieved when he walked into the garage before she could shut the door or even turn off the engine.

Liam unsnapped his seat belt and lowered his window. "I *horked* all over the schoolhouse," he told Travis gleefully. "People will probably talk about it for *years*."

"Excellent," Travis said with admiration. His eyes danced under the brim of his hat as he looked at Sierra over Liam's head, then returned his full attention to the little boy. "Need some help getting inside? One cowpoke to another?"

"Sure," Liam replied staunchly. "Not that I couldn't make it on my own or anything."

Travis chuckled. "Maybe you ought to carry *me,* then." His gaze snagged Sierra's again. "It happens that I'm feeling a little weak in the knees myself."

Sierra's face heated. She switched off the ignition.

Liam giggled, and the sound was restorative. "You're too big to carry, Travis," he said, with such affection that Sierra's throat tightened again, and she honestly thought she'd cry.

Fortunately, Travis wasn't looking at her. He gathered Liam into his arms, blankets and all, and carried him inside. Sierra followed with her son's things, scrambling to get her emotions under control.

"It's *arctic* in here," Liam said.

"You're right," Travis agreed easily. He set Liam in the chair where Sierra had sat writing in the diary of a woman who was probably buried somewhere among all those bronze statues in the family cemetery, and approached the old stove. "Nothing like a good wood fire to warm a place up."

"Drink your Gatorade," Sierra told Liam, because she felt she had to say something, and that was all that came to mind.

"Can we sleep down here again?" Liam asked. "Like we did when the blizzard came and the furnace went out?"

"No," Sierra answered, much too quickly.

Travis gave her a sidelong glance and a grin, then stuffed some crumpled newspaper and kindling into the belly of the wood stove, and lit the fire. Sierra shivered, hugging herself, while he adjusted the damper.

"Is something wrong with the furnace again?" she asked.

"Probably," Travis answered.

She was oddly grateful that he hadn't called her on asking a stupid question. But then, he wouldn't. Not in front of her son. She knew that much about Travis Reid, at least. Along with the fact that he was one hell of a lover.

Don't even think about that, Sierra scolded herself. But it was like deciding not to imagine a pink elephant skating on a pond and wearing a tutu.

"I think we should all sleep right here," Liam persisted.

Travis chuckled, more, Sierra suspected, at her discomfort than at Liam's campaign for another kitchen campout. "If a man's got a bed," Travis said, "he ought to use it."

Sierra's cheeks stung. "Was that necessary?" she whispered furiously, after approaching the wood box to grab up a few chunks of pine. If she was going to live in this house for a year, she'd better learn to work the stove.

"No," Travis whispered back, "but it was fun."

"Will you *stop?*"

Another grin. He seemed to have an infinite supply of those, and all of them were saucy. "Nope."

"What are you guys whispering about?" Liam asked suspiciously. "Are you keeping secrets?"

Travis took the wood from Sierra's hands, stuffed it into the stove. She tried to look away but she couldn't. "No secrets," he said.

Sierra bit her lower lip.

The kitchen began to warm up, but she couldn't be certain it was because of the fire in the cookstove.

Travis left them to go downstairs and attend to the furnace.

"I wish he was my dad," Liam said.

Sierra blinked back more tears. Lifted her chin. "Well, he's not, sweetie," she said gently, and with a slight quaver in her voice. "Best let it go at that, okay?"

Liam looked so sad that Sierra wanted to take him on to her lap and rock him the way she had when he was younger and a lot more amenable to motherly affection. "Okay," he agreed.

She crossed to him, ruffled his hair, which was already mussed. "Think you could eat something?" she asked. "Maybe some chicken noodle soup?"

"Yuck," he answered. "And I *still* think we should

sleep in the kitchen, because it's cold and I'm sick and I might catch pneumonia or something up there in my room."

The mention of Liam's room made Sierra think of Hannah again and Tobias. She went to the china cabinet, opened the drawer, raised the cover on the photo album. The journal was still there, and she looked inside.

Hannah's words.

Her words.

Nothing more.

Did she expect an answer? More lines of faded ink, entered beneath her own ballpoint scrawl?

A tingle of anticipation went through her as she closed the journal, then the album, then the drawer, and straightened.

Yes.

Oh, yes.

She *did* expect an answer.

The furnace made that familiar whooshing sound.

Liam muttered something that might have been a swear word.

Sierra pretended not to notice.

Travis came back up the basement stairs, dusting his hands together. Another job well done.

"It's still going to be *really* cold upstairs," Liam asserted.

"You're probably right," Travis agreed.

Sierra gave him an eloquent look.

Travis was undaunted. He just grinned another insufferable, three-alarm grin. "I'll make you a bed on the floor," he said, and though he was looking at Sierra, he was talking to Liam. Hopefully. "Just until it gets warm upstairs."

Liam yelped with delighted triumph, punching the air with one fist. Then, just as quickly, he sobered. "What about you and Mom?"

"I reckon we'll just tough it out," Travis drawled. With that, he went about carrying in a couple of sofa cushions to lay on the floor, not too close to the stove but close enough for warmth.

Sierra fetched a pillow and fresh blankets.

Liam stretched out on the makeshift bed like an Egyptian king traveling by barge. Sighed happily.

"Are you staying for supper, Travis?" he asked.

"Am I invited?" Travis asked, looking at Sierra.

She sighed. "Yes," she said.

Liam let out another yippee.

Sierra made grilled cheese sandwiches and heated canned spaghetti, but by the time she served the feast, Liam was sound asleep.

Travis, seated on the bench, his sleeves still rolled up from washing in the bathroom down the hall, nodded toward him.

"If I were you," he said, "I'd start checking out law schools. That kid is probably going to be on the Supreme Court before he's thirty."

Chapter 15

1919

Hannah's hands trembled slightly as she raised the cover of the family album and reached for the remembrance book tucked inside. She held her breath as she opened it.

Only her own words were there, alone and stark.

She was a practical woman, and she knew she should not have expected anything else. Spirits, if there was such a thing, did not take up pens and write in remembrance books. And yet she was stricken with a profound disappointment, the likes of which she'd never experienced before. She'd suffered plenty in her life, seeing three sisters perish as a girl and, as a woman grown, losing Gabe, knowing none of the brave dreams they'd talked about with such hope and faith would ever come true.

No more stolen kisses.

No more secret laughter.

No more cattle grazing on a thousand hills.

And certainly no more babies, born squalling in their room upstairs.

Hannah told herself, I will not cry, I have cried enough. I have emptied myself of tears.

So why do they keep coming?

"Hannah?"

She started, looked up to see Doss standing at the foot of the stairs. He'd been working in the barn, the last she knew, doing the morning chores. Chopping extra wood because there was another storm coming. It bothered her that she hadn't heard him come in.

"Tobias is worse," he said.

Alarm swelled into Hannah's throat, cutting off her wind.

She started for the stairs, but when she would have passed Doss, he stopped her.

"I'm going to town for the doc," he told her.

"I'll just wrap Tobias up warm and we'll—"

Doss's grip tightened on her shoulders. Only then did she realize he hadn't merely stepped into her path, he was touching her. "No, Hannah," he said. "The boy's too sick for that."

"Suppose the doctor won't come?"

"He'll come," Doss said. "You go to Tobias. Don't let the fire go out, no matter what. I'll be back as soon as I can."

Hannah nodded, bursting to get to her son, but somehow wanting to cling to Doss, too. Tell him not to go, that they'd manage some way but he oughtn't to leave, because something truly terrible might happen if he did.

"Go to him," Doss told her, letting go of her shoulders.

She felt as though he'd been holding her up. Swayed a little to catch her balance. Then, on impulse, she stood on tiptoe and kissed him right on the mouth. "You be careful, Doss McKettrick," she said. "You come back to us, safe and sound."

He looked deeply into her eyes for a moment, as though he could see secrets she kept even from herself, then nodded and made for the door. The last Hannah saw of him, just before she dashed up the rear stairs, he was putting on his coat and hat.

Tobias lay fitful in his bed, his nightshirt soaked with perspiration, like the sheets. His teeth chattered, and his lips were blue, but his flesh burned to the touch.

Hannah could not afford to let panic prevail.

She had mothering to do, and however inadequate and fearful she felt, there was no one but her to do it.

She pushed up her sleeves, added more pins to her hair so it wouldn't tumble down and get in her way, and headed downstairs to heat water.

Heedful of Doss's warning not to let the fire die, she added wood from the generous supply he'd brought in earlier without her noticing. She pumped water into every bucket and kettle she owned, and put them on the stove to heat. Then she dragged the bathtub out of the pantry and set it in the middle of the floor.

The instructions seemed to come from somewhere inside her. She didn't plan what to do, or take the time to debate one intuition against another. It was as if some stronger, smarter, better Hannah had stepped to the fore, and pushed the timid and uncertain one aside.

This Hannah knew what to do. The regular one stood

in the background, wringing her hands and counseling hysteria.

Tobias was practically delirious when Hannah roused him from his bed, an hour later when the tub was full of hot water, and half carried, half led him downstairs.

In the kitchen she stripped him and put him into the bath. Scrubbed him down, all the while talking quietly, confidently, without ever stopping to think up the words she'd say next.

"You'll be fine, Tobias. Come spring, you'll be able to ride your pony through the fields and swim in the pond. We'll get you that dog you've been wanting—you can pick him out yourself—and he can sleep right in your room, too. On the foot of your bed, if you want. You can call your uncle Doss 'Pa' from now on, and there'll be a brand-new baby in this house at harvest time—think of it, Tobias. A little brother or sister. You can choose the name—"

Tobias shuddered, chilled even in water that would be too hot to stand any other time.

Hannah dried him with towels, put him in a clean nightshirt, got him back upstairs again. Settled him into her own bed while she hastened to put fresh sheets and blankets on his.

All that morning, and all that afternoon, she tended her boy, touching a cold cloth to his forehead. Holding his hands. Telling him that his pa had gone to town for the doctor, and he needn't worry because he was going to be just fine.

They were all going to be just fine.

Tobias had occasional moments of lucidity. "Liam's sick, too," he said once. "I want to be with Liam."

Another time, he asked, "Where's Pa? Is Pa all right?"

Hannah had bitten her lower lip and reassured him gently. "Yes, sweetheart, your pa's just fine."

The day wore on, into evening.

And Doss hadn't returned.

Hannah put more wood on the fire, donned Gabe's coat and made her way out to the barn, through ever-deepening snow, to feed the livestock, because there was no one else to do it.

The wind bit through to Hannah's bones as she worked. Made them ache, then go numb.

Where was Doss?

The other Hannah, the fretful one pushed into the background, kept calling out that question, as if from the bottom of a well.

Where...where...where?

It was completely dark by the time she'd finished, and as she left the barn, she heard the faint rumble of thunder. Rare in a snowstorm, like lightning, but Hannah had seen that, too, there in the high country of Arizona, and in Montana, as well. A staggering sense of foreboding descended upon her, and it had nothing to do with Tobias being sick.

Hannah returned to the house, switched on the kitchen bulb before even taking off Gabe's coat, thinking somehow the light might draw Doss back to her and Tobias, through the storm. Even in daylight, and even for a man as tough and as skilled as Doss, navigating the most familiar trails would be difficult in weather like that, if not impossible. In the dark, it was plain treacherous.

"Ma?" Tobias called. "Ma, are you down there?"

It heartened her, the strength she heard in his voice, but her joy was tempered by worry. Doss should have been home by then. Unless—please, God, let it be so—he'd decided to stay in town.

"Yes," she called back, as cheerfully as she could. "I'm here, and I'm about to fix you some supper."

"Come up, Ma. Right now. That boy's here."

In the process of shedding the coat she'd worn to feed the livestock and the chickens and milk the cow, Hannah let the garment drop, forgotten, to the floor. She took the stairs two at a time and burst into Tobias's room.

With no lamp burning, it was stone dark. She made out the outline of Tobias's bed and him lying there.

"He's here, Ma," Tobias said, in a delighted whisper, as though speaking too loudly might cause his invisible friend to disappear. "Liam's here."

Hannah hurried to the bedside.

"I don't see him," she said.

Just then the sky itself seemed to part, with a great, tearing roar so horrendous Hannah put her hands to her ears. The floor trembled beneath her feet, and the windowpanes rattled. Light quivered in the room—she knew it was snow lightning, but it was otherworldly, just the same—and for one single, incredulous moment, she saw not Tobias lying in that bed, but another little boy. And she saw the woman standing on the other side of the bed, too. Staring at her. Looking every bit as surprised as Hannah herself.

Within half a heartbeat, the whole incident was over.

"Did you see them?" Tobias asked desperately, grasping at her hand. Clinging. "Ma, did you see them?"

"Yes," Hannah whispered. She dropped to her knees next to Tobias's bed, unable to stand for another instant.

Tobias had said "them." He'd seen the woman, too, then, as well as the boy. "Dear God, yes."

"She was wearing trousers, Ma," Tobias marveled.

Hannah raised herself from the floor to perch tremulously on the side of Tobias's bed. Fumbled for the matches and lit the lamp on the stand.

"Tell me what else you saw, Tobias," she said. Her hands were shaking so badly that the lamp chimney rattled when she set it back in place.

"She had short hair. Brown, I think. And she saw us, Ma, just as sure as we saw her!"

Hannah nodded numbly.

"What does it mean, Ma?" Tobias asked.

"I wish I knew," Hannah said.

Present Day

Sierra stood still at Liam's bedside, hugging herself and trembling, trying to understand what she'd just seen.

What the hell *had* she just seen?

Lightning.

A woman in an old-fashioned dress, standing on the opposite side of Liam's bed.

Hannah?

"What's wrong, Mom?" Liam asked sleepily. He'd protested a little, when she'd roused him from his slumbers in the kitchen and brought him up here to sleep in his own bed. Then he'd fallen into natural oblivion.

She couldn't catch her breath.

"Mom?" Liam prompted, sounding more awake now.

"We'll…we'll talk about it in the morning."

"Can I sleep with you?"

Sierra swallowed. Travis had gone back to his trailer several hours before. She'd sat downstairs in the study, with a low fire going, catching up on her email, checking in on Liam at regular intervals. Anything, she realized now, but open the family album and come face-to-face with a long line of McKettricks, every one of them a stranger.

The house seemed empty and, at the same time, too crowded for comfort.

"I'll sleep in here with you," she said. "How would that be?"

"Awesome," Liam said.

"Just let me change." Down the hall, she stripped to the skin, put on sweats and made for the bathroom, where she splashed her face with cool water and brushed her teeth.

Such ordinary things.

In the wake of what she'd just experienced, she wondered if anything would ever be "ordinary" again.

Liam was snoring softly when she got back to his room. She slipped into the narrow bed beside him, turned on to her side and stared into the darkness until at last she, too, fell asleep.

1919

While Doc Willaby's nephew was getting his medical gear together, Doss took the opportunity to slip into the church down on the corner. He hadn't set foot inside it since he and Gabe had come back from the army, him sitting ramrod straight on a train seat and Gabe lying in a pine box.

He'd had no truck with God after that.

Now they had some business to discuss.

Doss opened the door, which was always unlocked, lest some wayfarer seek to pray or to find salvation, and took off his hat. He walked down front, to the plain wooden table that served as an altar, and lit one of the beeswax candles with a match from his pocket.

"I'm here to talk about Tobias," he said.

God didn't answer.

Doss shifted uncomfortably on his feet. They were so cold from the long drive into town that he couldn't feel them. Cain and Abel had been fractious on the way, and he'd had all sorts of trouble with them. Once, they'd just stopped and refused to go any farther, and then, crossing the creek, the team had made it over just fine but the sleigh had fallen through. Sunk past the runners in the frigid water.

He'd still be back there, wet to the skin and frozen stiff as laundry left on a clothesline before a blizzard, if three of Rafe's ranch hands hadn't come along to help. They'd given him dry clothes, fetched from a nearby line shack, dosed him with whisky, hitched their lassos to the half-submerged sleigh and hauled it up on to the bank by horsepower.

He'd thanked the men kindly and sent them on their way, and then spent more precious time coaxing Cain and Abel to proceed. They'd been mightily reluctant to do that, and he'd finally had to threaten them with a switch to get them moving.

The whole day had gone like that, though the frustrations were at considerable variance, and by the time he'd pulled up in front of the doc's house, the worthless critters were so worn-out he knew they wouldn't make it back home. He'd sent to the livery stable for another rig and fresh horses.

Doss cleared his throat respectfully. "Hannah can't lose that boy," he went on. "You took Gabe, and if You don't mind my saying so, that was bad enough. I guess what I want to say is, if You've got to claim somebody else, then it ought to be me, not Tobias. He's only eight and he's got a lot of living yet to do. I don't know exactly what kind of outfit You're running up there, but if there are cattle, I'm a fair hand in a roundup. I can ride with the best of them, too. I'll make myself useful— You've got my word on that." He paused, swallowed. His face felt hot, and he knew he was acting like a damn fool, but he was desperate. "I reckon that's my side of the matter, so amen."

He blew out the candle—it wouldn't do for the church to take fire and burn to the ground—and turned to head back down the aisle.

Doc Willaby was standing just inside the door, leaning on his cane, because of that gouty foot of his, and dressed for a long, hard ride out to the Triple M.

"You ought to tell Hannah," the old man said.

"Tell her what?" Doss countered, abashed at being caught pouring out his heart like some repentant sinner at a revival.

"That you love her enough to die in place of her boy."

Doss heard a team and wagon clatter to a stop out front. "Nobody needs to know that besides God," he said, and slammed his hat back on his head. "What are you doing here, anyhow? Besides eavesdropping on a man's private conversation?"

The doc smiled. He was heavy-set, with a face like a full moon, a scruff of beard and keen little eyes that never seemed to miss much of anything. "I'm going out to your place with you. And we'd better be on our way, if that boy's as sick as you say he is."

"What about your nephew?"

"He'd never stand the trip," Doc said. "My bag's out on the step, and I'll thank you to help me up into the wagon so we can get started."

Doss felt a mixture of chagrin and relief. Doc Willaby was old as desert dirt, but he'd been tending McKettricks, and a lot of other folks, for as long as Doss could remember. His own health might be failing, but Doc knew his trade, all right.

"Come on, old man," Doss said. "And don't be fussing over hard conditions along the way. I've got neither the time nor the inclination to be coddling you."

Doc chuckled, though his eyes were serious. He slapped Doss on the shoulder. "Just like your grandfather," he said. "Tough as a boiled owl, with a heart the size of the whole state of Arizona and two others like it."

Getting the old coot into the box of the hired wagon was like trying to hoist a cow from a tar pit, but Doss managed it. He climbed up, took the reins in one hand and tossed a coin to the livery stable boy, shivering on the sidewalk, with the other. Cain and Abel would be spending the night in warm stalls, maybe longer, with all the hay they required and some grain to boot, and, cussed as they were, Doss was glad for them.

He and the doc were almost to the ranch house when

the lightning struck, loud enough to shake snow off the branches of trees, throwing the dark countryside into clear relief.

The horses screamed and shied.

The wagon slid on the icy trail and plunged on to its side.

Doss heard the doc yell, felt himself being thrown sky high.

Just before he hit the ground, it came to him that God had taken him up on the bargain he'd offered back there in Indian Rock at the church. He was about to die, but Tobias would be spared.

Someone was pounding at the back door.

Hannah muttered a hasty word of reassurance to Tobias, who sat up in bed, wide-eyed, at the sound.

"That can't be Pa," he said. "He wouldn't knock. He'd just come inside—"

"Hush," Hannah told him. "You stay right there in that bed."

She hurried down the stairs and was shocked to see old Doc Willaby limping over the threshold. He looked a sight, his clothes wet and disheveled, his hair wild around his head, without his hat to contain it. His skin was gray with exertion, and he seemed nigh on to collapsing.

"There was an accident," he finally sputtered. "Down yonder, at the base of the hill. Doss is hurt."

Hannah steered the old man to a chair at the table. "Are you all right?" she asked breathlessly.

The doctor considered the question briefly, then nodded. "Don't mind about me, Hannah. It's Doss—I couldn't wake him—I had to turn the horses loose so they wouldn't kick each other to death."

She hurried into the pantry, moved the cracker tin aside and took down the bottle of Christmas whisky Doss kept there. She offered it to Doc Willaby, and he gulped down a couple of grateful swigs while she pulled on Gabe's coat and grabbed for a lantern.

"You'd better take this along, too," Doc said, and shoved the whisky bottle at her.

Hannah dropped it into her coat pocket. She didn't like leaving the old man or Tobias alone, but she had to get to Doss.

She raised her collar against the bitter wind and threw herself out the back door. Out in the barn, she tossed a halter on Seesaw and stood on a wheelbarrow to mount him. There was no time for saddles and bridles.

Holding the lamp high in one hand and clutching the halter rope with the other, Hannah rode out. She soon met two of the horses Doc had freed, and followed their trail backward, until the shape of an overturned wagon loomed in the snowy darkness.

"Doss!" she cried out. The name scraped at her throat, and she realized she must have called it over and over again, not just the once.

She found him sprawled facedown in the snow, at some distance from the wagon, and feared he'd smothered, if not broken every bone in his body. Scrambling off Seesaw's back, she plodded to where he lay, utterly still.

She knelt, setting the lantern aside, and turned him over.

"Doss," she whispered.

He didn't move.

Hannah put her cheek down close to his mouth. Felt his breath, his blessed breath, warm against her skin.

Tears of relief sprang to her eyes. She dashed them away quickly, lest they freeze in her lashes.

"Doss!" she repeated.

He opened his eyes.

"What are you doing here?" he asked, sounding befuddled.

"I've come looking for you, you damn fool," she answered.

"You're not dead, are you?"

"Of course I'm not dead," Hannah retorted, weeping freely. "And you're not either, which is God's own wonder, the way you must have been driving that wagon to get yourself into a fix like this. Can you move?"

Doss blinked. Hoisted himself on to his elbows. Felt around for his hat.

"Where's the doc?" His features tightened. "Tobias—"

"Tobias is fine," she said. "And Doc's up at the house, thawing out. It's a miracle he made it that far, with that foot of his."

A grin broke over Doss's face, and Hannah, filled with joy, could have slapped him for it. Didn't he know he'd nearly killed himself? Nearly fixed it so she'd have to bear and raise their baby all alone?

"I reckon Doc was right," Doss said. "I ought to tell you—"

"Tell me what?" Hannah fretted. "It's getting colder out here by the minute, and the wind's picking up, too. Can you get to your feet? Poor old Seesaw's going to have to carry us both home, but I think he can manage it."

"Hannah." Doss clasped both her shoulders in his hands, gave her just the slightest shake. "I love you."

Hannah blinked, stunned. "You're talking crazy, Doss. You're out of your head—"

"I love you," he said. He got to his feet, hauling Hannah with him. Knocked the lantern over in the process so it went out. "It started the day I met you."

She stared up at him.

"I don't know how you feel about me, Hannah. It would be a grand thing if you felt the same way I do, but if you don't, maybe you can learn."

"I don't have to learn," she heard herself say. "I came out into this wretched snowstorm to find you, didn't I? After I suffered the tortures of the damned wondering what was keeping you. Of course I love you!"

He kissed her, an exultant kiss that warmed her to her toes.

"I'm going to be a real husband to you from now on," he told her. He made a stirrup of his hands, and Hannah stepped into them, landed astraddle Seesaw's broad, patient old back.

Doss swung up behind her, reached around to catch hold of the halter rope. "Let's go home," he said, close to her ear.

Hannah forgot all about the whisky in her coat pocket.

It was stone dark out, but the lights of the house were visible in the distance, even through the flurries of snow.

Anyway, Seesaw knew his way home, and he plodded patiently in that direction.

Present Day

The world was frozen solid when Sierra awakened the next morning, to find herself clinging to the edge of Liam's empty bed. Voices wafted up from downstairs, along with heat from the furnace and probably the wood stove, too.

She scrambled out of bed, finger combed her hair and hurried down the hallway.

Travis said something, and Liam laughed aloud. The sound affected Sierra like an injection of sunshine. Then a third voice chimed in, clearly female.

Sierra quickened her pace, her bare feet thumping on the stairs as she descended them.

Travis and Liam were seated at the table, reading the comic strips in the newspaper. A slender blond woman wearing jeans and a pink thermal shirt with the sleeves pushed up stood by the counter, sipping coffee.

"Meg?" Sierra asked. She'd seen her sister's picture, but nothing had prepared her for the living woman. Her clear skin seemed to glow, and her smile was a force of nature.

"Hello, Sierra," she said. "I hope you don't mind my showing up unannounced, but I just couldn't wait any longer, so here I am."

Travis stood, put a hand on Liam's shoulder. Without a word, the two of them left the room, probably headed for the study.

"Everything Mom said was true," Meg told Sierra quietly. "You're beautiful, and so is Liam."

Sierra couldn't speak, at least for the moment, even though her mind was full of questions, all of them clamoring to be offered at once.

"Maybe you should sit down," Meg said. "You look as though you might faint dead away."

Sierra pulled back the chair at the head of the table

and sank into it. "When...when did you get here?" she asked.

"Last night," Meg answered. She poured a fresh cup of coffee, brought it to Sierra. "I hope I'm not interrupting anything."

"Interrupting anything?"

Meg's enormous blue eyes took on a mischievous glint. She swung a leg over the bench and straddled it, as several generations of McKettricks must have done before her, facing Sierra.

"Something's going on between you and Travis," Meg said. "I can feel it."

Sierra wondered if she could carry off a lie and decided not to try. She and Meg had been apart since they were small children, but they were sisters, and there was a bond. Besides, she didn't want to start off on the wrong foot.

"The question is," she said carefully, "is anything going on between *you* and Travis."

"No," Meg answered, "more's the pity. We tried to fall in love. It just didn't happen."

"I'm not talking about falling in love."

Wasn't she? Travis had rocked her universe, and much as she would have liked to believe it was only physical, she knew it was more. She'd never felt anything like that with Adam, and she *had* been in love with him, however naively. However foolishly.

Meg grinned. "You mean sex? We didn't even get that far. Every time we tried to kiss, we ended up laughing too hard to do anything else."

Sierra marveled at the crazy relief she felt.

"Too bad he's leaving," Meg said. "Now we'll have

to find somebody else to look after the horses, and it won't be easy."

The bottom fell out of Sierra's stomach.

"Travis is leaving?"

Meg set her coffee cup down with a thump and reached for Sierra's hand. "Oh, my God. You didn't know?"

"I didn't know," Sierra admitted.

Damned if she'd cry.

Who needed Travis Reid, anyway?

She had Liam. She had a family and a home and a two-million-dollar trust fund.

She'd gotten along without Travis, and his lovemaking, all her life. The man was entirely superfluous.

So why did she want to lay her head down on her arms and wail with sorrow?

Chapter 16

1919

Come morning Hannah made her way through the still, chilly dawn to the barn. Besides their own stock, four livery horses were there, gathered at the back of the barn, helping themselves to the haystack. Remnants of harness hung from their backs.

Hannah smiled, led each one into a stall, saw that they each got a bucket of water and some grain. She was milking old Earleen, the cow, when Doss joined her, stiff and bruised but otherwise none the worse for his trials, as far as Hannah could see.

They'd shared a bed the night before, but they'd both been too exhausted, after the rigors of the day and getting Doc Willaby settled comfortably in the spare room, to make love.

"You ought to go into the house, Hannah," Doss said, sounding both confounded and stern. "This work is mine to do."

"Fine," she said, still milking. There was a rhythm in the task that settled a person's thoughts. "You can gather the eggs and get some butter from the spring house. I reckon Doc will be in the grip of a powerful hunger when he wakes up. He'll want hotcakes and some of that bacon you brought from the smokehouse."

Doss moved along the middle of the barn, limping a little. Stopping to peer into each stall along the way. Hannah watched his progress out of the corner of her eye, smiling to herself.

"I meant what I said last night, Hannah," he said, when he finally reached her. "I love you. But if you really want to go back to your folks in Montana, I won't interfere. I know it's hard, living out here on this ranch."

Hannah's throat ached with love and hope. "It is hard, Doss McKettrick, and I wouldn't mind spending winters in town. But I'm not going to Montana unless you go, too."

He leaned against one of the beams supporting the barn roof, pondering her with an unreadable expression. "Gabe knew," he said.

She stopped milking. "Gabe knew what?"

"How I felt about you. From the very first time I saw you, I loved you. He guessed right away, without my saying a word. And do you know what he told me?"

"I can't imagine," Hannah said, very softly.

"That I oughtn't to feel bad, because you were easy to love."

Tears stung Hannah's eyes. "He was a good man."

"He was," Doss agreed gruffly, and gave a short nod. "He asked me to look after you and Tobias, before he died. Maybe he figured, even then, that you and I would end up together."

"It wouldn't surprise me," Hannah replied. Dear, dear Gabe. She'd loved him so, but he'd gone on, and he'd want her to carry on and be as happy as she could. Tobias, too.

"What I mean to say is," Doss went on, taking off his hat and turning it round and round in his hands by the brim, "I understand what he meant to you. You can say it, straight out, anytime. I won't be jealous."

Hannah stood up so fast she spooked Earleen, who kicked over the milk bucket, three-quarters of the way full now, steaming in the cold and rich with cream. She put her arms around Doss and didn't try to hide her tears.

"You're as good a man as Gabe ever was, Doss McKettrick," she said, "and I won't let you forget it."

He grinned down at her, wanly, but with that familiar spark in his eyes. "I'll build you a house in town, Hannah," he said. "We'll spend winters there, so you can see folks and Tobias can go to school without riding two miles through the snow. Would you like that?"

"Yes," Hannah said. "But I'd stay on this ranch forever, too, if it meant I could be with you."

Doss bent his head. Kissed her. His hands rested lightly on the sides of her waist, beneath the heavy fabric of Gabe's coat.

"You go inside and see to breakfast, Mrs. McKettrick. I'll finish up out here."

She swallowed, nodded. "I love you, Mr. McKettrick," she said.

His eyes danced mischievously. "Once we get Doc back to town," he replied, "I mean to bed you, good and proper."

Hannah blushed. Batted her lashes. "When is he leaving?"

Present Day

Travis was packing, loading things into his truck. Even whistling as he went about it. Meg got into her car and drove off somewhere.

Sierra waited as long as she could bear to—she didn't know how she was going to explain this to Liam, who was sleeping off his flu bug—didn't know how to explain it herself.

She got out the album, for something to do, and set the remembrance book aside without opening it. Even after seeing Hannah and Tobias the night before, in Liam's room, she just didn't believe in magic anymore.

So she took a seat at the table and lifted the cover of the album.

A cracked and yellowed photograph, done in sepia, filled most of the page. Angus McKettrick, the patriarch of the family, stared calmly up at her. He'd been handsome in his youth; she could see that. Though, in the picture his thick hair was white, his stern, square-jawed face etched with lines of sorrow as well as joy. His eyes were clear, intelligent and full of stubborn humor.

It was almost as though he'd known Sierra would be looking at the photo one day, searching for some part of herself in those craggy features, and crooked up one corner of his mouth in the faintest smile, just for her.

Be strong, he seemed to say. *Be a McKettrick.*

Sierra sat for a long time, silently communing with the image.

I don't know how to "be a McKettrick." What does that mean, anyway?

Angus's answer was in his eyes. Being a McKettrick meant claiming a piece of ground to stand on and put-

ting your roots down deep into it. Holding on, no matter what came at you. It meant loving with passion and
taking the rough spots with the smooth. It meant fighting for what you wanted, letting go when that was the
best thing to do.

Sierra absorbed all that and turned to the next page.

A good-looking couple posed in the front yard of
the very house where Sierra sat, so many years later.
A small boy and a girl in her teens stood proudly on either side of them, and underneath someone had written
the names in carefully. Holt McKettrick. Lorelei McK-
ettrick. John Henry McKettrick. Lizzie McKettrick.

They wore the name like a badge, all of them.

After that came more pictures of Holt and Lorelei
together and separately. In one, they were each holding
the hand of a laughing, golden-haired toddler.

Gabriel Angus McKettrick, stated a fading caption
beneath.

On the facing page, Lorelei sat proud and straight in
a chair, holding an infant. Young Gabriel, older now,
stood with a hand on her thigh, his ankles crossed, with
the toe of one old-fashioned shoe touching the floor.
Holt flanked them all, one hand resting on Lorelei's
shoulder. The baby, according to the inscription, was
Doss Jacob McKettrick.

Sierra continued to turn pages, and moved through
the lives of Gabe and Doss along with them, or so it
seemed, catching a glimpse of them on important dates.
Birthdays. School. Mounted on ponies. Fishing in a
pond.

Sierra felt as though she were looking not at mere
photographs, but through little sepia-stained windows
into another time, a time as vivid and real as her own.

She watched Gabe and Doss McKettrick grow into young men, both of them blond, both of them handsome and sturdy.

At last she came to the wedding picture. Her gaze landed on Hannah, standing proudly beside Gabe. She was wearing a lovely white dress, holding a nosegay.

Hannah.

The woman with whom, in some inexplicable way, she shared this house. The woman she had seen in Liam's bedroom the night before, caring for her own sick child even as Sierra was caring for hers.

Sierra could go no further. Not then.

She closed the album carefully.

"Mom?"

She turned, looked around to see Liam standing at the foot of the stairs, in his flannel pajamas. His hair was rumpled, his glasses were askew, and he looked desperately worried.

"Hey, buddy," she said.

"Travis is putting stuff in his truck," he told her. "Like he's going away or something."

Sierra's heart broke into two pieces. She got up, went to him. "I guess he was just here temporarily, to look after your aunt Meg's horses."

Liam blinked. A tear slipped down his cheek. "He can't go," he said plaintively. "Who'll make the furnace work? Who'll get us to the clinic if I get sick?"

"I can do those things, Liam," Sierra said. She offered a weak smile, and Liam looked skeptical. "Okay, maybe not the furnace. But I know how to get a fire going in the wood stove. And I can handle the rest, too."

Liam's lower lip wobbled. "I thought...maybe—"

Sierra hugged him, hard. She wanted to cry herself,

but not in front of Liam. Not when his heart was breaking, just like hers. One of them had to be strong, and she was elected.

She was an adult.

She was a McKettrick.

Before she could think of anything to say, the back door opened and suddenly Travis was there. He looked at her briefly, but then his gaze went straight to Liam's face.

"If you came to say goodbye," Liam blurted out, "then don't! I don't care if you're leaving—*I don't care!*" With that, he turned and fled up the stairs.

"That went well," Travis said, taking off his hat and hanging it on the peg. He didn't take his coat off, though, which meant he really *was* going away. Sierra had known that—and, at the same time, she *hadn't* known it. Not until she was faced with the reality.

"He's attached to you," she said evenly. "But he'll be all right."

Travis studied her so closely that for a moment she thought he was going to refute her words. "I know this all seems pretty sudden," he began.

Sierra kept her distance, glad she wasn't standing too close to him. "It's your life, Travis. You've done a lot to help us, and we're grateful."

Upstairs, something crashed to the floor.

Sierra closed her eyes.

"I'd better go up and talk to him," Travis said.

"No," Sierra replied. "Leave him alone. Please."

Another crash.

She found Liam's backpack, unzipped it and took out the inhaler. "I've got to get him calmed down," she said quietly. "Thanks for…everything. And goodbye."

"Sierra…"

"Goodbye, Travis."

With that, she turned and went up the stairs.

Liam had destroyed his new telescope and his DVD player. He was standing in the middle of the wreckage, trembling with the helplessness of a child in a world run by adults, his face flushed and wet with tears.

Sierra picked up his shoes, made her way to him. "Put these on, buddy," she said gently, crouching to help. "You'll cut your feet if you don't."

"Is he—" Liam gulped down a sob "—gone?"

"I think so," Sierra said.

"Why?" Liam wailed, putting a hand on her shoulder to keep from falling while he jammed one foot into a shoe, then the other. "Why does he have to go?"

Sierra sighed. "I don't know, honey," she answered.

"Make him stay!"

"I can't, Liam."

"Yes, you can! You just don't want to! You don't *want* me to have a dad!"

"Liam, that is enough." Sierra stood, handed him the inhaler. "Breathe," she ordered.

He obeyed, puffing on the inhaler between intermittent, heartbreaking sobs. "Make him stay," he pleaded.

She squired him to the bed, pulled his shoes off again, tucked him in. "Liam," she said.

Outside, the truck door slammed. The engine started up.

And suddenly Sierra was moving.

She ran down the stairs, through the kitchen, and wrenched open the back door. Coatless, shivering, she dashed across the yard toward Travis's truck.

He was backing out, but when he saw her, he stopped. Rolled down the window.

She jumped on to the running board, her fingers curved around the glass. *"Wait,"* she said, and then she felt stupid because she didn't know what to say after that.

Travis eased the door open, and she was forced to step back down on to the ground. Unbuttoning his coat as he got out, he wrapped it around her. But he didn't say anything at all. He just stood there, staring at her.

She huddled inside his coat. It smelled like him, and she wished she could keep it forever. "I thought it meant something," she finally murmured. "When we made love, I mean. I thought it *meant something*."

He cupped a gloved hand under her chin. "Believe me," he said gruffly, "it did."

"Then why are you leaving?"

"Because there didn't seem to be anything else to do. You were busy with Liam, and you'd made it pretty clear we had nothing to talk about."

"We have *plenty* to talk about, Travis Reid. I'm not some…some rodeo groupie you can just have sex with and forget!"

"You can say that again," Travis agreed, smiling a little. "Do you mind if we go inside to have this conversation? It's colder than a well-digger's ass out here, and I'm not wearing a coat."

Sierra turned on her heel and marched toward the house, and Travis followed.

She tried not to think about all the things that might mean.

Inside she gestured toward the table, took off Travis's coat and started a pot of coffee brewing, so she'd have a chance to think up something to say.

Travis stepped up behind her. Laid his hands on her shoulders.

"Sierra," he said. "Stop fiddling with the coffee-maker and talk to me."

She turned, looked up into his eyes. "It's not like I was expecting marriage or anything," she said, whispering. Liam was probably crouched at the top of the stairs by then, listening. "We're adults. We had...we're adults. But the least you could have done, after all that's gone on, was give us a little notice—"

"When Brody died," Travis said, "I died, too. I walked away from everything—my house, my job, everything. Then I met you, and when—" He paused, with a little smile, and glanced toward the stairs, evidently suspecting that Liam was there, all ears, just as she did. "When we *were adults,* I knew the game was up. I had to get it together. Start living my life again."

Sierra blinked, speechless.

He touched his mouth to hers. It wasn't a kiss, and yet it affected Sierra that way. "It's too soon to say this," he said, "but I'm going to say it anyway. Something happened to me yesterday. Something I don't understand. All I know is, I can't live another day like a dead man walking. I called Eve and asked for my old job back, and I'll be working in Indian Rock, at McKettrickCo, with Keegan. In the meantime I've got to put my house on the market and make arrangements to store my stuff. But it won't be long before I'm at your door, with every intention of winning you over for good."

"What are you saying?"

Liam came shooting down the stairs, wheeling his arms. "Get a clue, Mom! He's in love with you!"

"That's right," Travis said. He gave Liam a look of mock sternness. "I *was* planning to break it to her gradually, though."

"You're in...?" Sierra sputtered.

"Love," Travis finished for her. "Just tell me this one thing. Do I have a chance with you?"

"Give him a *chance,* Mom!" Liam cried jubilantly. "That's not too much to ask, is it? All the man wants is a chance!"

Sierra laughed, even as tears filled her eyes, blurring her vision. "Liam, hush!" she said.

"What do you say, McKettrick?" Travis asked, taking hold of her shoulders again. "Do I get a chance?"

"Yes," she said. "Oh, yes."

"If you're going to work in town," Liam enthused, tugging at Travis's shirtsleeve by then, "you might as well just move in with us!"

Travis chuckled, released Sierra to lean down and scoop Liam up in one arm. "Whoa," he said. "I'm all for *that* plan, but I think your mother needs a little more time."

"You're not leaving?" Liam asked, so hopefully that Sierra's heartbeat quickened.

"I'm not leaving," Travis confirmed. "I've got some things to do in Flagstaff, then I'll be back."

"Will you live right here, on the ranch?" Liam demanded.

"Not right away, cowpoke," Travis answered. "This whole thing is real important. I don't want to get it wrong. Understand?"

Liam nodded solemnly.

"Good," Travis said. "Now, get on back upstairs, so I can kiss your mother without you ogling us."

"I broke my DVD player," Liam confessed, suddenly crestfallen. "On purpose, too." He paused, swallowed audibly. "Are you mad?"

"You're the one who'll have to do without a DVD player," Travis said reasonably. "Why would *I* be mad?"

"I'm sorry, Travis," Liam told him.

Travis set the boy back on his feet. "Apology accepted. While we're at it, *I'm* sorry, too. I should have talked to you—your mother, too—before I packed up my stuff. I guess I was just in too much of a hurry to get things rolling."

"I forgive you," Liam said.

Travis ruffled his hair. "Beat it," he replied.

Liam scampered toward the stairs and hopped up them as though he were on a pogo stick.

"Are you sure he's sick?" Travis asked.

Sierra laughed. "Kiss me, cowpoke," she said.

1919

Doc Willaby was with them for three full days, waiting for his bumps and bruises to heal and the weather to clear. He played endless games of checkers with Tobias, next to the kitchen stove, and Hannah and Doss tried hard to pretend they were sensible people. The truth was, they could barely keep their hands off each other.

"How come I have to move to the other end of the hall?" Tobias asked Doss, on the morning of the third endless day.

"You just do," Doss answered.

Early that afternoon, the sleigh came pulling into the yard, drawn by Cain and Abel and driven by Kody Jackson, from the livery stable. Two outriders completed the procession.

"Glory be," Doc said, peering out the window, along with Hannah. "They've come to fetch me back to Indian Rock." He looked down at Hannah and smiled wisely. "Now you and Doss can stop acting like a couple of old married folks and do what comes naturally."

Hannah blushed, but she couldn't help smiling in the process. "It's been good having you here, Doc," she said, and she meant it, too. "You saved Doss's life the other night, coming all that way to fetch me, in the shape you were in. I'll be grateful all my days."

He took her hand. Squeezed it. "He loves you, Hannah."

"I know," she said softly. "And I love him, too."

"That's all that counts, in the long run. Or the short one, for that matter. We each of us get a certain number of days to spend on this earth. Only the good Lord knows how many. Spend them loving that man of yours and that fine boy, and you'll have done the right thing."

Hannah stood on tiptoe. Kissed the doctor on the cheek. "Thank you," she said.

Doss came out of the barn to greet Kody and the other men.

They all went down the hill together to set the other wagon upright, leading the team along behind them. Doss put Cain and Abel away, while Kody drove the rig up alongside the house.

Doc was outside by then, ready to go, with his medical bag clutched in one hand and his cane in the other. He turned and waved at Hannah through the window, and she waved back, watching fondly as Doss and another man helped him up into the wagon box.

When Doss didn't come back in right away, Hannah busied herself making the kitchen presentable. Tobias was upstairs, resting in his new bedroom at the front of the house. Now that he'd adjusted to the change, he liked being able to see so clear across the valley from the gabled window, but what had really swayed him was the reminder that Doss and Gabe had shared that room when they were boys.

She swept the floor and put fresh coffee on to brew and even switched on the lightbulb instead of lighting lamps, as wintry afternoon shadows darkened the room.

Still, there was no sign of Doss, so she built up the fire in the stove, opened the drawer of the china cabinet, lifted the cover of the album and took out her remembrance book.

In the three busy days since she'd seen the other woman and her boy, up there in Tobias's bedroom, she'd thought often of the journal, and kept a close eye on the teapot, too.

Nothing extraordinary happened, but inside, in a quiet part of herself, Hannah was waiting. She carried the remembrance book over to the rocking chair drawn up close to the stove and sat down. Perhaps she'd begin making regular entries in that journal.

She'd write about her and Doss, and make notes as Tobias grew toward manhood. She'd record the dates the peonies bloomed, and tuck a photograph inside, now and then. Doss had promised her they'd build a house in Indian Rock, and pass the hard high-country winters there. She would capture the dimensions of the new place in these pages, and perhaps even make sketches. One day she'd take up a pen and write that the baby had come, safe and strong and well.

She was so caught up in the prospect of all the years ahead, just waiting to be lived and then set down on paper, that a few moments passed before she realized that another hand had written beneath her own short paragraphs.

My name is Sierra McKettrick.

I have a son, too, and his name is Liam. He's seven, and he has asthma. He's the center of my life.

You have nothing to fear from me. I'm not a ghost, just an ordinary flesh-and-blood woman. A mother, like you.

Hannah stared at the words in disbelief.

Read them again, and then again.

It couldn't be.

But it was.

The woman she'd seen was a McKettrick, too, living far in the future. She had the proof right here—not that she meant to show it to just everybody. Some folks would say she'd written those words herself, of course, but Hannah knew she hadn't.

She touched the clear blue ink in wonder. It looked different, somehow, from the kind that came in a bottle.

The door opened, and Doss came in. He took off his coat and hat, hung them up neatly, like he always did.

Hannah held the remembrance book close against her chest. Should she let Doss see? Would he believe, as she did, that two different centuries had somehow managed to touch and blend, right here in this house?

Her heart fluttered in her breast.

"Hannah?" He sounded a little worried.

"Come and look at this, Doss," she said.

He came, crouched beside her chair, read the two entries in the journal, hers and Sierra's.

She watched his face, hopeful and afraid.

Doss raised his eyes to meet hers. "That," he said, "is the strangest thing I've ever run across."

"There's more," Hannah said. "I saw her, Doss. I saw this woman, and her little boy, the night of your accident."

He closed a hand over hers. "If you say so, Hannah," he told her quietly, "then I believe you."

"You do?"

He grinned. "Does that surprise you?"

"A little," she admitted. "When Tobias mentioned seeing the boy, you said it must be his imagination."

Doss handed back the book. "Life is strange," he said. "There's a mystery just about everywhere you look, when you think about it. Babies being born. Grass poking up through hard ground after a long winter. The way it makes me feel inside when you smile at me."

Hannah leaned, kissed his forehead. "Flatterer," she said.

"Is Tobias asleep?" he asked.

She blushed. "Yes."

He pulled her to her feet, set the remembrance book aside on the counter and kissed her.

"I think we've waited long enough, don't you?" he asked.

Hours later, hair askew, bundled in a wrapper, well and thoroughly loved, Hannah sneaked back downstairs. She gathered ink and a pen from the study and lit a lantern in the kitchen.

Then, smiling, she sat down to write.

Present Day

Travis lay sprawled on his stomach in Sierra's bed, sound asleep. She sat up beside him, stroked his bare back once with a gentle pass of her hand. In the three days since he'd moved out of the trailer, he'd been back several times, on one pretext or another. Finally Meg had packed some of her things and some of Liam's, and the two of them had gone to stay in town with friends of hers.

"You two really need some time alone," she'd said, with a wicked grin lighting her eyes.

Sierra smiled down at Travis. So far they'd made good use of that time alone. They'd talked a lot, in between bouts of lovemaking, and they still had plenty to say to each other—maybe enough to last a lifetime.

She switched on the lamp, took Hannah's remembrance book from the bedside table, and opened it. Her eyes widened, and she drew in a breath.

Beneath her own entry, in the same stately, faded writing as before, Hannah had written:

It's nice to know there's another woman in the house, even if I can't see or hear you, most of the time. We must be family, since your name is McKettrick. Maybe you're descended from us, from Doss and me. I told my son, Tobias, that your name is Sierra. He said that was pretty, and he'd like the new baby to be called that, too, if it's a girl...

There was more, but Sierra couldn't read it, because her eyes were blurred with tears of amazement. She bounded out of bed, not caring if she awakened Travis, and hurried downstairs, switching on lights as she went. She had the album out and was flipping through the pages at the middle when he joined her, blinking and shirtless, with his jeans misbuttoned.

"What's going on?" he asked, yawning.

Sierra's heart thumped at the base of her throat.

She forced herself to slow down, turn the pages gently. And then she found what she was looking for—an old, old photograph of two children, smiling for the camera lens. The little boy she'd seen in Liam's room, with Hannah, holding a baby wearing a long, lacy gown.

Beneath the picture, Hannah had written Tobias's name and the baby's.

Sierra Elizabeth McKettrick.

Sierra put a hand to her mouth and gasped.

Travis drew closer. "Sierra—"

"Look at this," Sierra said, stabbing at the image with one finger. "What do you see?"

Travis frowned. "An old picture of two kids."

"Look at the baby's name."

"Sierra. You must have been named for her."

"I think *she* was named for *me*," Sierra said.

"How could *she* be named for *you*?"

"Sit down," Sierra told him. She reached for Hannah's remembrance book, offered it when he was seated. "Read this."

He read. Looked up at her with wide eyes. "You don't really think—"

"That I've been communicating with a woman who lived in this house in 1919, and probably for years after that? Yes, Travis, that is *exactly* what I think!"

"But, *how?*"

"You said it yourself, when I first got here. Strange things happen in this house."

"This is beyond strange. Are you going to tell anybody else about this?"

"Mother and Meg," Sierra said. "Liam, too, when he's a little older."

He reached for her hand, wove his fingers through hers, squeezed. "And me. You told *me,* Sierra."

"Well, *yeah.*"

"You must trust me."

She grinned. "You're right," she said. "I must trust you a whole lot, Travis Reid."

"Can we go back to bed now?"

She closed the album and tucked Hannah's remembrance book carefully inside. "Race you!" she cried, and dashed for the stairs.

* * * * *

Visit her Author Profile page at Harlequin.com,
or brendajackson.net, for more titles!

STAR OF HIS HEART

Brenda Jackson

To my Heavenly Father. How Great Thou Art.

"A good name is to be chosen rather than great riches, loving favor rather than silver and gold."
—Proverbs 22:1

Chapter 1

"Quiet on the set!

"Take one!

"Action!"

The director's voice blared from the bullhorn and the words sent a pleasurable thrill up Rachel Wellesley's spine. She had known before she'd uttered her first words as a child that she had an overabundance of artsy bones in her body.

The only problem was that as she got older, her choice of an artistic career would change from week to week. First she had wanted to become a painter, then a writer. Later on she had considered becoming a fashion stylist. But at the fine arts college she'd attended, after she took theory and practicum classes on beauty, she had finally decided on a career as a makeup artist and wardrobe designer. This was the life she lived for and what she enjoyed—being on the set of a movie. Or in this case, the TV set that was taping the popular prime-time medical drama *Paging the Doctor.*

It was day one of shooting for the second season. All the cast members from last season had returned except for Eric Woods, who'd played Dr. Myles Bridgestone. No one had been surprised to hear his contract was not renewed, especially with all his personal drama last season. The well-known Hollywood movie star had evidently felt it beneath him to do TV and to play a role other than a leading one. But the ratings of his last few movies had plummeted. Everyone who worked with him last season had been aware of his constant complaints. Eric was an egomaniac and a director's worst nightmare.

Rachel had managed to get along with Eric, but she couldn't say the same for others who considered him a pain in the rear end. But then, her older sister Sofia claimed Rachel could get along with just about anybody, and she would have to agree. It took a lot to rock her boat. She was easygoing by nature and was an all-around nice person. She figured some things just weren't worth the hassle of getting high blood pressure and stress.

A slight movement out of the corner of her eye made her shift her focus to the actor she'd heard would be added to the show this season in the role of Dr. Tyrell Perry. His name was Ethan Chambers.

He had been in Hollywood only a couple of years and already, at twenty-eight, he had taken the town by storm. And most noticeably, over the past few months, he and his playboy behavior had become quite the talk in the tabloids and gossip columns.

She gave him an appreciative glance. The only thing she had to say was that if the producer added Ethan to the show to boost the ratings, then he had hit the mark. Ethan was definitely eye candy of the most delicious kind. There was no doubt in her mind he would stir the interest of their female viewers, young and old, single or married.

And she couldn't help noticing he had already stirred the interest of several of the females on the set. He seemed oblivious to the open stares as he talked to a man she assumed was his agent. Although she found Ethan extremely attractive, she was too much of a professional to mix her private life with her professional one. And the one thing she detested above all else was being in the spotlight, which was something he evidently enjoyed since he'd managed to garner a lot of publicity lately.

She thought that his flashing white smile was as sexy as they came and figured he would be perfect for any toothpaste commercial. He was tall, probably six foot two, and powerfully built with broad shoulders, muscled arms and a masculine chest. He did a whole lot for those scrubs he was wearing. The company that manufactured the medical attire should be grateful, since he practically turned them into a fashion statement.

And last but not least was his cocoa-colored face with those striking blue-gray eyes—a potentially distracting pair for any woman fool enough to gaze into them too long—and his ultrasexy dimpled jaw. She had to hand it to him, he was as handsome as any male could get in her book, hands down.

A soft smile lifted the corners of her lips as she thought that this was bound to be an interesting season. Already a number of the women on the set were vying for his attention. The show's director, Frasier Glenn, would just love that.

"Cut! Good scene, everyone. Let's move on!"

Frasier's words had Rachel moving quickly toward the producer, John Gleason, and Livia Blake, a model and budding actress who would be guest-starring on the show for a few episodes as Dr. Sonja Duncan. The scene they had just filmed was an emotional one in which Dr. Duncan had broken the news to a devoted husband that his wife had died of cardiac arrest.

Livia would be in the next scene as well and it was Rachel's job to refresh her hair and makeup. And since Rachel was also the wardrobe designer for the show, she needed to verify John's request for a change in the outfit Livia would be wearing in the scene they would be shooting later today.

Rachel flashed a look back to Ethan Chambers, and her gaze raked over him once again. The man by his side was doing all the talking, and for a quick moment she detected a jumpy tension surrounding Ethan. She had been around enough actors on their first day on the set to tell he was nervous. That surprised her. If anything, she would think a man with his looks would be brimming over with self-confidence, even arrogance. If he wasn't, than he was different from Eric Woods in more ways than one.

Ethan Chambers took another sip from the water bottle, wishing it was a cold beer instead. He couldn't believe he had finally gotten his lucky break and was here, on the set of *Paging the Doctor,* playing the role of a neurosurgeon. He wasn't a hospital maintenance man or a victim who needed medical care but a doctor. He had landed the role of a lifetime on what was one of the most top-rated shows.

He would even go so far as to pinch himself if there weren't so many people around, and if his agent, Curtis Fairgate, wasn't standing right next to him, smiling, gloating and taking it all in. And of course, Curtis was ready to take credit for the whole thing, as if Ethan hadn't worked his tail off to get where he was now.

He thought about the three years he had studied acting abroad while doing some well-received but small theater gigs. He could finally say he was now building an acting career. Even his older brother, Hunter, who had tried pressuring him to stay in the family business, was happy for him now. And that meant a lot.

"You do know your lines, don't you?"

Ethan lifted a brow, not believing Curtis would ask such a thing. "Of course. I might be nervous but I'm not stupid. I'm not about to screw up my big break."

"Good."

Ethan pulled in a slow breath, wondering how he and Curtis had managed to survive each other for the past two years. Hollywood agents were known to be pushy, cynical and, in some cases, downright rude. Curtis was all three and then some. Ethan only kept him around because they had a fairly decent working relationship, and Curtis *had* managed to land him a spot on this show by talking to the right people. But Curtis probably would not have managed that if the sister of one of Ethan's former girlfriends hadn't been the current lover of one of the show's writers.

Curtis began talking, rambling on about something Ethan had no desire to listen to, so he glanced around, fascinated at how things were going and what people were doing. He had been on the set of a television show several times, but this was his first time on one that Frasier Glenn directed, and he couldn't help but admire how smoothly things were running. The word around Hollywood was that Frasier was a hard man to work for, a stickler for structure, but he was highly respected in the industry.

Ethan was about to pull his concentration back to the conversation he was supposed to be having with Curtis when his gaze settled on a gorgeous petite woman wearing a cute baby-doll top and a pair of wide-leg jeans. She was gorgeous in a restrained sort of way. He figured she was an actress on the show and wondered what role she played.

She couldn't be any taller than five foot two, but he thought she was a sexy little thing with her short dark hair and exotic looks. And she was smiling, which was a change of pace since everyone else seemed to look so doggone serious.

"Ethan!"

Curtis snapped his fingers in Ethan's face, cutting into his thoughts. "Don't even think it, Ethan," the man warned.

Ethan blinked, and an annoyed expression showed on his face as he met Curtis's gaze. "Think what?"

"About getting involved with anyone on this set, especially that hot little number over there. I know that look."

Ethan frowned. He liked women. He enjoyed sex. He did short-term affairs better than anyone he knew. The women he was involved with weren't looking for long-term any more than he was. "Why?" he finally asked.

"Frasier usually frowns on that sort of thing on his set, that's why."

Ethan took another sip of his water before asking, "Are you saying that he has a fraternization policy?"

"No, but a workplace romance isn't anything he gets thrilled about, trust me. It can cause unnecessary drama, and Frasier doesn't like drama since it can take away from a good day's work."

Ethan didn't say anything as his gaze found the object of his interest once again. For some reason, he had a feeling she would be worth any damn drama that got stirred. He shook his head, thinking he needed to put his player's mentality in check for a while, at least until the end of the season. Making his mark on this show was his goal, and now that he was in the driver's seat and pursuing his dream, the most important thing was for him to stay focused.

Although the urge to hit on the sexy pixie was strong, he would keep those longings in check. Besides, she probably wasn't even his type.

"I have a feeling you're going to be a big hit this season, Ethan."

Ethan glanced over at the woman who had introduced herself earlier as Paige Stiles, one of the production assistants. "Thanks."

"And like I said, if you ever need help with your lines after hours, just let me know. I will make myself available."

"I appreciate that, Paige." The offer seemed friendly enough, but he recognized it for what it was. The woman had been coming on to him ever since they had met earlier that day. She wasn't bad looking, in fact he thought her rather attractive; but she hadn't stirred his fire the same way the sexy pixie had.

Once the show had begun taping one scene after another, the petite brunette had all but disappeared. If she was an actress on the show then her segment was evidently being shot later. He was tempted to ask Paige who she was but thought better of it. The one thing a man didn't do was ask a woman who was interested in him about another woman.

"So where are we headed?" he asked as they moved away from the set toward an exit door.

"To the makeup trailer. That's also where wardrobe is located since the same person handles both."

He lifted a brow. "Is there a reason for that?" he asked, since that wasn't the norm, especially for a show of this magnitude. It was a lot of responsibility for one person.

"None other than that she wanted to do both, and Frasier obliged her. But he would since her last name happens to be Wellesley."

Ethan immediately recognized the last name. The Wellesleys were the brilliant minds behind Limelight Entertainment Management, one of the top talent agencies in the world. Their clientele consisted of some of the best in Hollywood, although in recent years they had expanded to represent more than actors. The firm now represented an assortment of talent that included big-name singers, set designers, costume designers, writers and makeup artists.

"Wellesley?" he asked.

"Yes, the high-and-mighty."

Ethan had the ability to read people, women in particular, and had easily detected the scorn in her voice. And because he knew about women in particular, he decided to change the subject. "How long have you worked for *Paging the Doctor?*"

She began talking and just as he'd done to Curtis earlier, he nodded while he tuned her out. His thoughts drifted back to the woman he'd seen earlier and he wondered if and when their paths would cross again and they would finally meet.

Finally a break, Rachel thought, sliding into a chair that was now empty. She had been in the trailer for the past five hours or so. She had sent one of her assistants out on the set to do those second-by-second touch-ups as needed while she hung out in the makeup/wardrobe trailer, making sure those actors shooting their scenes for the first time that day went through their initial makeup routine.

A couple of the scenes being shot today showed the doctors out of the hospital and in a more relaxed atmosphere either at home or out on dates, which called for a change from medical garments to casual wear.

John had approved her choice of outfits, and she felt good about that, especially since the outfit she'd selected for Livia hadn't been on John's preapproved list. And some of the artwork being used as props were her own creations. Other than Frasier and John, few people knew that when she left here at night she became Raquel, the anonymous canvas artist whose work was showcased in a number of galleries.

Her sister was worried that with being a makeup artist and wardrobe designer by day and a painter at night,

Rachel had no time for a love life. But that was the least of Rachel's concerns. She was only twenty-six and wasn't ready for a serious involvement with any man.

In her early twenties she'd dated a lot, but to this day she couldn't admit to ever falling in love. She would like to believe such a thing could happen for her. Her aunt and uncle had a loving relationship, and she'd been told her parents had had one, too. Regrettably, they had been killed in a plane accident before her second birthday.

Rachel eased out of her chair when she heard conversation outside her door and glanced at the schedule posted on the wall. She wasn't supposed to work on anyone for another hour or so. Who could be infringing on her free time?

There was a knock on the trailer door, followed by a turn of the knob. Rachel fought to keep the frown off her face when Paige stuck her head in. The twenty-four-year-old woman had gotten hired during the middle of the first season. For some reason they had rubbed each other the wrong way that first day and things hadn't improved since. Rachel still didn't know the reason Paige disliked her, but figured it had to do with Rachel's amicable relationship with Frasier and John.

"So you're here," Paige said in a voice that for some reason gave Rachel the feeling Paige wished she wasn't.

Determined to present a friendly facade despite Paige's funky attitude, she smiled and said, "Yes, I'm here. Was there something you wanted?"

"Frasier wants to go ahead and shoot the next scene as soon as lunch is over, which means you need to get started on this guy right away."

Paige came inside the trailer, followed by the hunky

and sexy Ethan Chambers. The moment Rachel's gaze clashed with those blue-gray eyes of his, she knew for the first time in her life how it felt to be totally mesmerized. And nothing could have prepared her for her hormones suddenly igniting into something akin to mind-blowing lust.

Chapter 2

So this was where his sexy pixie had gone to, Ethan thought, entering the trailer and glancing around. He pretended interest in everything inside the trailer except for the woman who'd been in the back of his mind since he'd first seen her that morning. And now here she was.

"Rachel, this is Ethan Chambers and starting this season he'll be a regular on the show as Dr. Tyrell Perry. Ethan, this is Rachel Wellesley, the makeup artist for the show. She's the wardrobe designer as well."

Again Ethan picked up a bit of scorn in Paige's voice, although she had a smile plastered on her face. But then it was evident her smile was only for him.

He crossed the room and extended his hand. "Nice meeting you, Rachel."

"Ditto, Ethan. Welcome to *Paging the Doctor*."

The moment she placed her hand in his he was

tempted to bring it to his lips, something he had gotten used to doing while living abroad in France. And when she smiled up at him the temptation increased. She had such a pretty smile.

"John wants him ready for his scene in thirty minutes. I'll be back to get him, so make sure he's on time."

Both Ethan and Rachel glanced over at Paige and watched as she exited the trailer, leaving them alone. Ethan returned his gaze to Rachel once again and couldn't help asking, "What's got her panties in a wad?"

Rachel couldn't help the laughter that flowed from her mouth, and when he joined in, she knew immediately she was going to like this guy. But then, what wasn't there to like?

Up close, Ethan Chambers was even more handsome than he had been across the room earlier. With him on the show, this would be a pretty good season. She couldn't wait to see them shoot his scene.

She finally answered him. "I have no idea," she said. "But we won't worry ourselves about it. My job is to get you ready for your scene."

"But what about your lunch? Shouldn't you be eating something?"

"I should be asking you the same thing, but to answer your question, usually I bring lunch from home and eat while taking care of business matters," she said, thinking about the order she had downloaded off her iPhone. *Libby's,* an art gallery in Atlanta, had just requested several of her paintings to display.

He nodded. "I'm too nervous to eat so I asked if I could go ahead and get the makeup part taken care of. I apologize if I'm infringing on your time."

She waved off his words. "You're not, so just go ahead and take the chair while I pull your file."

"My file?"

"Yes. Sorry, I can be anal when it comes to being organized, but there's no other way to work with Frasier and John. I have a file of all the scenes you'll be doing today, what you'll need to wear and the extent of lighting needed for that particular shot, although the latter is definitely changeable on the set. That gives me an idea of what kind of makeup I need to apply."

She tried not to notice how he slid into the chair; specifically, how his muscular thighs straddled it before his perfectly shaped backside came in contact with the cushioned seat. She grabbed the folder off the rack and tried to ignore the dark hair that dusted his muscular arms. However, something caught her attention. A tattoo of a cluster of purple grapes draped above his wrist.

"Grapes?" she asked, meeting his gaze and finding it difficult to breathe while looking into his eyes.

"Yes. It's there to remind me of home."

"Home?" she echoed, breaking eye contact to reach over and hand him a smock to put on.

"Yes. Napa Valley."

She recalled the time she'd visited the area years ago as part of a high school field trip. "I've been to Napa Valley once. It's beautiful."

"Yes, it is. I hated leaving it," he said after putting on the smock.

She glanced over and met those killer eyes again. "Then why did you?"

He would be justified to tell her it wasn't her business, she quickly thought, but for some reason she knew he wouldn't do that. They had met just moments ago, but she felt she knew him, or knew men like him. No, she corrected herself. She didn't know any man like him, and how she could say that with such certainty, she wasn't sure.

"I left to pursue my dream. Unfortunately, it wasn't connected to my family business," he said.

Now that she understood. Her sister and uncle always thought she would join them in the family business, but she hadn't. Limelight Entertainment Management had been founded by her father, John Wellesley, and his brother Jacob. It had been the dream they shared and made into reality, with the purpose of representing and building the careers of African American actors during a time when there were many prejudices in Hollywood. Today the company was still very highly respected and had helped many well-known stars jumpstart their careers.

"It's a nice tattoo, but I'll need to use some cream to completely cover it for the shoot. Dr. Perry doesn't have a tattoo," she explained, pressing a button that eased the chair into a reclining position

"That's no problem. Do whatever you have to do, Rachel."

It wasn't what he'd said but how he'd said it that sent sensuous chills coursing through her. For a timeless moment, they stared at each other as heat flooded her in a way it never had before. As the flames of awareness licked at her body, somehow a part of her—the sensible part—remained unscathed. In a nagging voice it reminded her that she needed to get back on track and prep Ethan for his scene.

She swallowed and broke eye contact with him again

as she turned to reach for her makeup kit. "Comfortable?"

"Yes."

"Then why are you so nervous?" she decided to ask him while checking different tubes of makeup cream for one that would work with his complexion and skin type. It was August, and although the air conditioner on the set would be on full blast, all the lighting being used would generate heat. She needed to prevent any facial shiny spots from showing up on camera.

He shifted in his seat and she glanced over at him. "This is the first day on the job of what I see as my big break," he said, straightening in the chair. "This is what I've worked my ass off for since the day I decided acting was what I wanted to do. I've done small parts in theater and guest spots on a couple of shows and was even an extra on *Avatar,* but being here, getting this opportunity, is a dream come true."

She nodded, knowing just how he felt. She had wanted to step out on her own without any help from her family's name. She had submitted her résumé to Glenn Productions and had gotten called in for an interview with both Frasier and John. Although Frasier had been a friend of her father's, and both men were well acquainted with Sofia since she was Uncle Jacob's partner in the family business, Rachel was convinced she had been given the job on her own merits and hadn't been given any preferential treatment.

This was her second season on the show and she worked doubly hard to make sure Frasier and John never regretted their decision to give her a chance. So, yes, she knew all about dreams coming true.

The first thing she thought as she applied a light

brush to Ethan's face was that he had flawless skin with a healthy glow. He had perfect bone structure and his lips were shapely and full. She bent toward him to gently brush his brows and was glad he had closed his eyes since crazy things were going on in the pit of her stomach. A tightness was there that had never been there before. She drew in a deep breath to relieve the pressure. His aftershave smelled good. Almost too good for her peace of mind.

"So tell me, Rachel, what's your dream?"

She smiled. "What makes you think I have one?"

"All women do."

She chuckled. "Sounds like you think you know us pretty well."

"I wouldn't say that, but I would think everyone has at least one dream they would love to see come true."

"I agree, and this is mine—being a makeup artist and wardrobe designer."

"You're good at it. Very professional."

He opened his eyes to meet hers and she was aroused in a way that just wasn't acceptable, especially for a woman who made it her motto never to mix business with pleasure.

"Thanks," she said, taking a step back and reaching over to grab a hand mirror to give to him. "You didn't need much. I don't believe in being heavy-handed with makeup."

"I can appreciate that."

She had made up enough men in her day to know if they had a choice they would gladly skip this part in preparing for their scene. "Now for that tattoo. I have just the thing to blend in with your skin tone that won't rub off. And later you can wash it off."

"Okay."

He held out his arm and she began applying the cream. Against her fingertips, his skin felt warm, slowly sending her body into meltdown. She could feel his eyes on her but refused to glance up and look at him for fear that he would know what touching him was doing to her. Instead she tried concentrating on what she was doing. This time, though, she was too distracted by other things, such as the feel of his strong veins beneath her fingers and the rapid beat of his pulse. Her body responded with a raging flood of desire that seeped into her bones.

Not being able to resist temptation any longer, she looked over at him. For a long, achingly seductive moment, they stared at each other. She wanted to look away but it was as if he controlled the movement of her neck and it refused to budge. She swallowed the panic she felt lodged in her throat as she slowly released his hand. So much for being a firm believer in the separation of business and pleasure. For a moment, no matter how brief, thoughts had filled her mind about how it would be to take her hand and rub it down his chest and then move her hand even lower to—

There was a quick knock at the door before it opened and Paige walked in. And for the first time ever, Rachel was glad to see the woman.

Chapter 3

"If he's as hot as you say he is, then maybe you should let him know you might be interested, Rachel."

Rachel wiped paint from her hands as she glared at the phone. If her best friend since elementary school wasn't there in person to see her frown, transmitting it through the speakerphone was the next best thing. "I'm not interested."

And because she knew Charlene would belabor the point, she went on the defensive and said, "Look, Cha, I thought you of all people would understand. You know I don't like mixing business with pleasure. Besides, I have plenty of work to do."

Charlene laughed. "You always have plenty of work to do. If becoming involved with a man is a way to slow you down, then I'm all for it. It's time you started having fun."

Rachel rolled her eyes. "I could say the same for you."

"Face it. Men aren't drawn to me like they are to you."

Rachel pulled in a deep breath knowing there was no use telling Charlene just how wrong she was. Her words would go in one ear and out the other. For once she wished Charlene would be the one to face it and see that she was beautiful and sexy.

Charlene had to be the kindest and sweetest person Rachel knew, but she always slid to the background when it came to dating and romance. Rachel blamed Charlene's parents, since they always thought their older daughter, Candis, was the "pretty one" and had always put her in the limelight. As far as Rachel was concerned, Charlene had a lot going for her, including a beautiful singing voice.

"I'm in no mood to argue with you, Cha. You know how mad I get when you put yourself down."

"I'm not putting myself down. I'm just stating facts."

"Then let me state a few of my own," Rachel said. "I'm the one on set every day surrounded by gorgeous men. The only problem is that those men are checking out the tall, slender actresses, not me."

When Charlene didn't say anything, Rachel had a feeling there was more going on with her friend. "Okay, Cha, what's wrong?"

There was another long moment before Charlene replied, "I talked to Mom today."

Rachel slumped down into a chair. Mrs. Quinn was the mom from hell, and that was putting it kindly. She'd always managed to boost one daughter up while at the same time tearing the other one down. "And?"

"And she wanted me to know that Candis made the cut for the *Sports Illustrated* swimsuit edition next year and will be staying in Paris for a while."

"That's great, and I'm sure you're happy for her." Rachel knew she could say that because deep down she knew Charlene was. Candis and Charlene had a rather good relationship despite the competitive atmosphere created by their mother.

"Yes, of course I'm happy for her."

"And?"

"And what?" Charlene asked.

Rachel pulled in a deep breath; her patience was wearing thin. "And what else did Mrs. Quinn say?"

"Just the usual about she still doesn't understand how Candis could be so pretty and me so plain when we had the same parents. She ended the call by even suggesting that maybe she and Dad got the wrong baby from the hospital. She said it in a joking way but I knew she was dead serious."

Rachel bet the woman had been dead serious as well, but she would never tell Charlene that. That was the kind of garbage she'd had to put up with all her life. "She wasn't serious, Cha. You and your mother look too much alike for you to be anyone's baby but hers."

Evidently Mrs. Quinn never took the time to notice the similarity. Or maybe she *had* noticed and since she'd never been happy with her own looks, she was passing her insecurities on to Charlene.

Rachel thought about her own situation. She had been raised by her uncle Jacob and her aunt Lily after her parents had been killed. Rachel had been only one year old and Sofia had been ten. Her aunt and uncle were wonderful and had raised her and Sofia as their own children, since unfortunately they'd never had any. The one thing Uncle Jacob and Aunt Lily didn't do was play her and Sofia against each other. Everyone knew that Sofia wanted to follow in their father's footsteps and take his place with Uncle Jacob at Limelight.

Although her uncle and sister would have loved for her to join them in the family business, Rachel had never been pressured to do so. She chuckled, thinking it was enough to have Sofia as her agent.

"Hey, let's do a movie this weekend," she suggested, thinking her best friend needed some chilling time.

"Sounds super, but don't you have a lot to do?"

Rachel laughed. "I always have a lot to do, but I need a break to have fun, and it sounds like you do, too."

A short while later, Rachel made her way to the kitchen, hungry after missing lunch. On the way home she had stopped by a restaurant owned by one of the cameramen's parents. She considered Jack Botticello her buddy, and his parents were truly a godsend. Whenever she dropped by their Italian restaurant, Botticello's Place, for takeout, they always gave her more food than she could possibly eat in one sitting. There would definitely be enough lasagna left for tomorrow's dinner.

As she sat down at the table to enjoy her meal, she recalled everything that had happened on the set that day, especially the scenes that included Ethan Chambers. She couldn't help but remember the moment he had walked into a patient's hospital room. To say he swaggered into the room would probably be more accurate. And when he began speaking in what was supposed to be a northern accent, all eyes and ears were on him. There was no doubt in her mind he was a gifted actor. It was as if the part of Dr. Tyrell Perry had been created just for him.

She couldn't wait for the airing of the show in a few weeks to see how he would be received by the viewing audience. It would probably be no different than the way he'd been received on the set. Women were all but falling at his feet, doing just about anything to get his attention.

He had mentioned to a member of the camera crew in between scenes that he was going to get a cup of coffee. The three women who'd overheard him had all but broken their necks racing across the room to the coffee cart to get it for him. She could tell he'd actually gotten embarrassed by their antics. That surprised her. Most men would be gloating about all the attention. But then, this had been his first day on the job. There was no doubt in her mind that eventually his media-hungry playboy tendencies would come out. It was only a matter of time.

Unbidden, the memories surfaced of what had happened during their makeup session that day. Had he deliberately tried to unnerve her? Break down her defenses so she would behave the way Tina, Cindy and Nina had done today with the coffee incident? It wouldn't surprise her to discover he was just as superficial as all the other playboys in Hollywood. And to think for a short while today she'd actually been attracted to him. But with his make-you-drool looks, the attraction couldn't be helped. It had a way of vamping your senses the first time around.

And his family had money. He'd mentioned his roots were in Napa Valley, but it was only later that day when she'd overheard some of the camera crew talking about how wealthy he already was that she realized he was one of *those* Chamberses. There were two African American families whose roots and vast financial empires were in Napa Valley. The Russells and the Chamberses. Both families' vineyards were known to produce some of wine tasters' finest.

So, okay, she had let her guard down and let herself be affected by him. But tomorrow would be better. She had gotten used to him and would be more in control.

With that resolved, she proceeded to finish her meal.

"Do you promise, Uncle Ethan?"

Ethan couldn't help but smile. "Yes, I promise."

"Truly?"

"Yes, truly."

His six-year-old niece, Kendra, had him wrapped around her finger and probably knew it, he thought. When his parents had mentioned to her that Los Angeles was close to Disneyland, she had begun asking him questions. Mainly she wanted to know if he'd seen any princesses.

Just to hear her voice was a sheer delight because Kendra hadn't done much talking since her mother had died three years ago in a car accident. She had pretty much been withdrawn and quiet much of the time. But she would always talk to her Uncle Ethan.

"Daddy wants to talk to you, Uncle Ethan."

"Okay, sweetheart, and always remember you're Uncle Ethan's cupcake."

"I remember. Nighty-night."

He then heard her hand the phone over to his brother, Hunter, after telling her daddy nighty-night, too and after exchanging an "I love you" and an "I love you back." It was only then that Hunter placed the phone to his ear. "What's going on, kid?"

Ethan couldn't help but chuckle. There was an eight year difference in their ages, and Hunter never let him forget it. But even with that big variation, they'd always gotten along. Like all brothers, they'd had their disagreements, but they'd never lasted more than a few hours. Except for that one time a few years ago when Hunter had tried pressuring him into staying in the family business and getting all those ideas out of his head about making it big in Hollywood.

Ethan had left home anyway to pursue his dream. It was only after the fatal car accident that claimed Hunter's wife's life—an accident that Hunter and Kendra had survived—that Hunter had understood why Ethan had to do what he did. He'd learned that life was too precious and fleeting to take for granted. Tomorrow wasn't promised to anyone.

"Nothing much is going on. Kendra talked a lot tonight," he said.

"Only because it's you. She loves her uncle Ethan. Besides, she wanted to ask you all about princesses."

Ethan grinned. "Yeah, I noticed. What's up with that?"

"*The Princess and the Frog.* She's seen it five times already. I should blame you since you're the one who got her the DVD as soon as it went on sale."

"Hey, there's nothing I wouldn't do for my cupcake," he said, meaning it.

He talked to Hunter for a few minutes longer before his brother passed the phone to their folks. In addition to the winery, Hunter and his parents ran a small four-star bed-and-breakfast on the property. It was always good to call home because he truly missed everyone, and updates were priceless.

"And you're eating properly, Ethan?"

He cringed at his mother's question, knowing he would have to tell her a little white lie, especially when at that very moment the timer went off to let him know his microwave dinner was ready. He had a beer to drink and his dessert would be a bag of peanut M&M's he'd grabbed out of the vending machine when he'd left the studio today. Paige had invited him to her place for dinner but he had declined.

He removed his dinner from the microwave and said, "Yes, Mom, I'm eating properly."

"Met any nice girls you want to bring home?"

She has to be kidding. The last few girls he dated weren't any he would dare bring home for his parents, brother and niece to meet. But then the face of his sexy pixie flashed across his mind and he couldn't help but think that she would work. For some reason he liked her, and the sexual vibes between them hadn't gone unnoticed, although it was evident she'd tried ignoring them.

Besides, he didn't have time to meet girls—nice or any other kind. He had lines to study every night, especially tonight. Frasier had been impressed with him today and had added another scene to his schedule for tomorrow.

"No, Mom, so don't go planning a wedding for me yet."

Later that night when he slid into bed, he couldn't help but think just how blessed he was. Both of his parents were alive and in good health. As the oldest son, Hunter had taken on his role with ease and was the perfect businessman to manage the family's vast wealth.

And Hunter had had the insight to utilize the property surrounding the winery to build the bed-and-breakfast, which was doing extremely well. The reservation list was always filled up a year in advance.

As much as he'd loved Napa Valley, Ethan had known it wasn't in his blood to the extent it had been in Hunter's. After college, he returned home and tried working alongside Hunter and his parents, but he hadn't been happy. Hunter had said it was wanderlust and that eventually he would get over it, but he never did. A year later he had made up his mind to pursue his dream.

So here he was, living in a nice place in L.A. and building the career he'd always wanted. Money was no object, thanks to a trust fund that had been set up by his grandparents as well as the financial standing of the winery, in which he was a stockholder. Of course, every once in a while some smart-ass reporter would ask him why an independently wealthy person would want to work. He was sure Anderson Cooper was asked the same question often enough, too. Ethan wasn't privy to Anderson's response, but his was simply, "Wealthy or poor, everyone has dreams, and there *is* such a thing as continued money growth."

He reached over to turn off the lamp light, thinking that things had gone better than he'd expected on the set today. His lines had flowed easily, and for a while he had stepped into the role of Dr. Tyrell Perry. To prepare, he had watched medical movies and had volunteered his time at a hospital for ninety days. He had come away with an even greater respect for those in the medical industry.

As he stared up at the ceiling his thoughts shifted to the woman he'd met that day, Rachel Wellesley. There

had been something about her that pulled her to him
like a magnet. Something about her that he found totally
adorable. Even among the sea of model-type women on
the set, she had somehow stood out.

And when she had leaned over him to apply whatever it was she brushed on his face, he had inhaled her
scent. With his eyes closed, he had breathed it all in
while imagining all sorts of things. It was a soft scent,
yet it had been hot enough to enflame his senses.

So he had sat there, letting her have her way with his
face while he imagined all kind of things, especially
the image of her naked.

More than once during the shoot, he had had to remind himself that he didn't really know her and that it
would be crazy to lose focus. But he would be the first
to admit that he hadn't counted on being bowled over by
a woman who had to tilt her head all the way back just
to look up at him. He smiled, remembering the many
times they had looked at each other and the number of
times they had tried not to do so. And nothing could
erase from his mind the sight of the soft smile that had
touched her lips when she'd seen his tattoo and when
he'd told her why he had it. If he had been trying to impress her, he would definitely have garnered brownie
points. But he wasn't trying to impress her.

He shifted in bed, knowing he had to stay focused
and not let a pretty face get him off track. All that
sounded easy enough, but he had a feeling it would be
the hardest thing he'd ever had to do.

Chapter 4

"Quiet on the set!

"Take four!

"Action!"

Rachel sat quietly in a chair and watched the scene that was being shot. When she heard two women, Paige and another actress on the set named Tae'Shawna Miller, whispering about how handsome and fine Ethan was, she had to press her lips together to keep from turning around and reminding them about the no-talking-during-a-take policy. But that would make her guilty of breaking the rule, too.

So she sat there and tried tuning them out and hoped sooner or later they would close their mouths. It didn't help matters to know that Paige was one of the women. Rachel figured she of all people should know better.

Rachel turned her attention back to the scene being

filmed and couldn't help but admire the way Ethan was delivering his lines. He was doing a brilliant job portraying Dr. Tyrell Perry, the sexy doctor with a gruff demeanor that could only be softened by his patients. And from the looks of things, a new twist was about to unravel on the show with Dr. Perry being given a love interest—another new doctor on the hospital staff, the widowed Dr. Sonja Duncan.

Rachel had been on the set talking to one of the cameramen when Ethan arrived that morning, swaggering in and exuding rugged masculinity all over the place. The number of flirtatious smiles that were cast his way the moment he said good morning had only made her shake her head. Some of the women were probably still wiping the drool from their mouths.

Why did women get so silly at the sight of a good-looking man? She would admit she had been attracted to him yesterday like everyone else, after all she was a woman, but there was no reason to get downright foolish about it.

"Freeze! No talking on the set!"

Frasier was looking straight at Paige and Tae'Shawna and frowning. He knew exactly who the noisemakers were, and to be called out by the director wasn't good. They had caused time to be wasted, and everyone knew Frasier didn't like that.

"Unfreeze!"

This time around, everyone was quiet while the shooting of the scene continued. In this scene, Dr. Tyrell Perry and Dr. Sonja Duncan were discussing the seriousness of a patient's condition. It was obvious in this scene that the two were attracted to each other. The television viewers would already know through the use of flashbacks that Sonja's late husband, also a doctor, had gotten killed when an L.A. gang, intent on killing a man being treated in the hospital, burst into the E.R. and opened fire, killing everyone, including the doctor, a nurse and a few others waiting to be treated.

Rachel figured since Livia was only a temporary member of the cast, there would not be too much of a budding romance between the two doctors, although it wasn't known just how Livia's exit would be handled. Frasier was known to leave the viewers hanging from scene to scene, so it would be anyone's guess what he had in mind. She couldn't help but wonder if the chemistry the two generated on the set would extend beyond filming.

She hadn't gotten a chance to get to know Livia. During the makeup and wardrobe sessions there hadn't been much conversation between them. Her initial impression was that Livia was just as shallow and self-absorbed as the other Hollywood types Rachel had met. She'd seen no reason for that impression to change. Livia had a reputation of being a party girl and as much the tabloid princess as Ethan was the tabloid king. So it would stand to reason the two would be attracted to each other both on and off the set.

"Cut! Good scene! Let's enjoy lunch. Everyone take an additional hour and be back to start again on time."

Rachel smiled, grateful for the extra time. It seemed a number of people were in a hurry to take advantage of Frasier's generosity...in more ways than one, she thought, when out of the corner of her eye she noticed several women bustling over in Ethan's direction. She rolled her eyes. My goodness, did they have no shame?

Interestingly, Livia walked away in another direction, as if the attention given to Ethan didn't concern her one bit.

Shaking her head, Rachel walked back to her trailer to grab her purse. She had a few errands to do before lunch was over.

Ethan watched Rachel leave before forcing his attention back to the two women standing in front of him. Tae'Shawna had all but invited him over tonight to go skinny-dipping in her pool. Of course he had turned her down. Paige had offered to come over to his place to help him go over his lines. He turned her down as well. For some reason, he wasn't feeling these two. If truth be told, he wasn't feeling any woman right now. Except for the one who'd just headed off toward her trailer.

"So what are you doing for lunch, Ethan? We would love for you to join us," Paige invited, interrupting his thoughts.

"Thanks, but I have a few errands I need to take care of," he said, knowing it was a lie as he said it. But in this case, he felt it was justified.

"No problem. Maybe we can help with your errands and—"

"Thanks again, but that's not necessary," he said, pulling his keys out of his back pocket. He had planned to wait until the weekend to shop for Kendra's gift, but now was just as good a time since these two were beginning to make a nuisance of themselves.

"I'll see you ladies later. I need to leave so I can be back on time."

For a second Paige looked like she was going to invite herself along. Instead she said, "Then I guess we'll see you when you return."

He only smiled, refusing to make any promises as he headed toward the exit. He was grateful for the additional hour and planned on making good use of it. Moving quickly, he reached for the door at the same time someone else did. The moment their hands touched he knew the identity of that person. Her scent gave her away.

"Excuse me."

"Excuse me as well," he said, taking a step back, opening the door and holding it for her to pass through. "You're taking advantage of the extra hour, I see."

Rachel smiled up at him. "I think everyone is." She glanced back over his shoulder. "Where's your fan club?"

His gaze scanned over her face and he saw a cute little mole near the corner of her lip. How could he have missed it yesterday? "My fan club?"

"Yes."

They were walking together as they headed toward the parking lot. "Trust me, there are some fans you can do without."

"And you want me to believe you're not flattered?" she teased, speaking in a low tone when a crew member passed them on the sidewalk.

He slowed his pace as they got closer to where the cars were parked in the studio lot. "Yes, that's exactly what I want you to believe."

She stopped walking and so did he. "Why? Why does it matter what I think?"

Ethan thought she had asked a good question. Why

did it matter what she thought? He knew the answer before he could pull in his next breath. He liked her, and if he had the time he would try to get something going with her. The thing was he didn't have the time. He had to stay focused and doubted he would have time to pursue a relationship, serious or otherwise, with any woman anytime soon. He kept reminding himself that this was his big break, and he wasn't about to mess it up by trying to get between any woman's legs. He had gone without for six months, and he could go another six months or more if he had to.

But that didn't mean that he and Rachel couldn't be just friends, did it? It would be nice to have someone who wasn't interested in anything more than friendship. The little attraction that had passed between them yesterday couldn't be helped. After all, she was a nice-looking woman and he was a hot-blooded man. But as long as they kept things under control, being just friends would be fine.

"It matters because I like you and I'd like for us to be friends," he said.

She pushed a wayward strand of hair from her face as she looked at him. "And why would you want us to become friends?"

Providing an answer to that question was easy enough. "The one thing I noticed yesterday was that you're genuinely a nice person." He chuckled then added, "Hey, you didn't rag on me about being nervous. And it's obvious everyone on the set likes you, from the maintenance man all the way up to the big-wigs. I figure with that kind of popularity, you can't be all bad. Besides, you and Livia are the only two females on the set that I feel pretty comfortable around."

She lifted a brow. "Livia?"

"Yes."

She tilted her head back as if to give him her full attention. "Not that it is any of my business, but I thought that maybe something was going on between the two of you."

He smiled. "There is, on the show. But it's all acting. She's supposed to be my new love interest for the next few episodes."

She nodded. "Your scenes earlier were pretty convincing."

He chuckled. "We're actors. They were meant to be convincing."

Ethan glanced at his watch. "I'd better get going. I want to pick up something for my six-year-old niece from the Disney Store. After watching *The Princess and the Frog* she's into princesses, so I thought I'd pick her up a Princess Tiana doll."

A smile touched the corners of her lips. "You have a niece?"

"Yes, Kendra. She's my older brother's little girl and, I hate to say it, but she's perfect."

She chuckled. "I believe you. And there's a store in walking distance on Hollywood Boulevard. I'm headed that way myself to pick up something from the art supply shop."

He turned the idea over in his mind only once before asking, "Mind if I tag along?"

He did his best not to watch the way her lips were tugged up in a smile when she said, "Sure, you can tag along, as long as we don't talk about work. We need to give our brains a break."

He jammed his keys in his pocket as he resumed walking by her side. It was a beautiful August day, and he had a beautiful woman strolling alongside him. Things couldn't get any better than that. "So what do we talk about?" he decided to ask her.

She slanted her head to look at him. "You."

"Me?"

"Yes."

"Hey, we talked about me yesterday."

Her mouth twitched in a grin. "Yes, but all I know is that you're from Napa Valley and you have a niece." She chuckled. "I guess I could go by what I've heard and—"

"Read in the tabloids," he said, finishing the statement for her.

"No, I don't do tabloids. It would be nice if others didn't do them either, then they would go out of business."

He glanced over at her and laughed. "You don't like the right of free speech?"

She laughed back at him. "More like the right of sleazy speech. Ninety percent of what they print isn't true, but then I guess that's the price of being a star."

He smiled, liking the way the sunlight was bouncing off her hair, making it appear even more lustrous. He liked the short cut on her. "Yes, it's one of the detriments, that's for sure. I just go with the flow. As long as I know what's true about me and what's not, I don't lose any sleep."

She didn't say anything for a while, and then replied, "I hate being in the spotlight."

She kept looking ahead, but he'd heard what she said. Clearly. If that was true, he wondered how she managed it, being a Wellesley. The company her family owned was so connected with this industry, and had been for close to thirty years, they were practically an icon in Hollywood.

He had researched information on Limelight when he'd returned to the States from abroad. He had even considered contacting them to handle his affairs before he'd chosen Curtis, who'd been a friend of a friend to whom he'd owed a favor. But he wouldn't hesitate to consider them again when his contract with Curtis ended. Lately, he'd begun feeling as if he was making his own contacts. Everyone he knew handled by Limelight was pleased with its services. Not once had they ever been made to feel like they were a passenger instead of a driver.

"Being in the spotlight doesn't bother me," he decided to say. "It comes with the territory. But then, my family is well-known in Napa Valley, so I got used to having a mike shoved in my face, only to be quoted incorrectly." He could recall a number of times when he'd been referred to as "the playboy Chambers" while Hunter had always been considered the one with a level head. The responsibly acting Chambers.

"And it doesn't bother you?" she asked.

He met her gaze. "A distortion of the truth will bother most people, and I'm no different. However, I don't lose sleep over it," he said, shifting his gaze to study her features.

But he had a feeling she would.

There had to be a reason, and the question rested on the tip of his tongue.

But he had no right to pry. This woman owed him nothing, had no reason to divulge her deep, dark secrets and innermost feelings. Not to him. They weren't husband and wife. They weren't even lovers. Nor would they ever be.

No, he reminded himself, he was trying out the friendship thing.

Chapter 5

Rachel could feel the power of Ethan as he walked beside her. And although it sounded strange, she could feel his strength. Not only did she feel it, she was drawing from it.

The very thought that such a thing was possible should be disconcerting, but instead the knowledge seemed to wrap her in some sort of warm embrace. That in itself was kind of weird since they'd decided to just be friends. She was fine with that decision. In fact, she refused to have things any other way. She didn't mix business with pleasure and she had too much on her plate to become involved in a serious relationship.

The last guy she had gone out with that she'd truly liked had been Theo Lovett. That had been a couple of years ago. They had dated for almost six months before she'd found out the only reason he'd been interested in her was as a way into her family's business. Luckily, she'd overheard him bragging to a friend on the phone when he'd thought she was in the shower and out of hearing range. Theo's explanation that he'd only been joking with his friend hadn't made her change her mind when she had kicked him out that day.

She stepped out of her memory and into the present. Apparently she'd missed some of what Ethan had said while she'd been daydreaming, because he'd changed the subject and was talking about his family.

"My older brother's name is Hunter. There is an eight year difference in our ages."

She glanced over at him. Despite the fact he was a lot taller than she, walking side by side they seemed to fit, and their steps appeared to be perfectly synchronized. How was that possible with his long legs and her short ones? He'd evidently adjusted his steps to stay in sync with hers. It was a perfectly measured pace.

"There is a nine year difference in me and my sister's ages," she said.

"Really? Was your sibling as overprotective as mine while you were growing up?"

Rachel made a face. "Boy, was she ever. She was ten when our parents were killed in a plane crash, and I was one. Our aunt and uncle became our legal guardians, but somewhere along the way my sister, Sofia, thought I became her responsibility. It was only when she left for college that I got some breathing space."

"Are the two of you close now?"

"Yes, very. What about you and your brother? Are the two of you close?"

"Yes, although I would be the first to admit he was somewhat of a pain in the ass while we were growing up. But I can appreciate it now since he covered for me a lot with my parents."

She could imagine someone having to do that for him. She had a feeling he'd probably been a handful. "Was your family upset when you decided not to enter the family business but to forge a path in a different direction?"

The corners of his lips lifted in a wry smile. "Let's just say they weren't thrilled with the idea. But I think it bothered Hunter more than it did them," he said. "The Chamberses have been in the wine business for generations, and I was the first to pull out and try doing something else. He lay on the pressure for me to stay for a while but then he backed off."

He placed his hand at the center of her back when others, walking at a swifter pace than they, moved to pass them. She could feel the warmth of his touch through her blouse. She breathed in deeply at the feeling of butterflies flapping around in her stomach.

"What about your family?" he inquired, not realizing the effect of his touch on her.

"Once I explained things to Uncle Jacob and Aunt Lily, they were fine with it. They wanted me to do whatever made me happy. But Sofia felt it was part of our father's legacy, that I owed it to him to join her and Uncle Jacob at Limelight. I had made up my mind on how I wanted to do things with my future, so instead of letting there be this bone of contention between us, she backed off and eventually gave me her blessings to do whatever I wanted to do with my life."

She chuckled. "As a concession, I am letting Limelight Entertainment handle my career. I'm one of their clients."

They paused a moment when they reached the security gate. They had deliberately walked the expanse of the studio lot to avoid running into the paparazzi that made the place their regular beat. Now that they were no longer in safe and protected territory, she noticed Ethan had slid on a pair of sunglasses. He had kept on his medical scrubs and had a stethoscope around his neck, and she wondered if anyone seeing him would assume he was a bona fide doctor walking the strip on lunch break.

She pulled her sunglasses out of her bag, too, although it had been years since she'd had the paparazzi on her tail. When she was younger, they'd seemed to enjoy keeping up with the two Wellesley heirs. She'd always found the media's actions intrusive and an invasion of her privacy. She could recall all the photographs of her as a child that had appeared in the tabloids. That was the main reason she much preferred not being the focus of their attention again.

She glanced over at Ethan when his hand went to the center of her back again. It was time for them to cross the street, and he was evidently trying to hurry her along before traffic started up again. Her pulse began fluttering, caused by the heat generated from his touch.

They increased their pace to make it across the street. She checked him out from the corner of her eye and saw how sexy the scrubs looked on him. They had agreed to be just friends, she reminded herself. And it meant absolutely nothing that they had a few things in common. Like the fact that they were both renegades. That they were both members of well-known families. That they both had siblings who'd chosen to go into the family business. Overprotective, older siblings who meant well but if given the chance would run their lives.

Rachel inconspicuously scanned the area around them and breathed a sigh of relief when she saw the paparazzi was nowhere in sight. But then they were known to bounce out from just about any place. Hopefully she and Ethan looked like a regular couple out on a stroll during their lunch hour.

A couple who were just friends, which was something she could not forget.

"You are such a good uncle."

Ethan glanced at Rachel while accepting his change from the girl behind the counter at the Disney Store. Had he used his charge card his cover would have been blown. Even through his sunglasses, he could see the woman was looking at him, trying to figure out if he was a doctor or someone she should know.

He smiled at Rachel. "I'd like to think so, especially since I doubt very seriously that Hunter will have any more children," he said, accepting the bag the cashier was handing him.

"Why is that?"

"He lost his wife in a car accident," he explained as they headed for the exit. "He took Annette's death hard and hasn't been in a serious relationship since. It's been three years now."

"Oh, how sad."

"Yes, it was. Hunter and Kendra were in the car at the time of the accident and survived with minor injuries," he said. He paused a moment and then added, "Kendra was three at the time and very close to her mother. She felt the loss immediately and withdrew into her own world and stopped talking."

The eyes that stared into his were full of sorrow and compassion. "She doesn't talk?"

He released his breath in a long and slow sigh, wondering why he was sharing this information about his family with anyone, especially to a woman he'd only met yesterday. But there was something about Rachel that was different from most women he'd met. For one, she wasn't trying to come on to him or jump his bones. It was as if she saw him as a person and not some sex symbol, and he appreciated that.

"She talks now, but not as much as she should for a child her age," he responded. "And she talks more with some people than with others. I happen to be one of those she will talk to most of the time. But it took me a while to gain that much ground again after the accident." He recalled the time he had come home from France to give his brother and niece his support. "But a part of Kendra is still withdrawn and so far no one has been able to fully bring her back. She's been seen by the best psychologists money can hire. They practically all said the same thing. Kendra suffered a traumatic loss, and until she's convinced in her mind that she can love someone again, become attached to that person without losing them all over again, she will continue to withdraw into her own little world."

He checked his watch and figured they needed to head on back. Prior to stopping at the store, they had stopped by an art supply place and picked up some new brushes. She'd told him that she liked dabbling with paints on canvas every once in a while and had promised to show him some of her work one day.

As they began retracing their steps back toward the studio lot, he had to admit he had enjoyed his time with her and knew that he was going to enjoy having her as a friend. An odd thought suddenly burned in his brain. What if they became more than just friends? He quickly forced the notion out of his head. The fact of the matter was they were just friends, or at least they were trying to be.

He glanced at her and saw her scan the surrounding area. He could tell she was nervous about the possibility of being seen by the paparazzi. So was he, but only because it bothered her. Despite the fact that only minutes ago he'd vowed not to pry, he couldn't stop the question now.

"Why do you avoid the spotlight, Rachel?" He could tell his question surprised her and suspected her reasons were deep-seated.

"I just do," she said.

She tried to act calm, like his question wasn't a big deal, but he sensed that it was. "Why?"

She frowned up at him, and the first thing he thought was that he'd made her mad. He hadn't meant to, but a part of him wanted to push her for an answer.

"Well?" he asked.

She didn't say anything as they kept walking. She had stopped glaring at him and was staring straight ahead. He'd almost given up hope for a reply when she began speaking. "I told you my parents were killed before my second birthday. Since my uncle and aunt who adopted us couldn't have any kids of their own, my sister and I became known as the Limelight heirs. For some reason we made news, and the paparazzi followed us practically everywhere we went—school, church, grocery stores…you name it, they were there. I couldn't tell you how many times when I was a little girl that I got a mike shoved in my face or my braid pulled by a reporter to get my attention. It was…scary.

"Things only got better when I went away to college. By the time I returned, the media interest was on someone else, thank goodness. But every once in a while someone tries to connect the dots to see what Sofia and I are up to. She doesn't mind being in the spotlight and uses it to her advantage."

Ethan took in what she said. The thought of someone harassing a child to get a story angered him, and knowing the child had been Rachel angered him even more. It was interesting that he felt such protective instincts for her.

A flicker of some sort of alarm flashed through his brain but he chose to ignore it. No matter what his mind thought, there was no way he would get in too deep with Rachel.

Chapter 6

Rachel stood by the window in her uncle's study and gazed out at the ocean. The sun was going down and she enjoyed watching it. Just like she had enjoyed being on the set the past two weeks.

Frasier and John were pleased with the tempo of the series. Ethan was working out perfectly as Dr. Perry, and the blossoming on-the-air love affair between the gruff doctor and the resistant Dr. Duncan had pretty much heated up. They had shot a love scene yesterday that had pushed the temperature on the set up as hot as it could get for prime-time programming.

She could definitely say she was pleased with this assignment and looked forward to going into work each day. The more time she and Ethan spent together during filming, the more they talked and bonded as friends. She found him fun to be around, and the two of them

would laugh together about some of the actresses' hot
pursuit of him. A few had tried some outlandish things
to get his attention. Like the time Jasmine Crowder
summoned him to her trailer to help rehang a photo
that had fallen off the wall. Instead of going, Ethan had
sent one of the cameramen, Omar Minton, in his place.
Poor Omar had walked into the trailer to be met by a
half-naked Jasmine draped across the sofa.

That had been just one of many times during the
past week that Ethan had had to foil seduction plots.
Just the fact that he'd done so impressed Rachel, and
she would be the first to admit that she was seeing him
not as the superficial playboy she'd originally thought
he was but as a focused, hardworking actor. That was
another thing they had in common. They believed in
professionalism on the job.

"Lily said I'd probably find you in here."

Rachel turned at the sound of her uncle's deep voice
and smiled. Since she'd been only one year old when her
parents had gotten killed, she didn't have a solid memory of them the way Sofia did. But what she did remember was her aunt and uncle being there for them, raising
her and Sofia as their own. Rachel appreciated having
been part of a family in which she'd always known she
was loved and always been encouraged to use her tal-
ents in whatever way she wanted to do.

She'd learned from her aunt and uncle that her
mother was a successful artist, and several of Vivian
Wellesley's paintings were on the walls in this house as
well as in a number of art galleries across the country.
Vivian had passed down her talent and love of painting;
Rachel really enjoyed the time she spent putting color
to canvas. She was definitely her mother's daughter.

And Sofia was definitely her father's. She had stepped into the role of the savvy and successful businessman that he'd been. And because Sofia had been the only child for almost nine years, she had been the pride of her parents' life and definitely the apple of her father's eye. Sofia had worshipped the ground their father had walked on and was still doing that same thing even though their parents had been dead for twenty-five years. Sofia thought John Wellesley was the most amazing person to have ever lived.

The man standing before Rachel was John's identical twin.

"Uncle Jacob," Rachel greeted, crossing the room to give her uncle a hug. She'd seen pictures of the brothers from years past, and to see one was to see the other. That said, she knew if her father had lived he would have matured into a rather handsome man. And at fifty-five, her uncle was definitely that, with a charm and charisma that should be patented. Ethan had told her about the close relationship he had with his niece, and she had fully understood because such a relationship existed between her and her uncle.

"And what honor has been bestowed upon me for this visit?" he asked, leaning back and scanning her from head to toe. "Hmm, I don't see anything broken or in need of repair, although I still keep plenty of bandages around."

Rachel could only laugh. While growing up she had been a handful, a tomboy in her earlier years. And anytime she got hurt, she would run to her uncle to fix her boo-boo.

"C'mon, Uncle Jacob, it's not like I never come to visit," she defended herself, laughing.

"No, but since you've moved to the other side of town we barely see you these days."

Rachel nibbled on her bottom lip. In addition to the enormous mansion her aunt and uncle owned in Beverly Hills, they also had this place, a luxurious oceanfront hideaway on Malibu Beach. A few months ago she had purchased a condo in the gated community of Friar Gate that was located on the outskirts of Hollywood. Before moving, she had lived in a condo that had been within walking distance of Rodeo Drive. It was fine until one of the Jonas Brothers had moved into the complex. There was no peace with the paparazzi, and she'd figured it was just a matter of time before they added others to their list to harass.

"I needed more space," she said and knew her uncle would understand. It was no secret she didn't like being in the spotlight.

He nodded. "And when will I get invited to your new place for dinner?"

She threw her head back and laughed again, knowing that was a joke since she didn't cook. The few times she'd tried, she had made a complete mess of things and decided there were too many restaurants serving good, tasty food to put herself through the agony of following some recipe.

"Just as soon as I get everything in its proper place. I still have a few boxes left to unpack, but I've been so busy on the set. And then there's that painting I want to finish before the gallery hosts that charity event next month."

"I understand," Jacob Wellesley said, leading her to the nearest sofa so they could sit down. "You are a very busy lady, just like your mother was. We would try and convince her there were but so many hours in the day, but she was always determined to stretch them anyway."

Rachel couldn't help but smile. She always liked hearing the stories her uncle and aunt would share about her parents.

"And how are things going for you at work? Frasier isn't working you too hard, is he?" he asked.

Frasier Glenn was not only an old friend of her father's but he'd been close to her uncle as well and had been one of Limelight's first clients. When she'd interviewed for the position of makeup artist and wardrobe designer for *Paging the Doctor,* Frasier had been up-front and let her know it was her own merit and work ethic, not the long-standing friendship he had with her family, that had gotten her the job. She had appreciated that.

"No, both Frasier and John are wonderful, and I'm learning so much from them," she said, leaning back against the sofa's cushions.

"Good. I understand Eric Woods's contract didn't get renewed."

"No, but we were expecting it with his behavior last season. I hear he's mouthing off to the tabloids that he had no idea he was getting the ax."

Jacob shook his head. "Oh, I'm sure he knew. Frasier doesn't work that way. When he makes a decision to let you go, you know why. Eric's just trying to save face. Everyone in the industry knows his last few movies bombed out, and because of his temperament, it's hard to find a director in Hollywood with the patience to take him on."

Rachel nodded. "This season is going to have a new

twist. They brought in a new doctor and I think his appearance will boost ratings."

"Really? Who is he?"

"Ethan Chambers."

A slow smile touched Uncle Jacob's lips. "I've never met Chambers but I've heard of him. Word's out that he's an actor who's going places. He received good reviews from the guest spot he did on CSI that one time last year. And there was that rumor earlier this year that he was being considered for *People*'s Sexiest Man of the Year. That didn't hurt. There hasn't been an African American male to get that honor since Denzel and that was close to fifteen years ago."

Rachel could see Ethan being considered. He was definitely a hot contender in her book.

"And how is Chambers working out?"

"I think he's doing a great job. It is difficult, though, to get the females on the set to concentrate on what they are supposed to do instead of on him. He has a way of grabbing your attention and holding it."

"Mmm, does he now?"

She smiled, knowing what her uncle was probably thinking. "Okay, I admit he's hot, but I'm beyond fawning over any man, Uncle Jacob. Besides, Ethan Chambers comes with something I could never tolerate."

Jacob Wellesley lifted a thick brow. "What?"

"The spotlight."

Later that night, after spending time in front of the canvas for a good part of the evening, Rachel's phone rang. She reached out and picked it up without checking caller ID, thinking it was either Charlene or Sofia.

"Hello?"

"Save me."

She blinked upon hearing the sound of the ultrasexy, masculine voice. "Ethan?"

"Yes, it's me."

She was surprised. They had known each other for two weeks now, considered themselves friends and had even exchanged phone numbers one day on the set, but he'd never called her before and she'd never had a reason to call him. And what was his reason for calling her now? Had he said something about saving him?

"What on earth is going on with you?" she asked, putting him on speakerphone while she dried her hands.

"I need a place to crash for the night. I came home and found the place swarming with paparazzi. Luckily they didn't see me, and I made a U-turn and headed in another direction. So, will you have pity on me and put me up for the night?"

She tossed the hand towel aside as she leaned against the kitchen counter. "Ethan, you know how I detest being—"

"In the spotlight. Yes, I know," he said interrupting her. "And that's the reason I hesitated calling you, but I need this favor, Rachel. I've been driving around for a few hours now and have periodically checked my rearview mirror to make sure no one is following me. They're probably still parked out front waiting for me to come home. They wouldn't think of looking for me at your place."

That was an understatement, Rachel thought. They probably figured he was somewhere warming some starlet's bed. He was single, sexy and a man who probably had needs that any woman would love filling. In that case, why couldn't he go back to his lady friend's place instead of putting her privacy at risk?

She began nibbling on her bottom lip. Tomorrow was Sunday and they were due back on the set Monday morning at eight. All she needed was for someone to get wind that Ethan had stayed overnight at her place, no matter how innocent it might be, and make a big deal of it.

Everyone on the set knew the two of them had become friends, but no one thought anything of it since she was friendly with just about everyone…except for Paige, who still had her panties in a wad for some reason. Besides, no one would assume something was going on between them because she wasn't the type of woman Ethan would be interested in. She was definitely not model material.

But still, she didn't want anyone assuming anything or, even worse, the paparazzi hunting him down at her place. Jeez, she didn't want to even think of that happening. One good thing was that she had a two-car garage, so his car wouldn't be seen parked in front of her place. And her gated community was known for its privacy and security.

"Rachel?"

She drew in a deep breath. "Fine, but if anyone from the media gets wind of this and starts harassing me, Ethan, you're dead meat."

She heard him laugh. "I don't want to be dead meat, Rachel."

She folded her arms across her chest and tapped her foot. "Well?"

"All right, I'll take my chances."

"With the paparazzi?"

"Heck no," he said. "I'll take my chances with you. I'm hoping our budding friendship will keep you from actually killing me. Besides, I've been around you enough to know that you do have a soft heart."

She either had a soft heart or a foolish mind, Rachel thought an hour later when she opened her door to Ethan. She also had a bunch of erratic hormones. The tingle started in the pit of her stomach when she looked at him, and it took a full minute to catch her breath. Not only did Ethan look good but he smelled good enough to eat.

She was caught off guard by her reaction to him. They'd agreed to just be friends, but at the moment friendship was the last thing on her mind. She couldn't stop her gaze from roaming all over him. He was leaning in the doorway in a sexy stance, wearing jeans and a button-down shirt with the top four buttons undone. She glimpsed his chest beneath, poking out like a temptation being dangled in front of her. If this was the way he showed up at his woman's home, no wonder he was in such high demand. And no wonder a rush of adrenaline jolted through her.

"And you're sure you weren't followed?" she asked, taking a step back to let him in. She figured conversation between them would distract her long enough to get her mind and body back under control.

He gave her a wry smile as he entered, moving over the threshold and filling the room the same way he'd filled the doorway...with dominating sexiness. "I'm positive. I drove around an additional twenty minutes or so to be sure. Those were good directions you gave me, by the way. I found this place without any trouble."

She nodded as she closed the door. That was when

she noticed the shopping bag in his hand. When she gave him a questioning look, he said, "I made a pit stop at a store to pick up a few toiletries."

"And you weren't recognized?" she asked, moving away from the door.

"No. I had my disguise on," he said, pulling a baseball cap and a fake mustache out of the pocket of his jacket.

Rachel lifted a brow while fighting back a smile. "That's the best you can do?"

He gave her a flirty smile. "Depends on what we're talking about."

He was flirting with her.

On a few occasions over the last couple of weeks, he'd turned on the charm and flashed his devilish smile that lit up his blue-gray eyes. But she'd just rolled her eyes at him. Tonight was different. Tonight she couldn't help her body's reaction to his flirting.

As much for herself as for him, she said, "We're talking about your disguise, Ethan."

"Oh." He glanced down at the items he held in his hand. "There's nothing wrong with my disguise. It served its purpose."

With a suddenly sweaty palm, she pushed her hair behind her ear and met his gaze. "We can only hope."

Then he flashed that devilish grin that she'd tried so hard to avoid. And something slammed into her. Awareness. Attraction.

Uh-oh, said the one remaining rational part of her brain. *You've made a big mistake.*

She had to agree. Letting Ethan stay overnight just might be the biggest mistake she'd ever made.

Chapter 7

Ethan gave Rachel a hot look because there wasn't any other type of look he could give her. He was totally taken with seeing her again. Had it been just yesterday when they'd last seen each other? Just yesterday when he had been alone with her in her trailer, reclining in the chair while she applied his makeup?

She had leaned over him and her scent had almost driven him crazy. They had agreed to be just friends, and God knows he'd tried keeping his desires under control with her on the set. But at night, alone in his bed, his dreams had been another matter. She was his friend by day and his dream lover at night. And the things that went on inside those dreams were enough to make a man stiff just thinking about them.

No woman had ever dominated his thoughts like she had.

As he'd told her, he had driven around a couple of hours before finally deciding to call her. There were a number of women he could have called, but she was the one he knew he could contact and not worry about anything getting leaked to the tabloids. But now he had to be honest with himself and admit the real reason he had sought her out. He had wanted to see her.

He pulled in a deep breath, and instead of standing there staring at her like she was a nice juicy steak he couldn't wait to eat, he glanced around, needing a distraction as much as he needed a cold beer. He saw several boxes and then recalled her saying she'd only been living in this place a few months. Obviously she hadn't finished unpacking yet. But it was a nice place, large and spacious and her choice of furnishings hit the mark. "Your place is tight, Rachel."

"Thanks. You want to see the bedroom?"

At his raised brow, she said, "I mean the one you'll use tonight. The guestroom."

He'd known what she meant but thought she looked cute when she blushed. He liked seeing her get all flustered. "Sure. But you didn't ask if I wanted something to drink, and I'm thirsty."

She rolled her eyes. "Are you going to be a pesky houseguest?"

"I'll try hard not to be but I do have another confession to make. I'm hungry, too."

Rachel shook her head, chuckling. "Then you're at the wrong place. I can give you something to drink, but for a meal you're out of luck."

"Why is that?"

"I can't cook, and before you ask, my aunt and uncle

always had live-in cooks and I never had a desire to learn."

He chuckled. "No problem. I know my way around a kitchen."

She laughed. "That's all nice but there's still a problem."

"What?" he asked.

"I don't have any groceries."

He lifted a brow. "Nothing?"

"Well, my best friend did feel sorry for my refrigerator and went to the store last week and picked up a few items like eggs, butter and bread. The basics."

A smile touched his lips. "That's all I need. Just lead me to your kitchen."

"That was simply amazing," Rachel said, leaning back in her chair. "If I hadn't seen it, I would not have believed it."

Ethan leaned back in his chair as well and laughed. "It was just an egg sandwich on toast, Rachel. No big deal."

"Hey, I beg to differ. I never got the hang of cooking an egg. Or anything else for that matter."

"Why would your friend buy eggs if you can't cook them?" he asked, taking a swig of his beer. He'd found several bottles behind all the art supplies she kept in her refrigerator.

"They can be boiled, you know," she said, taking a sip of her own beer, right from the bottle. "And I know it was just a sandwich but it was still good. I hadn't realized I'd gotten hungry."

"Hadn't you eaten dinner?" he asked, getting up and grabbing their plates off the table. They had used paper plates and plastic utensils so all they had to do was trash them. No dishes to wash. How convenient. That had been a good idea on her part.

"I had lunch with my aunt and uncle earlier in the day and when I got home, I started painting and lost track of the time." She got up from the table as well. "If you hadn't called, I probably would have ordered out for a pizza or something eventually."

He watched her stride across the floor to the sink to rinse out her beer bottle before tossing it into a recycle bin. She was wearing a pair of shorts and a top and looked pretty in them. He glanced down and thought she even had cute bare feet with polished toes.

"My uncle knows you or at least he's heard of you," she said, causing him to shift his gaze to her face. "He was very complimentary."

"Was he?"

"Yes. He believes you're a person who's going places."

A broad smile touched his lips. "That means a lot coming from the likes of Jacob Wellesley," he said before finishing off his beer.

He joined her at the sink and she slid over to give him room when he proceeded to rinse out his own beer bottle. She smelled good, he thought, pulling in a whiff of her scent through his nostrils. She smelled better than good. She smelled like a woman he wanted.

He smiled over at her and she glared at him. "What's wrong?" he asked, moving to place the beer bottle in the recycle bin. "I assured you that no one followed me over here."

"That's not what's bothering me, Ethan."

He leaned back against the sink. "Then what is bothering you, Rachel?" He had an idea but wanted her to tell him.

She had moved back to the table and stood with her arms crossed over her chest. "I think we need to reiterate a few things, like the fact that two weeks ago we decided to be friends and nothing more."

"I thought we were."

"I thought so, too," she replied. "But…"

He lifted a brow and tried looking baffled. "But what?"

"I'm getting these vibes."

"Really? What kind of vibes?"

When she didn't say anything, he crossed the room to her. "Rachel, just what kind of vibes are you getting?"

He was staring at her and those gorgeous eyes of his were probably seeing a lot more than she wanted them to. A lot more than she needed them to see. And that put her on the defensive.

"None. Forget I said that," she said.

"Not sure I can do that now," he said, eyeing her up and down the way he'd done the first day they'd met. Before they'd decided all they wanted between them was friendship. Her mind scrambled as she tried to recall that day. It had been his second day on the set. Had it really been two weeks ago already? They had walked to the Disney Store and Art World. He had purchased a Princess Tiana doll for his niece, and she had picked up some art supplies.

They'd both agreed they were not involved in serious relationships and wanted to keep things that way. Besides, she had painstakingly explained to him that she didn't mix business with pleasure. He had understood and said the same rule applied to him. That should have settled things...so why didn't it?

Why was he looking at her now in a way that made her so aware of her sensuality while at the same time reminded her that it had been a long time since she'd been with a man? Nearly two years, to be exact, and even then it hadn't been anything to brag about.

"You have no choice, Ethan," she heard herself say.

"I don't?"

At the shake of her head, he said, "And what if I told you I'm getting those same vibes, and that if we don't at least share a kiss, there will always be curiosity between us?"

Heat circled around in her stomach at his admission and his suggestion. "Maybe for you, but not for me," she said, lifting her chin.

He took a step closer. "And you want me to believe that you aren't curious?"

Of course she was curious. What woman wouldn't be when there were lips that looked like his? "No, not in the least," she lied while looking him straight in the eye.

Unfortunately, those eyes were staring right back at her, as if seeing straight into her. Heat crawled all over her skin and her heart thumped faster. And when the corners of his mouth eased into a sexy smile, she inhaled sharply.

She broke eye contact with him, not liking the look on his face. It was taunting her and tempting her, all at the same time. She nervously licked her tongue across her top lip as a sudden case of panic gripped her.

God, how he'd love to try out that tongue.

Thrumming heat raced through his gut. Funny the

difference a couple of weeks could make. His first days on the set, he was ready to push everything aside to focus on his role on *Paging the Doctor*. But now that he felt comfortable playing Dr. Tyrell Perry, he no longer went to bed with his lines infused into his brain. Instead something else—or should he say someone else—occupied his thoughts. And that person was standing right in front of him.

"You know what I think, Ethan?" she asked, interrupting his thoughts.

"No, what do you think?"

"You being here, claiming you needed a place to crash for the night, is part of some manipulating scheme." He could hear the sharpness in her tone and could see the fire in her eyes.

"Not true. I called you for the reason I told you. I didn't have anyone else to call."

"C'mon, Ethan. Do you honestly expect me to believe that? Of all the women you've been linked to, do you really assume I'm that gullible enough to think none of them would have let you stay overnight at their place?"

"I imagine one of them would." He paused a moment and then said, "Let me rephrase what I said earlier. There are others I *could* have called but you are the only one I *wanted* to call." Boy, if only she knew how true that was.

She got silent and he knew she was thinking, trying to make heads or tails of what he'd said. Then she simply asked, "Why, Ethan? Why was I the only one you wanted to call?"

He saw the frustrated expression on her face. But it was what he saw in her eyes that captivated him. Desire.

Although she might wish it wasn't there, it was and it was just as deep as what he was feeling.

But Rachel was a logical person who would not accept anything less than a logical and straightforward answer, so he said, "Because you are the only one I want."

Chapter 8

Speechless, Rachel could only stare at him while all the sexual desires she'd had for him since day one came tumbling back. Why was he trying to make things so difficult? Why was he forcing her to admit the one thing she had tried to deny? She was attracted to him something awful.

It would be so easy to let her guard down and walk across the room, wrap her arms around his neck and give in to temptation and indulge in a heated kiss. A kiss that would probably curl her toes and then some.

But she had to think logically. He threatened something she couldn't risk losing—her privacy. Any woman he was involved with would become just as much news as he was. The paparazzi would make sure of that. He was a man who spent his life, both personal and otherwise, in front of the camera, a place she tried to avoid.

She shook her head. Things were going all wrong. They had decided they wouldn't go down this road, so why were they? They were friends and that's all they would ever be. He knew it and she knew it, as well. If he refused to do what was best, then she would.

Rachel backed up and nervously tugged at the hem of her T-shirt. "C'mon, let me show you where you'll sleep tonight. I think you'll like this room since it has its own private bath."

He held her gaze and, for a moment, she felt a weakening she didn't want to feel. Those eyes were the reason and she understood what was happening. Ethan had invaded her space, both mentally and creatively. And she couldn't deal with it.

Instead of saying anything else, she walked off and drew in a deep breath when she heard him falling in step behind her.

Walking behind her had its advantages, Ethan thought, watching the sway of Rachel's curvy hips and the lushness of her backside in her shorts. She probably hadn't figured out yet that he was enjoying the back view, and it was just as well since he definitely needed to think.

Contrary to what she thought, when he had shown up tonight it hadn't been with the intent of jumping her bones, although he found such a possibility a very enticing prospect.

He followed her up the stairs and once they reached the landing, he glanced around. The second floor was just as large and spacious as the first. There were a number of hung paintings and he couldn't help but admire them.

"Are these your creations?" he asked when she turned around after noticing he had slowed down.

She followed his gaze from wall to wall and smiled. "Some of them." She pointed out those that were. "The others are my mother's. She was a successful painter. A few of her pieces are on display at the L.A. Museum and various others."

"They're all beautiful. You inherited her gift and it shows in your work."

"Thanks."

They began walking again and as before, he followed. When she paused by a door he moved ahead and glanced inside. It was a huge room with a small bed. But it was a bed and tonight he wasn't picky, although he would much prefer hers.

"This is it," she said, entering the room. "The bath is to your left and there are plenty of towels and washcloths. Everything you need for your overnight stay."

He didn't miss her emphasis on "overnight." She intended for him to be gone in the morning. "Thanks, I appreciate it, and no matter what you think, Rachel, I didn't have an ulterior motive for coming here tonight."

Instead of saying she believed him like he'd hoped, she merely nodded, turned and walked away. Instinctively, his gaze went to her backside, and a sizzling heat began building inside of him. Hell, he was a man and tonight he was reminded of just how horny he was.

A few hours later, Rachel curled up in her favorite spot in her king-size bed. Ethan had been in her home only a few hours and already her house smelled of man. And as much as she hated admitting it, she liked the scent.

She couldn't help but notice it after rechecking the doors for the night and walking up the stairs to get ready for bed. She had heard the sound of the shower and the fragrance of his aftershave had floated through the air. Immediately, tremors of desire had rippled through her, and upon reaching the landing she had quickly hurried to her room and closed the door.

While getting dressed for bed, she had heard him moving around. The sound of someone else in her house felt strange because other than Charlene or Sofia, she rarely had houseguests.

All was quiet, so she could only assume Ethan had settled in for the night. That was just great. He was probably sleeping like a baby, and here she was, wide awake and thinking about him and the fact that he'd wanted to kiss her. She could now admit to herself— although she would never admit such a thing to him— that she had wanted to kiss him as well and that she *was* curious. However, being curious wouldn't benefit either one of them. It would serve no purpose.

Yes, it would...if it didn't lead anywhere.

Rachel rolled her eyes. *Not lead anywhere? Yeah, right.* There was no doubt in her mind that kissing Ethan would probably lead right here to her bedroom. And they had agreed to be nothing more than friends, she reminded herself.

But since he seemed quick to break the rules, why couldn't she break a few of her own? As long as the kiss and anything that followed after the kiss was all there could ever be and they knew where they stood with each other, would it really hurt for them to indulge in something that her body was telling her she both needed and wanted?

Her ears perked up when she heard the sound of Ethan moving around. A smile touched her lips. It was two in the morning and she felt grateful he couldn't sleep any more than she could.

She sat up in bed when she heard his bedroom door opening and then picked up the sound of him going downstairs. Being hungry at this hour would serve him no purpose since she didn't have any food in the house, unless he was planning to make another egg sandwich.

Before she could get cold feet, she eased out of bed, deciding if a kiss was what he wanted, then a kiss was what he was going to get.

With a deep sigh, Ethan closed the refrigerator door after pulling out a bottle of beer. He was hot and needed to cool off. He'd tried to get some sleep only to be awakened with dreams of him and Rachel together in some of the most explicit sexual positions possible. If those dreams kept coming, they could possibly ruin him for future relationships—at least until he discovered how close his dreams were to the real thing.

After screwing off the beer bottle top, he took a huge swig, appreciating how the cold liquid flowed down his throat and hoping some would keep moving straight to his groin.

"I see you couldn't sleep either."

Ethan spun around. Rachel was the last person he expected to see. After showing him the guest room, she had made herself scarce, basically hiding out in her bedroom.

She crossed the room toward the coffeepot, and he wished he could ignore the tantalizing view of her bare legs and curvy backside in a pajama set that consisted of clingy shorts and a spaghetti strap tank top.

"No, I couldn't sleep," he answered, before taking a final swig of beer while wishing it had been something stronger.

"Why?"

He looked over at her after placing his empty beer bottle on the counter. "Why what?"

"Why couldn't you sleep?" Her expression grew troubled, showed her concern. "Isn't the bed comfortable enough?"

For a moment he thought about telling her the real deal, then decided she probably couldn't handle it if he did. "The bed is fine."

"Then what's your problem?"

He crossed his arms over his chest. "What's yours?"

Ethan hadn't meant for his tone to sound so gruff. Nor had he meant for his eyes to shift from her face to slide down to her thighs. But they did. Heat settled in his gut before he returned his gaze to her face. Just in time to see the corners of her lips lift in a wry smile. "Something amusing, Rachel?"

"You tell me." She began walking toward him and her scent—lush, exotic, jasmine and womanly—preceded her. He watched her as a sharp, tingling hunger swept through his groin, and suddenly, memories of the dream that had awakened him had his skin feeling like it was being licked with tongues of fire.

He never took her for a tease and hoped that wasn't her intent because he was not in a teasing mood. It wouldn't take much to push him over the edge right now. When she came to a stop directly in front of him, he inhaled and filled his lungs with her scent. And his testosterone level shot sky-high.

"Remember earlier when you asked me about those vibes, Ethan?" she asked.

"I remember," he said while thinking her mouth was almost too luscious for any woman's face.

"Well…"

He refused to let her get all nervous on him now. "Well what, Rachel?"

Ethan watched her take a long, slow breath. "You were right about that curiosity thing."

He didn't intend to make it easy for her. "What curiosity thing is that?"

She cleared her throat. "That curiosity thing about kissing."

He nodded slowly. "So are you admitting to being curious?"

"Umm, just a little," she said.

He went silent, deciding to let her think about what she'd said and, more importantly, what she planned to do about it.

Standing there facing Ethan, not all in his face but probably less than two feet away, Rachel concluded she had never felt anything close to the stomach-churning heat that had taken over the lower part of her body. It didn't help matters that he was shirtless with his jeans riding low on his hips. His muscular physique dominated her kitchen and reminded her that she was very much alone with a very sexy man.

And apparently he was a man who didn't forget anything, especially her evasiveness from earlier when she'd refused to elaborate on these vibes she was sensing. She was smart enough to know Ethan had no intention of letting her off the hook and was making her work for anything she got. That was fine with her, since she'd always considered herself a working girl.

He was a man who knew women. So he had to know she wanted him to kiss her. She hadn't been ready earlier tonight and hadn't been accepting. Now she was both ready and accepting. Nothing would change between them with one kiss. She was convinced of that now. Why would it? She wasn't his type and he definitely wasn't hers. Sharing a kiss wouldn't produce a marriage license or any document that said they would have to take things further than that. Monday, on the set, they would go back to being just friends. Nothing more. Nothing less.

"You think too damn hard."

She blinked upon hearing Ethan's blunt words and had to agree that she did think too hard. But then she'd always been the type of person to weigh the pros and cons before she acted. This was one of those times she had to really consider whether the pros outweighed the cons.

She quickly concluded that they did.

A smile touched her mouth when she took a couple steps closer to him, fascinated by the blue-gray eyes watching her. Now she *was* all in his face and decided it was time to do something about it. Granted, she wasn't the typical kind of woman he became involved with; however, she intended to show him that good things could come in small packages. With a pounding heart, she stood on tiptoe, reached out and placed her arms around his neck.

"Now, are we in accord?" Ethan asked, placing his

hands at her waist, drawing her closer and lowering his mouth toward hers, hovering mere inches from her lips.

She drew in a deep, unsteady breath, barely able to contain the heated passion taking over her body, filling her with all kinds of sensations. She had never responded to a man this way. Had never been this affected and bold. "Yes, we're in accord."

Fueled by a degree of desire she'd never felt before, she leaned farther up on tiptoes and whispered against his lips, "So, let's go for broke."

Chapter 9

Nothing could have prepared Ethan for the need that took over his body at that moment. Unable to hold back, he captured her mouth with a possession that fueled his fire in a way it had never been with another woman. He wanted to devour Rachel alive.

A part of him couldn't believe that she was in his arms and that he was taking her mouth like it was the only feminine one left on earth. For now, for him, it was.

For some reason, he couldn't control the rush of physical hunger consuming him. His tongue tangled with hers with a voracity that sent pleasure spiking throughout his body. He was kissing her hungrily, as if he was seeking out some forbidden treat and was determined to find it.

Moments later, only because they needed to breathe, he released her mouth and stared into her stunned gaze.

Refusing to allow her time to think again, he lowered his mouth once more and at the same time, he swept her off her feet and into his arms. Before the night was over, his touch would be imprinted on every inch of her skin.

Somehow he managed to get them up the stairs. Upon reaching the landing, he moved quickly toward her bedroom. She wanted to get it on and he was determined not to let anything stop them. Though he had wanted her from the first moment he'd laid eyes on her, he'd thought he would be satisfied with them just being friends. Well, he'd been proven wrong.

The moment he placed her on the bed, he joined her there, wanting to keep her in his arms, needing his lips to remain plastered to hers with his tongue inside her mouth and doing things so wicked it made his skin shiver. The kiss really had gotten ridiculously out of hand because never in his life had he been so damn greedy. So hard up to make love to a woman.

In an unexpected move, she pulled back, breaking off the kiss and drawing in a ragged breath. Her gaze latched on to the mouth that had just thoroughly kissed her, and he felt his rod pulsate when she took her tongue, that same tongue he'd tried to devour, and licked her top lip before saying, "I think we should get out of our clothes, Ethan."

He couldn't help but smile as he pulled up on his haunches. "I think you're right." He moved away from the bed to pull the jeans down his legs while flames of desire tore through him. He pulled a condom pack out of his wallet and ripped it open with his teeth. Sheathing his aroused member was an exercise in torture.

Without wasting any time, he returned to her. With a ravenous growl and a need he didn't want to question, he reached out and began removing the clothes from her body. The moment she was completely naked, the lusciousness of her feminine scent filled his nostrils and further stimulated every nerve in his body, making his protruding erection that much harder. He intended to stake a claim on every inch of her body. Beginning now.

He lowered his head and captured her mouth at the same time his hands reached around and began caressing her back and pulling her closer to the fit of him, his hard arousal pressing into her stomach.

He broke off the kiss and his mouth trailed lower, planting kisses over the soft swell of her breasts before taking a nipple into his mouth and sucking it with an intensity that made her groan.

Without losing contact with her nipple, he tilted his head and gazed up at her, saw the heated desire flaming her pupils. Returning his attention to her breasts he began kneading the other while continuing to torment the one in his mouth. He liked the feel and the taste of her and realized his desire for her was intrinsically raw.

"Ethan…"

He liked the sound of his name from her lips, and his erection throbbed mercilessly in response. "Tell me what you want, Rachel," he coaxed softly, planting kisses across her chest while his hands remained on her breasts. "Tell me what you like."

When she didn't say anything but let out a tortured groan, he blew his breath across a moist nipple. "You like that?"

She didn't hesitate, responding, "Yes."

"What about this?" he rasped in her ear before shifting, letting his wet, hot and greedy mouth slide down her body. She arched her hips the moment his mouth settled between her legs, and he could taste the honeyed sweetness of her desire on his tongue.

Her eyes were closed, her breathing was heavy. He knew she was feeling every bit of what his mouth was doing to her. With his hands he widened the opening of her legs as her taste consumed him and made him want to delve deeper into her womanly core. Her unique and sensuous flavor drove him to sample as much of her as he could get.

But he wanted to do more than that. He wouldn't be satisfied until he shattered her control the same way she had shattered his.

When he felt her body tremble beneath his mouth, he released her and pulled his body up and then over hers, easing between her legs and caging her hips with the firmness of his thighs just moments before thrusting into her. The force alone made her scream out her orgasm mere seconds before he released his.

A pulsing and fiery explosion rocked his body, which subsequently rocked hers. He leaned down and captured her mouth and knew what it felt to truly want a woman in every sense of the word.

Next time around they would go slow. And there would be a next time. He would make sure of it.

An aftermath of sensations consumed Rachel as she lay there, unable to move. Ethan excused himself to go to the bathroom, and she could barely nod in acknowledgment of what he'd said. Nor did she have the strength to turn over off her stomach and onto her back. She felt completely drained. And it wasn't because it was her first orgasm in two years. It was all about the man who'd given it to her.

Moments later, she heard him return and opened her eyes, only to see his naked body walking out of the bathroom. The dim light from the bedside lamp didn't miss his engorged erection. How could he be hard again so soon when she could barely catch her breath? And she couldn't help noticing he had on another condom. He couldn't possibly assume she had strength for another round.

The bed dipped beneath his weight as he slid in next to her. His hands began gently caressing the center of her back and the rounded curves of her buttocks. She closed her eyes again, enjoying the feel of being touched by him. When he replaced his fingers with the tip of his tongue and licked up and down her spine, a moan of pleasure escaped her lips.

Now she understood how desire could get stirred all over again so soon and gave herself up to the pure joy of it in his hands and mouth. She drew in a deep breath and then breathed out slowly, reveling in the passion building in every part of her body. It was a primitive force she didn't want to yield to again so quickly. She wanted to prolong the enjoyment.

"Turn over, baby."

She pulled in another deep breath and whispered, "Can't. Too weak."

"Then let me help you."

She heard his soft chuckle moments before he gently eased her onto her back. She stared up into his gaze, and the look in his eyes stroked something she hadn't counted on—intense desire even in her weakened state. Desire she couldn't resist or deny. She'd never wanted a man this much, so this was a first for her. And when he leaned down and claimed her mouth in a way no man had ever done before, a shiver of intense heat rode up her spine, renewing energy she didn't think she had. Her heart began pounding in her chest. At the same time, her body started shuddering with sensations she felt all the way to her toes.

With a burst of vigor that was rejuvenating every part of her, she lifted her arms and wrapped them around his neck while his mouth continued to mate with hers in a kiss that progressed from hot to scalding with a stroke of his tongue.

When he finally released her mouth it was only to shift his body between her thighs. She moaned, knowing he was about to soothe the ache at the juncture of her legs.

He reached out, cupped her bottom, lifted her hips and thrust deep inside of her. For a moment he didn't move. It was as if he needed to savor the feel of his erection planted so profoundly inside of her, pulsing, thickening and growing even larger while her inner muscles clamped down on him tightly.

Then, finally, he began moving in and out at a rhythm and pace that had every cell in her body humming, trembling and shuddering in pleasure. The muscles in his shoulders bunched beneath her fingers when he lowered his head to breathe against her mouth. Her breath hitched in her throat and then her lungs cleared in a precipitated slam.

"Ethan…"

He tasted her lips with his tongue as he drove into her. His hard thrusts made her bed shake, the springs squeak and the headboard hit against the wall. Not only was he drawing out a need and desire within her, he was fulfilling it to a degree that had her meeting him, thrust for thrust.

With one final thrust into the depth of her, her body spun into an orgasm of gigantic proportion. As she reveled in her climax, he kissed her with an intensity that elicited moans from deep in her throat.

At that moment, there was only one thing she could think of. So much for them being just friends.

Ethan eased from the bed and slipped into his jeans. Once he had snapped them up, he glanced back over his shoulder at the woman asleep in the bed. Never had any one woman touched him the way she had, in and out of bed.

And that was the crux of his problem.

He pulled in a deep breath and leaned down to brush a kiss against her temple and then quickly pulled away when he breathed in the scent of her, which had the power to render him helpless.

He rubbed a hand down his face. What the hell had he gotten himself into? Rachel had made it clear, exceedingly so and on more than one occasion, that she had no intention of getting involved with anyone she considered to be in the spotlight, anyone who would put the media on her tail. If she became involved with him, she ran the risk of that happening. He knew if there was any ounce of decency within him, he would grab his stuff and leave and when he saw her tomorrow he would pretend last night never happened.

Easier said than done.

He couldn't do that.

Something was forcing him to not only acknowledge

that it happened but to do whatever he could to make sure it happened again.

He shook his head in dismay as he left the bedroom, closing the door behind him. Wasn't it just a little over two weeks ago that he'd made the vow to focus on his career more than anything else, certainly more than any woman? But there was something about Rachel that called out to him at every turn.

He had gone back into the bedroom he should have been occupying to freshen up when his cell phone on the nightstand rang. He released a deep, annoyed breath when the caller ID indicated it was his agent.

"Yes, Curtis?"

"Ethan, where are you?"

He rolled his eyes. "Is there something you need, Curtis?"

"The paparazzi can't find you."

"That's too bad," he murmured with agitation clearly in his voice. "And how did you know they were looking for me?"

His agent paused a second before saying. "It's my job to know everything that's going on with you."

Ethan frowned. Was Curtis somehow responsible for the media hounds hanging around outside of his house last night? It wouldn't surprise Ethan, since his agent liked keeping him in the news. In the spotlight, as Rachel termed it. The thought that Curtis could be connected didn't sit well with him. "Your job is to advance my career, not fabricate lies about me and my love life."

"It's never bothered you before," his agent countered.

The man was right. It hadn't bothered him before.

"It does now, and it would behoove you to remember that. Talk to you later, Curtis."

Ethan then disconnected the call.

The sound of a ringing telephone worked its way into the deep recesses of Rachel's sleep-shrouded mind. Without lifting her head from the pillow, she reached out and grabbed her cell phone off the bedside table. "Hello," she said in a drowsy voice.

"I can't believe you're still in bed."

Rachel forced one eye open upon hearing her sister's voice. "What time is it?"

"Almost noon. You weren't at church today, and Aunt Lily wanted to make sure you were okay since it's not like you to miss service."

Rachel moaned, which was followed by a deep yawn. "I'm fine, Sofia." *Am I really?* "I overslept." That wasn't a lie.

She slowly pulled herself up in bed, surprised she had the energy to do so. Taking part in lovemaking marathons wasn't something she did often, and thanks to Ethan, her muscles had gotten one heck of a workout.

Ethan...

She glanced at the rumpled spot beside her in the bed. It hadn't been a figment of her imagination. He had been there. His masculine scent was still in her bedcovers. And she could hear him moving around downstairs, which meant he was still there.

She closed her eyes as memories of their lovemaking flowed through her mind. There were the memories of his hands all over her body, his tongue licking her nipple, his head between her legs, his—

"Rachel?"

She snapped her eyes back open. "Yes?"

"I asked if you wanted to do a movie later."

Sofia was a workaholic and any other time Rachel would have jumped at the chance to do something fun with her sister, but not today. But she knew better than to tell her sister the real reason. "Can I get a rain check? I want to finish this painting so it can be ready for the gallery's opening day."

"Sure, just let me know when."

They talked for a few more minutes and then Sofia had to take another call. Rachel disconnected the call and stretched her body in bed, thinking that as much as she had enjoyed making love with Ethan, it couldn't happen again.

She eased out of bed, knowing they needed to talk.

Few people knew that cooking was one of Ethan's favorite pastimes, so he wasn't taken aback by the look of surprise on Rachel's face when she walked into her kitchen. Her sexy-pixie expression was priceless.

Something else that was priceless was the way she was dressed. She had showered and was wearing a printed sundress with spaghetti straps at the shoulders and a cute pair of sandals on her feet. On anyone else the simple outfit would have been so-so, but not on her. It gave her an "at-home" look that couldn't be captured any day on the set.

There were a number of reasons for him to make that conclusion. Heading the list was the fact that this was the first time he'd seen her out of bed since they'd made love, so in his book she could have worn a gunnysack and she still would have looked good to him.

"Ethan, what are you doing?" she asked, glancing around her kitchen.

"I'm preparing brunch. I figured you'd be hungry when you finally woke up." He didn't have to say why he'd expected her to sleep late. Last night had been quite a night for them. He doubted either of them had gotten a full hour's sleep.

"But where did you find the stuff to prepare this spread?"

He smiled. "I went to that grocery store on the corner, and before you ask, no, I wasn't recognized. I wore my disguise and quickly went in and out."

"But your car..."

"I drove yours." At the lift of her brow he said, "I left a note just in case you woke up while I was gone."

"Oh." The thought of his male scent infusing the interior of her car was almost too much to think about. Now she would drive her car and think about him.

"You like cooking, I gather," she said moving across the room to the coffeepot. The coffee smelled good but she smelled even better. There was a sensuality to her fragrance that could reach him on a masculine level each and every time he took a whiff of her.

He chuckled. "You gathered right, although I didn't get an interest until college. It was a quick and easy way to get a girl up to your dorm room."

She glanced at him over her shoulder. "I'm sure getting a girl up to your room wasn't hard, Ethan."

A grin formed on his lips. "Should I take that as a compliment?"

"You should take it for whatever you want. I know it to be true. Most women would find you simply irresistible."

He tilted his head and looked at her. She was reaching up to open one of the cabinet doors, which was an almost impossible feat for her without stretching and standing on tiptoes. What flashed through his mind at that moment was a reminder of a position they had used last night when they'd made love standing up. Those same feet had been wrapped around him, locking him inside her body. "Do you find me irresistible, Rachel?"

She turned around to face him, leaning back against the kitchen counter as she did so. Her gaze roamed over him, up and down, before coming to settle on his face where she gave him her full attention. His stomach tightened at her perusal since it seemed as intimate as any physical caress could get. She pushed a few strands of hair behind her ear before a smile touched her lips. It was tantalizing in one sense but frightening in another.

"Yes, but not the same way that other women do."

Her words, spoken both seriously and honestly, had a profound effect because a part of him knew they were true. She had a way of seeing beyond what the media described as the "killer-watt" smile, past the persona of a jaw-dropping Hollywood leading man. In the two weeks they'd known each other, she'd shown him that she had the ability to get to know the real Ethan Chambers. She knew that what you saw was not always what you got.

And that made *her* irresistible.

Needing to touch her, wanting to kiss her, especially at that moment, he moved toward her and pulled her into his arms. She came willingly, without preamble, filled with all the grace and refinement that most women didn't possess. She had the ability to change the physical to the sensual the moment her lips locked with his.

She also had the intuition to know that when it came to an attraction between them, he needed more.

And more importantly, she was willing to give it.

He pulled her closer, wanting to seal every inch of space between them. She leaned up, wrapped her arms around his neck and tilted her head back automatically to meet his mouth that came swooping down on hers. He needed her in the way a man needed a woman.

A woman he was beginning to think of as his.

Nobody kisses like Ethan Chambers, Rachel concluded when she could manage to think again. She loved being held captive in his strong grip, loved being the recipient of his lusty and marauding tongue. And she loved the feel of her breasts pressed against the hard and firm lines of his chest. The same chest she had kissed every inch of last night. Even then she had felt the strength of it beneath her lips. Ethan had a body that was an artist's dream, and she would love to paint him one day, capture the essence of all his masculine beauty on canvas.

"Brunch has to wait."

Those words were barely out of his mouth before he swept her off her feet and into his arms. Once again she had managed to drive him out of control and she enjoyed every single moment of doing so. It was only last night that she had discovered her ability as a woman and the pleasure-filled places that skill could take her.

It might have been his intent to take her back to bed, but somewhere between the kitchen and living room he decided they couldn't make it that far. He headed for her sofa.

Her heart began beating rapidly because with Ethan

she had discovered you never knew what you would get, but the one thing you could expect was the most intense pleasure any man could deliver. And that knowledge caused an intense ache between her legs that only he could appease.

She caught her breath when she felt the sofa cushion touch her back, and he spread her out as if she was a sampling for his enjoyment. He would soon discover that he was also one for hers. His musky and ultrasexy scent was devouring all common sense in her body and replacing it with a spine-tingling need that had her moaning out his name.

"I'm right here, baby," he whispered while quickly removing the clothes from her body and then from his. When he stood over her naked, fully aroused and looking as handsome as any man had a right to look, she was filled with a craving that had her moving upward, launching herself at him and toppling them both to the floor.

He cushioned their fall, and they ended up with their legs entangled and her stretched out over him. Just the way she wanted. Some deep, dark emotion, an intense hunger he had tapped into last night, consumed her and she began licking him all over, starting with his broad shoulders and working her way downward.

Moving past his tight abs, she cupped his erection in her hands before lowering her head and taking him fully, needing the taste, texture and total length of him between her lips and as deep in her mouth as he could go.

"Rachel!"

His palms bracketed her head, his fingers dug into her scalp and his moan became music to her ears while she proceeded to torture him. She felt his shaft swell deep inside her mouth and she stretched to accommodate its size.

"I'm coming, baby."

And he did.

She appeased every deep craving she ever had, using her throat to prolong his orgasm. He seemed lost, powerless as he gave himself over to the magic she created. And she reveled in the control as she never had before.

When he could draw another breath, he pulled a condom pack from his jeans, sheathed himself and entered her. Quick work but thorough.

He began moving in and out of her, thrusting hard and deep, taking her to the brink where she'd led him moments ago. No matter what would come tomorrow, she knew she would have these memories of their lovemaking. Memories that would comfort her and tear at her heart long after he was no longer a part of her life.

But for now, for today, he was and because of that, she was satisfied.

It was time for him to leave.

After making love on her living room floor, they had returned to the kitchen and eaten the brunch he had prepared before going back up to her bedroom and making love some more. When they were spent, they had showered together, returned downstairs to devour the apple tarts he'd made for dessert, then he'd gone upstairs to gather his few belongings.

"Do you think the paparazzi have gone now?" she asked, walking him to the kitchen door that led to her garage where his car was parked beside hers.

"Yes. I spoke with the manager of my condo complex and she apologized profusely. The one thing I was assured of when I moved in was that my privacy would be protected. She doesn't understand what could have happened." He paused. "I think I do."

She lifted a brow. "What?"

"My agent. He thinks one of the ways to build my career is for me to stay in the spotlight, to keep my name in the news."

He could tell her mind was at work. Making that statement had made her remember her one argument as to why there could never be anything but friendship between them. For that reason, he was not surprised by her next statement.

"I refuse to think of this weekend as a mistake, Ethan, but it's something we can't allow to happen again. You are who you are and I am who I am. We live different lives and reside in basically different worlds."

"It doesn't have to be that way, Rachel."

"Yes, it does. I could never ask you to give up your dream for me, like you can't expect me to do the same for you."

He paused for a moment and then asked, "So where do we go from here?"

A sad smile touched her lips. "Nowhere. Let's chalk it up as nothing more than a one-night stand. This weekend is our secret. And it's up to us to know it was just one of those things that can't happen again."

He glanced down as if studying the floor and then he looked back at her. "What if I said I don't agree? That there has to be a way?"

A bittersweet smile touched her lips. "Then I'd say don't waste your time trying to figure one out. It doesn't exist. We are as different as day and night."

Ethan pulled in a deep breath and felt a tightening in his gut because he knew, in a way, she was right. Becoming a successful Hollywood actor was his dream, and it was a dream that didn't mesh with hers.

He leaned down and kissed her hard and deep. Only one thought pierced his mind then and again moments later when he walked out her door. How on earth was he going to give her up?

Chapter 10

"Quiet on the set!

"Take three!

"Action!"

Rachel could hear the sound of Frasier's booming voice carrying all the way into her trailer. Today they would be shooting mostly medical scenes, and several doctors from an area hospital were on the set to make sure that aspect of the show was done correctly.

She had arrived at work early, mainly to have herself together by the time Ethan got there. Like she'd told him yesterday, although she hadn't regretted any of it, their time together could not be repeated. For twenty-four hours she had let herself go and had made love to a man who had pleasured her body in ways probably not known to most men. All women should be made love to the way Ethan had done to her. Memories of their time together still made her skin hot whenever she thought about it.

When he had arrived this morning, he had not given her any more of his time and attention than he always had. There was no way anyone seeing them interact together would suspect they'd spent practically the entire weekend behind closed doors. There had been so much red-hot chemistry between them and they had taken advantage of it time and time again.

Although no one on the set had a clue, each and every time he glanced her way or gave her a smile, heat would begin simmering in the pit of her stomach. One look into Ethan's eyes had the power to send a rush of desire spiking through her. That was why she was letting Theresa work out on the set today, brushing up the actors during shooting, while she remained in her trailer applying the makeup for those in the next scene.

"You're quiet today."

Rachel blinked, remembering where she was and what she was doing. There never had been a time when thoughts of a man had interfered with her job. She looked down at Tae'Shawna Miller, the model-turned-actress from last season who played a nurse on the show. Tae'Shawna was known to be moody and self-centered and, not surprisingly, months ago she'd begun hanging around Paige.

Rachel wasn't sure what Paige might have told her, but lately Tae'Shawna had been acting even moodier where she was concerned. She'd even gone to John saying Rachel had applied her makeup too heavily last season and that she wanted to bring in her own makeup artist. John had denied her request.

"It's Monday," Rachel said, hoping that would end

things. It was a joke on the set that although Wednesday was considered hump day, Monday was pretty low-key with everyone trying to recover from the weekend.

"I hear you, girl. I could barely pull myself out of bed. If it wasn't for Ethan calling to wake me up this morning, I probably would have been late coming in today."

Trying to keep her hands steady and acting as nonchalant as she could, Rachel continued applying Tae'Shawna's makeup and asked in a casual tone, "Ethan Chambers?"

A smile touched the woman's lips. "None other. We spent some time together this weekend. I'm only mentioning this to you because I know you're the soul of discretion. Ethan would be upset if he knew I told anyone. He wants to keep things quiet since we're both working on the show."

The woman gave a naughty smile before adding, "Needless to say, I had to all but force him to leave last night."

Rachel managed to remain calm as she dissected the woman's words, hoping what Tae'Shawna was saying was more wishful thinking than gospel truth, especially since Ethan had been with *her* from Saturday night to late yesterday afternoon.

But she couldn't help wondering if he had left her bed and gone directly to Tae'Shawna's. And where had he been before coming to her place on Saturday night? She'd felt it hadn't been her place to ask. However, now the woman in her couldn't help wondering if Ethan had shared his weekend with her *and* Tae'Shawna.

That question was still on her mind hours later. For the moment, her trailer was empty and she slid into

the chair to take a breather, trying to fight the green-
eyed monster of jealousy consuming her. She pulled
in a deep breath, wondering why the thought of Ethan
being involved with Tae'Shawna bothered her and how
she could get beyond it.

The odds had been high when he'd shown up at her
place Saturday night that he would probably spend
some of his weekend with another woman. It would
have made perfect sense that he did. After all, he was a
known playboy around town. It really shouldn't concern
her since they had used protection every time they'd
made love, so she wasn't at risk. But still...

It disappointed her that, on the set, Ethan portrayed
himself as a man not giving any of the women who
came on to him the time of day. Although he was always friendly to them, she'd had no reason to assume
that things had been any different after hours. Was it
only an act? Was he involved not only with Tae'Shawna
but others as well, possibly even Paige?

She eased from the chair and began pacing. She told
herself she should not be bothered if he was also seeing other women. They hadn't set any rules or guide-
lines regarding their relationship. A frown deepened
her brow when she reminded herself they didn't have
a relationship. What happened this weekend was just
a one-time deal. She had made that clear to Ethan. But
why had he bothered to make it seem as if he hadn't
had sex for a while, certainly not that same day? Men!

She knew when it came to sex, men would get as
much of it as came their way and still want more. A
part of her couldn't help feeling somewhat disappointed
to discover he was one of those men and wasn't different at all.

"Looks like you're thinking too hard again."

She spun around to find the object of her deepest and most disappointing thoughts leaning against the trailer door. She hadn't heard him enter the trailer.

"And what's it to you?" she asked in a tone that sounded pretty snippy to even her own ears.

He shrugged. "With that attitude, nothing, I guess. Frasier gave everyone an additional hour for lunch again, and I was wondering if you'd like to take a walk over to—"

"No." And then because she knew there was no reason for her to have an attitude, she said, "Thanks for asking, but I have a lot to do here."

He nodded slowly as he continued to look at her. She wished he wouldn't do that. And she wished it didn't bother her, didn't make her feel those vibes again, especially when he probably looked at Tae'Shawna the same way. Not only Tae'Shawna but all the other women with whom he was probably involved.

"Is that why you haven't been out on the set today?"

"You could say that."

Avoiding his gaze, she moved around the trailer, picking up items to repack in her various makeup kits, as well as hanging up items of clothing that cast members had discarded.

"Is something wrong, Rachel?"

She glanced over at him. "No. What gives you that idea?" She then returned to what she was doing, basically presenting her back to him.

Moving away from the door, Ethan strode through the space separating them and came to stand in front of her, forcing her to look up and meet his gaze. "Hey, I knew yesterday you were serious about continuing this 'friends only' thing and, although I prefer more between us, I will respect your wishes."

"Do you?"

He had a confused look on his face. "Do I what?" His tone was low, gruff, with more than a hint of agitation.

"Do you prefer more between us?"

He released a frustrated sigh. "I told you I did."

She nodded slowly. "And what did you tell Tae'Shawna?" The moment the words left her lips, she wished she could take them back. She probably sounded like a jealous shrew. And she had no right to be that way, considering she had told Ethan there would be nothing between them. Ever.

She stared up at him to see even more confusion settle in his features when he asked, "Is this supposed to be a trick question or something?"

"Not a trick question, Ethan, just a curious one."

He crossed his arms over his chest. "And what does Tae'Shawna have to do with us?"

A shiver ran through her when he said the word *us*. Although when it came to them there was no "us," just hearing him say it did something crazy to her. "By 'us,' you mean you and Tae'Shawna?" she asked.

A smile that didn't quite reach his eyes touched his lips. "Was that question supposed to be a joke, Rachel?"

"What do you think?" She made a move to walk away but he reached out and gripped her arm, not too tight, but enough that the heat of his hand felt like a flame licking her skin. *Amazing,* she thought. Even when she wasn't happy with him, he had the ability to make her want him.

"Explain what you meant by that," he said. She thought she heard somewhat of a growl in his tone.

He was staring at her, and she returned his stare with no intention of breaking it. And she had no problem explaining what she'd said as well as elaborating on what she'd meant. "When I worked on Tae'Shawna's makeup earlier today, she took me into her confidence and shared information about you and her."

His expression seemed thoughtful. "Me and her?"

"Yes."

"And what did she say?"

She shrugged and then said, "Nothing more than that the two of you spent part of the weekend together and that you didn't leave her place until late last night and that you were her wake-up call this morning. I know you were with me from Saturday night until yesterday afternoon, but—"

"You're not sure about the time I wasn't with you?" he said, finishing her statement for her.

"Yes, but it really doesn't matter. Saturday night just happened between us. And it's not like I didn't know about your reputation."

He nodded as he held her gaze. "My reputation that you know about from a tabloid you *don't* read. Right?"

It was easy to see his expression had gone from thoughtful to rigid, as if he was struggling to contain the anger she could actually feel radiating from him. She was smart enough to take a step back when he took one forward, and she noticed the eyes staring at her had turned a stormy gray. Not a good sign.

She took another step backward only to have her spine hit a wall. He caged her in when he leaned forward, bracing his hands against the wall on both sides of her face. If his aim was to get her attention, he had it.

She lifted her chin and met his glare with one of her own. "What is this about, Ethan?"

"You tell me, Rachel."

"I told you. And I also told you that you don't owe me an explanation about Tae'Shawna because—"

"I wouldn't repeat it if I were you," he interrupted in a tone gruff enough to make her heed his warning.

He didn't say anything for a moment. He just stared at her. Then finally he said, "First of all, when I made love to you Saturday night, it was the first time I had been intimate with a woman in over six months."

She couldn't stop her mouth from dropping open. Nor could she disguise the flicker of surprise in her eyes. Both were probably what made him continue on to say, "This weekend I needed to get away, so I got up early Saturday morning and drove across the border to Tijuana. Alone. When I got back later that night, I discovered the paparazzi camped out at my place and called you. When I left your apartment Sunday afternoon, I went straight home. I don't know what make-believe game Tae'Shawna is playing but, unfortunately, it's not the first time and probably won't be the last time that some woman claimed we were together or involved in an affair when we weren't. That's how those tabloids you *don't* read are sold."

"Ethan, I—"

His sharp tone interrupted her. "The only thing I want to know from you now is whether you believe me or Tae'Shawna."

She frowned. "Does it matter?"

"To me it does."

She took a deep, uneven breath as she stared into his eyes, still jarred by his admission that their night together had been his first time in over six months. Her heart was pounding because he indicated what she believed mattered to him. And although she didn't quite understand why, she was glad that it did.

As odd as it might seem, she didn't want him to be involved with women like Tae'Shawna, women who would go so far as to invent a relationship with a man. Or even worse, women like Paige who would try anything to get him into their beds.

There was one thing that was actually making her feel somewhat warm inside—the fact that he hadn't wanted any of the model types. He had wanted her. And the strangest thing of all was that she didn't want any of those other women to have him either.

She couldn't explain the thought processes that supported her reasons, especially not to him when they were still somewhat foggy to her. But what she could do was give him the answer he was still waiting for. "I don't believe you're involved with Tae'Shawna, Ethan."

Ethan hadn't realized he was holding his breath until he released it after Rachel had spoken. Why what she believed mattered so much he wasn't sure, but it did. It might have everything to do with that bond he felt with her. A bond he'd never felt with any other woman. That bond had strengthened when they'd made love. He wondered if she realized it. If she didn't comprehend it now, he was certain she would later.

Needing to kiss her, he reached out and pulled her into his arms and captured her mouth with his. All the reasons this weekend had meant so much to him came roaring back to life like a living thing with a mind of its own. It had the ability to push him closer to her even when she wanted to keep him at a distance.

He tried to steady his heart rate and had almost succeeded until she wrapped her arms around his neck and pressed her body closer to his while returning his kiss with equal fervor. Her response was what he had hoped for and definitely what he was enjoying. It wouldn't take much for him to take her like this, standing up against the wall. He fought the temptation. Instead, he continued to make love to her mouth with a hunger that seemed relentless. The feel of her hardened nipples pressing against his chest was sweet agony, as was the rough texture of her denim jeans rubbing against his hard erection. He continued to fight the temptation, knowing what his body wanted would only lead to trouble.

That fight was taken out of his hands when they heard the sound of conversation right outside the trailer door and they quickly ended the kiss. He took a deep breath while forcing his body to cool down, which seemed nearly impossible to do.

He reached out and flicked the pad of his thumb across her bottom lip. "I know what you said last night, but I think we'll be doing each other an injustice not to explore what could be, Rachel. There will be risks but I intend to convince you they will be worth it."

He leaned down and swiped a quick kiss across her lips before moving toward the door.

Chapter 11

"Let me make sure I got this right." Wide-eyed, Charlene spoke in a low tone of voice as she leaned across the table while they waited in Roscoe's for their food to be served. Lower still, she said, "You spent the weekend with Mr. Drop-Dead Gorgeous himself? Ethan Chambers?"

At least Charlene hadn't blurted it out in a loud voice, Rachel thought, grateful for that, although it was evident Charlene was stunned. "Only *part* of the weekend," she quickly clarified. "He arrived around eight Saturday night and left Sunday afternoon around five. That's not even a full twenty-four hours." What she didn't have to say, and what Charlene could figure out on her own, was that a lot had happened during that period of time.

"Wow!" Charlene said, still clearly stunned. "Two

weeks ago you said the two of you were nothing more than friends. What happened?"

Rachel drew in a deep breath, wondering how she was going to explain to her best friend that lust happened. The man was simply irresistible, both in and out of bed. "Well, it happened like this…"

Charlene leaned even farther over the table. Not only were her ears perked but her eyes were bright with curiosity. Rachel figured she was more than ready to take in all the hot-tamale details. "Yes?"

When Rachel didn't say anything, Charlene lifted a brow. "Well?"

A smile touched Rachel's lips. "Well what?"

Charlene gave her a don't-you-dare-play-with-me-like-that look. "Tell me what happened."

"Whatever you can imagine probably did happen, Cha. The man knew positions that are probably outlawed in most states, and he has more staying power in bed than Peyton Manning has on a football field."

A huge grin lit Charlene's face as she sat back in her chair. She exclaimed proudly as she looked at her with envy, "What a woman."

Rachel shook her head as she recalled the past weekend. "No, what a man."

And she seriously meant that. Ethan had her considering taking risks she normally would not take. He said he would make it worth her while and, considering this past weekend, she had no reason not to believe him. After that incident in the trailer a few days ago, she had been trying to keep a level head around the set and handle things decently and in order. In other words, although she didn't try to avoid him, she didn't do any-

thing to seek him out either. But she was well aware that
he was waiting for her to make the next move.

She glanced over at Charlene. "What have I gotten
myself into?"

Charlene smiled naughtily. "His pants, for starters."

"Girl, be serious," Rachel protested.

"I am."

Rachel chuckled. Yes, her friend was serious and
also right. She had gotten into his pants and was looking forward to getting into them again. How shameful was that?

"It doesn't make sense," she said. "You know what
a private person I am and how I hate being in the spotlight. Anyone involved with Ethan will have their face
plastered all over the tabloids. There's no way to get
around that unless we sneak around."

"And how do you feel about doing something like
that?"

That was a good question and one she needed to
think about. Were earth-shattering, toe-curling orgasms
worth all of that?

"You know what's wrong with you, don't you?"
Charlene asked, smothering a giggle.

Rachel took a sip of her iced tea. "I don't have a
clue."

"You went without a hot male body too long. Trust
me, I know how it feels."

Rachel hated to admit that Charlene was probably
right. In the past, she'd always had enough on her plate
to keep her mind occupied so she didn't think about sex.
She was just as busy now as she was before, so what was
there about Ethan that made her want to make him a
top priority on her "to do" list? It wasn't like she wasn't

routinely surrounded on the set by gorgeous, sexy men. Why had her body decided Ethan was the one?

Before she could offer any more input to the conversation, her cell phone began vibrating. Caller ID indicated an unknown number. Normally she refused to answer those kinds of calls, but she felt a warm sensation in the pit of her stomach. She excused herself from the table and quickly headed toward the ladies' room.

"Yes?"

"This is Ethan. I want to see you."

So much for him waiting for her to make the next move.

The sound of his voice plunged her into a sea of desire so deep she felt herself going under. "Why? Do I need to save you again?"

"No, but I do need you to make love to me like you did last weekend."

If she hadn't been drowning before, she was certainly drowning now and there was no one around to throw her a life jacket.

"Ethan, I think—"

"You do too much of that."

For a moment she struggled with the possibility that maybe he was right. "One of us needs to."

"No, we don't. Just consider it something we both deserve. We work hard, so we should get to play harder."

He did have a point. Didn't he?

She drew in a deep breath, wondering where her logical mind was when she needed it the most. It had probably taken a flying leap with that first orgasm Saturday night. "We're risking the chance of you being followed."

"I have everything under control."

Including her, she thought, when she tried summoning the gumption to deny what he was asking. But then all she had to do was to remember Saturday night or the kiss they'd shared in her trailer earlier in the week. His lips had teased her mercilessly, and his tongue had nearly made her short-circuit.

"Rachel?"

"Yes?"

"Will you meet me?"

She nervously licked her lips. "Where?"

He rattled off an address that was followed by a brief set of instructions. "Do you need directions?"

"No, I'll use my GPS," she said, tucking the piece of paper she'd written on back in her purse.

Moments later, she hung up the phone with her heart pounding in her chest. Emotions she refused to put a name to stirred in her stomach, and she knew she was falling deeper and deeper into lust.

Slow down, buddy. The last thing you need is a ticket while racing across town for a night of hot and heavy sex.

Ethan flinched at the thought of that because he knew his meeting with Rachel was more than that. She was different and not just because she wasn't a woman anxious to blast their affair to all who'd listen.

And they were involved in an affair because neither of them was looking for any sort of heavy-duty relationship right now. He was satisfied to keep things under wraps as much she was, especially since he knew how she felt about the matter.

He had actually been followed for a short while after leaving his place. He had driven his car to the private parking garage of condos owned by a friend of Hunter's from college. If the person tailing him thought he was smart, Ethan intended to show he was smarter.

Ethan had parked his car in a designated spot and had donned his disguise before getting out of his car and getting into another vehicle—one owned by that same friend of Hunter's who was presently out of the country for the next month or so.

He had smiled upon leaving the garage and bypassing the photographer who was parked across the street, waiting for Ethan to come out. No doubt, the man would be there for some time while trying to determine what woman and at what address Ethan was visiting at this particular condo complex.

Ethan couldn't ever recall going through this much hassle to keep his interest in a woman hidden. If he wasn't so concerned about Rachel's feelings, he truly wouldn't give a damn.

But he needed tonight. He needed her. This had been one hell of a week, with Frasier in rare form, demanding more than perfection from everyone. The rumor floating around the set was that the man and his partner were having problems. Although Frasier's policy demanded all of them leave any and all personal matters at the door and not bring them on the set, evidently that rule didn't apply to Frasier.

Luckily, so far none of Frasier's tirades had been leveled at him but at a number of others, including Tae'Shawna when she had messed up her lines. After the lie she'd told to Rachel, the woman hadn't gotten any pity from Ethan.

He had come close to confronting Tae'Shawna on more than one occasion about the lie she had told. However, Rachel had asked him not to say anything. She worried that Tae'Shawna would resent her for breaking a confidence and possibly even retaliate in some way.

Ethan exited off the interstate and noted a lot of cars on the road for a Thursday night. He was in Industry, a city in the San Gabriel Valley section of Los Angeles. His destination was an old warehouse owned by Chambers Winery that was used to store bottled wine shipped from the vineyard. In other words, it used to be their off-site wine cellar. More than once he had considered the idea of fixing up at least part of the place as a possible hideaway when he needed peace from the media's scrutiny. This week he had acted on that idea, and after a few phone calls and explicit instructions, he had received word that the place was good to go. He couldn't imagine not bringing Rachel here to help christen the place.

More than once during the drive over, he had glanced back in his rearview mirror to make sure he was not being followed. Satisfied that he had not been, he pulled into the drive and around the side of the building that was away from the street.

Grabbing the pair of wine glasses off the seat beside him, he got out of the car and closed the door behind him. It was a beautiful August night with bright stars lighting the sky. The perfect night for a romantic rendezvous.

He had made good time, intentionally arriving ahead of Rachel. As he headed for the entrance with the wine glasses in his hands, he smiled. So far so good. His evening was going according to his plans.

Rachel pulled into the parking lot of the huge vacant building to park next to the vehicle already there.

Her heart began pounding and her hand on the steering wheel began trembling somewhat.

She glanced around through her windshield. She had followed Ethan's instructions to the letter, and the huge building looming before her appeared dark and scary. But she knew somewhere inside, Ethan was waiting for her.

She opened the car door and glanced around as she got out. It had been hard for her to consume her dinner knowing what her plans were for afterward.

If Charlene suspected anything was amiss, she hadn't let on. Rachel would give her best friend all the details later. But for now, the plan for tonight was something she hadn't wanted to share. She didn't want to take the risk of anyone talking her out of doing something she really wanted to do. She didn't want anyone to knock the craziness out of her and force her to go back to being her logical self.

She pushed the door and, to her intense relief, it opened, just like Ethan had said it would. The moment she stepped over the threshold, the smell of vintage wine consumed her nostrils. She could probably get intoxicated just from the scent alone.

The place was dark. The only light was a bit of moonlight shining in through one of the windows. She'd never been afraid of the dark but there was something eerie about this place. Her heart rate increased, and she fought back a nervousness that was about to consume her as she took a step back and bumped against the hard, solid wall of a masculine chest.

She gasped when a pair of strong, muscular arms reached around to enclose her within a powerful embrace. The familiar scent of him surrounded her and she breathed it in and relaxed against him. She could feel his hot breath at her neck, close to ear, when he whispered, "Welcome to my lair."

Her heart rate steadied when another type of response took control—not fear of the unknown but apprehension of the known. She knew why she was here, why he had asked her to come and how tonight would end up.

She released her breath with a shaky sigh when he turned her to face him and leaned forward to give her a more physical display of welcome, one she had no problem receiving.

His tongue tangled hotly with hers while his hands seemed to roam all over her, finding her bare skin not covered by her short skirt. And he was caressing her backside in a way that only he could execute. When he finally pulled back, she was grateful for his hands around her waist because her knees seemed to buckle beneath her, and she felt herself swaying against him.

He held her tight as he continued to rain kisses all over her face while his hands gently massaged her back. They stood that way for a while as their heartbeats and breathing returned to normal. But she was completely aware of the way her hard nipples pressed against the hard wall of his chest.

"Come on, let me show you around," he whispered against her temple.

He took her hand in his, and using a flashlight that he pulled from his pocket, he led the way. She glanced from side to side and saw rows and rows of wine bottles and immediately knew this was a place his family owned.

"There's usually a security guard around," he said.

"Clyde has worked for us at this place for years, making sure no one runs off with anything. I thought I'd give him the rest of the night off."

Instead of saying anything, Rachel nodded and merely followed him through another door and up a flight of stairs. She tried pushing back the question rushing through her mind. Why was she here and not at home in her own bed getting a good night's sleep? After all, it was Thursday and tomorrow was a workday for the both of them. But she knew the reason. Ethan had called and said he wanted them to make love again. She wanted them to make love again as well. For what other reason would she be here?

She knew getting involved with him, secretly or otherwise, was probably not a good idea, but then she could do casual dating just like the next man or woman. She wasn't looking for everlasting love. She liked her life just fine the way it was.

He used a key to open another door and it was only then that he put the flashlight away and flipped on a switch. She nearly closed her eyes at the brightness but not before she saw the immaculate-looking office.

She continued to glance around when he locked the door behind them. And when she gave him a questioning look, he smiled before taking her hand again and leading her through another set of doors.

She gasped when she saw what was in front of her. It was the most beautifully decorated room she could imagine, one designed as a lovers' hideaway, complete with a king-size bed and all the other matching furnishings. There was even an expensive throw rug on the floor and several beautiful paintings on the wall, lit candles around the room and a vase of roses sitting on a dresser.

She lowered her head when an errant thought hit her. Was this where Ethan brought all his conquests when he needed privacy? She glanced over at him and apparently the question was there, looming in her gaze, because he said, "I called and had this place renovated just a few days ago. I'm pleased with what they've done in such a short period of time."

And then in a voice that had thickened, taken on a rough edge in an ultrasexy sort of way, he said, "And let me go on record as saying that you're the only woman I've ever brought here, Rachel. I consider this place as ours."

Her breath caught in her throat as she took in all he said and all he meant. He had created this place for them? Did he assume there would be many more secret rendezvous for them? So many that they would need a place to slip away to and be together without prying eyes or stalking photographers hell-bent on fueling the tabloid frenzy?

The thought of such an idea—Ethan being so into her—was ludicrous. She could see him taking advantage of her willingness to engage in no-strings-attached sex a couple of times, but did he honestly think it would become a long-term affair? No, he probably knew that it wouldn't be and would be satisfied with the here and now. When she ceased being his flavor of the hour, he would replace her with someone else, someone more his style. More than likely it would be one of those leggy models his name was usually hooked up with. A woman who enjoyed being in the spotlight just as much as he did.

She fought the thick lump blocking her throat. Not wanting to put a damper on the mood he'd set for them tonight, she let her eyes roam around the room. The decor was simply beautiful in the warm glow of candlelight. Then her eyes lit on the glasses and the bottle of wine on a nightstand beside the bed.

"That's Chambers Winery's finest," he leaned over and whispered close to her ear. She glanced up into the depths of his eyes, saw all the desire embedded deep within them, and an unfamiliar sensation overtook her. It ran through her like a burning ball of heat and settled in the pit of her stomach as if it belonged there and had no intention of going away.

Mentally she weighed her options. She could take tonight and accept it for what it was—a night two sexually charged individuals wanted to enjoy each other. Or she could go along for the ride as long as it lasted and as long as they took all the measures necessary not to get caught—providing it was all enjoyment and no emotion. There *had* to be a no-emotional-attachment policy.

Deciding which option she would go with, she eased closer to him and said, "I can't wait to have a glass."

The tips of her nipples were beginning to heat up, and she intentionally rubbed against him to bring her breasts in contact with his chest. The hitch in his breath let her know she'd made a hit. It seemed Hollywood's newest heartthrob wasn't immune to her charms. Just the thought that she had enough to hold his interest made her heart pound and her entire body begin to tremble inside.

The look in his eyes told her that he knew exactly what she was doing and was willing to let her take the lead for now.

"And there's something else I can't wait to have," she said, tilting her head back to meet his gaze.

"What else do you want, Rachel?"

The huskiness of his voice made a shiver ripple through her. She lowered her gaze to his chest and then lower still to his crotch. She'd never been fascinated with the makings of an aroused man before, but now she couldn't help marveling at what a fine specimen of a man he was. His erection nearly burst through the zipper of his jeans, and she felt proud of herself that she had caused his intense arousal.

"I want this," she said, reaching out and groping that part of him. She heard his low growl and glanced up. His eyes could not hide the desire she saw in them.

"Sweetheart, I'm going to make sure you get everything you want." And then he swept her off her feet and into his arms and carried her over to the bed.

There was something about Rachel's scent that got to him every time. It was an intimate fragrance that seemed to beckon him on a primitive level that even now had every muscle in his body rippling in a way he found tormenting.

He undressed her and then undressed himself. He had seen the way she blushed when he tossed several condom packets on the nightstand and took a step away from the bed to put one on. She watched him sheath himself and the thought that she was doing so sent a rush of blood to his loins.

Silence dominated the room and for a heartfelt moment he wished some type of music was playing to set the mood. Too late now. But next time…

And there would be a next time. He was going to

make sure of it. Like he told her, this was *their* place. When he'd made the arrangements on Monday, it had been with her and only her in mind. He hadn't wanted any other woman in that bed with him.

He flinched at the thought, like he always did when his mind would begin thinking of more than sex between them. During those times, he would do whatever was needed to get his thoughts back in check. The only reason he and Rachel were drawn to each other was their intense sexual chemistry. And they were well aware that the attraction could never go beyond what they were sharing now. Neither of them had plans of ever falling in love.

He moved back toward the bed and she shifted on her haunches and met him, reaching out and taking hold of his throbbing erection. She tilted her head back and stared into his eyes for a long moment. Something was passing between them, and he felt it in the hands holding him as well as in the eyes locked with his.

"Tomorrow will we be able to pretend tonight didn't happen?"

Her question broke the silence. "Yes, it's going to be hard but we'll manage it."

She leaned up and licked the side of his face. "You think so?"

"Hell, I hope so, but I'll be the first to admit, every time I see you on the set, I want to tear your clothes off."

He heard her snort at that. "You would have a hard time convincing me of that with that love scene you did today."

He lifted a brow. Love scenes were staged and she was well aware of that. Surely she didn't think any part of them meant anything to him. He was simply follow-ing the script. Did he hear a bit of jealousy in her voice?

"Then I need to do whatever it takes to erase that scene from your mind," he said, and for emphasis he reached out and pulled her closer toward him.

He felt the shiver that passed through her and, in re-sponse, a slew of emotions flowed through him, nearly taking his breath away. A need for her filled him to ca-pacity, and for a moment he could imagine her with him even when he was in his eighties.

At the thought, he went momentarily still. Where had that come from? He knew there was no way he could consider anything with her beyond this affair.

He reminded himself of that again as he captured her mouth with his and lowered her body to the bed.

There was something about being pressed into the mattress by the man you wanted. A man who was hold-ing her gaze as he entered her slowly, as if he was sa-voring the journey.

The last time they'd made love he had taken her hard and fast, and now the slowness was driving her mad. She could only ask, "Why?"

He knew what she was asking and said throatily, "There's no rush. We have plenty of time and I want to take things slow, draw it out and make you scream. A lot of times."

She could feel the hardness of him grow inside of her and knew he intended to make some point. Being the skilled lover he was, he'd succeed in making all his wishes come true.

Chapter 12

"Quiet on the set!

"Take one!

"Action!"

Rachel fought back the rush of jealousy as she watched yet another love scene being shot between Dr. Tyrell Perry and Dr. Sonja Duncan. Did Ethan have to appear to be enjoying it so much?

Usually she stayed in the trailer working with the actors, but today she decided to venture out and would be the first to admit a part of her had wanted to see Ethan. More than once he had accused her of hiding out in the trailer, so today she had decided to be seen.

Although, she thought as a smile touched her lips, hiding out in the trailer hadn't stopped him from seeking her out on occasion and making the find worth his while. He had introduced her to quickies. She didn't want to think about the risk they took of someone discovering their secret. So far no one had, and she was thankful for that.

It had been a week since that night when they'd started their secret rendezvous. Most of the time they would meet up at their hideaway haven but on occasion he would come to her place. So far he was still outsmarting the paparazzi.

She smiled, thinking about how Ethan had bought her a disguise—a honey-blond wig and green contacts. And because she was a makeup artist, it hadn't been difficult to add her own camouflage to make herself unrecognizable when they'd made a decision to branch out beyond the bedroom to grab something to eat. They had even risked going to a movie together.

On more than one occasion she had found herself thinking just how a normal relationship with him would be, one where they wouldn't have to sneak around to be together. But she knew such a thing wasn't possible.

"Cut!"

The production crew rushed around trying to get the props changed for another taping, and it was then that Ethan glanced over at her. When he winked and smiled, she couldn't help smiling back. Last night they had spent the night together at *their* place, and he had surprised her by having an easel with art supplies waiting for her when she had arrived. After having made love, he reclined on the bed while she painted him, something he had surprised her by agreeing to do. It would be her own personal painting of him in all his naked splendor to be shared with no one.

She had returned to the trailer when her cell phone

went off. Caller ID indicated it was Charlene. "Yes, Cha?"

"I know you don't read the tabloids so I feel I should give you the scoop."

She raised a brow. "About what?"

"Ethan. He's driving the paparazzi crazy by eluding them every chance he gets. They've begun wondering what's going on with him and who the woman he's intent on hiding is."

Rachel felt a knot in her stomach. "Do they have any idea? Did they mention a name?"

"No, but they have vowed to find out, so you might want to cool things with him for a while."

Rachel began nibbling on her bottom lip. Yes, that would be best, but it would be hard to do.

"The media can be relentless when they want to find out something," Charlene added.

Rachel knew that to be true. "Thanks for keeping me in the loop. I appreciate it."

"What are you going to do?"

Rachel drew in a deep breath. She had few options and knew there was only one thing that she could do. Regardless of whether she liked it or whether she was ready for it to happen, their affair had run its course. "I'm going to talk to him."

"And if the two of you meet up somewhere to have this talk, you might want to be looking over your shoulder. Disguise or no disguise, the two of you will have the media hounds on your heels for sure."

Ethan glanced in his rearview mirror. He was being followed. A deep frown set into his features. He'd been trying to elude the guy now for a full hour without any success.

He was to meet Rachel at *their* place and he couldn't do so as long as this reporter was still on his tail. Even switching cars and donning his disguise hadn't helped. This guy was on to him and seemed intent on letting him know it.

When his cell phone rang, he almost snatched it off his belt and his frown deepened when he saw the caller was Curtis. He had been trying to avoid his agent for a week or so now. "Yes, Curtis?"

"Damn, Ethan, are you trying to mess up a good thing?"

Ethan glanced into his rearview mirror, getting more agitated by the minute. He needed to get rid of this reporter so he could hook up with Rachel at their scheduled time. "What are you talking about?"

"The tabloids. You've become elusive over the past few weeks, annoying the hell out of several tabloid reporters who even claim you've purposely given them the slip."

Ethan rolled his eyes. "And?"

"And they are wondering why and just who you're trying to hide. Someone has connected you to a nameless married woman and has vowed to uncover her identity."

Ethan's hand tightened on the steering wheel. That was not what he wanted to hear. He of all people knew how tabloid reporters could make a pest of themselves more so than usual when they thought they were on to a story.

"I'd like to see them try to uncover anything," he

said, almost in a growl, knowing he would do whatever it took to protect Rachel's identity.

"So you're admitting to being involved with a married woman?"

"I'm not admitting to anything, but if I were, it would be my damn business," he responded.

"Not here in Hollywood, Ethan, and not while we're trying to build your career. You were doing a great job wining and dining the ladies, causing others to take notice and earning the title of this town's newest heartthrob. All of that is what we need to continue to build your image the way we want. I know how important that is to you."

Ethan pulled in a deep breath. Yes, it had been important to him at one time, but now...

"And in that same vein, I have a suggestion for a date for you on Saturday night."

Curtis's words pulled Ethan's concentration back into the conversation. "Excuse me?"

"I said that I have a suggestion for a date for you on Saturday."

Ethan frowned. "What are you talking about, Curtis?"

"I'm talking about Faith Pride. I got a call from her agent who suggested it might be a good idea if the two of you attended the event together."

"I know nothing about an event next Saturday night."

"Sure you do," Curtis insisted. "I sent you the invitation with a mailing confirmation so I know you got it."

He might have gotten it but, like the rest of his mail, he hadn't opened it. His time and the majority of his attention had been given to his sexy pixie, with no regrets. He looked back in his rearview mirror. The man was still there. Damn.

"I'm not going anywhere Saturday night, Curtis."

"What? You can't be serious, Ethan. You have to go. You're hot news and expected to be there. If I didn't know better I'd think you didn't give a damn about your career anymore. I assume you still want one, right?"

"Of course I do!"

"Good, but it sounds like you have a distraction and that isn't good. Get rid of her."

"Come again?"

"I said get rid of her, Ethan. I don't know who she is and frankly I don't care. She's interfering with your life in a negative way. Your actions in keeping her a secret mean she isn't someone you want to be seen with." Curtis paused a moment then said, "Oh, hell, please tell me the person is a she and not a he."

Ethan fought the urge to tell his agent just where he could go. Instead he said, "Bye, Curtis."

"Hey, you didn't answer me."

"And I don't intend to. If you don't know the answer to that then it's time I start looking for another agent."

"Wait, Ethan, I think we—"

Angrily Ethan clicked off the phone. He then glanced back in his rearview mirror and saw the bastard was still on his tail. Deciding he'd had enough, he figured it was time to seriously lose this guy. Increasing his speed, he darted in and out of traffic before making a quick exit off the interstate, only to make a quick right and then a quick left into the parking lot of a car wash.

He smiled, thinking it was his lucky day since there weren't many cars around and immediately drove around the side of the bay. A glance in his rearview mir-

ror showed his stalker speeding by. Backing up, Ethan
quickly pulled out and headed back toward the interstate, satisfied for the time being that he'd lost his tail.

Rachel continued to pace the bedroom floor. Ethan
had called to say he was on his way but would be late
due to "unforeseen circumstances." He hadn't elabo-
rated.

She paused by the bed and drew in a deep breath,
remembering her conversation with Charlene. Rachel's
common sense was basically telling her that continuing
to take risks at this point would be acting irresponsibly.
She was an intelligent woman and Ethan was an intelligent man. They had enjoyed each other's companion-
ship but both fully understood that they could not have
a future together of any kind. And that was where their
similarities ended. Their connection over the past three
weeks had only been physical. He didn't love her and
she didn't love him.

Then why was the thought of not being with him, not
sharing stolen moments any longer, causing her heart
to ache?

She began moving again, pacing the floor. He would
know something was bothering her the moment he saw
her. For one thing, she still had her clothes on, and usually if she was the first to arrive, she would be naked
in the bed waiting on him.

She turned when she heard the sound of footsteps
and felt the fluttering in her chest when the door slowly
opened. She couldn't deny the excitement and joy she
felt when her gaze met his blue-gray eyes. It was the
same moment of elation she felt whenever she saw him.

He closed the door and leaned against it, holding her

gaze for a moment, and then he began slowly unbuttoning his shirt. She knew she should stop him, tell him what she'd heard and that they needed to talk about it.

But she couldn't now.

Her hands automatically went to her skirt and undid the zipper, then slowly shimmied out of it before pulling her blouse over her head. She then kicked off her sandals and by the time they met next to the bed they were both completely naked.

As they tumbled together on the bed, one thought ran through her mind. *So much for talking.*

Chapter 13

An hour or so later, a very satiated Ethan was stretched out in the bed with Rachel in his arms and their legs still entwined. Mentally he was ordering his heart rate to slow down, but it wasn't listening. And his brain cells, which had gotten scrambled after a couple of back-to-back orgasms, were still a jumbled mess. But he didn't mind. In fact, he couldn't imagine it any other way. He was precisely where he wanted to be and was with the one person he wanted to share his time.

He raised her hand to his lips to kiss it and in response she snuggled even closer to him. Her body felt warm all over, and he liked the feel of spooning her backside, cradling her hips.

"So tell me," he leaned down and whispered close to her ear. "Why were you still wearing clothes when I got here?"

He noticed the exact moment her body stiffened and he tightened his arms around her. Only a man who had been a lover to this woman could detect at that moment she was bothered by something. He shifted his weight, turned her in his arms to face him and his eyes met hers. "What's wrong, Rachel?"

For a moment he wasn't sure she would answer him, and then in a soft voice she said, "My friend Charlene called today."

He was sure there was more. "And?"

"You were in the tabloids. It seems reporters are trying to figure out who's your flavor of the month."

"They wouldn't have to try and figure it out since I'd be glad to tell them, if you would let me."

She stared at him through long lashes, surprise showing in her eyes, and he understood why. This was the first time he'd ever suggested they take their affair public. The only reason he'd never done so was because he knew her feelings on the matter.

"Ethan," she breathed out in a regretful tone. "I can't."

In other words, you won't, he thought and fought back the frustration he felt. He thought about the party and knew he didn't want to take any other woman but her. He pulled in a deep breath, wondering at what point he had decided he wanted more than a fling with her. When had sneaking around with Rachel become something he did only because that was the way she wanted it?

"Okay, you can't," he said, trying to keep the sting from his voice. "What does a tabloid reporter have to do with you having your clothes on when I got here?"

She turned her head to look at the painting of him

that she had done and hung on the wall. It was a good thing they were the only ones with keys to this room in the building. He would hate for anyone to ever walk in and see that painting of him. She called it art; he thought of it as borderline X-rated. The only thing keeping him from being completely nude was the very thin piece of cloth that covered a certain part of his body at the juncture of his legs.

"Rachel, you're thinking too much again."

She returned her gaze to his. "Tabloid reporters are trying to figure out who you're spending your time with. You and I know if they keep snooping then it's only a matter of time before they find out, and I can't let that happen, Ethan. I can't risk being placed in the spotlight ever again. And then there's my career I have to think about. I've worked too hard building myself as a professional in the industry to risk losing everything."

He pulled in a deep breath. Those damn reporters had definitely done a job on her when she was a kid for her to have this intense fear. He could just imagine the hell she went through. He pulled her tighter to him, trying to imagine life without her. He would still see her on the set but he had begun thinking of these interludes with her as their time. He looked forward to them. In a way, he needed them. They had stopped being just sexual escapades a while ago. There were those times like these where he would hold her in his arms and savor what they shared, both the physical and the emotional.

"You won't lose anything, Rachel. I told you our secret is safe. No one knows about us or this place."

"For now, but how long will it be before they—"

"Once they see I'm no longer worth their time and effort, they will leave me alone," he interrupted her.

"Hmm, as much as I don't want to attend that function Saturday night, maybe I should."

Rachel lifted a brow. "What function?"

"Some charity function Curtis wants me to attend with a date to calm the waters with the tabloids. Maybe if they see I'm a boring person who's gotten so absorbed in my career and nothing more, they will move on to someone else."

He could tell by the look in her eyes that she was confused. "But I thought you wanted to court the media, build your career that way as a playboy."

He studied her features. *I thought so, too,* he said to himself. And instead of trying to determine why he'd had a change of heart, he said, "There are other ways."

He pulled her closer into his arms. "Come on, we've talked enough. Let's get some sleep."

She pulled back. "Sleep?"

He smiled. "Yes, but if you prefer that we didn't…" He leaned over and kissed her in a way that had her body quivering. And when she responded by returning the kiss he proceeded to deepen it.

This was what he wanted and what he needed. Tabloids or no tabloids he intended to keep her by his side, even if they had to continue to sneak around to do it.

Rachel wrapped the sheet around her as she sank into the chair across from the bed. She needed to think and she couldn't do so wrapped in Ethan's arms. She had to have distance.

She closed her eyes and could clearly recall how it felt to be accosted by a crowd of reporters shoving mikes in your face, pulling on your hair to get your attention and all but screaming questions at you. She would try hiding behind her aunt and uncle, and later behind Sofia, but they would get relentless, their questions more demanding, the hordes of reporters even bigger. Then there was the period where she'd had nightmares about them and how they would all enjoy making her life unbearable.

And it had kept up that way until after she'd finished high school and then decided to travel abroad for a while. When she returned home, all the attention had shifted to other heiresses and up-and-coming starlets and actors. They forgot about her, practically left her alone, except for those times when the Wellesley family appeared together at a social function.

Over the years she had worked so hard to avoid that, as well as strived to be taken seriously in the industry as a makeup artist and wardrobe designer. To land a job on one of the most popular television shows was definitely a feather in her cap, one she refused to lose.

But she didn't want to lose Ethan either. She glanced at him, asleep in the bed. She enjoyed these times with him when she could be herself. Although they made love, they spent time talking as well. He had become her lover but he was still her friend, a very good friend. And it was a friendship that she cherished.

"Rachel?"

She heard the sound of her name and glanced toward the bed again. Ethan had awoken and had stretched his hand out to her. Without a moment's hesitation, she eased from the chair, dropped the sheet and went to him.

He gathered her into his arms and whispered, "You're thinking again and that's not a good thing."

She pulled back and looked up at him and smiled. "It's not?"

"No."

"Well, then, can you come up with a better pastime?"

He rubbed his nose against her neck. "Um, I think I can," he said throatily before capturing her mouth.

He released her mouth and eased her down on the bed. "Yes," she managed hoarsely, as her body began shivering in a need only he could satisfy, "I believe you can."

A few days later Rachel looked down into the face of the actress reclining in her makeup chair and smiled before handing the woman the mirror. "There you go. Your makeup looks good on you, as always."

Livia studied her features in the mirror and smiled. "And, as always, you did a wonderful job, Rachel. You certainly know your stuff."

Rachel thanked her. Livia Blake was always giving her compliments about her work. Unlike Tae'Shawna Miller. The woman was still living in a fantasy world, still weaving the story of a secret affair with Ethan. Rachel figured she was the only one the woman had probably shared her lie with, probably because she figured Rachel was the only person gullible enough to believe her.

"You're one of the few people I'm going to miss when I leave the show," Livia said, easing up in her chair and handing the mirror back to Rachel.

Rachel knew she was going to miss Livia as well. Over the past weeks, she'd discovered her earlier assumptions about the woman had been all false, especially when she'd taken time to compare her to Tae'Shawna. Both were beautiful women who turned men's heads without much effort. But their attitudes and the way they treated people were totally different. Livia wasn't shallow or self-absorbed at all. Tae'Shawna took all those honors.

"You know how directors are. They may decide to rewrite the script and keep you on."

Livia shook her head sadly. "I doubt that will happen, although it would be wonderful. I'm thirty and nearing the end of my modeling career and although it's been a good one, it's time I moved on, although I haven't figured out to where just yet. *Paging the Doctor* has been a stepping-stone in the right direction. I've met some good people on the set, and—" she threw her head back and chuckled "—a few not so good ones."

Rachel smiled. Livia didn't have to tell her who the "not so good ones" were. Everyone had figured out by now there were several women on the set who were jealous of Livia's beauty, with Tae'Shawna heading the list.

"Well, I wish you the best," Rachel said sincerely.

"And I wish you the best, as well." Livia paused and then said, "Can I offer you some advice, though?"

Rachel raised a brow. "Advice about what?"

"Not what, but who. Ethan Chambers."

With effort, Rachel kept her features expressionless as she continued to pack away her cosmetics. "Ethan?" she asked, fighting to keep her voice steady. "And what kind of advice do you want to offer me about him?"

Livia paused, as if trying to choose her words carefully, and then she said, "I know the two of you are fiercely attracted to each other and..."

When Rachel began shaking her head, trying to deny it, Livia waved her off. "Hey, I felt the vibes between the two of you, even during his hot and heavy love scenes with me."

"But I—"

"Want to deny it," Livia said, smiling. "I don't know why you would want to when you're both beautiful people. Look, I'm sorry if mentioning it got you all flustered. That wasn't my intent. I just don't know why the two of you are keeping it a secret."

Rachel dropped down in the nearest chair, totally outdone. She and Ethan had worked so hard not to give anything away on the set, yet Livia had picked up on it. She met Livia's curious gaze. "Do you think others noticed?"

Livia shrugged. "Probably not. I'm just good at reading people and picking up vibes. I doubt Tae'Shawna noticed, since she's under the illusion he's all into her, and Paige isn't any better. Those are the only two still hanging on, hoping he'll give them some attention. I think the other women on the set have decided he's truly not interested."

Rachel didn't say anything for a moment, and then asked, "What did we do to give ourselves away?"

Livia chuckled. "The way the two of you look at each other when you think no one else is noticing, and I'm sure no one else is noticing but me, only because I have a tendency to notice everything. But I still don't understand why the two of you are keeping it a secret."

Rachel nibbled at her bottom lip. "It's complicated. I prefer not being in the limelight and he's a person who can't help but be there, dead center."

"Well, I hope things work out for the two of you because I think you're a good match, and you and Ethan truly deserve each other. Since I've gotten to know the both of you, I can easily see you're good people."

Livia glanced down at her watch. "It's time for me

to get ready for my next scene. I'm not sure how they plan to write in my exit from the show since I'm supposedly Dr. Perry's love interest with emotional baggage. I think I'm supposed to pack up and leave when things between us get hot and heavy because I haven't gotten over my husband's death."

Rachel nodded. It was either that or killing Dr. Duncan off, but she couldn't see them doing that. Still, on the set, you never knew how things would go.

"Ethan, can I see you for a moment?"

Ethan kept the annoyance out of his face as he turned around. "Yes, Tae'Shawna, what is it?"

She smiled up at him. "I have tickets to the premier of *Saturday's Hussle*. Would you like to go with me tonight?"

Ethan knew just where he planned to be tonight, and Rachel's arms were far better than any movie premier. Even if he and Rachel hadn't made plans to meet up later, Tae'Shawna would be the last woman he'd go out with. "Thanks, but I have plans already."

"Oh. Maybe next time."

He doubted it. In fact, he knew for certain there wouldn't be a first time or a next time. "I'll see you later," he said, turning to leave.

"Umm, you don't know how I wish on that one, Ethan."

He kept walking, refusing to turn back around and respond to her flirty comment. His workday had ended, and for him, the fun was about to begin with the woman he wanted.

Chapter 14

Rachel glanced over at Charlene as they got out of the car. They were at a karaoke bar for a girls' night out. It was Saturday night and Ethan had decided to go to the charity event solo, against his agent's wishes. He'd insisted he would not take a date.

"Are you ready to have some fun?" she asked her friend. Rachel knew she needed to cheer Charlene up since her mother had hit again, calling her and telling her younger daughter all the reasons why she couldn't get a man.

"Yes, although you should have let me spend the weekend alone getting wasted."

Rachel laughed. "Neither one of us can handle too much booze and we both know it. Come on, let's enjoy ourselves."

A few hours later they were doing just that. Rachel

was trying to talk Charlene into competing in the singing contest to win the five-hundred-dollar prize. Everyone knew what a beautiful voice she had.

"You really think I should?" Charlene asked.

Rachel smiled. Charlene had a dynamite voice but she'd always had this thing about singing in public. She much preferred staying behind the scenes, working as a voice coach at one of the local schools. "Hey, so far I haven't been impressed by the others I've heard. The sound of your voice has spoiled me. Personally, I think you have a good shot at winning. Just think of what you could do with the money." And Rachel could see from her best friend's expression that she was thinking the same thing.

"I don't know, Rachel."

"Well, I do, so just think about it. You have time to make up your mind. We're going to be here for a while."

And she meant it. She wasn't ready to go home to sit around or go to bed wondering if Ethan was having a good time at that event without her. No doubt there would be plenty of women there throwing themselves at him. She pulled in a deep breath. By mutual agreement, they were in an exclusive relationship. She knew she hadn't dated anyone else since they'd begun sleeping together and he'd said he hadn't either.

"Okay, I'm going to do it!"

Charlene's exclamation interrupted Rachel's thoughts and she smiled over at her friend. "Good. I have a feeling that you won't regret it."

The hounds were on Ethan the minute he got out of his car.

"Chambers? Where have you been hiding?" a reporter asked as a mike was shoved in Ethan's face and cameras went off from all directions.

Stepping into his role, he smiled for the cameras. "I haven't been hiding."

That began a series of other questions and he answered every last one of them with the intent of diffusing their curiosity and getting them interested in his role in *Paging the Doctor* instead. After a while it worked, although there were still a couple of reporters who seemed determined to dig into his personal life. Years of being one of the heirs to the Chambers Winery had taught him how to handle that kind.

"No date, Ethan?" one of the two resilient reporters asked.

"No, no date. Is there anything wrong with a man coming alone?"

"Not when he doesn't have to," was the other resilient reporter's quick comeback.

Ethan smiled. "I call it freedom of choice."

He answered a few more questions before bidding the reporters good-night. He knew he would be tailed when he left the event, but he figured eventually they would reach the conclusion he was no longer newsworthy and go find someone else to harass.

"I can't believe I won!"

Rachel smiled brightly over at Charlene who was holding a bottle of champagne in one hand and a check for five hundred dollars in the other. "I told you that you would. I keep telling you that you have a beautiful voice. Maybe one day you'll finally believe me." Charlene had done a beautiful rendition of "Bridge Over Troubled

Water" and brought everyone out of their seats. "You sounded like a young Aretha."

Charlene waved off her words. "You're my best friend, so of course you'd think so, and you know how much I love me some Aretha."

Yes, Rachel did know, but no matter what Charlene thought, she was dead serious.

"Excuse me, ladies."

Both Rachel and Charlene glanced at the man standing by their table. "Yes?" Charlene asked.

"I hate interrupting, but I wanted to congratulate you, Ms. Quinn. You did an outstanding job. And I want to introduce myself. I'm Jason Burke, a talent scout," he said handing Charlene his card. "Please call me. I would like to discuss a few things with you. The company I represent would love to bring you on board."

Rachel could tell from the look on Charlene's face that she wasn't taking the man seriously. Playing along with him, Charlene slid his card into her pocket and said, "Sure, I'd love to contact you. Will next week be soon enough?"

The man smiled brightly. "Yes, and I'll look forward to that call." He then walked away and out of the club.

Charlene rolled her eyes. "Does he really think I'm going to call him?"

Rachel took a sip of her drink. "You said that you would."

"That was to get rid of him. Please. I can sing but not that good. And he's probably not who he's claiming to be."

"Let me see his business card." Rachel waited while Charlene dug it out of the pocket of her jeans.

Rachel studied the card. "I think you should call

Sofia and let her check him out to see if he's legit. If he is, I would follow up with him if I were you."

Charlene waved off her words. "Whatever. Hey, let's forget about Jason Burke and have a good time. We need to get on the dance floor and celebrate my win."

Rachel laughed as she followed Charlene onto the floor to shake their booties for a while.

It was past three in the morning by the time Rachel had showered and slid between the sheets. She was about to turn off the lamp when her cell phone rang. Thinking it was Charlene still on a high from that night's win, she answered the phone saying, "Hey, haven't you gotten enough already?"

"Of you? Never."

Her body immediately began throbbing at the sound of the deep, husky voice. Her eyes clouded over in desire just from hearing it. "Hey, lover boy, haven't you heard it's not nice to call a girl after midnight?"

His soft chuckle came through the phone and touched her in places she'd rather leave untouched. But since he was going there, she might as well let him finish. "I prefer being there in person but some ass is parked outside the complex, waiting for me to leave. So I guess I'll stay in and engage in some sex talk with you."

She chuckled. "Sounds like a winner to me. Speaking of wins, Charlene won a singing contest at the club tonight. A whopping five hundred dollars and a bottle of champagne. And a talent scout approached her afterwards."

"I'm happy for her."

Although Ethan and Charlene had never officially met, they knew a lot about each other thanks to Rachel.

"I'll tell her you are." There was a pause, and then she asked, "And how was your night?"

"Boring."

"Did you change your mind about taking a date with you?"

"No."

Rachel tried not to feel giddy at that one single word but couldn't help it. She had convinced herself that she could handle it if he'd decided to take a date. After all, they were nothing more to each other than occasional bed partners. She drew in a deep breath, not wanting to think about it or how depressed she'd get when she did.

"So what are you wearing?"

His question made her smile. "What makes you think I'm wearing anything?"

He chuckled. "You only sleep naked when you're with me."

"Says who?"

"Says me. The man who has made love to you a lot of times."

"Hmm, how many?" she asked in what she hoped was a sexy, low tone. And he was right. He had made love to her a lot of times.

"Was I supposed to be counting?"

"I was."

He laughed. "Okay, then how many?"

"Tally up your own numbers, Chambers."

"If I were there, I would tickle it out of you."

"If you were here, Ethan, I'd make sure you put your hands to more productive use."

When Rachel hung up the phone an hour later she drew in a deep breath. Ethan's smooth, hot talk had almost made her come several times, it definitely had made her consider leaving her house and meeting him somewhere. But luckily her common sense held tight. They had agreed to throw the paparazzi off their scent by not meeting at their place anytime during the coming week. That meant when they did get back together for some bed time, they would have a whole lot of making up to do.

Ethan left his home on Sunday morning to go to the diner for some coffee and a roll. When he walked out with his purchase, he noticed one of the reporters from last night was waiting on him, braced against Ethan's car. The man was Joe Connors and he was known to be as tenacious as they came.

Since he was wearing the same clothes as he'd worn yesterday when he'd followed him, Joe had apparently slept in his car. And because Ethan considered himself a good guy, while buying breakfast for himself he'd also grabbed something for Joe.

"Looks like you could use this as much as I can," Ethan said, handing the man the extra breakfast sack he had in his hand. "All the creamers, sugars and artificial sweeteners you'll ever need are in that bag," he added.

The man accepted the offering. He then took a sip of the coffee, drinking it black. "Good stuff. Thanks."

"You're welcome." Ethan took a sip of his own coffee and asked, "Now, why don't you be a nice guy and leave me alone."

Joe chuckled as he shook his head. "No can do. I have to make a living."

"Don't we all?" was Ethan's dry response.

The man eyed him curiously. "Since you're in a giving mood, Chambers, how about an interview?"

Ethan shook his head. "I gave you an interview last night. You asked your questions and I answered them."

"Yes, but you refused to talk about your love life."

Ethan smiled. "What makes you think I have a love life?"

The man shrugged. "I just figured you did. This time last year you were dating anything in a skirt, and now for the past month you've been cooling your heels, so to speak, which can only mean you've been caught."

"Caught?"

"Yes. Some woman's got your heart. Is she married?"

Ethan threw his head back and laughed. "What is this obsession that I'm involved with a married woman?"

"What other reason would make you go to great pains to hide her?"

Ethan fought back the temptation to respond by saying he wasn't trying to hide Rachel. He would be perfectly happy if they made their affair public but...

"Um, look's like you started to say something and then changed your mind. Did I get close to the truth or something?"

"No."

"You sure?"

"Positive."

Joe looked at him for the longest time. "Then what was that funny look about?"

"Nothing. Eat your food, Joe. It's getting cold."

After pulling a warm croissant from the bag, Joe tilted his head and looked at Ethan. He grinned and said, "Hey man, you're not such a bad guy."

Chapter 15

"Have a nice evening, Rachel."

Rachel smiled over at one of her assistants. "You do the same, Loraine."

"And don't hang around here too late. They start killing the lights around seven," Loraine advised.

"Thanks for letting me know that."

There were only a few more weeks of filming left before the final shoot of the season. A wrap party was already being planned and Frasier was going all out to make it a monumental affair.

As she thought about the season ending, Rachel was happy that Livia's character was not killed off. It left the door open for a possible return next season. Just as she had predicted, Dr. Duncan was not emotionally ready for a hot and heavy love affair with Dr. Perry so soon after her husband's death. The season would end with her asking to be transferred to another hospital in Florida. That meant Dr. Perry would be free to pursue another love interest next season.

Livia would be joining her and Charlene for dinner over the weekend. Ever since Livia had mentioned that she was aware of her affair with Ethan, the two of them had become friends. Rachel appreciated Livia not gossiping about her and Ethan; apparently somebody in Hollywood could keep a secret.

Rachel's cell phone went off and she pulled it out of the pocket of her smock. "Yes?"

"Whooo, Rachel, you'll never guess what happened to me!"

Rachel couldn't help but hear the excitement in Charlene's voice. "And what has happened to you?"

"That guy Jason Burke is legit. Sofia checked him out. He works in A&R for the big music company that distributes Playascape."

Rachel lifted a brow. Playascape was a well-known recording company. One of the biggies. "Are you sure?"

"Sofia verified everything."

Then that settled it. Sofia knew just about everyone in the music, movie and television industry through Limelight Entertainment.

"And guess what?"

"What?"

"They want me to come in and meet with them."

Rachel couldn't help but be ecstatic as well. "Wow, Cha, that's fantastic."

"I think so, too, and Sofia suggested I send them a copy of that demo tape I did a while back."

"That's a smart move."

"Sofia's managing everything for me."

Rachel's smile widened. She knew her sister's abilities when it came to working deals. "Then you're in good hands."

Rachel heard a sound and turned around. Her breath caught in her throat when she saw Ethan. He had entered the trailer and was leaning against the closed door. Their eyes met and she watched as he reached behind him and locked it. The click sounded loud.

"Cha, that's good news but I need to call you back later."

"You okay?"

Evidently Charlene had heard the change in her voice. "Yes, I'm fine. I'll call you when I get home." She then clicked off the phone.

"Ethan, what are you doing here? I thought you'd left hours ago."

He crossed his arms over his chest. Instead of answering her, he had a question of his own. "And why are you still here?"

"I had some paperwork to do."

He checked his watch. "It's late."

"I know but I'm fine. The security guard patrolling the studio lot is still here."

He was still leaning against the door, but now his hands were tucked into the pockets of his jeans. Although they saw each other every day on the set, they hadn't been together intimately for over a week thanks to that tabloid reporter dogging Ethan's heels. But they did talk on the phone every night and had made plans to try and sneak away to Tijuana this weekend.

"Go ahead and finish what you have to do. I'll wait and walk you out to your car."

She swallowed the lump in her throat. "That's not necessary."

"I think it is."

Instead of arguing with him she slid behind her small desk and began going over the paperwork she needed to give John in the morning. Out of the corner of her eye she saw Ethan had moved away from the door to straddle one of the chairs.

The air-conditioning system was working but she was beginning to feel hot. She was also feeling his eyes on her, singeing her flesh. In the quiet, she couldn't help but be aware of him. He'd been in the trailer with her lots of times while she'd applied his makeup, and because of where they were, things had always been professional between them. But she'd always been tempted with him reclining in one of her chairs and her over him and breathing in his scent.

Deciding the trailer was too quiet, she opted to share Charlene's good news with him. "Isn't that wonderful?"

"Yeah, I think it's great," he replied. "I hear they have a good outfit over there."

Rachel continued working, going through John's requests for the season finale. Out of the corner of her eye, she saw that Ethan had moved again. This time he'd gone over to the watercooler to get something to drink. She turned to look at him at the exact time he tilted the cup up to his lips to take a swallow.

The way his throat moved as water trickled down it did something to her. And when he licked his lips as if the drink had been one of the most refreshing things to go into his mouth, she actually began envying the water.

"How much longer before you're done?"

She blinked and realized he had spoken to her. In

that case, he'd probably caught her staring. She drew in a deep breath as she looked down at the papers. "Not long. If you need to leave then I—"

"No, I don't need to leave. But I do need you."

Now *that* she heard. And upon doing so, she couldn't smother the heated sensations taking root in the pit of her stomach or the hot tingle between her legs. This was where she worked, her business sanctuary. Actors came and went and usually she was too busy, too involved to connect the insides of this trailer to any one particular person. But for some reason, she had a feeling that was about to change.

Deciding not to respond to what he'd said, she turned her attention back to the papers in front of her. Ten minutes later, she was signing off on the last sheet. She opened the top drawer to slide them inside.

"Finished now?"

She glanced over at him and met his gaze. He had gone back to straddling one of the chairs. "Yes."

"Good." He stood. "Come here, Rachel."

She continued to hold his gaze, felt the heat zinging between the two of them. She didn't have to ask what he wanted; the look on his face told her what he needed. It was there in his expression, in the chiseled and handsome features. Not to mention those beautiful eyes staring back at her.

Instead of putting up any fuss, not that she would have, she crossed the room without a word and walked straight into his arms. He pulled her to him and she felt it all. His heat, the pounding of his heart against her chest and the engorged erection pressing at the juncture of her thighs.

"It's been hell these seven days without you," he whispered against her lips.

"Actually, it's been eight but who's counting?" she said as her arms automatically went around his waist and she rested her head against his chest. She had to fight hard to keep from being overwhelmed by him. When she felt his erection throb against her thigh, she pulled back and glanced up at him.

"We'll be together Saturday," she reminded him.

He smiled down at her but she still saw the tension in his features. "I can't wait. I need you now."

As he spoke, he backed her against the wall. Already his hands at her waist were lifting her up. Instead of wearing jeans today she had decided to wear a skirt. *How convenient for him,* she thought.

And for her.

Her legs automatically wrapped around him and his hands were busy under her skirt, pushing her panties aside before unzipping his pants and freeing himself. By mutual consent, he had stopped using condoms when she'd told him she was on the pill.

His finger slid inside her as if to test her readiness, and the feel of his touch had her moaning.

"Shh," he whispered in her ear. "There's no need to bring the guard in here to check out things."

No, there was no reason, which meant she couldn't let go and scream. How was she going to stop it? He always made her scream.

His finger inside her was driving her to the brink. He'd said he needed her and he was taking his time to make sure that she also needed him. She should tell him doing so wasn't necessary. She did need him. She did need this.

"Baby, you're hot and your scent is driving me insane," he whispered before taking her mouth in a kiss that told her this was just the beginning.

He covered her lips, captured her mouth in a combination of hunger and tenderness that zapped her senses. And when his tongue began doing its thing, exploring her mouth as if it were conquering unfamiliar territory, she went weak in the knees. But he held her, making sure she didn't go anywhere. She had detected his hunger the minute he'd entered the trailer, and now she was experiencing it firsthand.

Her body was responding to him as it always did and as it always would. Whenever it came to this kind of mutual satisfaction, they were always in accord. A deep, throbbing ache within her intensified and, of its own will, the lower part of her body rocked against his. She clung to him as his mouth clung to hers, plundering it, stirring sensations all the way down to the soles of her feet.

For one fleeting moment she felt the silky head of his erection probe her womanly core, then he entered her in one smooth stroke. She wrapped her legs around him to take him in fully.

She moaned into his mouth and gripped tightly to his shoulders, surrendering to the feel of him being embedded within her, stretching her wide. He deepened the kiss and at the same time he began to move, thrusting back and forth inside of her, feeding her hunger while making her skin tingle all over. Her breasts felt heavy, full and sensitive to the chest rubbing against them.

He was deep inside her and with each thrust he was going deeper still. As he rocked his hips against her, he used his hands to cushion her back from the wall.

He pulled his mouth away and whispered against her lips, "Come for me, baby. I need to feel you come."

As if his words were a command for her body to obey, she felt herself begin to shatter into a million pieces. She clenched her teeth to hold back her scream, and when his mouth came down on hers she gave in and felt every part of her body explode in a climax so intense she trembled all over.

"That's it, baby. Now I'm yours," he uttered huskily right before his body ignited in an explosion as well. She felt the hot, thick essence of him shoot all the way inside of her in the most primitive way, and she called out his name.

He responded in kind, and the sound of her name on his lips sent everything within her throbbing for more. She only knew this kind of pleasure with him. She only wanted this kind of pleasure from him.

Sensation spiraled inside of her and she knew at that moment that Ethan Chambers had captured her heart.

Chapter 16

"Ethan, wait. I need to see you for a moment."

Ethan looked over his shoulder and turned around. "I was on my way out, Paige. What's up?"

Joe Connors had finally stopped being his shadow, but that didn't mean he and Rachel could let their guard down. They'd been careful since that amazing night in the trailer, not hooking up until last weekend in Tijuana. Their Mexican rendezvous had been special, and they'd made up for the time they'd lost. Now they would be spending the night at *their* place and Ethan couldn't wait. He didn't need Paige Stiles delaying him.

"Evidently you're up, big boy," she said in that flirty voice that annoyed the hell out of him. "I need a date to the wrap party."

He chuckled softly. "And?"

"And you're going to take me."

He was surprised by her bold statement. He had finally gotten Tae'Shawna out of his hair by his persistence in letting her know he wasn't interested. Paige, on the other hand, was not getting the message. He'd just have to be more explicit. "I'm not taking you anywhere."

"Yes, you are. At least, you will if you want me to keep your secret."

He felt the hair stand up on the back of his neck. "And just what secret is that?"

"You banging Rachel Wellesley. She never fooled me. I figured she had the hots for you just as bad as the next woman, and I was wondering how long it would take for you to be lured by her bait." The woman then chuckled. "Seriously, Ethan, are you *that* hard up? You couldn't do better than Rachel? If I was picking someone that you'd want to mess around with, it wouldn't be her. And don't deny the two of you are involved because I can prove it."

He drew in a deep breath, not sure if she could prove it but truly not caring. "No, I seriously don't think I can do better than Rachel. Now if you will excuse me, I—"

"I mean it, Ethan. You make plans to get something going with me or else."

"Or else what?"

She smiled sweetly. "Or else everyone, especially Frasier and John, will know that Rachel isn't the sweetie pie they think she is."

Now that pushed his anger to the top. "I don't know what game you're playing, Paige, but keep Rachel out of this."

"Sure, I'll keep her out of this, but only if you give me what I want. My name connected to yours will open doors. I not only want those doors opened, I want to walk through them."

"It won't happen."

She wiped the smile from her face. "Then I suggest that you make sure it does."

She walked away.

On the drive home, Ethan tried to figure out the best way to handle Paige. Reasoning with her was out of the question since the woman was vindictive and obviously intent on hurting Rachel. He had detected her dislike and jealousy from the first.

The one thing he'd learned growing up as a Chambers was to not let anyone bully, or in this case blackmail, you into doing something you did not want to do. He had no intention of taking Paige or any other woman to the wrap party. The only woman he would take was the woman he wanted and would always want: Rachel.

He thought about telling Rachel about Paige's threats, but he could just imagine what her reaction would be. He wanted to save her from that worry. And he wanted to save himself from seeing it. No, he would simply ignore Paige as he had Tae'Shawna and hopefully she would forget about her foolish threat.

He had no problems with his and Rachel's relationship going public and he'd pushed for that several times with Rachel—only to meet a brick wall. For some reason she thought news of their involvement would diminish the professional career she had created, and then there was her intense desire not to be in the spotlight.

There was no one who could say his and Rachel's relationship on the set had been anything other than professional. And as far as her being in the spotlight, he thought she didn't give herself enough credit for handling things. He knew the media could sometimes be relentless, but because of their families, he and Rachel had been born into the spotlight anyway and the key was not avoiding it but dealing with it.

As he continued on the drive home, he finally admitted something else. Something he'd known for a while but just hadn't acknowledged. He had fallen in love with Rachel. And because he loved her, he didn't want to sneak around to be with her. He wanted everyone to know the woman he loved and adored, the woman who could make him smile just by being close to him. The woman he wanted to bring home to meet his family.

The woman he wanted to marry.

He wanted Rachel, and only Rachel, to become Mrs. Ethan Chambers. He wanted her to be the mother of his children. To walk by his side for always.

He gripped the steering wheel, knowing those thoughts were true. Every single one of them. But they were thoughts he could not share with Rachel. She didn't love him, and she didn't want to share a future with him.

Two days later Paige was back in his face again, reiterating her demands.

Ethan gave her his total attention, squaring off and looking her right in the eyes with an adamant expression. "Look, Paige, I told you once before that I'm not taking you to the wrap party and I meant it. My feelings haven't changed."

He saw the anger build in her features. Her jaw clenched and her eyes narrowed. "Then you leave me no choice. Now everyone will know what you and Rachel have been doing behind their backs."

Then she walked off.

Ethan got into his car, pissed but still positive he was handling the nagging woman the only way he could. He decided to forgo the air-conditioning on the ride home, preferring the warm breeze against his face. He imagined the stench of Paige Stiles being blown off him.

As if he'd warded it away, any thought of the encounter dared not enter his mind. Until the next night when his cell phone rang.

How Joe Connors, of all people, had gotten his cell phone number, Ethan didn't know and didn't waste his time asking.

"What do you want, Connors?" he asked instead.

"I like you, Chambers. You're different from most of the stars out there who can be anal, so I'm giving you a heads-up. You and your lady have been exposed. Not by me, but by a tip we received. And there are pictures, nothing sleazy, but pictures that will substantiate this person's claim. They are pretty damn excited over here, and I understand the article, pictures and all, hits tomorrow's paper."

Ethan felt his heart drop to his feet. He drew in a deep breath, knowing he had to get in touch with Rachel. She had volunteered to be a chaperone to Disneyland for a group of kids who attended the school where Charlene worked as a voice coach. She wasn't scheduled to return until late tonight.

When Ethan didn't say anything, Joe Connors continued, "I can't give you details but I can tell you the headline of the article isn't pretty."

Dread turned to anger, and it raced through Ethan. "Thanks for the heads-up."

Ending the call, he tried to reach Rachel. He had to

prepare her for whatever the article said and assure her they would handle it, work through it and deal with it.

He only hoped she'd believe him.

Rachel finished taking her shower and was about to settle in for the night when she checked her messages on her cell phone. She lifted a brow. She had several missed calls from Ethan and just as many text messages and they all said the same thing: "Call ASAP."

Wondering at the urgency, she was about to punch in his phone number when there was loud knock at her door. After running downstairs she took a quick look through her peephole and saw Ethan. She quickly opened her door.

"Ethan, what is—"

He suddenly pulled her into his arms and kissed her, kicking the door closed behind him as he continued kissing her and sweeping her off her feet, into his arms.

She always enjoyed being kissed by him and today was no exception. His lips moved hungrily over hers and instinctively she melted against him, loving the feel of being in his arms. She whimpered his name when moments later he pulled his mouth away.

"Rachel, sweetheart, we need to talk."

She saw they were no longer at the door, but he had carried her across the room and had taken a seat on the sofa with her cradled in his arms. She had been so wrapped up in their kiss she hadn't noticed the move-ment.

It was then that she remembered the missed calls and text messages. "What about?" Her voice sounded wobbly from the impact of his kiss.

He continued to hold her tightly against him and

when he didn't answer her, she glanced up into his eyes. She had been with Ethan long enough to know when he was deeply troubled. She pulled herself up. "What is it, Ethan?"

"I need to prepare you for something."

"What?"

"The tabloids know about us, thanks to Paige, and *The Wagging Tongue* is breaking the story tomorrow. Someone I know on the inside called and gave me a heads-up."

Rachel felt as if someone had just doused her with a pail of cold water right in her face. She jumped out of his lap. "What?"

"Yes, baby, I know. This is not how you wanted things, but together we'll deal with it."

She backed away from him. "No, no, this can't be happening…" Shaking her head as if to get her thoughts in order, she asked, "What does Paige have to do with it?"

Ethan rubbed his hand over his face. "Earlier in the week she approached me claiming she knew about us and threatening to go to Frasier and John if I didn't begin dating her. She figured her name connected to mine would take her places. I flatly refused and two days ago, when she approached me again and I refused again, she got mad. I guess this is her way of getting retaliation."

Rachel's head began pounding. "She approached you earlier in the week and you didn't mention it to me?"

He came to his feet and faced her. "I didn't want to upset you and I was hoping she would drop it."

Rachel pulled in a deep breath. "Paige is like a sore that only festers. She's never cared for me, Ethan. Jealousy is deeply embedded in any decision she makes about me. She's always wanted you, and for her to find out you and I have been involved in an affair, there's no way she would have dropped it. You should have told me."

"Maybe I should have, but I didn't want you upset."

"Well, now I am upset. I am livid. I am mad as hell."

He reached out for her. "The truth is out, baby, and we'll deal with it."

She pulled away from him. "It's not that easy, Ethan. It's my privacy and professionalism being threatened."

"And I still say we will deal with it, Rachel. When we're approached we'll tell them the truth."

"No, we won't! We will deny everything. They can't prove anything."

"I'm not sure about that. The person I talked to claims there are pictures."

"Pictures! Oh my God!" She dropped down on the sofa and covered her face with her hands.

Ethan went to her and pulled her into his arms. He'd never seen her this upset. "Rachel, the best thing to do is not to deny anything. We're two consenting adults who—"

"Should not have let things get out of hand. We should not have gotten involved in the first place since we knew what was at risk."

"But we did and we need to own up to it and not let the tabloids or anyone else control our lives or our relationship."

She jerked out of his arms. "No! You make it sound so easy and it's not. Don't you understand what I'll be going through, Ethan? Don't you understand? You like this sort of stuff. It makes you who you are, but it can only destroy me."

"Rachel, we can deal with it. Together."

"No! That's just it. We can't be together. That will just be more fuel for their fire. We have to end things between us now."

"That's not going to happen, Rachel. I won't give you up because of any damn tabloid," he said angrily.

She glared up at him. "You don't have a choice because I'm ending things between us, Ethan. I can't sacrifice a professional career I've worked hard to build or a private life I've tried hard to preserve. Besides, our affair was about nothing but sex anyway."

Her words were like a backhanded slap to Ethan's face and he felt the pain in the depths of his heart. "You don't mean that, Rachel," he said softly.

He refused to believe all the time they'd spent together had been about nothing but sex. Maybe that had been the case the first few times, but there was no way he would believe she didn't care for him the way he cared for her. No way.

"I love you, Rachel. Our times together weren't just about sex for me and I refuse to believe that's the way it was for you. And I won't deny what we shared to anyone. I won't make it into some backstreet, sleazy affair. I've never loved a woman before you, and I hope that you'll realize that our love—yes, our love—will be able to deal with anything. Together. You know how to reach me when you do."

He then turned and left.

Chapter 17

By noon on Saturday, Rachel was ready to have a stiff drink. The entire bottle, if necessary. Her phone hadn't stopped ringing. Some calls she had answered and some she had not.

Ethan's calls were some of the ones she had not.

It seemed everyone was shocked by the tabloid's allegations that she'd been having a secret affair with Ethan, but they were happy if she had. Uncle Jacob and Aunt Lily told her not to be bothered by the accusations. Sofia inquired as to how she was holding up but didn't ask any specifics about the affair. So far no one believed the tabloid's headline that she only got involved with Ethan to further her career. That was so far from the truth. She had already had an up-and-coming career before Ethan appeared on the scene. But the goal of the tabloids was to sell papers, and with those kinds

of accusations and the photos of them kissing in the
studio lot, they created the sensationalism they craved.

Thanks to Charlene, who'd shown up for breakfast
with a copy of *The Wagging Tongue* in her hand, she'd
been forced to see the article. She wished she could
claim the picture plastered on the front page had been
doctored, but it hadn't.

Evidently, Paige had been around that night Ethan
had shown up in the trailer unexpectedly. After they'd
made love, he had walked her to her parked car. Since
it was late, they assumed everyone had left and, before
getting in her car, Ethan had pulled her into his arms
and given her a very heated kiss. What she considered
a special moment between them had been reduced to
something sleazy, thanks to Paige and her cell phone
camera.

She looked up from the book she'd been trying un-
successfully to read when her house phone rang. She
hoped the caller wasn't Ethan again. She couldn't help
but smile when she heard the voice of Carmen Aiken
on her answering machine.

"Rachel, I know you're there, so pick up this phone!"

Carmen was an Oscar-winning actress who was married to director/producer Matthew Birmingham. She
and Carmen had become good friends when Carmen,
new to Hollywood at the time, had been cast in one of
Matt's movies. Rachel had been the makeup artist on
the set.

She reached for the phone and answered, "Okay, so
you knew I was here."

"You've been holding back on me, girl. Ethan Chambers! Why did you keep that hunk a secret?"

Rachel wished it had been a secret she could have

shared, but the only people who'd known about her affair with Ethan had been Charlene and Livia. "You know why, Carmen."

"Yes, I know how brutal the tabloids can be. Remember, I was a victim of their gossip for a while. Even after Matt and I remarried, they claimed we did it as a way to get publicity for his next movie."

Rachel was aware of that lie. Carmen and Matt had been divorced for a little over a year and had remarried last month. Rachel was glad they had worked out their differences and had gotten back together. She didn't know of any couple who deserved each other more.

"It really doesn't matter what those reporters think. It's how you feel, Rachel. I can tell from the photo that was one hell of a kiss he gave you. You're probably the envy of a lot of women today."

Rachel drew in a deep breath. Charlene had said the same thing, but it really didn't matter. She wanted no part of the tabloids and no part of Ethan.

She couldn't help but remember what he'd said before leaving and in the messages he'd left on her answering machine and cell. He said he loved her.

Well, she loved him, too, but in this case love would not be enough.

Carmen breached her silence. "I don't want you to make the same mistake I made, Rachel, by letting the tabloids rule your life."

Moments later when Rachel ended her call with Carmen, she knew it was too late. The tabloids were already ruling her life.

"What do you want, Curtis?"

"I like the publicity, Ethan, but you could have

hooked up with another woman. It would have benefited your career a lot more had she been a model or an actress. She's a makeup artist, for crying out loud, regardless of the fact her last name is Wellesley."

An angry Ethan slouched back against the sofa with a beer bottle in one hand and his cell phone in the other. He didn't give a royal damn whether Curtis liked the publicity or not. That last comment alone meant the man's days as his agent were numbered.

When Ethan didn't say anything, Curtis continued, "Now what we need to do is to play our cards right with this publicity and keep it moving. But you need to get rid of the broad in that picture and get someone more newsworthy. Someone like Rayon Stewart. We can work the angle that Rachel Wellesley was just someone you were sleeping with while waiting for Rayon Stewart to end things with Artis Lomax."

"Go to hell, Curtis."

"Excuse me?"

"I said, go to hell. By the way, as of now, you're no longer my agent. You're fired."

He then hung up the phone and took a swig of his beer. He refused to let anyone put Rachel down. She was the best thing to ever happen to him, and he loved *her* and not some model or Hollywood actress.

He reached for his cell phone and punched in her number. He knew she was at her condo hiding out. He'd tried calling her all day but she refused to take any of his calls.

Joe Connors had been right. The article hadn't been pretty and had made Rachel look like a schemer who had used their affair to build her career. No doubt that was the story Paige had told the tabloids and they had run with it. If anyone would have bothered to check, they would have known it was all lies fabricated by a jealous woman.

When Rachel didn't answer, Ethan clicked off the phone before standing and moving to the window. The paparazzi was out there and had been all day, waiting for him to come out with a story. Well, he didn't have one. At the moment, the only thing he had was heartache.

Rachel braced herself for work Monday, knowing everyone had probably seen the tabloid's article. She had decided the best thing to do was to deal with it and move on. She had worked too hard to build her career to do otherwise.

Ethan had continued to call her through late last night and had called her again this morning. By her not answering his calls, she hoped he now realized she hadn't changed her mind. Ending things between them had been the best thing to do. It was important that anyone expecting drama would get the professional she had always been.

She appreciated that the studio lot was private. But that didn't stop the paparazzi from being crowded out front with their cameras ready to get a shot of her when she arrived at work. A few even tried blocking her car from going through the gate.

From the way everything got quiet when she walked onto the set, it was obvious she had been the topic of conversation. She gave everyone her cheery hello as usual while heading toward the trailer, but she didn't miss Paige's comment, which was intentionally loud enough for anyone to hear. "And she actually thought someone like Ethan Chambers could be interested in *her?*"

Rachel refused to turn and comment, but she couldn't help the smile when she heard Livia speak up. "Evidently he was interested in her, since she's the one with him in that photo, Paige."

Livia's words had no doubt hit a nerve with Paige, since everyone on set had seen her flirting outrageously with Ethan. Tae'Shawna had been just as bad. Some people on set had placed bets on which of the two—Paige or Tae'Shawna—would finally get his attention. Neither had.

Rachel kept walking to her trailer, intent on not being around when Ethan arrived. It would be bad enough having to work with him on the set knowing they would be the subject of everyone's attention. She needed to get herself together before seeing him.

She appreciated her two assistants giving their support with words of encouragement and letting her know if she and Ethan were an item, that meant he had good taste.

For the next hour or so she went about her day as usual, and when it was time for her to go out on the set she left her trailer. The last thing she wanted was to give the impression she was hiding out.

Ethan and Livia were in the middle of a scene where Dr. Duncan was explaining to Dr. Perry why they couldn't be together and why they needed to end things. Boy, that sounded familiar.

Several people turned to look at her, including Frasier and John, who both gave her nods. If they believed the tabloid story, then they knew she and Ethan had broken the show's rule. In which case, she knew her job was in jeopardy. If they had to choose which of them to keep, no doubt Ethan would stay, since he was their star.

"Freeze! Rachel, kill that shine on Ethan."

At Frasier's command, she moved forward. The set got quiet and she knew everyone was looking at her. At them. She greeted him only with his name when she stopped in front of him.

He did the same.

Their greeting sounded stiff. Being the professional she was, Rachel was determined to do her job. She took her makeup brush and swept across the bridge of his nose. She tried to ignore his scent, something she'd gotten used to, and the sound of his heavy breathing.

But she couldn't ignore the blue-gray eyes that seemed to watch her every moment. Emotions stirred within Rachel but she fought hard to keep them at bay. Making sure she didn't take any more time than necessary, she gave him a smile and said, "All done." And then she quickly walked away.

"Unfreeze!"

They resumed shooting the scene, and when she glanced over at Paige, there was a malicious smirk on the woman's face. Paige doubtless assumed it was Ethan who ended things between them and not the other way around. She was probably also thinking that although she might not be his date at the wrap party, neither would Rachel.

She didn't want to be the object of discussion and speculation. But since she was, she would do everything she could to stay professional and put her and Ethan's affair behind her.

No matter how much it hurt.

"Ethan, wait up."

He glanced around and saw Tae'Shawna approach with a smile on her face. Out of the corner of his eye, he saw Paige watching. She'd had the good sense to avoid him today.

"What is it, Tae'Shawna?"

"I see you're scheduled for makeup with Rachel tomorrow."

"And what of it?"

"If you're uncomfortable about it, I'll speak to John for you to have one of her assistants do it."

He didn't need Tae'Shawna to tell him of his schedule. He knew Rachel would be doing his makeup, which meant they would be alone in the trailer for a short while. But he figured to keep talk down, Rachel had already arranged for one of her assistants either to do his makeup or be there with her when she did it. He doubted very seriously they would be alone.

He looked at Tae'Shawna. "Why would I be uncomfortable with Rachel doing my makeup?"

She shrugged. "I just assumed since the news is out about how she came on to you to boost her career that you are leery of her now. Coming on to you was unprofessional on her part."

Ethan put his hands in the pockets of his jeans and he didn't care one iota about the fierce frown that settled on his face. He was sick and tired of people assuming the worst of Rachel. Bottom line was he had pursued her, he had wanted her. He still wanted her.

"First of all," he told Tae'Shawna, "anyone with good sense knows most of what's printed in those tabloids isn't true. Second of all, Rachel is one of the most professional women I know. She didn't have to come on to me because I found her attractive from day one. I saw in her something I haven't seen in a lot of woman lately."

Tae'Shawna lifted her chin and he could tell his words had hit a nerve. "And what is that?"

"Unselfishness. She is not self-absorbed and I doubt that she has a shallow bone in her body. In fact, she never came on to me, but *you* did, many times, right here on the set. So who should I think is the professional one? Now if you'll excuse me, I need to call it a day."

A few hours later, in the privacy of his home, Ethan sank down on his sofa frustrated as hell. He hadn't tried making any type of contact with Rachel while on the set but he had called her several times since getting home, and she still would not accept his calls. If the paparazzi were on her tail like they were on his, he could imagine what she was going through, but that was no reason to block him out of her life.

Considering everything, he had expected her to withdraw for a day or so, but he hadn't expected her to put up an emotional wall that he could not penetrate.

For the last three days on the set she had been cordial yet distant, as if to prove to everyone that they were not together. When she looked at him, it was as if she was looking straight through him. He knew she was trying hard to maintain a mask of nonchalance where he was concerned, determined to avoid any situation that would compromise her professionalism.

He had tried not to be angered by her actions but a part of him couldn't help it. And now in the comfort of his home, lonely as it was, his anger was turning into intense hurt.

Why was he letting her do this to him?

Because, as he had told her, he loved her and a part of him believed she loved him back. And he believed that one day she would realize that nothing, not the paparazzi and not the threat of jeopardizing her career, was worth sacrificing their love.

Rachel cuddled on her sofa and pressed the replay button to pick up her last call.

"Rachel, this is Ethan. I know what you're going through but I wish you would let us go through it together. When you hurt, I hurt. I love you and I know you love me. Baby, please don't do this to us."

She glanced over at the beautiful bouquet of flowers that had been delivered to her from Ethan by way of Charlene. Her best friend had dropped by with the flowers earlier that evening. The card attached simply said:

I love you.
Ethan

Tears rolled from her eyes. She didn't think it would be so hard giving him up. She hadn't counted on the agony and the pain, the feeling of loneliness and heartbreak. It was hard during the day to see him and try to ignore him. Alone in her trailer, she would feel alienated. Even after three days, everyone on the set was still abuzz about her and Ethan breaking the rules, but so far neither Frasier nor John had approached her or Ethan. She figured they were probably waiting for one of them to approach them first, so tomorrow she would.

Tomorrow... Tomorrow she was scheduled to do Ethan's makeup. Typically they would be alone in her trailer, but she didn't want everyone speculating about what they were doing or saying behind closed doors. To have one of her assistants fill in for her would indicate she wasn't professional enough to handle a controversial situation. So in a way it was a "damned if you do and damned if you don't" situation.

Livia had come to her rescue. She volunteered to be the buffer by being in the trailer at the same time Ethan was there, on the pretext of repairing a broken nail or something. Rachel hoped the ploy worked.

Ethan knew all eyes were on him as he headed for Rachel's trailer. No doubt there were some who had their watch set to see how long he stayed inside alone with her.

"Ethan, wait up." He stopped and glanced around. Livia was walking toward him. She was one of the few women on set who hadn't tried coming on to him. Like Rachel, she was a specialist in her craft. Even with all those love scenes they'd done, they had still maintained professionalism.

"I need to see Rachel a minute myself," she said, smiling. "Broken nail."

He smiled, seeing through her ploy. Rachel was her friend and she was making an attempt to avoid gossip and speculation.

From the look on Rachel's face when they entered her trailer, Ethan knew for certain that Livia's appearance had been planned. Rachel showed no surprise at seeing them both walk in.

"Hello, Ethan, you can take my chair. And Livia, I'll fix that nail in a minute, just as soon as I finish with Ethan."

"No problem," Livia said, smiling. "I'll just sit over here."

"You can go ahead and take care of Livia and then do me," Ethan suggested. Only after the words had left his mouth did he realize their double meaning.

"No, Livia can wait until I finish with you," Rachel insisted.

"And I don't have a problem with you doing her first."

Before Rachel could open her mouth to retort, Livia spoke up. "Look, guys, evidently you two need time alone to clear up a few things."

"No, we don't."

"Yes, we do."

Livia shook her head. "Since the two of you can't agree, I'll make the decision for you," she said. "Rachel, you can work on Ethan while I excuse myself a minute to go to the ladies' room." Livia then headed toward the back of the trailer where the dressing room and bathroom were located.

Rachel watched her friend's retreating back.

"You can take care of me now, Rachel."

Rachel turned and glared at Ethan. "Do you not care about my career?"

His face rigid, he returned her glare. "And do you not care about my heart? Or yours?"

Her stomach twisted with his question, and she forced herself to ignore the stab of pain that ripped through her. "I care, but there's nothing I can do about it, Ethan. Please just let me make you up so I can be ready for the next person."

"Fine, get to it then."

He reclined in the chair and she stood over him. She hesitated a moment and looked into the eyes staring back at her. Just like always when she looked at them, she was in awe of their beauty, but this time she saw the anger and pain in their depths.

Drawing in a deep breath, she brushed foundation

across his cheekbones, then around his mouth, and she couldn't help but focus on his lips. Lips she had kissed so many times. Lips she wanted to kiss again. But she fought doing so.

Those lips moved and she heard the husky but low tone of his voice. "I love you, Rachel."

She dropped the brush from her hand and took a step back. "I'm finished, Ethan."

He eased out of the chair, his long legs bringing him to stand directly in front of her. "You might be finished but I'm not, Rachel. At least not where you're concerned. What we've shared is too precious and I won't give up on us. Admit that you love me as much as I love you."

She looked up at him, her heart full, but was unable to say the words he wanted to hear. "Ethan, I—I can't say it."

He reached out and gently pulled her into his arms and she could not have pulled out of them even if she wanted to. He lowered his head and, of their own accord, her lips parted as she sighed his name. The moment his lips touched hers she felt soothed by something she had missed for the past couple of days, something her body had gotten used to having.

A sensuous shudder passed through her as his tongue reinstated its rights to her mouth, letting her know that no matter how she continued to deny them, put distance between them, there would always be this—a passion so intense and forceful, it would take more than negative publicity to destroy it.

When he angled his head to deepen the kiss, she stretched up on tiptoes to get the full Ethan Chambers effect. And it was worth every effort. He was kissing her like a starving man, and in kind, she was kissing him like a starving woman. Her heart swelled with every stroke of his tongue, and she knew in her heart what she refused to speak out loud.

He finally pulled his mouth away and tenderly touched her cheek. "One day you will tell me that you love me and I'll be ready to hear it when you do." His tone was raw and husky and sent sensuous shivers all down her spine.

He leaned down and brushed a kiss across her lips before turning to walk out of the trailer.

Chapter 18

Rachel's lips twitched in a smile when the limousine pulled up behind Amaury's, an exclusive restaurant in Hollywood whose doors usually were closed until eight every night. Only Sofia, with a list of connections and contacts a mile long, could make the impossible happen.

For the past week, other than leaving for work, Rachel had pretty much stayed in and not ventured out with the paparazzi breathing down her neck. Although the breakup between Rayon Stewart and Artis Lomax and rumors of another adoption by Brad and Angelina now dominated the headlines, there were a few reporters who just didn't know when to quit.

"We're here, Ms. Rachel."

"Thanks, Martin," she said to the man who'd been the limo driver for Limelight Entertainment for years. She could recall sitting in the backseat of the huge car, with him behind the wheel, while being transported to and from private school as a child of no more than eight or nine. During those days, he kept her entertained with his own rendition of the animated voices of Bugs Bunny and Daffy Duck. He used to be so good at it.

Moments later, he was holding the door open for her as she got out. Amaury Gaston met her at the door and gave her a big hug.

"Sofia is already seated and waiting on you, Rachel," he said in a heavy French accent.

"Thanks."

"I've prepared your favorite," he added.

Rachel licked her lips. Chicken cordon bleu, she guessed, and Amaury's was the best. "You like spoiling me and Sofia," she said, smiling.

"Yes, just like I used to enjoy spoiling your parents. They were two of my first customers, and your father proposed to your mother right here one night. It was very special."

Rachel had heard the story before but didn't mind hearing it again. According to everyone who knew them, her parents had been very much in love.

"And I know if they were alive, they would want me to treat their girls just as special as I thought they were," Amaury added.

Moments later, Rachel made her way toward the table where her sister sat waiting. Sofia saw her approach and smiled. With her beauty and tall, slender figure, Rachel thought Sofia could have easily been a model or actress. Instead, she had followed in their father's footsteps and had taken his place in the family business working alongside Uncle Jacob. Despite their

age difference, she and Sofia had maintained a close
relationship, especially now that Sofia wasn't as overprotective as she used to be.

Sofia stood and Rachel walked straight into her sister's outstretched arms. Then Sofia took a step back
and studied her from head to toe. "Hmm, it doesn't look
like the tabloids have beaten you up too badly, although
I'm sure there are scars on the inside that I can't see."

Rachel felt a thickness in her throat. She hadn't intended to let Sofia know just how shaken up she really
was. Ethan's kiss yesterday had done that enough. She
had expected him to call last night, but he hadn't. She
wasn't sure what she would have said if he had.

"Are you okay, Rach?" Sofia asked, looking into her
eyes.

"Yes."

"You sure?"

Rachel forced a smile. "Yes, I'm fine. Come on, let's
let Amaury know we're ready to be served. I'm starving," she said, moving to her chair and away from her
sister's intense scrutiny.

"Okay, but don't think you're not going to tell me everything," Sofia said, taking her own seat again.

"Everything like what?"

Sofia held her gaze with that "let's get serious" expression on her face. "Everything like how you really
feel about Ethan Chambers."

"Maybe we ought to buy stock in those tabloids since
you seem to be in them quite a bit these days, Ethan."

Ethan closed his refrigerator after pulling out a cold
beer. He juggled the phone as he twisted off the cap. His

heart had begun pounding in his chest when the phone had rung, in hopes the caller was Rachel. Instead it was Hunter. "That's a possibility."

"So is any of it true?" his brother asked.

"The only thing I will admit to is an involvement with Rachel. Her motives were exploited falsely. Our being together was mutual and she didn't need me to advance her career. She did that on her own."

"Pretty defensive, aren't you?"

"Can't help but be where she's concerned. I love her."

There was silence on the other end, and Ethan was well aware that his brother was recovering from what he'd said. In all his twenty-eight years, he'd never admitted to loving any woman. While his brother was pondering what he'd said, Ethan took a swig of beer.

"This is serious," Hunter finally said.

"I hope she realizes that it is. She's tabloid shy."

"And you're just the opposite," Hunter pointed out. "For as long as I can recall, you enjoyed getting in front of a camera."

Ethan shrugged, remembering some of his wild escapades while in high school and college. "Not when they portray my woman in a bad light."

"Well, we're all looking forward to meeting her. And since things are that serious, don't forget the traditional Chambers vineyard weddings."

Ethan smiled. "I won't, but first I have to convince her that she loves me and that I will make her life with me worth anything the tabloids might put her through."

"Good luck."

Ethan drew in a deep breath. "Thanks." He knew he was going to need it.

* * *

Sofia took another sip of her wine. "And you think Livia Blake might be looking for another agent?" she asked.

"Yes," Rachel said, eager to keep her sister talking about something else other than her and Ethan. "Livia says at thirty her modeling days are coming to an end, and she wants an agent who will take her acting career to another level and run with it. Of course, she's heard about Limelight Entertainment and would love to talk to you, but she's heard how selective you are."

Sofia didn't deny what Rachel said. She *was* selective. "I've been keeping an eye on Livia Blake's modeling career for a while now and wondered if she planned on doing anything beyond that. Limelight is definitely interested, so have her give me a call."

Rachel looked at her sister and could tell she was bothered about something and that it was something other than what was going on with her and Ethan. "You've been working a lot lately, Sofia. When do you plan on taking another vacation?"

Sofia smiled. "Hmm, a vacation sounds nice but I won't be going back to the islands any time soon. My clientele has doubled, and I have to find work for a lot of people." She took another sip of her wine, leaned back in her chair and asked, "Did you know Uncle Jacob is thinking about retiring?"

Rachel's eyes widened. "No. I talked to him a few days ago and he said nothing about that. But I can see him wanting to just chill, take it easy and travel. He and Aunt Lily have been saying they want to build that house in Barbados for years."

"Yes, I'd love for him to retire and enjoy life, too, but not if the rumors I'm hearing are true."

Rachel lifted a brow. "What rumors?"

Although there weren't others in the restaurant, Sofia leaned over the table and said in a low tone, "I've heard that he's thinking about selling his interest in Limelight to Ramell Jordan at A.F.I."

Rachel's expression denoted her surprise. Artists Factory Inc. had been a rival talent agency of Limelight Entertainment for years. In fact, Ramell's father, Emmett, had been a close friend of her father's, but for some reason they were not on good terms at the time of her dad's death. And because of Sofia's close relationship with their father, Rachel was not surprised that her sister would not favor a possible merger.

"What you heard is probably just a rumor," Rachel said, hoping that would smooth her sister's ruffled feathers.

"I certainly hope so. I can't believe Uncle Jacob would consider doing such a thing."

Rachel could see why he would. Although her father and Emmett Jordan had ended on bad terms, Uncle Jacob and Emmett had remained somewhat friendly.

"Ramell Jordan is nothing more than the son of a backstabber after what Emmett did to Dad," Sofia said angrily.

Rachel lifted a brow. "And just what did he do to Dad?"

She'd always believed there was more to the story than either she or Sofia knew, but no one would ever say. In fact, Sofia was the only one who'd ever made such accusations about Emmett Jordan. All Uncle Jacob would say was that it had been a misunderstanding between the two men and that had her father lived, his and Emmett's relationship would have been restored to a close friendship.

"You're better off not knowing."

Rachel only shook her head. For years that had been the same response Sofia gave her whenever she asked. Maybe she was simply better off not knowing.

"And now that you've tried to get me to avoid talking about you and Ethan Chambers, I think that we need to finally get to the meat of your problem."

Rachel pushed away her plate. Dinner had been delicious and now she was ready for desert and coffee. But she would wait awhile until after she answered the questions she knew her sister had for her.

"There's really nothing to tell, Sofia. You know how I detest being in the public eye and Ethan's popularity right now puts him there, as well as any woman he's involved with."

"So the two of you *are* involved?"

Pain rolled through Rachel. "We *were* involved."

Sofia studied her sister's features, saw the pain that settled in her face. "The two of you kept things between you a secret from everyone—including me—which evidently was working for a while. So what happened?"

Rachel took a deep breath, and then she told Sofia about what Paige had done.

A deep frown appeared on Sofia's face. "And this Paige person works on the set of *Paging the Doctor*?"

"Yes, she's a production assistant."

"Not for long," Sofia muttered under her breath. "Tell me something, Rachel. Did your affair with Ethan have substance or was it all about sex?"

Rachel met her sister's inquisitive gaze. It would be so easy to claim it had been nothing but sex, but this was Sofia and she'd always had a way of seeing through any lie Rachel told. Besides, she would tell Sofia what she hadn't told anyone, not even Ethan.

"I love him, Sofia. It wasn't all about sex."

Her sister stared at her for a long moment, and then a smile touched her lips when she said, "Then I can see no reason why the two of you can't be together."

Rachel rolled her eyes. In a way she was surprised at her sister's comment, since Sofia of all people knew how she guarded her privacy. "You know that's not possible, Sofia. Ethan is an up-and-coming star, and being the focus of a lot of attention is what will boost his career. I can't risk that kind of publicity with the career I tried so hard to build."

"And what else?"

Rachel gave her sister a confused look. "What do you mean what else?"

Sofia leaned in closer. "This is me, and I can read you like a book, Rachel. So level with me and tell me the real reason you and Ethan can't be together. Since I'm always on the lookout for potential clients, I'm well aware that Ethan Chambers is hot news. I'm also well aware that during the time the two of you were having your secret tryst, his name wasn't linked to any Hollywood starlet, which made the tabloids wonder exactly what he was doing and who he was doing it with. And when it seemed he had decided to just live a boring life, they backed off. When the news hit the papers about the two of you, the tabloids had basically given him a rest."

Sofia paused to take a sip of her wine and then asked, "And what's this I hear about you taking a temporary leave from the show?"

Rachel placed her wine glass down after taking her

own sip. She didn't have to wonder where Sofia had gotten the news. Few people knew that Frasier considered himself as their godfather. "I thought it would be best, and I met with Frasier yesterday. He wasn't all that keen on the idea but said since there was only a week left for filming, he would go along with it. But he wanted me back on my job when they began the new season. I can handle that."

Sofia lifted a brow. "Can you? They aren't writing Ethan out of the script, so he'll be returning, too. Will you be able to handle that?"

"I don't have a choice."

"Yes, you do. For once you can fight for what you want, what you have every right to have."

Rachel was still surprised by her sister's attitude. She'd expected her to be the voice of reason and agree with her that the best thing was to put her career ahead of anything else. That was certainly what Sofia was doing these days. She couldn't recall a time when her sister had gotten serious about a man.

"You don't think my career is important, Sofia?"

Sofia waved off her words. "Of course I do, but your heart takes priority."

At Rachel's frown, Sofia reached out and captured her hand in hers. "Hear me out for a second, Rach." She paused and then said, "This is the first time I can truly say I believe you're in love. It shows on your face every time you say Ethan's name. You, little sister, are truly in love and I don't believe it's one-sided. I've been waiting to see how Ethan was going to respond to the tabloids. He hasn't denied the two of you are having an affair. In fact, he's gone on record with Joe Connors to say that you were not using him to boost your career. Other than that, he's been low-key about everything, which shows me he's doing whatever he can to protect you, and I like him for that. He could take all this publicity and run with it, but he hasn't. He's trying to fade to black."

Rachel had to agree with Sofia on that. Ethan was keeping a low profile these days.

"A man like that is worth keeping, Rach. And it's time you do what I haven't been able to do yet."

"And what is that?" Rachel asked, taking another sip of her wine.

"Stop hiding behind your career as an excuse to avoid falling in love. It's an unfortunate Wellesley trait. I'm guilty of it, too. We're both scared that if we love someone, they will abandon us like Mom and Dad did."

Rachel met her sister's gaze. Is that what she had been doing? Was that the reason she'd deliberately kept men at arm's length? Although she was barely out of diapers when her parents were killed, and her uncle and aunt had always been there for her, she had grown up feeling a tremendous loss. It had been hard during her early years when all her friends had had someone to call Mom and she had not. A part of her had always had that inner fear that to love also meant to lose. Wasn't it time for her to finally take a chance on love and believe she was deserving of a forever kind of love like everyone else? Did she want to live the rest of her life afraid of the unknown? Wasn't a life with Ethan better than a life without him? In her heart she knew that it was, and it was time for her to take a leap of faith and take control of her life.

A smile touched Rachel's face when she recalled the party planned for the cast and crew this weekend. "You're right. It's time for me to stop hiding."

Chapter 19

"You look simply beautiful, Rach," Charlene said, smiling as she gazed at her best friend from head to toe.

"And I feel beautiful," Rachel responded, looking at herself in a full-length mirror. She glanced over her shoulder at the woman who was smiling proudly at her handiwork. "Livia, I'm thinking that maybe I ought to be worried. You could take my job as a makeup artist."

Livia chuckled as she waved off her words. "You don't have to worry about that, and thanks to your sister I won't either. I appreciate you putting in a good word for me. It's a dream come true to be represented by Limelight Entertainment."

Rachel smiled as she looked at herself in the mirror again. Sofia had gone shopping with her and helped her pick out her dress, Charlene had selected the accessories and Livia had done her makeup and hair. She felt like

Cinderella about to go to the most important ball of her life. And her Prince Charming was waiting.

At least she hoped he was waiting.

She'd heard from Livia that Ethan had gone home to Napa Valley last weekend and that on the set for the season finale he had thrown himself into his work and pretty much kept to himself. More than once she was tempted to call him but decided to do things this way. Now nerves were setting in and all those "what-ifs" were stirring through her mind.

She turned to her two friends. "Are you sure he's coming to the wrap party tonight, Livia?"

Livia smiled. "I heard him assure Frasier that he'll be there to walk the red carpet."

Rachel nodded. "What if he brings a date?"

"I doubt that, and I even heard him tell Frasier that he's coming alone," Livia responded. "And just so you know, Paige was dropped from the show. All I know is that she got called to John's office and he told her she was no longer needed. So the only thing she gained by stirring up that mess with the tabloids is an unemployment check." Livia smiled and added, "And I heard she's having trouble finding a job. Seems like someone put the word out around town about her."

Rachel didn't have to guess who. Her sister was that influential.

"I think it's time for you to leave now," Charlene said, glancing out the window. "Martin just pulled up."

Nervous flutters raced through Rachel's stomach. Sofia had called her from London, where she'd gone to meet with a client, and given her another pep talk. Then Uncle Jacob and Aunt Lily had called and told her to follow her heart, and since they would be at the wrap party, they would see her later.

Rachel knew she was doing the right thing. Ethan had said he wanted her to tell him that she loved him and she was prepared to do that. And it no longer mattered who would be listening. She did love him, and she needed him in her life more than anything. It was about time that he knew it.

Ethan drew in a deep breath when the limo he was riding in alone pulled to a stop in front of the red carpet. The crowd was massive and, as usual, reporters were out in droves. People were standing behind the roped areas, and cameras were flashing from just about every angle.

More than anything, he wished Rachel would have been there with him, by his side, to bask in the moment of his accomplishments. He had worked hard to reach this point in his career and, more than anything, he wanted the woman he loved to be with him.

He had told her that he loved her and now the next step would have to be hers. And he could only hope that sooner or later she'd make it.

He had to believe that one day she would realize that together their love was strong enough to withstand anything. Even this, he thought, glancing out the car window at the crowd that seemed to be getting larger by the minute.

As soon as he stepped out of the car, flashbulbs went off, momentarily blinding him, and he was immediately pulled center stage to be interviewed. The cheering crowd made him feel good, but nothing could heal his broken heart.

"Everyone, we have Ethan Chambers, who this season became known as Dr. Tyrell Perry on *Paging the Doctor.* And how are you doing tonight, Ethan?"

Ethan smiled for the camera while giving his attention to the red-carpet host for the evening, Neill Carter. "I'm doing great, Neill, and looking forward to a wonderful evening."

Neill laughed. "I can believe that, but you came by yourself, man. Surely there was a special lady who would have loved to make this walk down the red carpet with you."

It was Saturday night and, more than likely, millions of people were sitting in front of their television sets watching the festivities, including his family. He hoped Rachel was one of those watching because he intended to give her a shout-out. Even if no one else knew whom his message was meant for, she would.

"Yes," he said, looking directly into the camera. "There is a special lady for me and I want her to know that I…"

He stopped talking when he glanced over Neill's shoulder and saw a woman strolling toward them. He blinked. She was beautiful, from the way her hair was styled on her head to the gorgeous red gown she wore—down to the silver shoes that sparkled on her feet.

His gaze returned to her face and for a moment he didn't believe what he was seeing. Rachel was here, in the spotlight, and it was obvious she wasn't there to make anyone up behind the scenes tonight. She was standing out and she was walking toward him.

All eyes were on her, including his. When she reached his side, she smiled and leaned closer and whispered in his ear, "I love you, Ethan. Thanks for waiting on me."

He couldn't help the smile that touched his lips. He

had waited on her. And that wait had not been in vain. He pulled her into his arms and lowered his mouth to hers, kissing her right there in front of everyone. It was a move that caused the crowd to roar with excitement. Photographers snapped pictures, taking it all in. When Ethan finally released Rachel's mouth, he grinned down at her as flashes continued to go off around them.

"I take it you two know each other," Neill said with a teasing grin.

"Yes, we know each other," Ethan said, pulling her closer to his side. "This is my special lady, and she has something I've never given another female."

"And what's that?" Neill asked.

"My heart."

Later that night, Ethan opened the door to *their* place and swept Rachel into his arms. The party had been great. He'd made more contacts and had gotten numerous offers from new agents looking to fill Curtis Fairgate's place.

But the highlight of the entire evening was the woman in his arms, the star of his heart.

He tried to maintain control as he carried her to the bed. His hands began shaking as he slowly undressed her, hoping and praying this wasn't a dream and he wouldn't wake up to an empty room.

It was only after he'd gotten them both undressed and eased on the bed with her, right into her outstretched arms, that he finally accepted this was the real deal. He took her face in his hands and stared into the darkness of her eyes as his heart swelled even more. "I love you, Rachel."

Her smile brightened his whole world, and her voice

was filled with sincerity when she said, "And I love you, Ethan."

For a suspended moment in time they stared at each other, and then he captured her lips with his as joy bubbled within him. He knew at that moment that he'd been made to love her, to be her shelter from the storm, to protect her, to honor her for always.

He deepened the kiss and felt her body tremble. When he settled his body over hers, he knew he was almost home.

He had wanted to take things slow with her, but it had been too long since they'd been together like this and his body was craving to get inside of her. When she moaned his name he knew he couldn't wait any longer.

He broke off the kiss to gaze down into her eyes at the same time he thrust inside of her, entering her with a hunger that shook every part of his body. As her scent swept through his nostrils and her inner muscles gripped him for everything they could get, he threw his head back and surrendered to her.

"Rachel!"

His sexy pixie was making her mark, and each time she lifted her hips to meet his thrusts, stroke for stroke, he was pushed even more over the edge. When he felt a mind-blowing explosion on the horizon, he glanced back down into her face and saw his passion mirrored in her eyes.

When the climax hit, he could swear bells and whistles went off. Their bodies exploded together, escalating them to the stars and beyond. They shuddered together as the power of love drenched them in an orgasm so potent he wondered if they would ever be able to recover.

But deep down he knew they would—only to take the journey over and over again, for an entire lifetime.

When their bodies ceased shuddering, he rolled to the side, pulled her into his arms and held her close to his heart. Just where she would always be.

Rachel lay contented in Ethan's arms. She hadn't realized how much she'd missed coming here, being here with him, until they'd stopped being together. But never again.

They had made love several times, and she kept telling him how much she loved him because she loved hearing herself say it and he seemed to enjoy hearing it. And he told her how much he loved her as well. She knew now that together they could face anything. She was no longer afraid of what the tabloids might print or how her career could be affected.

Tonight Frasier had congratulated everyone and indicated that he expected them all back for the new season. Everyone except Paige, of course, who ironically wasn't invited to the wrap party she'd been dying to attend with Ethan. And Tae'Shawna Miller. Apparently she had whined one time too many, because rumor had it she'd been released from the show as well.

Rachel shifted her body to glance up at Ethan. "You're quiet. What are you thinking?" she asked him.

He smiled down at her. "I was thinking about how surprised I was to see you tonight. Surprised and happy. What made you come?"

She reached up and her fingers touched his cheek. "You. I knew I loved you and you kept telling me that you loved me, breaking down my barriers." She paused a moment and then said, "And I also realized Sofia was right. I was hiding my love on the pretense of protecting my career when I was really afraid to admit loving you. I was afraid I wouldn't be able to handle it if you were to leave me the way my parents did."

Ethan held her gaze. "I'll never leave you, sweetheart. And by the way, while you were talking to Frasier tonight, I got a call on my cell phone. It was my mother. She was watching the whole thing on television and heard me when I said you had my heart. So she wants to know when's the wedding."

Rachel laughed. "The wedding?"

"Yes. I told her I hadn't gotten around to asking you yet." He pulled her closer into his arms. "So, baby, will you marry me?"

She smiled up at him. "For better or for worse?"

He nodded. "And richer or poorer."

"In sickness and in health?"

He chuckled. "Until death do us part."

She leaned up and threw her arms around his neck. "In that case, I accept!"

He wrapped her in his arms and kissed her, sealing what he knew would be a Hollywood marriage that would last forever.

* * * * *

HARLEQUIN
PLUS

Try the best multimedia
subscription service for romance
readers like you!

Read, Watch and Play.

Experience the easiest way to get
the romance content you crave.

Start your **FREE TRIAL** at
<u>www.harlequinplus.com/freetrial</u>.